"*Dark Ride* is Dante's *Infern...* dose of Stephen King thro... a pitch-perfect new voice i...

Coke Sams
Film maker ("Blue Like Jazz"
and "The Second Chance")

"*Dark Ride* carries tones reminiscent of C.S. Lewis's *The Lion, the Witch and the Wardrobe*. Four teenagers from the town of Cassidy, Tennessee find themselves trapped inside a ride called The Enchanted Forest at Storybook Hollow Amusement Park. Their adventure takes a supernatural turn for the worse. 'A chilling tale for the ages.'"

Ken Beck
Author, Editor, former Newspaper Columnist
for *The Tennessean*

"Put down the technology and get lost in the lives of some students who go on an interesting ride of their own. Enjoy a day of twists and turns that you will never forget."

Robert Oglesby
Center for Youth and Family Ministry
Abilene Christian University

"Todd Loyd's creativity and storytelling ability will delight and encourage readers young and old. He uses his love for Christ and his dramatic skills to weave a story that both teaches and entertains.

Jeff Walling
Author, Speaker, and Senior Minister
at Providence Road Church
in Charlotte, North Carolina

"For more than a decade now I've witnessed Todd Loyd's compelling, engaging, and even hilarious creativity draw teens into a story bigger than themselves — God's story. Dive in for a read and enjoy the ride."

Chris Seidmon
Author and Senior Minister at
the Farmer's Branch Church, Dallas, Texas

DARK RIDE

TODD LOYD

FRANKLIN GREEN
PUBLISHING
www.franklingreenpublishing.com

Dark Ride

Copyright © 2012 by Todd Loyd

Published by
Franklin Green Publishing
PO Box 51
Lebanon, TN 37088

ISBN 978-1-9364 - 8722 - 6

Printed in the United States of America
10 9 8 7 6 5 4 3 2 1

Acknowledgements

Thanks to Jacob Michael for his mentoring and experience that guided me through this process. I would like to also thank my "creative brotherhood" which consist of; David Skidmore, David Rubio, Jon Shoulders, and Dave Clayton. If not for an especially productive night on the steps of the Otter Creek stage this story would have never been told. Thanks to Chris Lee for showing me this could be done, to Zach Watson for laboring through the first edit, and to Steve Davidson, for just about everything (except comic genius). Thanks to Steve Kenney and Josh Cherry for their input and friendship. Of course, most of all, thanks to my wife, Amanda and three boys for sharing and enduring the formation of this story over the last 5 years.

Visions of a carefree holiday had been shattered, and it was only the second day of summer. It didn't matter that it was his last three months at home before going off to college. The ultimatum was this: he was going to get a job.

Well, it was actually nicer than that. His parents said something to the effect of, "If you work now, we'll help you with school, but if you don't, you're on your own." So off to work he went in khaki shorts, a polo shirt, which was some disgustingly teal color, white socks, and white shoes with no lettering or logos visible. This, aside from the optional sunglasses, was the official attire for every employee at Storybook Hollow Amusement Park. A nametag topped off his garb—"Doug."But no one called him Doug. It was always Douglas. Except when he was in trouble with his dad, and then it was Douglas Edward Finch. Or when his mother talked to him. To her, he was Dougy—her attempt to freeze him forever at the age of three and a half.

Working at an amusement park with the tagline "Where Everyone Experiences Their Happily Ever After" seemed like a fun option. And Douglas didn't think the first day was so bad; he got the lay of the land, filled out paperwork, filled out more paperwork, and he learned where to punch in and how to work the time clock so he could get paid.

But the second day was a completely different story. It was work. Dull, tenuous work—and not very fun at all. He'd drawn the lot of being trained by Clyde, a legend of sorts...or more like a fixture. The old man showed Douglas the ropes by barking out orders, filling his head with endless facts, and going through a mental checklist that the old grizzled veteran had probably never written down. After they had been at it for nine hours and walked through every inch of the place, Douglas wondered, "Does this guy ever stop?"

He received his answer by hearing more statements such as, "In case the toilets back up, you got plungers in that shed there or behind the water ride," . . . "Never let anyone park in that spot. It's reserved," . . . "That's where the breakers are...unless it's at night. Then you gotta flip the power switch in the carousel, but only after priming the charger plate," . . . "That right there? Pixie's? Best funnel cake in the park...if you ever have a hankerin' for that kind of stuff."

On and on it went.

Their goal that day was to simply make sure everything was ready for the opening weekend. But Douglas was still trying to learn his way around

Storybook Hollow. It was like a maze. Even when Douglas came as a kid, he'd always get lost. Clyde said the place was "intentionally made that way. Keeps people in the park longer. They get lost. Decide to get on another ride. Spend more money. Hope we never have a fire emergency—whole place'll burn all the guests." Douglas couldn't tell if his mentor-slash-boss was serious or not. Old Clyde never seemed to laugh.

Clyde had always been at Storybook Hollow. At least as far as Douglas could remember. But both the park and Clyde were showing their age. Douglas longed for the old man to simply say, "Okay that's it for today," but instead, he heard, "Now for the Dark Ride."

The Dark Ride, like Clyde, was a legend of the park. The main attraction, actually. One of those "get in a car and drive through the dark" rides that teens like to steal a kiss on, scares little kids, and parents dread. But the story of the ride was what made it fun because it found a way to blend together all of the old stories and fairytales. Douglas had many good memories of the ride, and even though it'd been a long day, he was a little excited to see the ride "behind the scenes."

They entered the musty old building. Clyde said, "Now we're gonna need to make sure everything's in order. Calibrate the runners. Tighten the ratchets on the anti-rollbacks. Streamline the—"

"The anti-roll what?"

"Keeps the car from rolling back-erds." But then Clyde stopped and took a closer look at Douglas. "You need to be writin' any of this down, or you got it?"

"I think I got it."

"Then stop interruptin'."

Clyde went on about the "car barn" and the "Linear Induction Motor" and the "Friction Bars" until Douglas felt like his brain was melting out of his ears, which could be due to info-fry or to the fact that the air conditioning hadn't been turned on and it was about 100 degrees inside, even at 10 p.m.

Aren't there laws against slave labor? Douglas wondered, trying to squelch his growling stomach.

Clyde was busy working on an electronic short of some kind, fixing it with saliva and black electrical tape. "Yeah, that'll hold."

Douglas thought, *At this rate, we'll be here till sun-up.* He asked, "You think I can go on ahead? Check out anything on down the road?"

"The *track*. On down the track." An electrical ZAP sent Clyde's fingers to his mouth and he sucked on them to ease the sting. "Yeah, go on ahead. Make sure there's no debris or anything, then meet me two rooms up. We gotta check a couple of props, which is a two-man job, and then we'll call it a night."

Douglas pushed through two heavy doors. The power was on but Clyde had turned the cars off so neither of them had to avoid the large moving vehicles that carried guests on their tours through the ride. Although two feint lights glowed overhead, they were almost useless. He had relied on Clyde's large black flashlight to provide light, but now he reached into his canvas work belt and grabbed the one he'd gotten on the cheap at Barney's, the local discount store. Shining the flashlight from corner to corner, he knelt beside the tracks, illuminating the curving trail all the way to the next set of doors. Nothing. All was clear. He kept moving. The faster this went, the better. He was looking forward to getting home to finish the remains of a large mushroom and green pepper pizza from the night before, which was nestled into the top shelf of the Finch family fridge.

Then he heard music.

Douglas stopped and craned his neck to make sure he wasn't making up the sound. He wasn't. Sure enough, a strange, soft tune was being emitted from behind the wall to his left.

Sounds like a calliope, he thought.

Stepping over to the wall, he listened some more. Sure enough, he wasn't hearing things.

He called out, "Hey Clyde? Do you hear that music?"

"What was that?" came the muffled response from the other side of the doors. "Did you say music?"

"Yeah. Sounds like a calliope or something."

"How you know what a calliope sounds like?"

"You know…like the merry-go-round plays."

"You're hearing things, captain. Ain't no calliopes in this place."

Douglas liked the fact the Clyde called him captain. He knew it was something he called everyone, but it made him feel important.

He turned his attention back to the wall; the music kept on playing. It was also getting louder. Douglas moved along the wall, trying to find the focal point of the sound. As he approached the spot on the wall where the sound was the loudest, he slowly raised his hand to feel for any vibration. At a spot above his head there was a buzzing, static sound, as if someone had just turned on a fluorescent light. A sign he had not noticed before flickered to life. It simply read, "ENTER" in dim glowing green.

As the sign glowed to life, so did the edges of a door with a faint, green glow illumined all around it. Then a push-bar emerged. *Weird,* thought Douglas. The music kept playing.

The old man called, "Almost done in here, your music still playing?"

"Yeah. I think I see where it's coming from. Gonna check it out." Douglas, slightly apprehensive but more curious, gripped his flashlight, pushed the bar, and went through the door.

Darkness. Complete, utter darkness. It wouldn't be long before the cycle began again. Now it's just anticipation, waiting for the distant whispers, the shrieks of fear, the bravado mocking. It's quiet, black, still.

Suddenly, there's light everywhere. Blinding light.

Here we go. A barrage of sound erupts, but the different noises can't be deciphered. It's confusing, but amidst the chaos… it's her—the girl in red. She's twenty feet away.

I have to catch her. This time'll be different. I'll succeed.

There's running, pushing, dodging, and lunging.

Just as fingertips are about to reach her dress, a mechanical juggernaut blocks the path.

Ear splitting screams fill the air.

No! She's getting away. Just like last time. And the time before. And the time before. And the… An invisible force that feels like a hand clasping, choking, and pulling,

The light fades.

Voices fade.

There is no sound.

Then the light wisps out.

Back to nothingness.

Next time… next time I'll catch her.

More waiting. Waiting till it begins again. The cycle.

"The teens prove clever avoiding the beast.
One false move and they would have been its feast.
To survive in the story, their wits must be keen,
For in this wood there's far worse yet unseen."

Chapter 1

It's a cool July morning. The fog lifts over the town, and the sun hides behind the haze. Slowly, the streets of Cassidy Falls come to life. A newspaper delivery boy wheels his bike along the quiet streets and flings newspapers at dew-covered targets. Men and women in business attire clasp cups of coffee as they shuffle lazily to their high-priced SUV's. The mammoth vehicles grunt and whirl to life.

In his suburban house at 1223 Crockett Way, Jack Braddock's alarm clock goes off. Reading the numbers in red, he slaps the snooze bar and turns over, thinking another ten minutes of sleep will not delay him. But, after three more minutes of tossing and turning, he lumbers out of bed like a zombie. His eyes are caked with sleep, and he presses his index fingers into their corners, rubbing the dried substance from his eyes and massaging them to prepare for another day. Looking out his second story window, Jack peers into the summer sky to check for rain, then down into his neighborhood, scanning the lawn to see if paperboy has come. *Not yet, good,* he says to himself, hoping to get downstairs in time to witness the entertaining morning ritual.

Opening the door to his room, he almost runs head first into his sister, Blair, who is standing at the door. It startles him, and he wonders, *What is she doing up so early?* She has an intense glower on her face. Jack knows this look well. Evidently, he has made her mad yet again. She is two years older and will be a junior at James K. Polk High School in the fall. She is popular and snooty, and their relationship is more than tumultuous. In fact, it is downright hostile. She has something to say, but Jack fears that listening to her may prevent him from getting outside to witness the morning spectacle.

"What were you doing in my room last night?" she asks. Jack knows that in her mind an intrusion is a capital offense with the only suitable punishment being death by some ancient Chinese torture.

"Uh…nothing."

"I saw you. My room is off limits to losers, and you are a loser."

"Maybe you were dreaming."

"Wide awake. Nice try."

"Was anything missing?"

"No."

"Was anything moved?"

Blair thinks a moment. "Not that I noticed."

"Don't you think if I was in your room, or even within ten feet of your room, I would have done something to annoy you? You know, like, take something or move something? Maybe?"

Jack knows it is a convincing argument, but she's not letting him off the hook that easily. "I better not find anything missing. And if my iPod playlist has been altered in any way, I know where you sleep."

She storms off, but before she gets too far, Jack stops her with, "Oh and, be sure to tell Colton Spurlock hello when you meet him at the mall later tonight."

With the mention of the boy's name, Blair's face turns red.

Gotcha, thinks Jack.

He had learned through his vigil outside her door that Blair, unbeknownst to her parents, was planning on meeting the boy at the mall. His parents did not like Colton.

"Stay out of my room. Stay out of my way. And stay out of the air I breathe."

"Okay, logically, how am I supposed to do that? The air you breathe? Really?"

"And if mom or dad find out I was talking to Colton, I'll know who told them."

"It's not like they can't just log on and check the cell—"

"I mean it, you little brat. Off limits! And if they hear about me and Colton, I've been reading up on Chinese bamboo torture."

"Umm, don't you gotta have bamboo for that to—"

"Mom? I need to get some bamboo for a school project. Can we get some today?"

A sweet voice from downstairs floats up, "Sure thing, dear."

Blair sasses a smile, cinches her robe tighter, and storms off.

Jack just shakes his head. He waits for the slam of her door that he knows is coming.

Slam! Jack smiles to himself. If Blair is one thing, she is predictable, a fact he can always count on—and take advantage of. He checks a clock on the wall and thinks, "Oh, no. I'm gonna miss it."

Jack launches himself down the steps as fast as his morning legs can take him. He eyes the front door, ignoring his father, who is already watching the morning news in the living room. Bursting out the door, Jack waits at the end of the drive, spying eagerly at the yard of his neighbor Mr. Lambert. *No paper,* he contemplates. *Just in time! Okay Lambert, where are you hiding today?* Scanning his neighbor's driveway, he finds Ronald Lambert dressed in work clothes and crouching behind a large Ford truck, one of those four-door, jacked-up monsters that makes more noise than a dump truck. From his vantage point, he sees Teddy Zuckerman peddle down the street launching papers to the right and left. Jack watches as the boy slows for his approach in front of the Lambert's.

From behind his hiding spot, Lambert runs out from his cover and says, "Don't you dare, boy...." But it is too late. Zuckerman is good. He is already hurling the paper with the precision of a professional quarterback. The package lands perfectly on top of the cab of the behemoth truck. Zuckerman waves at Jack as he peddles forward, and Jack grins as Teddy tosses a copy of the *Cassidy Falls Herald* to his feet. Jack steals a glance at the undersized Lambert, who is jumping up and down muttering inappropriate words. He's trying to fetch the paper from its perch, which is just out of his reach.

Jack knows he shouldn't laugh, but he can't resist. Every morning for the past three months, Teddy Zuckerman has launched newspapers in hard-to-reach places. Jack is a fan of a well-played prank, and watching this prank always starts his day off right. Pulling the paper from its plastic sheath and loosening the rubber band, Jack walks back into his two-story domicile ready to comb the headlines and catch the scores of last night's hockey game. As he closes the door, he notices that Mr. Lambert, who has grabbed a broomstick, seems to be attempting to play hockey as he tries to free his newspaper. Jack chuckles at the spectacle of the portly man hiking himself on his tip toes, and then losing his balance a couple of times before finally knocking the paper to the asphalt driveway. Giving one last look behind him at Mr. Lambert, he walks into his house.

Jack turns back toward his house as he unwraps the paper and glances at the top headline: *"End of the Story for Storybook Hollow."* He freezes.

Chapter 2

It's been two hours since Jack read the haunting words. Sitting on the corner of his bed, he reads the article again for perhaps the fiftieth time.

End of the Story for Storybook Hollow

After decades of entertainment, Storybook Hollow will be shutting its gates for good, making this the park's final weekend. It is a sudden end for the Park, which has been open for nearly 60 years. The current owners of the once popular local amusement park, Newcastle, Inc., sighted decreasing attendance and rising maintenance fees as the reasoning. Senior spokesman, Art Snodgrass, told *The Herald* that they intend to build a new outdoor mall where the park has stood since 1952. The original owner sold the park to the group before his passing in 1989. Many locals hoped that the sale would revitalize the park since many of its attractions had become dated. The park has suffered major losses within the past ten years, and many locals have considered the park an eyesore.

Snodgrass continued, "While we hate to let go of this part of Cassidy Falls' past, judging by the recent attendance lull, we feel like today's consumers want a totally different experience."

Hopefully the new outdoor mall can pump some energy into an area in need of a facelift.

The last few words reverberate in Jack's mind. Swiping his falling bangs from the corner of his left eye, Jack blinks back tears that have been waiting to gush out for the last two hours. Storybook Hollow had been his palace, his escape, and the home of his fondest memories. He thought that maybe if he just read the article one more time he would see that it was just a hoax.

"Jack!" his father yells from downstairs. "Where is the paper?"

The thundering voice of his father wakes Jack from his self-induced stupor.

"I have to leave for work soon, and I want to see if the letter I wrote made the editorials."

Readying himself to reveal the horrible news to the rest of the family, Jack slowly descends down the steps.

The Braddock family mornings were always the same. His mom, Brenna, would scrap together some breakfast for his dad, but the kids were forced to scavenge for themselves. This suited Jack just fine. He simply raided the pantry, looking for the white powdered doughnuts his mom always said were bad for him but bought anyway because he asked her to.

"So what's the game plan for today?" his mother cheerily calls to him. "Another day of fun at the pool? It's the last days of summer. You should take advantage of them."

Jack does not respond.

His father, Wallace Braddock, proud partner of Gaylord and Braddock Accounting, waits in anticipation. Grabbing the paper from Jack, he greedily he scans the editorial page.

"Here it is! They printed another one of my letters."

His father's obsession with writing letters to the local paper has gotten out of hand. The letter writing has become a badge of pride to Wallace and a bane to Brenna. He reads it aloud as if the family has actually never heard it, forgetting he read it to them at least five times before he sent it off.

> When will the city see the injustice? Just because our elected officials cannot meet a budget, it does not give them the right to allow the citizens of Cassidy Falls to be hounded on the highways and intersections by their very own police officers. There are more speed traps in this town than there are streets. Why are we being punished? Because drivers roll two miles an hour over the speed limit?

Ignoring the victorious dramatic reading of her husband, his mother can see that Jack is in a daze and asks, "Jack, are you okay?"

"Brenna here is the best line," Wallace says then continues reading, "'It seems to at least this citizen that their relentless pursuit of speeding fines keeps them from doing more important things like keeping the citizens of Cassidy Falls safe.'" Wallace looks over to his wife. Scanning her face looking for praise, he is sorely disappointed by her lack of adulation.

"Wallace, hush. Jack, what is wrong with you? I thought you were meeting the boys at the pool?"

With the scolding fresh in his mind, Wallace Braddock finally looks at his son and sees the boy's dropping demeanor. For all of the good intentions of Wallace Braddock, he is a businessman through and through. There have been one too many days when Wallace has simply ignored the kids.

From the corner of Jack's eye, he sees Blair turn her attention away from some reality show and focus on him.

"They're closing Storybook Hollow."

Not missing a beat, his dad isn't surprised at all and says, "'Bout time."

"Wallace." His mother attempts to redirect her husband.

"Well, look at it this way, son, that area of town was really going downhill fast."

Again Brenna rebuffs, "Wallace, really?"

"What?"

She gestures to Jack, who is on the verge of tears. Her eyes shoot daggers at Wallace, and the man retreats into his letter to the editor.

Jack is aware of the conflict. His mother has been on his dad's case for years. He overhears her in quiet conversations with his dad at night, saying things like, "You have other responsibilities, Wallace," and, "The kids really need their father right now." The pleas are always met with his father's irritated retorts, such as, "I do the best I can, Brenna. When are you going to appreciate the fact that my work is what keeps food on the table?" For years the cycle has continued behind closed doors. Now it is happening right in front of Jack's eyes. Dad is thinking about his business and his letters, and mom is irritated.

His mother turns to Jack. "I'm sorry, dear. Those things tend to happen, though. Part of growing up."

"But they're gonna build a mall on top of it."

This has Blair's full attention. "A mall? Sweet! Think we'll get an Abercrombie and Fitch?"

Brenna begins to play referee. "We can't afford that place, sweetie. Not many people around here can."

Pouting, Blair says, "I can browse."

"Nobody cares that a local icon is going to be bulldozed?" Jack angrily scolds his family.

Brenna finally stops what she's doing, goes over to Jack, and as tenderly as she can, responds, "What can we do?"

Out of the side of his mouth, Wallace offers, "I can write a letter."

"Dear?" instructs Brenna, which is code for Wallace to shut up.

Jack considers a moment, then states, "I want to go. Tonight or tomorrow."

"Not by yourself," Brenna advises.

"Then you or dad can take me." Jack includes his mother because he's being nice. The whole family knows that Brenna, after having had a bad experience with Blackbeard's Pirate Ship as well as a bad funnel cake a few years ago, proclaimed she would never set foot near the park again. So, all eyes turn to Wallace.

"Oh no. The only night we have free this week is Friday. And that's game night."

"Dad, come on. How many more game nights at the Zuckerman's are you gonna have versus how many more times can I go to the park?"

Wallace Braddock stares back at his son. "Let's don't get overdramatic, Jack. Talking to me like that is not going to get you anywhere."

"Wallace, Jack is very upset. Perhaps you could make up for some lack of sensitivity by overlooking his tone just this once?"

Jack can see that his mother is on his side. He looks at the businessman, clad in suit and tie, to see if her persuasion is registering.

"Okay Jack, I'll take you tomorrow night."

It is a victory, but Jack is still in mourning and too upset to even acknowledge his father's acquiescence. He gives a nod to his mother, who came through for him, and simply turns and walks back up the stairs. A bittersweet victory. He would go to the park tomorrow. One last glorious night at the Hollow.

Chapter 3

"I saw it, too, Jack. You're the first person I thought of. I know you're, like, super bummed. We all are," says Mason Chick, speaking gravely to his friend.

Jack had been downright despondent ever since stepping foot into the local swim club. Mason, a taller boy, terrifically tan and built with muscle beyond what a fourteen-year-old's frame should carry, looks years older than Jack although he's only a few months his senior. As Jack knows to be his fashion, Mason launches into an inspirational speech.

"Jack, look, this is the last weekend of the summer. You have to make a choice. We can either walk around for the next two days like a pack of mope-a-sauruses or you, Scotty, and I can have the time of our lives tomorrow night."

"Can you believe they're out of bottle pops?" says another voice coming up from behind the two boys.

It belongs to the pudgy Scotty Carnahan. Pushing his glasses up from the bridge of his nose, Scotty's face holds a since of bewilderment. "First the park and, now, no bottle pops. Is there any justice in this world?"

The smell of chlorine is overwhelmed by the wafting scent of suntan lotion, and Scotty's pale belly bears the white greasy evidence of a fresh coat.

Mason playfully punches Scotty in the arm and says, "Look the park is closing, we can't change that. Take the rest of the day to sulk if you guys want, but I refuse. Tomorrow night I better have the old Jack back, or it's going to be a waste of time." Walking away from the others, Mason walks to the steps of the taller of the two springboards.

"He's right, you know," Scotty relents.

"You always think Mason is right."

And, he did: in all the years Jack has known Scotty, he's hardly ever crossed Mason. While Scotty is Jack's friend, Scotty worships Mason.

Jack's mind is awash with emotion and thinks, *How can these two take this so lightly, after all of the good times they have had at the park?*

Splash. A torrent of water drenches the two boys. Mason swims over and tells them, "That was my best splash all day."

Ignoring the wall of water that has cascaded over him, Scotty tries to cheer his friend. "If it makes you feel any better, Jack, what if we all got some matching T-shirts at the airbrush stand in the park? They could read something like, 'The three amigos' last night in the Hollow.'"

"Scotty, that is the single most stupidest idea I've ever heard. I wouldn't be caught dead in an airbrushed T-shirt," Mason retorts.

Jack decides not to comment. He agrees with Mason, the suggestion is pure Scotty, who happens to be the shortest of the three and not the most socially gifted. While Mason is always about sports and girls, the heavyset Scotty is a hopeless nerd. He loves to read, but not anything cool like comic books. He has an unnatural fascination with reading and studying about old folk stories and fairy tales. In fact, Scotty is quite the expert on Grimm's, Hans Christian Anderson, Tolkien, and others—a trait that qualifies him for über-nerd status. Other kids at school tease him relentlessly, unless Mason is around. The fact that Scotty and Mason are friends at all is one of the school's ongoing mysteries.

Just then, an idea pops into Jack's head. "Mason, I think Scotty has a point."

"Are you kidding me, Jack? Look you two can get your little T-shirts, but I am not making that mistake. Do you have any idea what a babe like Lauren Van Wormer would say if she saw me in something like that?"

"No, Mason, I have a better idea. What if we grabbed something from the park like a keepsake?"

"Go on, I like the way you're thinking, Braddock."

"I remember when they closed the Dairy Dipper over on Campbell Lane. One of my sister's friends grabbed a sign from inside one of the walls. It says something like, 'Try the Dip's Mango Monster Shake.' Blair has it hung up on the wall in her room."

Mason grins. "I get it. We can take something from like inside the Enchanted Forrest! That's your favorite ride. It would be like a keepsake."

"Wouldn't that be stealing?" interjects Scotty.

"Can it, Scotty, I like it. Maybe having a memento like that will bring Mr. Poopie Pants out of his slump?"

"If we could get something cool, it would be like a little bit of the park will remain with us," Jack confides.

It doesn't take much to convince Mason of questionable behavior. "Okay, I'm in. We'll all get a prop from inside the Enchanted Forrest. Besides, it won't be stealing since they're just going to bulldoze the place anyways, right?"

"If you think it's all right, then I'm in," Scotty says.

"Great! One last hurrah at Storybook Hollow. Now, I'm going to make a wave so large that the lifeguard up there will never forget the name Mason Chick."

Jack cycles through his mind about the ride, his ride. The Enchanted Forrest is the park's only dark ride and his favorite attraction. But what would he take? There are dozens of props small enough to sneak out of the ride, but how could he actually get one of them without anyone seeing?"

Mason makes another thunderous splash, and a pretty teenage lifeguard blows her whistle and screams, "You little troublemaker! Get out of the pool and sit your butt on the side!"

"She's hot, Mason. Better lay low for a while," Scotty warns.

"I know she's hot, that's why I did it. I need to go home anyways. Dad wants me to mow the yard. So, tomorrow night, it's a deal."

Scotty follows Mason as he scampers over for a towel and leaves Jack, once again, to his thoughts. The idea has cheered him up a little, but something inside tells him that perhaps Scotty's reservations are right. Still, he tells himself, *Nah I need something, I deserve something. After all, no one loves that place, that ride, more than I do. I will claim some Storybook Hollow history for myself tomorrow night!*

Jack makes his way to the front gate where his Schwinn bicycle is chained to the rack. Suddenly, an image pops into his head. As he hops on the bicycle, he knows exactly what he is going to take.

Chapter 4

For 50 years, Clyde Spahn has spent his entire working life in the park. He cannot help but feel a twinge of remorse. He was only 18 when the original owner, Mr. Ross, hired him on to do cleanup work. He wonders where the time has gone. The last two days have been filled with questions:

what would Edna think of all this, and what would he do now? Retirement hadn't been something Clyde was waiting for since his job wasn't just about the money. It was about being useful and doing something with his hands. With a grunt, Clyde comes back to reality and pulls a hose from a shed behind the Tilt-A-Whirl.

"So, this is the last weekend. It just seems so sudden," says Gwen Purvis, his assistant for the summer. She comments as if the old man had not already churned that fact over in his mind dozens of times.

Clyde thinks, *She is making small talk, that's what Gwen does. Ever since she was hired, that college student has babbled incessantly.* Still, Clyde did not mind the girl. He actually found her constant chattering comforting, but, tonight, he would prefer if she just kept her thoughts to herself.

Hosing down the floor of the Ice Cream Shack, the star-filled sky provides just enough light for Clyde to mark his progress. It's obvious the employees here have been careless. Ice cream coats the cement floor. *Since when did we sell purple ice cream?* Clyde wonders.

Gwen pipes up again, much to Clyde's chagrin. "It's been a fun summer, you know. I never dreamed this would be the last. I thought I could work here next summer as well."

She pauses, hoping for some response but gets none, so she presses on. "You would think they could have given us more notice. I mean none of the employees had a clue 'til that stinking newspaper article came out today. Don't they have to give us, like, 30 days' notice or something?"

No response again. Changing the subject, Gwen looks for something to say that will solicit a response. "Want me to put the hose up?"

This time Clyde graces her question with a simple, "Yep."

Shutting off the hose, Gwen rolls it back on its wheel. When she moves on to store it, Clyde takes himself back again. *What will I miss the most? No question, the kids.* While he and Edna have two girls of their own, he always felt like the kids who came to the park often were like his extended family. He had kept this place running for decades and seen thousands of smiles, and realizes that he will miss the little screams of glee. His nostalgic moment is interrupted, though, as Gwen returns.

"Okay, captain, time to hit the Forrest. It was running fine today, so all we really need to do is make sure there is no debris on the track."

"Got it."

The Dark Ride stands silent in the back corner of the park. It is the oldest and most famous ride in the park and has developed into Storybook Hollow's version of a Haunted House. Clyde anticipates the maintenance check to go quickly, after which he could go home to a TV dinner and some late night television. Rubbing his grey beard, Clyde pushes through the heavy black doors into the ride along with Gwen. A memory pops into Clyde's head, but before it has the chance to stake a more permanent claim, Clyde shudders and forces himself to do something, anything, to not remember that night. It is like this every time he walks in, a nightly battle in his head.

"Gwen, don't wander too far off now." Not wanting to voice his reasoning, Clyde adds, "It's awful dark in here and you might hit your head on something."

"Clyde, we have been in here every night this summer, and you tell me that at least three times a night. You know, I'm almost 20 years old."

Chuckling, he chides himself for his paranoia and thinks, *We have been in here every night. And I have been in here hundreds of times with no cause for alarm. Except for that time I caught a stray cat...and the time I found a couple of teens sneaking around after hours...and that night twenty-two years ago.* There it was again: the memory Clyde refuses to give life to.

Walking slowly and bending to pick up the occasional box of popcorn to sling into the black waste bag, Clyde opens the doors into the next room. Looking around, he watches as Gwen passes by and seizes a half-eaten candy apple with her gloved hands.

This bristles Clyde. "What a waste, twenty years ago, no kid in his right mind would have just tossed a perfectly good apple on the tracks. Kids are just spoiled these days. Oh, there I go again, sorry to sound like a—." He pauses mid-sentence and calls out, "Gwen?"

His young assistant is gazing towards the wall on the far end of the room.

"Do you hear that?" she asks.

"What?"

"Music."

Before the next words come out of his mouth, every hair on his body is standing at attention. "What music?"

"You know like a calliope. You hear it don't you"

A flood of memories tears down every restraint he has built up, and he thinks, *It is happening again.*

He says, "Gwen there's nothing we can accomplish tonight that I can't just do in the morning. Let's get out of here. It's awful late."

"Clyde, you don't hear that music? Aren't you curious?"

"Gwen, I'm tired. Let's pack it in."

"But, Clyde, it's coming from that room just ahead. Don't you think—?"

"I think I'm tired. We're leaving." His bright blue eyes look directly at the girl. Motioning to the door behind them with his head, he leaves no more room for argument.

He did not care if she was confused. He simply wanted them out now. "Let's go," he says and gestures for her to lead the way. After shaking her head in utter confusion, she does.

Clyde lingers a moment, straining to hear the music he's imagined all these years, but all he hears is… nothing. He didn't hear anything that night twenty-two years ago, either. The night Douglas Finch went missing for good.

Chapter 5

The Enchanted Forrest sits still. It will be another 12 hours before the park opens its doors. Standing motionless, a figure is waiting patiently, somewhere in his own world of dreams, thinking, *It will come like it always does, but this time I'll do it. This time, I'll succeed.* The thoughts tantalize him and comfort him, although he knows it will be the same result. He muses, *There she is, the girl in red. Standing, tempting, mocking.*

He plays the scenario over in his mind, wondering what he can do differently. *How can I reach her? What if I jump as soon as I hear the whirl?* Deciding to play this new scenario out in his mind, his arms move. He moves on his own. His hand rises in front of his face, and his eyes blink. With shock and elation, he realizes he has control. There is no music, no lights, no chaos, and yet he can move. With a sudden jolt of freedom, he lunges at the girl, although every joint prepares to be halted in the air. Headlong, he smashes into the girl. The pain of the fall is of no consequence; he got her. He looks at his victim joyously. The years of failure have now been rewarded. Saliva runs free. His jaws flex, and his teeth shimmer. Preparing to tear at the girl, a strange realization interrupts the joy.

What is this?

He rips and slashes for signs of blood, or any life. He growls.

A replica? This is no girl. She was real, the girl is real. All these years, and now that I am free, someone has fooled me. Replaced her with this. A plastic statue. A new feeling rips through his mid-section. He is famished. He must feed. How long has it been? The pain is so intense that it seizes his stomach into a convulsion. The instinct is overwhelming.

Food. The girl. I will find the girl. She must be here. She will be mine, and then I will feed. Now that I am free, I will feed!

Chapter 6

The sign outside the door reads, "Employees Only – Break Room." But it's not much of a break room. A relic of a coffee maker sits atop a counter next to a grimy sink, a solitary drink machine offers sodas that passed their prime five years ago, and leaning against an unused wall is a yellow-stained, folded-up card table. Clyde, hands on his hips, tries to forget what happened last night. He shoves a hand into his back pocket and removes his wallet and opens the black leather flap. There she is: Edna. The picture was taken for an old church directory back in '74. Instinctively, any time Clyde is at a loss, he thinks about Edna. She passed away ten years ago, but looking at her picture brings him comfort. Relishing the respite, Clyde speaks to her.

"Well, Edna, last night was something else, huh?"

Clyde remembers back when the Enchanted Forrest first opened. Originally it was a kiddie ride until Mr. Ross decided that the park needed something a little more edgy and had all of the scenes altered to make it more frightening.

A well-rusted hinge signals that Clyde is about to have company. It's Gwen.

"Clyde, I was in the Enchanted Forrest this morning."

"You what?"

"Look, I was just curious about that music, and I was looking around when I noticed that the Wolf is gone."

"The Wolf is gone? You have got to be kidding. How? That thing weighs a ton."

Of all of the special effects in the Enchanted Forrest, the Wolf in the Red Riding Hood Room, which is placed on a track so that it startles the riders, is by far the best scare of the ride.

Clyde wonders if this has something to do with the music but tells Gwen, "Bet it was some college kids pulling the ultimate prank." Clyde wonders who the culprits could be.

Gwen offers, "I bet that Colton Spurlock is behind this. He and those guys over at the Midway games are always up to no good." She pauses, then adds, "Oh brother, Mr. Snodgrass is going to be angry."

"Oh no. We're not calling him."

"But that's what we were told to do in training."

Clyde stows his wallet and replies, "No need Gwen, let me take care of this."

"But Mr. Snodgrass is already on his way."

"You called him already?"

She nods, a bit sheepishly, and Clyde's face falls. To say that this is not exactly what he wanted to deal with today would be an understatement. Handling delinquent teenagers is easy, and making adjustments for stolen property at a closing park is manageable. But, dealing with the manager, Mr. Snodgrass—pull out a calculator and start adding.

Chapter 7

The Braddocks' kitchen counter has seen better days. Large clunks of peanut butter and jelly are smattered here and there, along with an empty milk jug, a half-full bag of chips, and some bills and coupons messily stacked next to Brenna's purse. Jack walks into the living room with his recently constructed sandwich to see if anything good is on TV, simply looking for a way to kill time until 6 p.m. when his dad takes him to the park. Jack considers laying on the couch to doze off. He had not gotten much sleep last night due to envisioning exactly how he would pull off grabbing his prop from inside the Dark Ride.

Flopping down on the couch, he tries to catch up on some sleep, but, once again, thoughts of how to get the prop disturb him. His target would be a small golden statue inside one of the first few rooms that make up the Enchanted Forrest. Within the ride, there are several rooms that revolve around the fairy tale of "Jack and the Beanstalk," the old familiar story where the character Jack climbs a beanstalk, enters a giant's castle, and steals a goose that lays golden eggs to help his family out of poverty. Obviously, by sharing his name with the hero of the tale, Jack thought there would be no more appropriate keepsake than a small golden statue of a goose that the ride displays in the "Giant's Room." The statue rests on a fireplace. The major problem would be getting out of the small moving vehicle in order to snatch the item. He had to figure out some way. *The statue is just too perfect,* Jack reasons. Just like his namesake, Jack would take the golden goose.

His plan to sprawl out on the couch and take a nap is futile. He cannot sleep while wrestling with the problem. Jack contemplates, *How can I get out of the train to get the goose? Will I be able to leave the ride and hop back on before it gets away from me?*

Just then Blair waltzes into the room, phone to her ear, as always. "I know they are just obnoxious sometimes, no all the time...one day he will get what he deserves... that will be too sweet."

Jack is curious as to whom his sister is speaking, but decides to ignore her. Flipping on the TV, a commercial for Titus Chick, Mason's dad, is on.

"*Do you need someone in your corner? Have you been arrested for a D.U.I.? Have your rights been infringed? The law office of Titus J. Chick is here to help.*"

"That was Denise," Blair says. His sister reaches down and grabs the remote, flipping off the TV.

"Who's Denise?"

"Can it, egghead—you know exactly who Denise is."

"No, I don't."

"Uh, yes you do. She happens to be the lifeguard your little friend soaked yesterday afternoon with his little cannonball routine."

"And this matters to me because?"

"You tell that brat that next time Denise will have him expelled from the pool—for good."

"She can't do that. Besides, she's a lifeguard." He repeats the word slowly for emphasis, "Lifeguard. Isn't she supposed to get wet? I say occupational hazard."

"Oh, you guys think you're so cute. You know, your little pranks are going to catch up with you one day. What if Denise was mad enough to call her boyfriend, who's on the wrestling team, by the way? She could simply say one word like, 'sick 'em,' and Mason would be begging for mercy."

"'Sick 'em' is actually two words."

"Oh, you are really smug, aren't you?"

"What are you gonna do, have Colton Spurlock beat me up? Maybe you guys can talk about that at the mall tonight. You can arrange your hit then."

Jack could see Blair reaching her breaking point. And like all good younger siblings who smell blood, Jack goes in for the kill. "Maybe mom and dad would be interested to know Colton is on your speed dial. I think that information would intrigue them since you were forbidden to date him."

"You little!" Blair's face twists into an angry snarl.

Evasive maneuvers are required. The sandwich drops to the floor, and Jack leaps off the couch and heads for the stairs. Turning to gauge the distance between him and Blair, he realizes that her arm is coming forward with an object in it. Jack ducks as the phone whistles through the air.

Crash! The projectile smashes into a family portrait hanging above the piano.

Both siblings look at the portrait in horror.

The picture is one of those false illusions. All four of them dressed in khaki pants and white button downs sitting on the beach. It's their mom's favorite thing in the entire house. She paid a photographer loads of money while the family was on vacation to come and snap the photo. Jack always gets a kick out of how happy and peaceful they all look. Mere seconds before the photo was taken, Jack had been arguing with Blair, and their mom had been riding Wallace about taking a call from work on the beach.

A thorough investigation reveals a small chip in the glass.

"Now you're in for it, Blair. Looks like someone is going to get grounded."

"Mom will never notice. You better keep this quiet."

"Oh, mom won't notice, huh?"

"No, she won't unless some useless little brat tattle-tells."

The insult inspires Jack to push on. "So mom won't notice what you did, huh?"

The sinister idea just pops into his head. Jack bends down and lifts the phone to the picture. With a quick forward motion he slams the instrument hard against the crack.

A thin trial of shattered glass stretches out from the original crack like a spider web.

"I think she'll notice now. Looks like someone is in big trouble."

"You… you!" Blair screams.

Blair's scream is so loud that Brenna Braddock is called away from folding clothes upstairs. The familiar footsteps patter down the carpeted steps.

"What in the world are you two fighting about now?"

Neither Blair nor Jack makes a move.

Brenna scans the room. "My picture!" Her face shows a look of total despair.

"Blair did it, mom. She got so angry, she threw her phone at me."

"No, he did it. Mom, he took my phone and slammed it into the picture!"

"Enough!"

The ferocity of his mother's voice sends a cold chill up Jack's spine. He realizes this is serious. The look, the tone—they were reserved for capital offenses.

"I have had it up to here with your antics, both of you. Where did I go so wrong that my two children treat each other like this?" She pauses, red-faced, to think. "You're both grounded for at least a week."

"But mom, it was all Blair's fault."

"I don't care whose fault it was. One week—no TV, no movies, no car, no anything! You will be in your rooms, unless you're doing chores. The chores will commence tomorrow morning."

"Mom, I was going to the mall tonight."

"No, ma'am, you will be staying right here."

Blair storms up the steps. *SLAM!*

Jack is in total shock. He wonders, *What about tonight?* His little stunt has completely backfired. He thinks, *She cannot mean this. Time for some smooth talk.*"Mom, I'm sorry about what happened. It just got out of control."

He waits a second and then risks it.

"Can I still go to the park tonight? I mean, it's closing and all."

"Jack, you're not talking your way out of this one. You should have thought about the consequences when you and your sister decided to destroy my picture."

"But, mom!"

"Not another word, Jack. I hate that I have to do this, but you and Blair have to learn to coexist." Jack's world has just caved in. "One week," his mom says, and then, after pausing thoughtfully, "and no park tonight."

Chapter 8

With mallet in hand, Clyde examines his latest handy work. He has just placed a "Park Closing" sign up in front of the main ticket gate, another painful reminder that he only has two more days on the job. He notices a slick black, top-of-the-line BMW pull into the parking space reserved for Howard Snodgrass.

"The boss is here," Gwen announces gloomily, holding the season pass sign that she just took down.

Oh brother, here we go, Clyde says to himself as he takes a deep breath and prepares for the impending conversation.

The stout man struggles against his own girth to pry himself out of the front seat. Finally freed, Howard Snodgrass slams the door and ambles towards Clyde and Gwen, obviously irritated.

"So what's this about a wolf being gone? And why, pray tell, did I have to come all the way down here to see about it?"

"All the way down here: meant five minutes.

Gwen clears her throat and says, "Mr. Snodgrass, I thought—"

Clyde cuts her off, thinking, *No need for the kid to get involved,* and says, "Looks like we had some vandals last night." He turns and nods to Gwen. "Mr. Snodgrass, I thought you needed to see for yourself." Even though Clyde is 20 years Snodgrass's senior, Howard makes everyone address him as mister. Clyde often wonders if Mrs. Snodgrass had to, too.

"So. You've dealt with vandals before, Clyde. Just do your job."

Clyde's job description never included night watchman. Those guys had been let go years ago, after the park's financial trouble had started. Still, Clyde had dealt with lots of things that were not his job. At this point, Clyde decides not to mention the incident with the music from the night before. He is already trying to suppress the memory, and it wouldn't really matter. Snodgrass will ignore him.

"Actually, Mr. Snodgrass, I was the one—"

Clyde cuts her off again. "I did not want to bother you, sir, but the fact is that the wolf is a major part of the Enchanted Forrest. The park guests will be upset if it's not there."

"Oh, horse hockey. We only have two miserable days left in this miserable little park. Who cares if someone stole a wolf statue? They could steal the roller coaster and I would not care at this point. Now, explain to me why I was called down here?"

Again, Gwen continues, trying to take the bullet, "Sir, in orientation—."

Again, Clyde interrupts her to cover. "I thought since you were the operations manager you would be concerned, that's all." Her intentions are noble, but he's not letting her fall on the sword.

"So what am I supposed to do? Call the cops?"

"Well, maybe."

"Clyde, we are not about to call the police down here about some stupid little prop. Do you have any idea what kind of paper work I would have to fill out? Plus, don't the police have something better to do than worry about this kind of garbage?"

"Yes, I guess so."

"Good. Now go back and do all those important things that you maintenance people do like pick up some trash or fiddle with your thumbs. I'm going home. And, Clyde?"

"Yes, sir."

"Remember, this park is done. Consider this your two-day notice."

"You were right," Gwen declares as Snodgrass ambles back toward the parking lot. "Thanks for covering for me."

"Don't mention it." Clyde peers at the backside of the departing Snodgrass. It takes all of Clyde's reserve not to tackle the man right then and there. He stews, *His flippant attitude about the closing is one thing. What does he have to worry about? After all, his rich daddy, Art Snodgrass, CEO of Newcastle, Inc., will probably give him some cushy job. But the fact that he does not even care enough to step in and at least check out the disappearance is revolting.* Howard Snodgrass has never cared about the park or its guests, and that, at least to Clyde, is a major reason the park is closing.

Chapter 9

"You have got to be kidding, Jack." Mason says. His irritation coming through the phone is more than justifiable. "This just won't do—no, not at all. We're leaving in like an hour."

"I know, I know. But I'm really up the creek here. Look, I blew it this time. How many times do I have to say I'm sorry?"

"Jack, what about our plan? The three of us, taking a keepsake from the Enchanted Forrest. There has to be a way you can get out of this."

"Dude, I'm stuck here. I'm just as hacked as you are. You two will just have to go without me. Other than sneaking out tonight, I really have no other options. My mom is not going to give."

"That's a good idea!"

"What?"

"Sneak out."

"Oh… I don't know, Mason. I'm already in the doghouse."

"But it's our last night at the park—your park."

"Sneaking out? That's about as bad as it gets. If I get caught, I may be grounded forever."

"Don't get caught. Jack, how late do your parents stay out at the Zuckerman's?"

"Oh, I don't know, around 10, but sometimes later."

"Okay, that's it. We simply get you home by 9:30."

"My folks leave around 5. How am I supposed to get over to the park? I can't ride my bike—that would take over an hour."

"Look I will come to your house around 5:15. I'll call Scotty and tell him we are coming to his house to hitch a ride. We can ride our bikes over there in less than ten minutes. The Carnahans will have no clue you're sneaking out. It's perfect."

Jack thinks, *You do want this really bad. It's worth the risk.*

A feeble, "Okay," escapes from Jack's mouth before he can second-guess the heavy decision.

"Good, Jack, see you then. You won't regret this."

He's right, Jack says to himself, *Everything will work out fine... I hope.*

For the next hour, Jack whirls about his room in quiet preparation. In order for this to go smoothly, he has to account for Blair. She would be lurking around the house, and if she got the slightest notion of his plan, he would be busted.

Years ago, there had been no sibling rivalry. There are scrapbooks filled with happy pictures that bare proof. One shows Blair, age five, holding little Jack. Another is a shot of them as small children with paint-covered faces, grinning at the camera. And another has Blair, age nine, and Jack, age seven, standing in three inches of snow, proud of a four-foot snowman built with themselves. But those photos, those happy memories, are mere shadows of the past. The rivalry and hostility began the instant Blair turned 12.

It was an elaborate party. Wallace and Brenna had gone all-out with cake, balloons, family, and friends, all filling the Braddock living room. Brenna had even given Blair a new white dress to wear to the party. It was exactly what Blair wanted, a tribute to her. Blair no longer saw herself as a little girl, and this marked the culmination of her transition out of childhood with a towering birthday cake celebrating the coming of age of one soon to be crowned princess.

For his part, Jack wanted to do something special as well. He was a prankster, of course, and a trip to the novelty store had provided him with trick candles, ones that would re-light after being blown out over and over again. Jack beamed with pride as he relished in the joke. He thought it would be perfect and that everyone would love it. On the day of the party, he had taken every precaution to make sure no one saw him replace the ordinary candles with the trick ones. During the celebration, Jack watched from a distance, simply awaiting the cake and his moment. His eyes followed the cake as it was brought from the kitchen. Blair stood at the end of a table, flanked by an assortment of 12-year-old girls and one boy, her current "boyfriend," a blonde-haired kid named Grayson. This was her day, and she glowed with pride. The white cake was lowered to the table, and the guests began to sing. Twelve candles were lit. They sparked and flared to life.

Jack eased forward to get a good view. Before blowing them out, Blair thanked everyone in a diva-like salute. Jack could hardly contain his excitement. Then Blair began to blow out the candles. With a rather ladylike gust of wind, she puffed several times, and the candles went dead. Jack starred, anticipating what was to come next. The candles, one by one, sparked back to life. A few laughs rippled through the mass of guests. Blair looked slightly embarrassed and repeated her dainty gusts. The scene repeated itself. Jack could not contain his own pride. He wanted everyone to know this was his joke.

"Gotcha good, Blair," he announced.

After few more laughs, Jack looked for approval, but he was disappointed. The girl made an unfamiliar face, one of anger and irritation. She was determined not to allow the prank to spoil her party. She climbed up on a chair, hovering over the cake itself. Forgetting her ladylike charms, she sucked in lungs full of air and blew down upon the cake candles. Her face showed determination; this time she would win. But as she blew out the wind in her cheeks, her right arm gave way. Her entire body lost balance and she collapsed head first into the cake. Her dress was ruined, her cake was ruined, and, by all accounts, her perfect day was ruined as well.

Jack was punished for the prank, even though he said, "But I didn't mean for that to happen."

His mother was furious and responded, "But it did."

It was that event that marked the change in their relationship. Blair never got over the embarrassment of that day. It was supposed to have been the greatest day of her life. For his part, Jack had never gotten over being punished for the good-natured prank. It made little difference that it was one isolated incident up to that point. From that moment on, the sibling rivalry had begun, and since then, things between Blair and Jack have never been the same. No matter how small the offense, the slightest argument would turn into a global conflict. Now, Blair saw Jack as her irritating little brother, and she took joy in getting him in trouble. In Jack's eyes, Blair was his nosy older sister, so tonight, as he prepared to sneak out of the house, he would have to watch out for her.

He and Mason had carefully talked over the plan. The review had taken quite some time from start to finish, but Jack felt ready. He pulls out the fire escape ladder from underneath his bed. He had never used it, so he familiarizes himself with how it works. There will only be a few minutes between the moment his parents leave and when Mason shows up to aid in his escape. He looks at the backpack in the corner. It is the perfect vessel for stashing the golden goose. He grabs an old red-hooded sweatshirt from his drawer and places it inside his backpack along with a T-shirt. He always packs an extra shirt just in case he gets wet on one of the water rides. Finally, He snags a pack of Twizzlers, his favorite candy, from the nightstand and then stands, scanning the room for anything else he might want or need.

From underneath a pile of socks, hastily placed in the corner of his closet, he removes a small plastic hippo. The container bought at the Louisville Zoo when he was six has faithfully served as his piggy bank. He pulls out a wadded up $20 bill and three fives.

A knock on his door causes him to quickly sling the bank back in the closet.

"Who is it?"

"It's mom, I'm coming in."

The ladder! remembers Jack.

With cat-like agility, Jack leaps over to the ladder and kicks it under the bed. He then assumes the proper hurt-slash-penitent look of sitting on the edge of his bed and staring at a spot on the wall, looking completely bored with a little bit of "my cat just died" thrown in.

His mom walks into the room with a casserole dish in her hands.

The smell of his mother's tuna casserole fills the room. Ugh, Jack says to himself. The vile concoction has made Jack sick more than once.

"Jack, your father and I are leaving."

Jack can see the outline of his father coming up from behind his mom.

"Jack, I simply want you to do the right thing. Today you made a bad choice and that has to be addressed."

"I said I was sorry."

"There are still consequences, Jack. You know that."

In another desperate plea, Jack says, "But I'm being punished for something Blair did. She started the whole—"

"I don't want to hear it, Jack. The decision is made." Brenna chews on her lip a moment, trying to figure out how to soften things. She goes with,

"I love you, Jack. I want you to learn to be the man your father and I hope you'll be, okay? And that's not someone who antagonizes others."

The feelings of guilt wash over Jack. His mom had played the "I love you" card. He reprimands himself for even thinking about sneaking out and surmises, *I can't do that now.* Somehow moms know exactly when to say those three little words. Jack is convinced that his mom has been a part of some underground secret mother society where she worked on using guilt as a weapon.

"Jack," his father interjects. "This kind of behavior is not acceptable. I hope you take the hurt of tonight and channel it into improved behavior. You have so much potential. We need to see a drastic change for the better soon. " It is a typical Wallace Braddock moment. He speaks to Jack like an employee he is threatening with a pink slip.

Brenna steps in front of Wallace, a gesture to show that he isn't speaking for the both of them, and says, "We'll be back before 10. Just… make wise decisions, okay?"

Before she exits, she leans over and kisses him on the forehead. "Bye, Jack, don't stay up too late. I have a list of chores we need to tackle first thing in the morning."

Exiting, his father nods to him and closes the door.

The guilt settles somewhere in Jack's head and seers his conscience. There is no way he can sneak out now. Locking the door behind his parents, Jack grabs the backpack, unzips the bag, and pulls out the contents.

After a few moments, he hears the front door close and his father's Toyota Camry start. He sulks over to retrieve the plastic hippo when he hears an odd sound.

Ping, ping.

The sharp noise is coming from the window. Jack takes four steps and looks through the pane. The car is gone. He scans the yard…nothing. Then, another *ping.* Looking straight down below him he sees Mason hidden amongst the shrubbery and dressed head to toe in black. Something large is draped over his shoulder.

Jack can't believe this. *He's here already?* he thinks. *How can I tell Mason I'm not going through with this?*

Jack lifts the window. "Mason, the coast is clear. You can get out of our bushes."

Before leaving his hiding spot, Mason gives a comical exaggerated glance to his right, then to his left. He slings whatever is draped over his shoulder to the lawn and then dives from the brush and rolls into the lawn. He looks around again, and in a loud whisper, he calls up to Jack, "Okay, Braddock, the great escape begins now."

Oh man, thinks Jack, *better just say it.* He explains, "Uh... Mason, I'm not going."

"What?"

"I said I'm not going."

"Why, what's gotten into you?"

"Well, I...." Jack thinks, *I can't tell him my mom said "I love you." I would never hear the end of that. Think fast.* He says, "Uh, I've got homework." Immediately, he tells himself, *Oh no, no, no that's not good.*

"You've got homework, Jack? It's summer! Are you kidding me?"

"Uh, yes—I mean no—I've got homework—like, work to do at home."

"Jack, you're chickening out."

"No, I'm not. Just got a lot of chores."

"Jack, we only have fifteen minutes to get over to the Carnahans'. Need I remind you that tonight is the last night we will ever be able to go to the park? We have plans, awesome plans. You're not going to let me down, are you?"

Oh brother, thinks Jack, *Now Mason has played the "let me down card." What am I going to do?* Jack stares down at Mason and realizes, *This will be my last chance. Mason has gone to a lot of trouble.*

Jack nods at his friend and removes the escape ladder from its resting place. The ladder latches to the window frame easily and chain link steps flow down to the ground. Mason grabs the thing from the lawn and struggles up the ladder.

At the window, Mason slings the large item from his back. To Jack's astonishment, he sees that it's a dummy dressed in a green T-shirt and jeans. The head is made out of a volleyball, complete with a brown wig.

Knowing that secrecy is the upmost priority, in a whispered hush Jack asks the obvious, "What are we gonna do with that?"

A whispering Mason responds, "We're going to place this thing in the bed. Just in case your sister comes into the room. It took me three hours to make it this afternoon. I stuffed it with grass cuttings."

"You're gonna put your backyard in my bed?"

"Yeah. But it doesn't look like my backyard." Mason sidles up next to the dummy and smiles as if Jack's got a camera.

"Fine."

"What was that all about anyways? You were backing out."

"No, my parents really gave me a bunch of stuff to do."

36

He didn't mention that his mother had prepared the list for tomorrow. Mason seems appeased but leery. Shrugging off the uncomfortable moment, the two friends finagle the dummy in the bed.

"What made you think of this?"

"Jack, this is not my first escape. This Chuck is just the latest of many."

"It has a name?"

"Of course, it's Charles Coltraine Higgenbotham. Chuck, for short."

"I don't care."

Mason covers the dummy's ears and says, "You'll hurt his feelings." He spies a tinge of reluctance on Jack's part. "Come on, always works for me."

"Look, this is stupid."

"We need to go, the Carnahans are expecting us." Mason sneaks over to the window and drapes his right leg over the ledge. "Come on, Jack."

The time is come for Jack to decide between enjoying the park or dealing with the guilt. Mason is already out of sight. *Okay,* Jack says to himself, *let's do this.* The decision has been made, the plan is back on.

Jack looks down at the backpack and quickly replaces the removed items before slinging it over his shoulder.

Someone knocks on his door.

"Jack, Jack. What's going on in there?" asks Blair.

Chapter 10

Jack panics. Rushing over to the window, he unlatches the ladder.

"Umph."

A quick glance out the window by Jack reveals Mason lying in an awkward pile upon the lawn.

"Who are you talking to in there?"

"Who's talking?" If he does not open the door soon, Blair will ruin the whole thing. He sees Chuck in the bed. After yanking the sheets over the dummy, he knows he has to position himself in front of his sister. She cannot enter the room or else he is busted.

"Jack, you're up to something."

"You always think that."

Opening the door, Jack tries to force any remnant of guilt from his face.

"Now what do you want?" Jack asks.

"Who were you talking to?"

Jack sees the phone in her hand. "Who are you talking to?"

"No one."

"Then me neither."

"I'm not an idiot."

"Debatable."

"Ha ha. Very funny. Perhaps I should call mom and dad and tell them you have a friend in your room?"

"Oh, now I understand. You heard me talking to Mason."

"Mason Chick? What's that little troublemaker doing here?" Blair attempts to look behind Jack, but Jack, equally as tall, maneuvers to block her view.

"He was on the phone, Blair."

Jack knows that he must draw her attention away from the room. Jack steps out into the hall, shutting the door behind him. He must draw her away. Jack wants more than anything to check on Mason and escape, but for now, putting Blair's suspicion at ease is top priority. He needs to turn this around.

"Talked to Colton tonight?"

"None of your business."

"Blair, I will be listening tonight. Mom and dad told me to keep my eye on you," says Jack, and then he thinks, *This is good.*

"They what?"

"You heard me. They think you're going to try something sneaky."

Jack lures Blair away from the doorway and walks toward the staircase.

In pursuit, Blair trails behind, agitated. "Look, you little toad, for your information, you ruined everything. Because of you, Colton is mad at me."

"Think he will find another cheerleader to hit on at the mall?'

"You are so full of yourself. You make me so...."

Jack waits for the final words of her insult, but realizes something is wrong. Blair is giving him a suspicious look.

"Jack, what's that backpack for? Are you going somewhere?"

A lump forms in the pit of Jack's throat. He forgot about the backpack draped across his shoulder. He must think fast, but, then again, thinking fast is Jack's forte.

"Oh, this? Well, if I'm going to be stuck in my room for a week, at least I can be comfortable. I don't see why this is any of your business. I'm going downstairs to get some snacks for the prison."

Jack walks hastily down the steps and into the kitchen, acting out his latest rouse. Blair follows, watching him. He snags a roll of powdered doughnuts and a box of granola bars and places them in the backpack.

"Sure hope things turn out okay with Colton. I would hate to think I'm the reason your latest love connection failed."

He knows he is milking the whole Colton thing, but it's working. The more he can get Blair focused on her would-be-boyfriend, the less she would wonder what he is up to.

The two siblings walk back up the stairs. Now, Jack puts the final touches on his scheme. "Look the best thing either one of us can do is just stay out of each other's way. I'll be in my room, and you can text whoever you want in yours."

Pausing at her door, Blair considers the deal and then replies, "That's the smartest thing I think you've ever said, loser."

Slam!

Back in his room, Jack pulls the sheet down again, revealing only the head of Chuck. He turns his backpack upside down emptying it of the items he had just grabbed. He slings the pack back over his shoulder and carefully hides the snacks.. He turns off the lights and makes one last survey of his room. He imagines Chuck will do a fine job and tells himself, *Looks like I'm sound asleep.*

Jack makes his way quietly back through the door. From years of sneaking into Blair's room, he knows the exact path to take to avoid any spots in the floor that might squeak beneath him. On tip toes, he walks past Blair's room and hears Coldplay blaring from the stereo.

The escape route is clear. Jack moves through the front door and shuts it with careful precision. Wasting no time, Jack circles the house to the spot beneath his window. Mason is nowhere in sight. Jack risks a hushed call. "Mason?"

"Over here."

From behind one of the large holly bushes that surround the house Mason is sitting next to the wall ladder crumpled at his feet.

"What happened up there? Did the ladder slip?"

"Blair."

"Blair did it? She saw—?"

"She didn't see anything. I took care of it. You okay?"

"I'm fine. My ankle twisted and my knee hit me in the chin, but I'm no worse for wear. Next time we sneak out through the window, though, you're going first." He rubs his jaw. "The bikes are next door in the ditch. Let's go."

Hunkered down like a hunchback, Mason creeps to the neighbor's lawn. Jack thinks, *Mason is enjoying this a little too much.*

Everything is on schedule.

Chapter 11

Jack is plagued with worry from the moment he steps out of his neighbor's yard. Everything had gone smoothly up to this point, but he couldn't help but think that Blair might walk into his room at any minute. He is taking a big risk. He had decided against locking his bedroom door because that would have only heightened suspicion, but now he starts to second guess himself. He knows that the odds of Blair actually going into his room are slim, and consoles himself thinking that even if she does, she would see Chuck and probably be delighted that she could speak freely in her room without worrying about a spy being outside the door. Still, there is always a chance she could blow the whole plan to smithereens.

Wrapped up in his own thoughts, Jack takes little notice that the truck he is in is pulling into Storybook Hollow. As the vehicle stops, though, he hears the familiar sounds of the King Midas Roller Coaster. Waking from his fear, all worry and doubt are gone in an instant. The park is calling to him. The Carnahans had to use two vehicles to transport the party to the park. In addition to Jack and Mason, the Carnahans also have their four children with them: Scotty, age 14; Amy, age 13; and the twins, Abigail and Ashley, age 8. The boys were relegated to Mr. Carnahan's '78 Ford pickup while the four girls rode in Mrs. Carnahan's Nissan van.

Jack takes in the sights and the smells. Colored lights are flashing, and the smell of cotton candy is wafting through the air. He is at his home away from home.

Once inside the gate, the Carnahans give final instructions before the boys are allowed to set off on their own.

Mr. Carnahan instructs, "We will meet back here at 9:15, no later, boys. Mason has to get home early." Houston Carnahan is a tall muscular man with long black hair and a rather intimidating Fu Manchu mustache. He is the polar opposite of his son, to whom he adds, "Scotty, call us if you need us. Make sure your phone is off vibrate. You never answer it unless you hear it. We are probably going to be spending most of the night over in the kiddie area."

With the speech over, the boys know it's time to conquer the park. But as they turn to go in the opposite direction toward the roller coaster, Mr. Carnahan gives one last order, "And Scotty, Amy is going with you guys."

Upon hearing these last words, Scotty drops his mouth in shock and Mason casts an angry look at Jack while slamming his left fist into his open right hand. Jack can only nervously brush his bangs up from his eyes as he's made uncomfortable by Mason's obvious irritation. The news flash has the opposite effect on Amy, however, and the girl smiles.

Scotty voices the protest. "Dad, why?"

"Because Amy is old enough now and we are not going to force her to ride kiddie rides with the twins all night."

"Oh man," Mason confides to Jack. "Are they serious? She'll ruin everything."

Seeing the reaction of his crew, Jack decides to act as if this bothers him as well. The truth of the matter is that Jack has no problem with Amy. He has always gotten along fine with her.

As Amy extends her arm to get a few extra dollars from her dad, the three companions have a council. Mason makes sure Amy is out of earshot and then says, "Oh man, I can't believe that tonight, our last night, we're gonna to have to deal with a tag along." His agitated voice gives way to a sinister grin. "Okay boys, we're going to have to ditch her."

"Ditch Amy? I can't do that. My parents will kill me."

"No, Scotty, we have too. We can't let her screw up the plan. Remember, we are here for the props. Right, Jack?"

"Uh… yeah, right."

"Okay, but if I get in hot water over this…."

"You'll what, Scotty?" challenges the taller Mason.

"Oh, never mind. You're right."

"Look, the hall of mirrors will be the perfect place. We can ride the roller coaster and the Dutch Swings, then we lose her in the hall." Mason waits for acknowledgement from the other boys.

"Okay," Scotty says and nods in agreement.

Jack thinks, *She would be a hindrance to the plan, but it's just so mean.* "Jack?"

"Yeah, I guess."

"Okay then."

As Amy approaches, the boys break their huddle.

Walking next to Jack, a quiet almost apologetic voice escapes from the girl. "Jack, I know you guys would rather be alone."

"No, it's cool," Jack lies.

"No really, I had no idea my dad would let me go with y'all tonight."

"Really, it's cool, Amy."

"Thanks for saying that, Jack, but I don't think Mason and Scotty are cool with it."

"Never mind them, they'll get over it," he lies again.

"I really wanted to come with you guys. I mean, I don't think I could have taken another night of riding those mindless kiddie rides. They are all the same—'round and 'round in a circle. You can ride on the back of a dragon, 'round and 'round, or there is the excitement of riding in a police car, 'round and 'round."

"Amy, it's all right, you're not a kid anymore." Jack watches as the tense smile loosens on the girl's face.

Without saying one word to her, Mason and Scotty start walking to the far side of the park where the rickety old wooden roller coaster, King Midas, dwells.

"Awesome—no line. Let's you and I sit up front, Scotty," Mason, wild with excitement, blurts as he runs ahead of them.

Mason and Scotty high-tail it through the queue.

Amy tells Jack, "I guess you're stuck riding with the tag along."

"Amy, really, it's okay. You don't have to apologize all night. You want to sit behind the guys?"

"Sure."

The park is nearly empty: only a hundred or so people are there. This surprises Jack, who wonders, *Don't people want to say goodbye to the park?*

Jack pulls the iron bar down and anticipates the slow climb up the first incline.

"You know, I've never ridden King Midas before," Amy confesses.

"Are you serious? All the times you've been here and…."

"Nope, never."

"Well hold on tight."

For years, Jack had found himself playing peacemaker between Mason, Scotty, and Amy. The two boys were merciless in their abuse of her. Jack wouldn't have been able to explain why he never felt like joining in, since it wasn't like he had any love for girls. After all, his own relationship with Blair is downright ugly. Still, he could not help but feel a little sympathy for shy Amy.

"This is the best view in all of Cassidy Falls," Jack proclaims.

He watches with interest as Amy ducks her head, ready for the first big drop.

Jack grins. He likes this. Something about the vulnerability intrigues him.

Whoosh, whisp, zoom!

A knot in Jack's stomach tickles him as they plummet down the hills and whizz around corners. Amy is laughing and no longer seems intimidated by the thrill ride.

"Isn't this great?" Jack yells.

After another corkscrew and a quick plummet, the voyage is over. It's only taken 30 seconds, but they have enjoyed every last twist.

"That was great! You guys wanna ride again?" asks Amy, who is excited by the thought.

"Nope, Amy. We have a tradition here. Now we go on to the Dutch Swings." Mason points to the next destination just ahead.

"That was a blast, Jack. I can tell tonight is going to be great."

The other two boys are up ahead. A twinge of guilt rises somewhere within Jack. He hesitates and then says, "Yep, we're going to have fun." But, he thinks, *At least three of us are,* with a hint of disappointment in himself.

Chapter 12

Just outside of the Hall of Mirrors Mason pulls Jack towards him. "Just follow our lead." From the corner of his eyes, Jack watches as Scotty distracts Amy.

"All right, Jack, we only have one shot at this. We all know the place pretty well. You hang back a little behind Amy with Scotty and me when we get about halfway in. When she climbs through the spinning tunnel, we all high-tail it back to the entrance and go to the Enchanted Forrest without her."

Mason waits for confirmation from Jack.

Hesitantly, Jack nods.

"Jack, what's gotten into you? You are with us, right?"

"Sure, I'm with you." Even as he says the words, Jack knows he does not want the plan to work. It seems a little cruel to him, and he's really not minding Amy's company.

Scotty calls to the other boys. "You guys ready?"

The companions move to the front doors. "After you, mi-lady," Mason says with more than a little deceptiveness in his voice.

Stopping at mirror after mirror, they enjoy the various reflections the mirrors cast.

At one particular mirror, Scotty laughs at how stumpy the mirror makes Amy look.

"Gosh, Amy, you look like a hobbit."

"Thanks, Scotty, these mirrors are supposed to do that."

"I know, but you look ridiculous," Scotty giggles.

"Knock it off."

Jack wonders, *Is Amy upset? Surly she knows Scotty is only kidding? She did look kind of funny—everyone did.* Still, Jack cannot deny that in spite of whatever she looked like in the mirror, Amy Carnahan is one very cute girl. As soon as the thought pops into his head, he chastises himself, thinking, *Where did that come from? That's it, one step over the line. I'm actually checking out Scotty's little sis. Gross, Jack, she's practically your sister, too.* But, try as he might to force the attraction out of his mind, he is defenseless against the new line of thought. It's like he's seeing her in a whole new light. He tells himself, *This is the girl who was obsessed with Barbie dolls and tea parties not four years ago. Now she's attractive? Stop it Jack,* but then has to reconsider, *No, Amy Carnahan has become a babe.* His attention is now focused on the girl. He can't take his eyes off her. He watches her closely and soon gathers that something is wrong. Her demeanor has changed. She's obviously avoiding the mirrors. Jack wonders if Scotty's insult bothered her that much? Although Jack will admit that he does not understand the opposite sex—by a longshot—he knows it has something to do with the way she feels about herself.

Jack's psychoanalysis comes to a halt when Mason blurts out, "Looks like were coming to the middle of the hall. We can only go through the spinning tunnel one at a time. Amy, you go first." Looking to make sure the others are behind him, Mason holds up a hand, signaling for the two boys to stop.

This is it, Jack realizes, *This is where we are supposed to run.*

"Oh man, I can't keep my balance," Amy says while laughing.

Jack hears Amy's words as the blurring figure of Mason runs past him with Scotty hot on his heels. Now it is his turn to run. He half-heartedly follows.

The boys clear a couple of rooms. They can hear Amy calling to them just over the piped in music. "Guys, where are you?"

"She'll be on to us soon," Mason calls, ducking past an overweight man in a loud Hawaiian shirt.

Jack decides it's time to act. He refuses to allow this to go down. Hanging back slightly, Jack executes a dramatic trip.

"Oww!" he calls in fake pain.

Scotty immediately turns upon hearing Jack's staged yelp. Scotty doubles back to Jack.

"I'm fine. Just tripped, that's all. I might have turned an ankle or something. I was in such a rush… man, I am such a klutz." By now Mason has rejoined the two.

"You tripped?" asks Mason, giving Jack a questioning eye.

Jack wonders, *Does Mason suspect?* He continues his charade, though, and says, "Sorry, guys. Let me get up and see if I can walk." Using all of his acting skills perfected by playing Col. Von Trapp in his fourth grade presentation of *Sound of Music*, Jack hobbles to his feet. "Looks like I am good to go, let's get to the exit before—"

Amy, panting, has caught up to the boys. "What are you guys doing? Are you trying to ditch me or something?"

Thinking fast and not wanting to bust his friends, Jack makes quick reply. "Uh, no, we just decided to go on to the Enchanted Forrest. Mason here was getting nauseous with all the mirrors and stuff, so we decided to get out of here fast before he barfs. We were going to wait for you outside."

"Yeah, I am feeling a little light-headed," lies Mason.

Pacified, Amy walks out through the entrance with Scotty. Mason grabs Jack's arm, slowing him down so they can talk. "Great, Jack, just great. You just tripped, huh?"

"Yeah, I don't know why."

"Look, I don't know what's going on with you, but you are the reason we are going to have to drag her with us into the Forrest. All I know is that she better not keep me from getting my prop. We have a deal, right?"

"Yep, no one is going to stop us." Jack tries to sound as positive as possible. He is not completely sure, but he has to be careful with Mason, who suspects things too often.

"If she gets in the way and we get busted, I am going to tell everyone who will listen that this whole plan was your idea. You know Scotty will back me up. Try not to… trip… again."

Now he is sure Mason is on to him. Jack knows he better come through tonight.

Chapter 13

The crew waltzes past many of the other attractions at the park, intent on their plan to hit the Forrest. To Jack's astonishment, the plan is actually the last thing on his mind right now. While Scotty and Mason are talking about a new video game, Jack is still debating in his head what to do with this newfound admiration of Amy. His head tells him to let it go, but his heart tells him to take the opportunity to hang back and focus on Amy. His heart wins.

"Oh man, I love Blackbeard's Pirate Ship." The girl looks longingly at the ride as they pass.

"My mom hates it. She won't even step into the park because she got so sick on it once."

"Really? That's too funny." Amy brushes her bangs over her ear and giggles at the absurdity of Jack's statement.

"Hey Jack, let's ride it. Can we?"

Is she asking me to ride? Just me? Jack wonders, allowing himself to think of Amy and him alone on the ride.

"Get the guys to stop," she urges.

Snapping out his fantasy with a little disappointment, Jack calls ahead to the guys. He has to play this right. If they think he is acting on her behalf, there's no telling about the ribbing he would take.

"Hey, Mason, Scotty, hold up. Let's ride Blackbeard."

"I thought we were headed to the Forrest?" Scotty says.

"We have another two hours, plenty of time to jump on the ship for a ride."

This time Mason agrees. "Okay, Jack, but why the sudden interest? You hardly ever ride the ship."

"Oh, I don't know. Call it a trip down memory lane. A last voyage."

They make their way past an employee dressed like a buccaneer and take their place on the ship. Mason slips past Jack and settles down next to Amy. Paranoid, Jack hopes Mason's maneuver is unintentional.

"Amy, you sure you are up to riding the Enchanted Forrest?" Mason coyly asks.

Jack knows immediately that Mason is in the midst of another scheme. The ship begins its gentle rock.

Mason continues, "You know what happened to Douglas Finch, right?"

"Of course, everyone knows that urban legend," Amy responds.

"Oh, it's no legend. It happened. My dad told me all about it. He was involved in the lawsuit. Finch was in the ride with that creepy old maintenance man, and no one ever saw him again. I think that old guy murdered him."

This was too much. Jack had developed a friendship with old Clyde over his many trips to the park. He counters by saying, "Mason, even if that really happened, Clyde had nothing to do with it. He's harmless."

The ship steadily rises.

"Sure, whatever you say, Jack. I just wanted to make sure Amy knew what she was getting into. It's not a kiddie ride."

"Come on, Mason, it's not like Amy hasn't ridden it dozens of times."

"Actually, Jack, this will be the first time."

"Gee, Amy, first King Midas and now the Forrest. You have no idea what you've been missing."

Jack wonders what it is about Amy tonight and why he has this new feeling for the girl. He thought it was so fun seeing her react to King Midas, and now he has the chance to show her his favorite attraction. He decides to make sure, though, that Mason does not sit between them on that ride as well.

Jack is a decent looking boy with a thin frame and youthful, ruddy looks. His unkempt brown hair is his signature trait, and he is constantly brushing his bangs from his eyes. In spite of this, he has had very little experience with girls. Although he'd had a couple of "girlfriends," they were the kind of relationships that you have in fourth grade—having a girlfriend just so you can say you have one. In fact, Jack had probably talked to those girls less when they were his "girlfriends." The closest thing Jack had ever had to a romantic interlude was in sixth grade at the Brentwood skating rink. The announcer had called out the dreadful words "couple skate," and Jack consigned himself to the Miss Pac-Man machine, waiting for the song to end. While he was looking down at the screen waiting for his turn, Jenny Pappadill came skating up from behind.

"Jack?"

He turned to see the fifth grade girl. He couldn't recall if he'd ever spoken to her before. "Wanna skate?"

The invitation evoked a tingling feeling in his face—a couple skate with a girl.

"Umm…." he stuttered. "I'm not a great skater."

"That's okay, neither am I."

With a nod, Jack took his position beside her, almost tripping as he stepped down onto the hardwood floor. The song was by a band called R.E.O. Speedwagon. The floor was dark, lit only by dim red lights that hazed off and on. Jenny reached out her hand and clasped it with Jack's.

This was a first, and a totally new sensation filled Jack's body. He felt flushed, but he liked it. Unsure of his footing with the boat-like skates, Jenny steadied him more than once. It was total euphoria. But, just as Jack allowed himself to let the sensation wrap around him, he felt a heavy blow in the small of his back, which caused him to topple backwards, and his head struck the hardwood floor.

Instantly, the music stopped and the lights flashed on. Mr. King, the sixth grade physical education teacher, was already kneeling over him.

"You okay, Jack?"

Lindsey Cho was there as well, a tiny fifth grader who was apologizing over his dazed head.

Great, thought Jack, *I've been pummeled by a fifth grade girl. Of all the embarrassing things.* He replied, "I'm fine, just help me up." He grumbled with a touch of anger.

Then he heard, "Jack, Jack!"

Oh no, realized Jack. *Mom's here.* His mother, who was chaperoning the event, was running out to him. Three other male teachers had joined the rescuers. Before Jack could protest, the men lifted him and carried him to a bench in the food court like pallbearers at a funeral. This was beyond humiliating. The whole time, his mother wailed, "Jack, are you okay?"

After being laid out on the bench, Jack caught a glimpse of Jenny. Seeing that he was okay, she skated off. Jack never spoke to her again, except for once when she asked him if he could give a note to another boy.

During the whole bus ride back to Cassidy Falls from the skating party, Mason had dogged Jack about the ordeal. And, now, as luck would have it, when he is perhaps in the throes of his first real crush, Mason, instead not Jack, is enjoying the ride beside Amy.

The pirate ship slows and creaks to a stop.

"Well, if we still have time tonight, we'll have to ride Bigfoot's Rapids," Mason crows in high spirits. "But now it's time we hit the Forrest."

Mason's tone implies that all is good between Jack and him, but just to make sure, Jack approaches his friend and asks, "Ready to roll, Mason?"

"Yep, are you?"

"Of course."

"Just watch where you step, Jack. Don't trip."

Chapter 14

In the back corner of the park, the Enchanted Forrest casts a dark shadow over a large swath of the area. The foursome approaches the ride and immediately Jack knows something is wrong. The lights are off. No music pipes through the outdoor speakers. There are no screams of fear or cries of delight.

In front of the ride, Jack notices Clyde speaking to another employee.

"Well I don't think we should try again." It's the girl speaking. Jack does not like what he hears.

The trusty old man sees them approach.

"Jack, good to see you, captain. I was wonderin' if you were gonna come see me before we closed."

"Clyde, what's up? Why are the lights off?"

The old man gives an exaggerated sigh and wipes his forehead with a towel. "Well, Jack, we've been having a heckuva time with the ol' girl tonight. Electrical problems. Every time we think we got her fixed, the blasted power shuts off again.

No, not tonight, thinks Jack. "Are you serious?" he asks, "Is it closed for good?"

"Well, yes, I was just about to call it a night, in fact. Probably won't have her running again by the time we shut the park down."

"Clyde, you have to let us ride one last time. With the park closing and all, we just have to."

"I know how you feel, cap. It's just the Forrest has been acting strange for the last two days. I would hate for you kids to get stuck in there."

"But this is our last night. You know how much I will miss this ride." Jack shoots his best puppy dog eyes at the old man.

"There's really little I can do. This one's got us over a barrel." Clyde looks at his watch, then at Jack. "I tell you what. Only for you, captain, will I try to crank her back up again. It will take a while, so you kids go have fun for 20 minutes or so. Come back here, and if we have power I'll let you take her for one last spin."

"Great, let's go ride Bigfoot's Rapids, then we can get back to the Forrest," Mason suggests.

There is nothing on earth at that moment that Jack wants more than one last trip on the Dark Ride. Clyde has given them all a glimmer of hope. "Thanks, Clyde," says Jack. Clyde offers a short wave as the kids move along.

Mason pulls Jack aside. "Good job with the codger back there."

Jack feels relieved that Mason seems to have forgotten about his missteps.

"If you hadn't pulled that off, I would have never forgiven you for letting us miss our chance. Your little trip and the whole pirate ship deal could have cost us our shot."

So much for Mason letting it go, thinks Jack.

Chapter 15

Jack is trying to figure out some way to get Mason off of his back about the whole Amy situation. He thinks, *Please come through for me Clyde, or I will never hear the end of this.*

"One dolla', a throw. Win the lady a prize!"

A row of carnival games stretches out in front of teens. The mid-way games line the path to the Rapids. College-aged workers bark at and challenge perspective contestants to test their skills while blinking lights and fanciful decorations enhance the lure of the games.

"It's so simple, a baby can do it blindfolded. Toss the ring over any one of these bottles!"

"Shoot the ball through the hoop. Win the lion!"

"One dollar for a lifetime of memories!"

Jack asks Scotty, "You think Mason can make it past without playing one of these mind-numbing games?" Then he realizes, *That's it.*

If there is one thing the taller, faster, and stronger Mason Chick enjoys, it's showing off. It comes naturally to Mason, alpha male, son of local high school sports legend Titus Chick. While Jack could never hope to equal his friend on the physical fields of athletic combat, Jack knew for sure he had the edge with his mind.

This is my chance, thinks Jack, who knows that the large stuffed animal prizes are like precious metals to Mason. He would win one and almost always force Scotty to lug the thing around the park—that is, unless a pretty girl was walking by. It was like Mason thought a gorgeous high school cheerleader-type would see that Mason had won a stuffed hippo and fall head over heels in love with him. Last summer, Mason won a huge purple gorilla that was so big, it took up two seats in Mr. Chick's BMW. Jack wondered where in the world Mason put all of those things. He imagined that Mason had a garage full of the stuffed relics.

"You there with the lady, why don't you win her a nice big stuffed bear?" Jack turns to see who the barker is talking to. But the barker stares straight at him. He realizes that he is with a lady: Amy is right beside him. Jack watches as Amy blushes.

"Come on, strapping lad like you, make the lady's day. Simply shoot the water in the clown's mouth."

"Uh, Mason," says Jack. "Why don't you play? I'll pay."

Like a fish going after a worm, Mason jumps at the offer.

"Okay, Jack, deal… but if I win I get the prize."

"Of course," Jack relents. Mason is playing right into his hands.

Mason hops on a stool in front of the "Crazy Clowns" booth. Jack, Amy, and Scotty prepare to watch Mason compete against a couple of older teens dressed in black with piercings, and all sorts of various tattoos arranged in scattered patterns on every visible inch of flesh on their arms and legs. Seated next to them, also competing for the prize, is a small freckle-faced boy, probably around eight years old, who is being watched with one eye by his mother standing a mere two feet behind him. Her other eye rests firmly on the two blacked-out teens. A voice yells at Jack from behind. "You there, don't let your friend have all the fun." Jack turns to see another park employee motioning toward him. It's Colton Spurlock, the very same one who his sister gushes over. He stands in a booth manning his own game of chance.

Oh no, thinks Jack. *He could blow the whole evening. What if he recognizes me? He'll text Blair.*

"Come on, kid. Think you can outwit me?"

Kid, huh? thinks Jack, who is actually relieved that Colton has no clue about his identity.

Normally, Jack would have ignored the challenge, but the prospect of perhaps outwitting Blair's love interest and maybe impressing Amy in the process is too much to ignore. Jack shuffles towards the booth followed by Amy and Scotty. Their curiosity is peaked as well.

"So what's the game?" Jack asks.

"It's called the shell game, kid. All you have to do is keep your eye on the ball. I will place it underneath one of these three cups and then shuffle them. When I'm finished, simply show me which cup hides the ball and you win a prize."

"Sounds easy enough," Jack declares, laying a dollar on the counter.

"Pay attention, Jack, these guys are good," Scotty points out.

Colton places the ball under a cup and begins to whirl the cups in and out of one another. At first Jack has a hard time keeping his eye on the ball, but as Colton continues to maneuver the cups, Jack's confidence rises. Finally he stops.

"So which cup is it under?" Colton asks with a cocky grin.

"That one." Jack points to the cup on the left.

The smile on Colton's face disappears. "No way!" He lifts the cup Jack selected, revealing the red ball.

"Good going, Jack," Amy says and laughs.

Jack beams with pride.

Obviously not pleased, Colton continues, "Good job, kid. How about best two out of three? You're not going to be so lucky twice."

As Jack ponders playing again, Mason strolls up to the party. He is carrying a huge blue stuffed bear. Jack looks to Scotty, who marvels at Mason, not realizing he has been doomed to lug a bear the size of a medium-sized dog around the park for the next two hours.

Colton coaxes Jack, trying to win back his pride. "Look, I'll let you play for free. You win again, and I'll give you the biggest prize I've got."

With Mason already winning the bear, Jack has no desire for the gang to be saddled with two such monstrosities. However, he likes the feeling of besting the older boy. It gives him something to tease Blair about.

"You're on," he accepts.

Colton repeats the shuffling again, but this time he's faster, concentrating on making it extra hard. When he is finished, he confidently announces, "No way you followed that."

Jack shrugs and calmly points to the cup in the middle. This time Colton is incredulous. "No way!" He lifts the cup, and once again, the ball is revealed.

"You've got to be kidding me. No one has ever been able to beat me twice!"

"I guess I've got beginner's luck," says Jack, who likes this game that he is obviously good at.

"Wow, Jack, you're a natural," says Scotty, applauding.

"What prize do you want?" the defeated Colton asks in an irritated voice.

Jack looks at Amy and asks, "You want something?"

A small blush of red appears on the girl's cheeks. "Thanks, but no thanks. I don't need another stuffed animal."

"Come on, Jack. Get that big orange rhino," encourages Mason, who points to the colossal beast hanging above their heads.

"Uh, no thanks," Jack declines.

"What? Come on, chicks dig these things." Colton pats his blue bear.

"But, you won. You need to choose something," Spurlock offers.

Jack thinks for a moment, looking at the cups. "I tell you what, do you have another set of those cups and a ball. I think I like this game?"

"Yea, we've got plenty of them. You want a set? You can have one. I'm sure the boss would rather part with a set of these cheap, ten-cent cups over a five-dollar animal." Colton ducks behind the counter and pulls out a set of grey cups and a bright red ball.

Jack thanks him and places them into his backpack.

"You should have taken the rhino," Mason advises.

Jack ignores the statement but makes sure to stroke Mason's ego. "So, I see we both won. You sure know how to play these games."

"It was nothing—like taking candy from a baby." Mason beams with pride. Looking down at his prize, he declares, "I think I'll call him Lucky. Here ya go, Scotty. Take care of this for a while for me."

As they head off, Mason's glowing, like he just won a championship or something. He's even strutting. Jack and Amy share a glance and then a chuckle at Mason's expense.

Chapter 16

Bigfoot's Rapids is one of the "improvements" Newcastle, Inc. brought to the park. A large whitewater raft ride. It's not something anyone would expect from a small, local amusement park. Nonetheless, Storybrook Hollow has it, a hulking attraction that roughly covers a third of the park's land. For a while it drew the crowds as thousands of people surged into the park the first summer it was running to get a taste of the Falls, but the novelty wore off quickly. This resulted in Newcastle, Inc. not spending any more money on new attractions from that point on.

Amy is waltzing on cloud nine. This night has been perfect for her. That her parents had let her go off on her own had been a huge victory, but on top of that, Jack Braddock is paying a lot of attention to her. While she would never admit it publically, she had liked the boy ever since she was old enough to like boys—about the time she was five. Now, she allows herself to wonder, *Maybe Jack is interested in me?*

She stays close to Jack in an effort to avoid being stuck beside Mason on another ride. To her, Mason Chick is the spoiled brat who tormented her childhood. She can't even begin to count the number of times he had destroyed her toys playing Godzilla with her Barbies. When this happened, Scotty would never say a word, but Jack, on the other hand, would at least try to distract Mason. He had always been so nice.

While waiting in the small line at the Rapids, Amy sees Mason grab the bear from her brother. Not knowing why, she looks around.

"Nice bear, Chick," The voice belongs to a slender blonde-haired girl wearing a button-up white polo top and a plaid skirt that Amy would feel indecent wearing in public. It is the one and only Lauren Van Wormer. The girl stands just ahead of them in line, flanked by a redhead and brunette.

Lauren Van Wormer, who's in the ninth grade, is that type of girl who sets such an unreachable standard of wealth and beauty that even seniors in high school tremble in her wake.

"This thing? Yeah, I didn't want to have to lug it around, but Braddock begged me to win something."

What a jerk, surmises Amy. *Does he think they're impressed?*

Shooting a glance at Scotty, she sees her brother mesmerized by the blonde. Then she looks at Jack, who looks like even he is trying to push out his chest. *Boys,* she thinks.

"We tried to get our parents to take us to the mall, but they were dead set on making us come here one last time. Lame, right?" Van Wormer makes a face like she's just smelled some bad cheese.

"Yeah, you said it," Mason blurts. "We got stuck here, too."

Amy says to herself, *Won't this line move any faster? What is going on? The park is nearly empty, what is with this line?*

The redhead says, "Oh, how nice you've brought your baby sis to tag along, Scotty. How cute."

The wry grins of the girls send Amy into a helpless tailspin.

"It's Annie, right?" the redhead concludes.

"Her name is Amy," asserts Jack.

"Oh that's right, Jack… Amy. Well, Amy, I hope you are tall enough to ride some of the big girl rides," Lauren coaxes.

Mason gives the girl a chuckle, acknowledging that he is on their level.

Trying to hide, praying that they will move along, Amy turns away from the girls. Why would she think anyone would be attracted to her? These girls have it all. Amy chides herself, thinking, "*What could Jack Braddock, or any boy for that matter, see in me? Everything about me is nothing compared to them. These ugly freckles, auburn hair, off-the-rack T-shirt, and khaki shorts.*

The ride attendant breaks the uncomfortable silence. "You guys are next. How many in your party?"

"Three." And with that, the girls walk forward and into one of the large black rafts.

"See you later, Mason."

"Yeah, cool."

Stepping up in line, the four of them await their turn.

"Don't mind them, Amy," Jack says as he looks at her, "They say that stuff to make themselves feel better."

Amy tells herself, *But they are better.*

"Okay, we're up, Amy…. Amy?"

Amy is torn away from her own self-loathing by Jack's repeated calling of her name.

Jack waves and points her to a couple of seats on the far side of the raft. Scotty and Mason are already buckled and ready to ride. The large bear is strapped across Scotty's chest. An older couple fills out the raft. After Jack and Amy are settled, the raft stutters and shakes down a ramp into the man-made river.

"I've got this strategy. I always pick the seats that are the driest. That's where the people who didn't get wet sat. Like the signs say, on this ride you *could* get soaked." Jack recites.

"Does it work?" Amy asks, thankful for the small talk that eases Lauren Van Wormer and her gang out of her mind.

"No, hardly ever. I am like a water magnet."

This makes Amy laugh. She can breathe freely again.

The raft bounces all over the watery course. A huge rapid washes over the older couple. The man's three grey hairs stand at attention atop his head. After another spin and a whirl, a huge wave hits the side of the boat where Scotty sits.

"So much for staying dry," a soaked Scotty chuckles.

"No one gets away from Bigfoot unscathed!" Mason cheers.

"So far, so good. We're dry," says Amy, who crosses her fingers playfully.

"Oh great, now were jinxed for sure." Grinning, Jack mockingly puts his head under his barricading arms.

The raft jets up and down over rushes of water. The cave is just ahead.

Inside the cave, a large Bigfoot dummy, holding a boulder above his head in a threatening stance, growls piped in sound effects at the riders.

The raft spins. Jack and Amy's backs are to the front. Just then, the raft dips and a monstrous flood of water spills over the front of the raft, soaking Jack and Amy.

The ride ends shortly after the drenching, and the attendant laughs at the soaked crew.

"Look at me, not a drop of water!" Mason crows.

Amy cannot believe how water logged she is.

Now we have to walk around like this. It will take forever to dry. Jack thinks.

Upon seeing the monstrous damage, the attendant throws Jack a towel.

"Thanks."

Jack takes the towel and begins to wipe it across his chest when he stops.

"Here, Amy, you first."

The act is so unselfish, so kind. While she stops herself from taking it too seriously, she can't help but let the small, simple offer warm her heart. In spite of the Tennessee summer heat and the sun's departure, the sudden soaking has sent Amy chattering.

Jack goes on, "Hey, wait a second. Here, take this Amy." From his backpack, Jack produces a red hooded sweatshirt. "Try this on. At least it will keep you warm."

"Thanks, Jack."

Now she can't help but take the second act to its logical conclusion. Something about the boy has changed. This was not a simple action. This was a deliberate act of chivalry. Jack Braddock has been intentionally thinking of her.

Drying his glasses with his shirt tail, Scotty offers, "Think Clyde's got the Forrest on line? It's been 27 minutes. Let's get back."

Chapter 17

A little train with seats for eight riders, two per cart, wheels past Clyde.

"Looks like we're open for business." Clyde declares.

"So you gonna let the kids ride?" Gwen's statement reveals that she is still not sure about the reopening.

"Well, I haven't been flipping switches for nothing. I should have said no. I wish I had. Would have saved us some time, but it's Jack. Ever since he was a little runt, he's been haunting this park from open to close every other day or so. It's not just that. There are lots of kids like that. Heck, I've seen most of this town get older. But Jack, well not many kids take the time to talk to this old man. He's been tugging on my shirt tail for years, and this ride… well, it's almost his ride."

"Okay, I just don't want to have to go in and bail them out of there."

"Neither do I. That's why I'm going with them. The power should hold up as long as they go ahead and get here. It's been holding steady for about 40 minutes at a time. "

"Here they come, Clyde."

The motley crew of four sees the trains move, they hear the sound effects and the piped in screams. Clyde watches as their pace quickens.

"Looks like the power's on—you did it, Clyde!" Jack beams.

"Yep, and you and your crew better hop on now. Not sure exactly how long it's going to stay."

"Come on Scotty," Mason calls, "front row." Mason clambers forward, blowing past Jack. Scotty places Lucky in the cart behind him, carefully lowering the bar over the stuffed bear.

Jack takes the seat behind Lucky and looks to make sure Amy follows.

"Okay, Gwen, I've got my radio. If the power shuts off, I'll let you know where we are."

Jack shoots a quizzical look up to the old man. "Clyde, are you coming with us?"

"Yep, just to make sure I don't have to go in and fish you out if there's a problem." The old man lowers himself in the final cart. "Oh man, they don't make these little trains for people my size do they? Urgh, it's been years since I have actually gotten in one of these. Too many TV dinners I guess."

Mason clears his throat and calls back to Clyde, "Hey, thanks for fixing the ride and all, but you don't have to babysit."

Clyde can see disappointment in the Chick boy's face. *What's that all about?* wonders Clyde. *That Chick boy, never got a good feeling around him.*

"No problem, I want to ride, captain. Gonna take her for one last spin for old time's sake."

The sound system, which has not been updated since the 70's, cackles to life.

"Welcome to the Enchanted Forrest, please keep all hands and
feet in the train until the journey is through. Enjoy your visit,
and beware, the Enchanted Forrest has frightening images not
appropriate for younger guests. Now, enjoy your journey into
the woods… if you dare!"

The train pulls out of the entrance cue and rambles forward under a large black metal archway, the official entrance to the ride. Etched into the cast iron frame are the words,

The Enchanted Forrest.

Just under the sound effects and piped-in music, Clyde hears what he thinks is calliope music. He swallows hard and thinks, *No it's just in your head. Anyway, too late to get off now, let's just get this over with.* A singular face forces its image into his mind—Douglas Finch.

Chapter 18

Things have suddenly gotten very complicated for Jack, and the timing could not be any worse. With Clyde behind him and Amy beside him, would Mason still expect him to somehow take the golden goose from the ride? *It's Impossible,* thinks Jack. He chides himself for thinking up the plan in the first place. There is no doubt in his mind that the mission is off. Surely Mason would not go through with it? And, why should he be worrying about it anyways? This is his last ride. He wants to enjoy it.

The ride itself tells the hair-raising story of four fairy tale characters lost in the woods. Each room reveals another scene in the story. The story is "told" by a mannequin who appears in most of the 16 rooms. He is an older gentleman dressed in a white suit with shaggy white hair and a beard, and he carries an open oversized book in his hands as if he were reading. Jack always thought he resembled the author Mark Twain

The narrator stands still as the first lines of the story pipe over the speakers while they pass by.

"Once upon a time…"

And with that, the cart rolls through two large black doors that automatically open into the second room of the ride.

Jack glances over at Amy. "So this is your first time?"

"I know, I just, well, it always frightened me as a kid and I never got around to it."

"It's not so bad. I'll give a shout when something scary is about to happen. Don't worry, the next couple of rooms are a breeze."

Haunting music chimes over the speakers, and Jack takes pleasure in seeing Amy grip the handle bar so hard that her knuckles turn white. Also, she scoots, ever so slightly, closer to Jack, who thinks, *This is going to be good.*

Passing by the doors, the cart begins a slight climb up a hill. Plastic trees and a green floor give the allusion that the woods are getting thicker. Two mannequins, a boy and a girl in playful poses, occupy the space to the train's left during the slow climb. The mannequins look like the ones you would see at department stores, except they are not modeling the latest fashions. Both show signs off age: the peach paint is wearing off the boy's face and the girl with a red-hooded cape is missing her left pinky finger.

The narrator speaks again.

"Jack and Jill went up the hill to fetch a pail of water."

"Blair always tells me this Jack looks better than me."

"Well, she's wrong."

Heat rises up into Jack's face while he wonders, *Is she flirting with me?*

"Your face isn't peeling off."

At the top of the rise, just to the left, an old fashioned wishing well sits to the side of the next set of doors. It has become a tradition for riders to throw coins into the well for good luck.

From his vantage point, Jack watches as Scotty and Mason throw coins at the well. He sees Mason raise his hands in victory. The doors open into the second room.

"Hold on, Amy."

The train—with a sudden jolt—rushes down a short incline.

"Jack and Jill fell down the hill:
It had been a nasty spill.
All the way into the woods the children lay.
Jack tells Jill, 'Let's have a look around today.'"

At the bottom of the hill, the two plastic children are on their knees recovering from the fall. The atmosphere of the ride changes for this room, everything is much darker. Sound effects of hooting owls and howling wolves play loudly. It is clear to Jack that the sounds are having their desired effect on Amy. The girl nudges herself closer to Jack. Now Jack is sure things are going his way. He wonders, *Should I take her hand? No, not yet. There is still some time.*

Traveling on the track toward the next set of doors, Jack breathes deeply. He allows himself a moment of victorious thought. For the first time in his life, he's experiencing the excitement of a real budding romance. Of course, Jack does not count Jenny Pappadill.

A large vulture on a string falls from the ceiling.

Jack ducks. He had forgotten about the startling bird.

A playful laugh escapes Amy. "Oh, so the brave Sir Jack has a chink in his armor?"

Embarrassed, but not above giving a playful laugh, Jack excuses himself. "I forgot about it, that's all. Nothing much in the next room. But from there…."

"Well, maybe I should be the one looking out for you?"

The playfulness in the girl's voice warms Jack's heart.

The next room introduces the other main characters of the ride. To the left of the tracks stand a tailor and his apprentice, who look ready to enter the woods. The tailor is adorned with a large gold badge. The apprentice holds a silver trumpet.

Up ahead in the front seat, Jack can hear Scotty playing know-it-all for Mason.

"In German fairy tales, the tailor is renowned for killing giants," Scotty lectures.

Scotty knows just about everything there is to know about this stuff, and he's a little too quick to point this fact out.

"The brave Tailor called to the wood.
There with his apprentice the brave man stood.
To kill a beast, his goal that day.
The reward, the king's daughter to live with him always."

The train approaches the figures. Mason turns to Jack and shoots him a wink.

What is he up to? wonders Jack.

Then, with catlike reflexes, Mason leans over the side of the train and yanks the badge from the tailor's chest. A patch of white shirt rips, and the tailor hobbles forward. The mannequin appears about to lose its balance but steadies itself with its own weight.

Jack asks himself, *Did I just see that?* Looking at Amy, hoping the girl did not witness the theft, he relaxes a little to find Amy staring up at the ceiling, perhaps scouting for another vulture.

Then Jack realizes, *What about Clyde!* Instantly, Jack turns to Clyde and thinks that Mason is perhaps the luckiest kid on earth or that maybe the coin in the well worked. Clyde is looking down behind them at an entire tub of popcorn an earlier guest had discarded on the floor.

"No respect for anything these days. See that mess back there, Jack? You know who will have to pick that up tonight?" Clyde pauses for effect and then says, "Gwen." The old man gives a chuckle at his own joke.

Shocked at the boldness of Mason, Jack realizes the quandary now. The plan is still on, and Mason will expect Jack to come through. He has to get the goose. The gauntlet has been thrown down.

Chapter 19

The first three rooms have been relatively devoid of anything all that startling. The trip through the Forrest begins slowly; it was designed that way. The masterminds behind the reformat had deliberately planned to make riders feel a false sence of security before the real haunting starts.

Jack knows that the biggest scare of the ride is looming through the next set of doors. Even after having been in the Little Red Riding Hood room countless times, Jack continues to always be startled. This is his least favorite room in the ride. Normally, he would duck down a little and turn his head away from the impending appearance of the Wolf, but tonight, he has to act brave. Somehow, he will have to face the rolling predator. At least he can take a little delight in watching to see what Amy will do when the beast appears.

> "The children split up to see what they could find,
> But before Jill knew it, she was in a bind.
> She did not know she would be attacked that day,
> And Jill, in her red riding hood, ran and barely got away."

The narrator stands among dense trees that mostly fill the room, giving way briefly to a small clearing. The train approaches the clearing and slows down a little on the tracks. Jill, the plastic girl, is also supposed to represent Little Red Riding Hood. Her little mannequin stands up to the right of the tracks in the clearing.

Jack informs Amy, "From here on out, a bunch of villains narrowly miss the kids, and the tailor saves them in the end."

Jack's tour guide lecture helps to ease the tension of what is on the horizon. Gripping the iron bar he prepares to be startled, thinking, *"Don't embarrass yourself again."* He tenses up. His hands grip the bar. He had not actually looked at the Wolf in dozens of trip because it is just so vicious looking. The massive hideous wolf should soon be rolling along a track and pitch down just above the riders' unsuspecting heads. Mason points to the spot, and Jack closes his eyes instinctively—but only temporarily. He quickly opens them again, fearing Amy will laugh.

Brace yourself, Jack tells himself. *Here it comes.* Bravely turning to face the impending beast, he

grips the bar with resolve. *Do not turn away,* he thinks and says, "Okay, Amy, here it comes."

The sound of a snarling growl fills the air. The tension is so thick. Jack hears a whispered

"yelp," like that of a pup, escape from Amy's mouth.

There is a flash of light and then….

Nothing.

No wolf? thinks Jack.

The light reveals empty tracks and gears where the beast had been anchored for years.

Mason turns to Jack, yelling from the front car, "What happened, where's the wolf?"

Jack turns to Clyde.

"I don't know, captain. We think some pranksters took him away. He's probably in some dorm room as we speak."

"So we missed something big, right?" Amy asks.

"Yep, the best scare in the whole ride." Jack, as much as he feared the wolf, is utterly disappointed. "I can't believe someone could steal that thing."

"I know. That wolf is so heavy. Must have been four or five guys. How they got him out without anyone knowing baffles me. Gwen just discovered him gone yesterday. Makes me downright angry."

By this point, Clyde is talking loud, almost shouting over the sound system. "I mean people these days. Just think they can take anything they want. We've been dealing with this crud a lot lately, people wantin' to grab themselves a piece of the park before it closes, I guess. They may think it's cute, but it's stealing."

Ouch, thinks Jack. *Is Clyde on to us? No, he couldn't be.*

Amy sulks, "I finally get on this thing, and I'll never know what I missed—this stinks. I hope they catch whoever stole that stuff. It's just so wrong."

Amy's disappointment and condemnation settle it for Jack. Even if Mason were angry for the rest of his life, Jack decides he will not be taking anything out of the ride tonight. The golden goose is only a couple of rooms away. But, with Amy beside him and Clyde behind him, Jack realizes that there is no way he could pull this off.

The ride continues to the next room. Another narrator dummy with its large book mimics the lines of the story.

"Jack finds a beanstalk large enough to climb.
He scales the stalk to see what he can find."

This room, much smaller than the others, is filled by the massive green stalk. The train rolls around the perimeter and moves upward on the rising track. The next set of doors open to reveal the inside of what is supposed to be the interior of the Giant's lair, the room containing the goose.

"So, we went up the beanstalk, and now we're in the Giant's castle. I'm tracking," Amy happily chimes.

In the room, oversized tables and chairs and a huge bookcase are designed to give riders a dwarfed feeling. In the corner to the right are scarier props, such as a stack of bones and skulls, brought in to create chills. To the immediate right is a tremendous fireplace, complete with a "fire," created by red paper over a fan. It is adorned by a rake and shovel, and next to them is the Golden Goose.

"Jack found where the Giant did roam.
He knew pretty quickly he should go home."

Although the narrator's voice is audible, the builders had not bothered to place a mannequin here.

"But before he fled, his eyes spied a surprise.
He thought to himself, I could escape with a prize.
Yes, a goose made of gold next to a fireplace rake
Just waiting for a boy like Jack to snag and take."

Scotty had often complained that the ride should have had a real goose since in the story it was not a statue of a goose that laid eggs. Jack knew this complaint was more about Scotty showing off his knowledge rather than a serious complaint. He figured that surely Scotty must know some artistic license is required on a ride like this.

The goose itself is small and painted gold, the kind of ornament you could buy at a crafts store. As the train rolls by it, Jack feels a tug at his heart. He broods, *There it goes. Mason is never going to let me live this down.* "Is anything going to happen in here?" Amy wonders out loud.

"When we get past the table, we will hear steps and the table will rattle. Bats will fall down on wires."

"Oh, I hate—"

The train makes a sudden jolt. The dim lights flicker once, a second time, and completely shut off followed by a blurring of the sound effects before they whine and go silent.

With a sparkle and crack, two small emergency lights spur to life, but they only provide enough light for Jack to see outlines of shapes. Behind him, Clyde grumbles, "Dagnabit, here we go again."

Chapter 20

The Braddocks roll toward home after their brief outing.

"I really thought we had you two on the ropes," Wallace Braddock confides to his wife from behind the steering wheel.

"Oh, please! You guys haven't beaten Freda and me in months. I was just about to play the Queen of Diamonds when Freda ran to the bathroom. I hope she's okay." Brenna comments, assuring her husband that her team had been in control.

"Yeah, I haven't seen anyone turn that green since the last time Jack ate your tuna casserole."

Brenna eyes her husband, not pleased with the implication. "Wallace, I don't think my dish had anything to do with Freda's spell."

"No offense, dear, just putting two and two together." Wallace grins trying to lighten up the tension.

"Well you can keep your investigation to yourself, Sherlock."

"I'm just saying."

"You're being a jerk—everyone loves my casserole. Just because Jack got sick once—"

"Twice."

"Oh, stop it, Wallace. You're really getting on my nerves."

"I'm just playing with you, dear."

She knows full well he is not playing at all and that this is just his way of avoiding further escalation. Still, Brenna decides to let him off the hook by changing the subject.

"I wonder how the kids have gotten along tonight?"

"We've only been gone a couple of hours. I am sure they have been wonderful, those two angels. I bet they're baking cookies and playing Monopoly, as happy as clams."

"Wallace, would it kill you to spend more time with them?"

"Why do you want to start that again?"

"Because, you never spend time with them. Maybe if their father would take some time and give them more attention, it would help ease whatever it is that they are going through."

"Honey, they're teenagers. What they're going through is natural. Brothers and sisters fight."

"I didn't fight with my brother like that."

"Give it time, Brenna. When Blair leaves for college in a couple of years—"

"A couple of years? I can't deal with this for two more years."

The two drive in uneasy silence for a bit.

"I was too hard on them today. I should have let Jack go to the park. The whole time we were at the Zuckermans' I couldn't help but think I took something away from him."

"There you go again. Look, we baby them too much. He has to learn from this. Perhaps the whole reason they fight like they do is because we have looked the other way too often. No, do not second guess yourself tonight. It was the right thing to do."

"I know, but I just feel so bad."

The vehicle rolls into the driveway.

"Well, since we're home early, I might write a letter to the mayor. It's high time I contacted him instead of just writing to the paper."

Wallace's keys jingle as the door is unlocked.

"It's Friday night, Wallace… oh, never mind."

"What?"

Inside, everything appears to be in order to Wallace and Brenna, at least downstairs. They perceive no signs of fighting, and Blair's music blasts away upstairs.

"I'm going to check on the kids," says Brenna.

The door to Blair's room is cracked, and Brenna looks in.

"Honey?"

Blair is texting away on her phone, oblivious to her mom. The blaring music is not coming from the stereo but the headphones gracing her daughter's head.

"Blair, you're going to go deaf!" Brenna yells and thinks, *She's in her own world. Didn't she know she was grounded from everything? I'll take the phone away tomorrow. Too much drama for one night.*

Leaving Blair to her domain, Brenna takes ten steps down the hall and to the right to Jack's room. She slowly opens the door and sees her son sleeping like a baby. She thinks, *That's it, Jack, get some rest. We'll talk tomorrow.*

Shutting the door behind her quietly, Brenna cannot help but chide herself again for prohibiting the boy from enjoying the park one last time.

Chapter 21

"Okay, kids—sit tight, don't panic," says Clyde. He thinks, *Why did I ever agree to this? I knew this would happen.*

Clyde reaches into his work belt and pulls out his trusty flash light. Clicking the red button near the nozzle, he waits for the stream of white light to cut through the darkness.

"Look, I'm going to lead you out of here, back the way we came."

"Can't you just fix it? I mean we're halfway through the ride." Jack's voice is full of emotion, crushed and disappointed.

"Jack, there's got to be a short somewhere. Gwen and I thought we had found the wire giving us all the fits, but now I'm not sure. We're basically grasping at straws."

"But the power—it's been coming back on."

"Yeah, but so far, only after we jiggle a few wires at the box. It's not an exact science. For all I know, the power just comes on when it feels like it."

"Clyde, let us wait here. You can go mess with the box. If, or better yet when, the power comes on, we can finish the ride."

Clyde knows this is an exaggeration, but he can't blame the boy for trying.

Amy chimes in, "Clyde, what could go wrong?"

That was the wrong thing to ask, and suddenly the old man is re-established in his firm stance.

"I can't just let you kids sit in here in the dark."

"Clyde," responds Jack, "There are four of us, and we're not kids. I know this ride better than anyone, except you. Just let us finish, please. This is our last ride, ever."

The box is only a couple of rooms back, and Clyde tells himself, *The kids are right. The power has been cutting back on all night. What would it hurt to let them finish? There are four of them.* He says, "Okay, look, it's not like I am going to lose my job over this. It's everyone's last ride. I'll make a deal with you. Sit here in the cart, and then when the power comes back on, finish the ride. If the power shuts off again stay wherever you are and I'll come get you."

"Thanks, Clyde!" They each say with various degrees of sincerity.

Climbing out of the ride, Clyde is at peace with his decision to comply with the will of the riders but reminds them again, "Stay put. If the power does not come on, I need to know I can find you here."

"Sure thing, Clyde!" Jack calls. All four teens nod in unison.

Walking away, Clyde gives one last look back at the teens.

Better make this quick, thinks Clyde, who second guesses himself, wondering, *This is the right thing to do, isn't it?* One last time for emphasis, he tells them, "I mean it… stay in the cart."

Chapter 22

"I don't like it," Mason offers dramatically.

"You don't like what?" Scotty inquires gullibly.

"Don't you guys think the old man was a little too eager to get outta here?"

"Don't be ridiculous, Mason, I begged him to let us stay," Jack retorts. "What do you mean?"

"Oh, I don't know… like, maybe the old man set this whole thing up. You know, to get us all in here by ourselves."

Jack knows this tone. Mason is trying to scare them.

"I bet this is exactly what happened to Douglas Finch. The old man lured him in, then deserted him in the dark. Just like in one of those horror movies, he hunted him down and offed him, hiding his body somewhere in the ride."

"Okay, that's enough, Mason. I told you that's just a myth," Jack defends.

"And I told you, Finch really did disappear."

"If Clyde had something to do with it, don't you think the cops would have figured that out?"

"I don't know, Jack. You ever watched CSI?"

"Mason, just be quiet, you're not helping." The tone in Amy's voice gives away her feelings. Jack can see Amy is not comfortable with the present situation. She is rubbing her hands together and scanning the room.

Taking the opportunity to look around the room himself, Jack's eyes slowly become accustomed to the dim lighting. The room has never looked so frightening to him. His eyes check every corner.

Scotty has his cell phone out, providing just enough extra light to make some of the room's objects visible. On the fireplace, Jack eyes the goose. *There it is for the taking,* he thinks. In his wildest dreams, this could not have been set up for him more perfectly. Now the moral dilemma begins anew, for he could easily get off the ride. It almost seems like this is meant to be, but Jack still wonders what Amy would say.

From the front of the cart, Jack hears an iron bar jiggle. Turning to see what's going on, he can see Mason slide up and force himself out of the cart.

"Sit down, Mason," says Amy with newfound courage brought on by nerves.

Mason rubs Lucky's head as he passes the second cart. He strolls around the room and says, "I always wanted to be able to just get out and explore this place. What about you, Jack?"

There is an unmistakable emphasis on Jack's name. *Mason is suggesting something—something more than just getting out of the cart,* knows Jack.

"Jack, don't leave," Amy pleads. "Clyde said to stay put. What if the power comes on and you're not on the ride?"

Now Jack is in a quandary. He must choose between disappointing Amy and irritating Mason. And, he has already pushed it with his friend. His eyes rest on the goose; he knows what Mason is getting at. It is a challenge and the golden opportunity. Before, with Clyde behind him, there was no way he was going to get his prop, but now it is almost like the ride wants him to take something.

"No worries, Amy. If the ride starts back, I'll jump in. It's not like this thing is very fast."

Risking the scorn of Amy, he squeezes himself from behind the bar and joins Mason near the fireplace. Amy's glance is painfully disapproving.

In low tones, Mason whispers to Jack, "Now is your chance. I saw you looking around. This is perfect. I can't believe we're having so much luck. Did you see me grab the badge?"

"Yea, you almost got us busted. That mannequin thing almost fell over."

"But it didn't."

"What gave you the idea to snatch that badge?"

"I don't know—it just called out to me, like, 'Here's your chance.' I knew the old man wouldn't see."

The old man, thought Jack. Just moments before, he had resigned himself to not steal anything. If Clyde found out, Jack would be devastated. *Still,* Jack thought, *This is a clear cut chance.* A chance to get the goose. *They are closing the ride. It's not like anyone is going to miss something now.*

"Jack, you don't even have to worry about anyone seeing like I did. This is a lay-up. You can get whatever you want from in here with no worries," says Mason.

The phrase "no worries" brings Jack's eyes to Amy, and he tells Mason, "I don't want Amy to know."

"Why not?"

"I just don't want to drag her into this, okay."

"Jack, you sure are acting all protective and stuff of her. What's going on?"

"Nothing, I just mean, in the unlikely case that we get busted, she should not get in trouble. She's not in on this. Got it?"

"Okay, I'll go over and distract her. You get what you want and come back when you're done."

With that, Mason strolls over to Amy. Jack can make out the small talk from where he stands.

"So what do you think about the Enchanted Forrest, Amy?" Mason rests an arm on the side of the train, coolly making conversation.

Scotty has left his seat, as well, and is walking around looking at the table. Jack wonders if he is searching for his prop as well.

With Mason taking Amy's focus off of him, Jack goes to work. Moving backwards, he slips his hand around the neck of the goose. The goose lifts easily. He had thought it could have been glued down or something, so he is relieved. Turning his back to the train, he glides his other hand over the golden statue. It is smooth and solid, weighing about as much as one of his mom's 10-pound aerobic hand weights. Unzipping his backpack, the goose slides in easily.

"Jack, what are you doing?" asks Amy. She has turned her attention back to him.

Did she see me? wonders Jack, who turns back towards the girl with the goose tucked away inside the backpack. He replies, "Just walking around a bit. Always wanted to do this. In all my years of riding this ride, I have never gotten to just walk around. It's pretty cool. You should come out— uh, what do you see over there Scotty?"

"You guys need to get back in the cart now." Amy starts to sound like a broken record.

"Come on, sis, lighten up," Scotty calls.

"No, you lighten up, Scotty. You guys are going to get us all in trouble."

Jack shoots a wink towards Mason to let him know that the mission is accomplished. A feeling of satisfaction washes over Jack. In his wildest dreams, Jack could not have imagined how perfect everything has fallen into place. He has the object of his desire, and Amy is none the wiser.

Detaching himself from his small talk with Amy, Mason gives Jack a nod toward Scotty.

"Let's go see what Scotty's up to," Mason says, which Jack understands as code for "Let's help Scotty find something." Mason and Jack walk over to the other boy standing underneath the oversized table.

With a spark, a grind and a flash of the dimmed lights, sound crackles through the speakers. The train lunges forward.

"Guys!" alerts Amy.

The power is on. The boys are caught flatfooted standing twenty feet away from the train. All three boys dash to the carts, but they cannot catch the little vehicle. All Jack can do is catch Amy's scolding and frightened gaze as she disappears through two large black doors.

Chapter 23

The train pulls Amy into a new room. The doors slam behind her.

She thinks, *Those stupid boys. We are going to be in so much trouble.* She didn't say this just because they had disregarded Clyde's instructions. Mainly, she had been so demonstrative in hopes that they would re-join her for the reason that she had no desire to be left alone in such a spooky place. Despite this, though, Amy finds herself alone.

Winding up in a mess caused by Mason Chick reminds Amy of previous experiences with him. Oftentimes when they were younger, before Mason could stay alone at his house, he would spend two or three agonizingly long days at Amy's when his bachelor father was working on an especially rough case. One event in particular that had cemented her dislike for Mason occurred when she was in second grade. Amy was playing with one of her dolls in her room. She was setting up a surprise birthday party for Barbie and had arranged her other dolls around the dream house to surprise the doll. Her playtime was disturbed when Mason waltzed in carrying one of Scotty's dinosaurs. He started snarling and hissing, stomping around the room.

"Stop it, Mason! You're knocking over my dolls."

"Godzilla not care, must destroy!"

He threw down the play toy and apparently decided he would play the role of the giant lizard. Grabbing and slinging her dolls recklessly around, he hissed and growled, mocking the monstrous cries of Godzilla. He proceeded to stomp and break more than one doll. This was more than she could bear. She slung herself at his legs and tried to make him stop. With his left leg, he slung her into the dream house, cracking it in two. She was mortified with a combination of tears, rage, and hurt. Mason simply looked at her and snickered.

Then he ripped the head off of Barbie and roared, "Godzilla—king of monsters—rahhhhhh!" And with that, he was gone.

Amy heard that, as a result of this incident, Mason had gotten in trouble. However, he had never apologized to Amy, and despite the fact that they were only little kids when it happened, she had never forgiven him.

The cart Amy is in slows to a crawl for riders to get a good view of the room. To her left is a campfire scene. Green lights provide the forest-like atmosphere, and a small tent provides shelter for what looks to be an old-time spinning wheel. Gold strands of what appears to be hair are draped over a wicker basket. Amy immediately recognizes the scene as one from Rumpelstiltskin.

The train stops, the sounds fade, and the lights cut off. The power seems to be off again. Looking backwards, Amy waits for the boys to spring through the doors. The two dull emergency lights provide little comfort for her. She is afraid.

Waiting patiently, though, she sits and says, "I am supposed to stay in the cart. Clyde said to stay in the cart."

Nonetheless, her resolve to stay in cart is immediately tested. She imagines that the walls are closing in. Then she hears a crackle noise from behind, followed by a pop from above. Craning her neck to catch the cause of the noises, she tries to settle herself, thinking, *It's nothing, just like at home when the house settles. The boys will be here in a moment.* Amy takes another look at the door. On it are odd shadows that resemble a man. *That's just plain creepy*, thinks Amy who starts wondering what exactly happened to Douglas Finch. She tells herself, *It's just a story, Amy, stop it.*

But, she realizes that all she has to protect herself with is Lucky, the stuffed bear, and, after a bizarre whirling sound exudes from the wall to her left, she feels so much apprehension and fear welling up inside her that she can no longer tolerate sitting there.

She thinks, *What if Mason was right? What if Clyde.... Stop it, Amy, get a hold of yourself.*

Regardless, she can stay put no longer. After wrangling herself from behind the iron bar, Amy steps out into the room. It is remarkably still.

Amy looks at the train and sees Lucky in the second cart. She heads toward the large bear and lifts him from the seat. "So you're stuck in here, too? Mason is such a jerk for leaving us here. Scotty was simply doing what he thought Mason would like, and Jack... well... what was Jack thinking? Boys. Don't worry, Lucky, they'll be here in a second.... Won't they?"

Amy strolls over to the campfire. A collection of sticks are stacked up against each other to form the structure. One stick in particular appears loose, and it grabs her attention.

"Good idea, Lucky. It wouldn't hurt to have that, just in case. She lifts the object from its rest and holds it firmly with her right hand. The stick is solid wood and roughly three feet long, similar to a softball bat.

In fourth grade, Amy's dad had made her go out for softball. She absolutely hated it at first. The practices were pure drudgery. But this changed after she played in her first real game. The crowd, the competition—they fueled her. Ever since that first game, she was hooked.

Amy cradles the stick and squeezes her hands around the solid wood exterior, thinking, *Like to see someone try and get us now.*

From the wall to her left, sudden music startles Amy. She wonders, *What's that? Is the power coming back on?*

After rushing back to the train, she pauses. The train doesn't stir. The green tinted lights don't flicker to life. But the music continues. It's calliope music. Amy ponders, *I didn't think we were that close to the carousel.*

Amy is now filled with confusion but also curiosity. *Where is that music coming from?* she wonders and takes cautious steps toward the wall, scanning for the point of origin. Above her head, a neon green sign glows to life. It reads, "Enter." The outline of a door is now apparent on the wall. Amy thinks, *Is this a way out? Could I walk out the doors and back into the park? No. Then it would be labeled "Exit," not "Enter."* She notices a crash bar at her waist protruding from the door.

"What do you think, Lucky? Wait for the boys? Right, let's go back and wait in the cart."

Turning back to the vehicle, she gives another glance at the door. The music grows louder.

Chapter 24

A barrage of activity, lights, sounds, and motion comes all at once. The three boys wheel around, but it's too late to catch Amy. As a result of their foolishness, they turn just in time to see her carried through the large doors.

Jack arrives at the doors first. Desperately, he flings himself at the door, expecting it to give way, but a dull thud is heard as his shoulder strikes the barrier.

"They won't budge."

"You serious? Back off, let me try," offers Mason.

Relenting to let the "macho man" try, Jack watches as Mason grunts with his shoulder pressed on the door.

"Oh, man, you're right. Come on, help me here."

Jack takes a position directly beside Mason.

"Okay, we push on three," states Mason.

Scotty, willing to help, looks up at the other two boys and asks, "Hey, where do you guys want me?"

Dismissing the offer, Mason growls, "You'll just get in the way, Scotty. We'll take it from here."

Scotty, however, ignores the rebuff and finds a place to push beside Mason, who looks at Jack and says, "One, two, three."

The door does not give, but Scotty's footing does. He slides face first towards the floor, and his hands search for a steadying hold. They find Mason's shirt, which rips at the collar and results in the larger boy falling down on top of Scotty.

In the ensuing confusion, Mason ambles to his feet and yells, "Scotty, you klutz! I told you to stand back. You almost strangled me. Now get back and let us handle this."

Reproached, Scotty wanders a few feet back while rubbing a bright red spot on his forehead. Still wanting to help, he offers, "But if we just wait for the next train to come through, we can catch up."

"He's right, Mason, another train should be here any minute."

On cue, the hum of the sound system throttles off and dim lights flash bright and then go out, leaving only the emergency lights that lazily give off their glow. The power has died again.

"No use in waiting for another train now," says Jack. A dark thought clouds his mind: *Did the ride respond to our plans? No, that's ridiculous.* Scotty remarks, "It's like the ride heard you, Jack."

"Shut up, Scotty," says Mason, who's assessing the damage to his shirt.

"Well, at least this buys us some time. Amy's train won't be going anywhere 'til the power cuts back on. Come on, Jack. We need to hurry. The power might cut back on soon." Mason says.

After another three-count followed by straining and groaning, a slight budge gives way. However, it's not enough for any of them to squeeze through.

"Oh man, we're in for it now, Mason. Clyde is going to know that we got out of the ride. He's going to know we were up to something, and Amy—she's . . . ."

Jack stops mid-sentence before revealing a deeper level of concern for the girl.

"Calm down, Jack," assures Mason. "We're going to get through that door."

Still, Jack's mind races, *"What was I thinking? Everything had been so perfect. She's out there all alone, and I left her."*

Mason instructs, "Jack look around. We need something to pry them open."

Every second wasted in the room, causes more stress to envelop Jack. He realizes that Amy's cart could be two rooms ahead now.

Thankfully, Mason is keeping his cool. He says, "There—against the wall—that stack of bones," and saunters to the pile. Examining the collection, he pulls a leg bone from the stack. "This will do."

Scotty starts, "You want me to—?"

"Can it, Scotty, you've helped enough."

The mood is tense, and even Jack pays little attention to the harsh treatment of Scotty.

"We're gonna push one more time. Give it all you've got, and when we get a gap, I'll do the rest. One, two, three."

Jack slams his shoulder hard into his door with desperation fueling his effort. As the others exert their will as well, the doors open slightly. While Mason grinds his left shoulder on the left door, he extends his right hand and lodges the bone into the crevice. Then, using the bone as a wedge, Mason forces the small opening to extend. A loud cracking sound occurs as the bone snaps in two and Mason spills back onto his posterior. Nonetheless, the left-side door flings open due to the hinge giving way against the strain.

"It worked! Let's go! Hurry!" Jack implores.

Mason flings a piece of the broken bone to the side and clambers to his feet, joining the other boys in making a break through the open door, which leads into the Rumpelstiltskin Room.

Chapter 25

Scotty is the last one into the room. He is hurt. Mason has rarely been so critical of him before, and it stings. He is not sure what is more painful, the lump forming just below his hairline or the insults Mason threw his way.

Sulking and feeling useless, the boy decides to let the other two be the heroes by rescuing the damsel in distress. Instead of following the other boys to the center of the room, he slumps away from them to explore the room. After all, he, too, had never been able to walk around the ride like this. He examines the tent set up in the room as well as the spinning wheel and the fake bonfire. Although the sticks were toppled over, this didn't faze Scotty as being all that unusual, but out of the corner of his eye, he spies something shinning and wonders, *What's this?* It turns out to be a shiny pair of large silver scissors at the base of the spinning wheel. His eyes are transfixed on the sheers. Marveling at the imagination of the creators of the ride for their realism, he stands before them as an idea flashes in his mind: *My prop! I bet Mason thinks I was going to chicken out. Well, I'll show him. He'll have to be impressed. Maybe he will forget about my fall back there.*

Glowing with pride, he scoops up the scissors, thinking, *Now we all have what we came for. Mission complete!* He calls out, "Guys, look what…. Guys? What are you looking at?"

Then, looking down, he gasps at what the other two are staring at: an empty train with no sign of Amy.

Chapter 26

"This is way too creepy deepy. So, Lucky, do we go through the door or stay in here? We could wait for the boys."

After further consideration, Amy says, "No, it serves them right. We should leave them. I bet this door will lead us right out of here. The power is off again, and that music has to be coming from outside the ride. Come on, let's go. Oh, this is ludicrous: I'm talking to a stuffed bear. What? Don't look at me like that."

Amy thinks about waiting for Jack but then tells herself, *"He left me sitting there on the ride, too. He's no better than the others."*

She pushes the bar, and the door under the "Enter" sign gives way. A small black tunnel is revealed behind the door.

"Jackpot, Lucky! This is a service exit."

Another single door illuminated by two glowing emergency lights appears at the end of the tunnel.

Slowly and cautiously, Amy takes one step at a time. The lights at the end of the hall provide little comfort for the shaken girl and her bear.

"When we get to that door and find Clyde, we are not covering for them, you know," Amy says aloud, and then

thinks, *The faster I get out of here, the better.*

As Amy quickens her pace, the calliope music grows louder. *Maybe the carousel is just on the other side*? she considers. But when she pushes against this second door, the music stops as the door opens to reveal another room. Amy realizes she is still in the ride and thinks, *Oh, just great.*

She sees a gingerbread house positioned in the center of the large room. The house stands there made entirely of candy. It is a life-sized version of one of those gingerbread houses she used to make with her grandmother during Christmas break. Trying to make sense of the situation, Amy thinks, *I just took a cut through to another part of the ride.*

From somewhere up above, a speaker cracks and buzzes. Amy looks in the direction of the sound and is startled to see a narrator mannequin with a large book in hand. Amy, reassuring herself that the figure is not real, waits for the rhyme.

> "Little Red all alone had made a wrong turn.
> A poor choice, she made the boys to spurn.
> If she had some wisdom on this ominous night,
> She would realize her peril and at once take flight."

Amy thinks, "*Little Red, wrong turn, boys? What peril? Wait a minute, is he talking about me? This can't be happening. It has to be a coincidence.* Just then another ominous fact makes her dizzy. She says, "Wait a second, isn't the power off? How is that speaker...?"

Talking to the bear is absurd, she knows, but it helps calm her a little.

"Okay, Lucky, that's enough. Let's go find the boys."

Amy turns around to reach for the door and exclaims, "What in the world!?"

The handle and the door are both missing. She scratches and pries along the wall trying to find the door, but it's no use. The entrance has completely disappeared.

Panic takes hold of Amy, and she yells, "Jack! Scotty! Help! Somebody!"

Chapter 27

The fact that Amy is not in the room confuses Jack. *Where is she? he wonders.*

"Okay, this is not good," Scotty informs the others.

"Understatement of the year," Mason sourly snaps.

"She's not here?" Scotty continues.

"That's enough, Captain Obvious. We can see that. We know this is not good, we know Amy is not here, we know we're in deep trouble, we know something—"

"Okay, Mason, I think he's had enough. You're not helping."

"All right, Jack, since you're the one who knows everything about this ride, where did she go?"

"I don't know," Jack answers disturbed. "Well… she had to leave this room. Probably when the power shut off."

"Why didn't she wait for us?" Scotty wonders aloud.

"I don't know," Jack answers again.

"You don't know much, do you?"

Cross at Mason's attitude, Jack snaps back, "None of us know what happened in here! All we know is that Amy is gone."

He tells himself to remain calm and says, "Look, she probably just walked over to the next room." Jack takes long strides to the door to the next room and tries to open it. "This door won't give just like the last one."

Jack thinks, *Amy where are you?*Mason starts, "Maybe she got out before the doors were—"

"You guys hear that?" asks Jack.

"Yeah. Music," says Scotty who looks in the air for the source.

Pointing above Mason's head, Jack asks, "Where did that come from?

"The music?" Mason cocks his head listening.

"No. That."

Scotty and Mason look up to see an illuminated "Enter" sign glowing above a door. C

alliope music floats through the room.

"That's where she went, come on," commands Jack. He pushes on the crash bar, and the three boys enter the tunnel and amble down the dim hallway to the far door.

"I bet she walked down this hallway," Scotty suggests. "That door probably is an exit."

Jack nods in hopeful agreement to Scotty's observation. He opens the door, and the boys are stunned by the sudden appearance of a new room.

"I have never seen this one before," says Jack, who looks around, marveling.

"Neither have I," adds Mason.

"You think this is like some cast aside part of the ride they don't use anymore?" Scotty asks.

"It has to be," Jack says.

Suddenly, the narrator mannequin speaks.

"The shaken boys have made a quite a blunder
In their haste for items to plunder.
The mistake had been made for personal glory
Now they must make amends to finish the story.
But they cannot go back: the girl is lost.
Must find her at once, but at what cost?"

For a few seconds, none of the boys speak. There is an uncomfortable silence.

Breaking the tension, Jack offers, "Okay, that's bizarre."

"It was talking about us," Scotty, eyes wide open, suggests.

"Oh, Scotty, that's garbage," Mason counters, dismissing the rhyme.

Jack ponders the meaning of the words. "No, Scotty is right. How did it know about us—and our props and Amy?"

"He, or, uh, it doesn't. It's just a coincidence. Has to be," declares Mason, who appears to be trying to convince himself of the truth of his own words.

Jack walks up to the narrator slowly. He's apprehensive that the mannequin might actually be real. Glaring over the shoulder of the fake man, he, for the first time, examines the large book. Jack has always wondered whether the creators of the ride had taken the time write words in the large books, but there it is on the paper—the exact rhyme that had blared over the cracking speakers.

"What's with the house?" Mason quips.

"Oh," answers Scotty, "I imagine it's a scene from Hansel and Gretel. You know, the German fairy tale recorded first by the Brothers Grimm. It was—"

"Okay, Scotty, I get the point. What do we do now, fearless leader?" asks Mason while staring at Jack.

This situation surprises Jack more than a little. He knows the ride well, but this is new territory, and Mason is actually ready to take orders.

"She can't be far. There are a set of doors over this way. She must have gone through here."

A munching sound catches Jack's attention. He asks, "Scotty, what are you doing?"

"It's candy, real candy."

Disgusted, Mason mocks a puking lurch, then says, "Oh, you're sick. You have no idea how long it's been sitting here."

"No, it's good! It tastes fresh. Here, take a bite."

Scotty pulls a peppermint stick from the frame of a tiny door.

"No thanks, I'm good. What's gotten into you? I can't believe you're just going to eat that." But Mason actually finds the whole affair not surprising. Scotty is pretty well-known for his cast iron stomach.

"I'm nervous. I get hungry when I'm nervous. Plus, I was curious."

"I don't care how curious I am, I am not going to go munching on some house in a creepy dark ride," Mason chides. Then, he remembers something and asks, "Hey, what happened to Hansel and Gretel when they ate off the house?"

Between bites of candy, Scotty says, "A witch came and imprisoned them in a cage to fatten them up so she could cook them in—"

Scotty stops chewing for a moment when he realizes how similar his situation is to Hansel and Gretel. He looks around. Jack and Mason, too, are scanning the room, but the coast is clear.

Scotty says, "I don't see any witches," and he continues chowing down.

Still, Jack is growing nervous about the whole situation. "Guys, something about this room seems different. It's 'off,' you know?"

"What do you mean, Jack?" grumbles Scotty while munching on a piece of red licorice from the window sill.

"I don't know, it just feels… odd." And after another pause, he says, "We need to find Amy, and then we should get outta here."

Chapter 28

The troubles in the Dark Ride have caused Clyde headaches for three days. He wondered why he had not simply closed the Enchanted Forrest down, but the answer to that question is obvious. In spite of the trouble, it is a popular attraction, and he hated the thought of shutting her down before fans had an opportunity for a farewell ride. In fact, he was willing to fight the ride all night if he had to just to let kids like Jack have one more moment. This perseverance had resulted in at least fifteen trips to the large breaker box located in the rear of the Jack and Jill Room. There, he would simply jiggle a few wires and flip a couple of switches, and the ride would groan back to life. However, Clyde was beginning to think that what he was doing at the box had nothing to do with the power coming back on at all.

Still, Clyde heads for the box. His flashlight cuts through the low-lit rooms, but as he reaches his destination, the light from his flashlight begins to waiver and then goes out. Clyde thinks, *I changed those batteries just yesterday. Cheap off-brand. You get what you pay for.*

There is no reason for Clyde to continue. The emergency lights in the ride would not give enough of a glow for him to be able to see the components of the box. *Great. Just great,* he thinks.

In one last attempt at light, Clyde bangs the flashlight against his open palm, but nothing happens. After unscrewing the base of the light, he yanks out the batteries and replaces them in a different order inside the chamber. He knows it is probably futile, but he tries anyway. This, also, has no effect, and Clyde thinks, *All right, bub, what ya gonna do now? Go back to the kids? Fool with the box anyways? Maybe I can get Gwen to bring her flashlight in, get the power back on, and get those kids on their way.*

Once again, Clyde second guesses his decision to let the kids stay behind, but he assures himself that he made the right move. Since there were four of them, he told himself nothing was going to happen. There is safety in numbers, he concludes. He decides to get the light from Gwen, so he pulls his radio from his waistband and holds the instrument to his mouth.

"Gwen, you out there?"

After a pause, she answers, "Go ahead, Clyde."

"My flashlight is dead. You got yours on ya?"

"What's going on in there, Clyde? Whatcha need a flashlight for?"

"Well, I can't see anything in the box unless I have more light. Bring yours in here."

"I don't understand, Clyde. Did you get out of the train?"

"Gwen, the power's out. I just—"

"Clyde, what are you talking about? The ride has been running fine."

"Gwen, I assure you, the power is out in here."

There is another pause, and Gwen says, "Clyde, I don't understand. The carts are rolling on the tracks, the music is on, and all the strobes out here are flashing fine. I expected you guys to roll out here any minute."

"Okay, Gwen, this isn't funny. There are four kids in here stuck up in the Giant's lair."

No response comes from Gwen. Clyde grows agitated at the young employee.

"Gwen! Gwen, come back!"

Looking at the radio, he sees the battery light has changed color to red. He tells himself, *This is getting ridiculous.* Violently, Clyde bangs the radio against his hand, snaps off the back of the radio, and flips the square battery out of place. After waiting ten seconds, he replaces it into its position. A green light glows on top of the radio for a second but then switches to red.

"Blast!" says Clyde, who consoles himself a little by thinking, *At least I'll never have to fool with these stinkin' radios again after this weekend.* But then a twinge of finality hits him, and he regrets the thought. He is actually thankful to have been kept busy all night because the problems of the ride have been somewhat of a distraction from the reality that his life in the park is about to end.

Clyde tells himself, *Calm down, old fellow. We've been through worse than this. Maybe I'll just mess with that box, light or no light.*

Turning back to the area where the box hangs on the wall, he chuckles to himself and thinks, *I guess someone's having one last joke on the old man.*

Chapter 29

There has been no sound from the boys and the last few minutes have been tense. Amy is waiting, nervously biting her fingernails and cracking her knuckles—a habit inherited from her mom. She begins to think about the words of the narrator, and as she wonders, *What did he mean by peril?* The hair on the back of her neck begins to tingle. But, she consoles herself by thinking, *Come on, Amy, there's no way he was talking about you.*

The only sound is the dull hum of the emergency lights. Tracks on the floor end abruptly at the gingerbread house. At first, Amy guesses that the structure is some sort of hub where they keep extra carts but then realizes it is too small. With the mysterious disappearance of the door, she decides to move on and takes the only set of doors available to her.

She finds herself in another room. Standing just inside the doors of the new space, she takes inventory of the surroundings and scans for another door that could get her out of here.

"Lucky, do you get the feeling we're just getting more lost? When we see the boys, I'm telling Mason you're with me. Would you like that? Serves him right, troublemaker."

Amy wonders if the power had come back on. The new room looks alive. Bird sounds and chirping cricket noises reverberate in the room, and there are dozens and dozens of trees.

Taking the stick she acquired from the bonfire, she strikes the side of one of the larger trees and says, *Man, that thing is solid. Whoever designed this room outdid themselves.* At this point, Amy's neck begins to tingle. An overwhelming sensation that someone is following her envelopes her. She can't explain how she knows, she just does. It is the same feeling she got every time she played hide-and-go-seek with her sisters at home. She thinks, *Maybe it's the boys—or Clyde? But, what if it isn't?* If she had not already been scared, she probably would have simply called out to the pursuer, but the words of the narrator, "Realize her peril and at once take flight," had made an impression. She tells herself, *Hide, Amy—now!*

A particularly large tree trunk is on the right side of the room. Quickly, Amy and Lucky duck behind its cover, and Amy hears the doors she entered quietly open again followed by clicks on the floor and then the sound of sniffing and panting. She realizes this is not the boys and certainly not Clyde. While trembling and gripping the stick, Amy thinks, *Do I dare sneak a peek?* She hears deep breaths and more panting coming closer to her.

She asks herself, *Should I run? No, wait, whoever it is will—*

The panting stops. There are no more clicks on the floor.

Did they leave? Amy wonders. She decides to take a quick glance and stands upright and carefully looks around the corner of the tree. The first thing she sees is a pair of eyes—enormous green eyes staring directly at her. Amy dashes toward doors at the rear of the room. However, before she can makes much headway, her pursuer cuts off her path to the door. They stand looking directly at each other in full view. In front of Amy is the most hideous creature she has ever laid eyes on, a wolf standing upright wearing a black coat and a stovetop black hat. It has wild eyes and a gaping mouth full of awful fangs. Amy thinks it can't be real, that this has to be a prank.

With her throat full of bile, Amy can't scream. Instead she yells, "What do you want?"

"You."

The eerie voice of her costumed tormentor shakes her to her core, and she asks, "Why?"

In a thick snarling accent, it answers, "Because you are the girl and I am the Wolf. You are what I have always craved."

The wolf steps closer.

"Stop right there. I don't understand." Amy thinks, *This has to be a prank?* and then asks, "What's going on? Are you an employee? Why do you want.... ?"

The wolf does not stop.

Amy contemplates, *Run? No, I can't outrun it.*

Suddenly, with wild abandon and fury, the wolf snarls and leaps at Amy. Her only option available is to defend herself. Amy drops Lucky to the floor and instinctively swings the stick, which cracks against the attacker's gaping jaws.

It makes a hideous yelp followed by an ear-splitting howl.

Amy thinks, *Run. Don't look back—just run. The doors are just ahead.* She runs.

Chapter 30

The boys try to open the door on the little ginger bread house, but it's locked. Chomping on a last bit of candy, Scotty wipes his hands against his knit shirt. Mason, who is watching his friend with disgust, mockingly asks, "Finished?"

"Yep."

"That was disgusting," responds Mason.

"All right," Jack says, "Let's move. We've wasted too much time in here." Jack motions to a set of doors to the right side of the room. "Okay, she had to go that way."

The words of the narrator have bothered Jack, and Mason's attempts at dismissing the rhyme have done little to comfort him. To Jack, there's no way around it—somehow, someway the ride has spoken to them. However, Jack doesn't have time to sit and mull over any possibilities. In spite of the lingering questions simmering in his head, his attention is focused elsewhere. Right now, they have to find Amy.

Since it took a lot of effort to get through the first set of doors, Jack prayed that this next set would let them through without putting up a fight. Thankfully, the doors open without a struggle, and the boys walk through.

"Whoa, this is amazing," says Scotty, wide-eyed and looking at the various trees.

"Jack, what is going on in here?" asks Mason. "Where are we?"

"I don't know. This is new to me." He pauses, then calls,

"Amy!" The other two boys call.

"She's not in here," Mason declares. "For all we know, she never has been."

"Then where did she go?" Scotty asks.

Mason starts, "Maybe she—"

"Guys," says Scotty.

"What, Scotty?" answers Jack.

"She's been here."

Scotty points at a particularly large tree. There at the base, Lucky, the large blue bear leans up against the trunk.

"Lucky!" Mason shouts.

"Okay, guys, we know she's been here," Jack announces. "That means we're on the right track."

Scotty pushes his glasses back up the bridge of his nose and asks, "Why did she leave him here?"

"Who knows," replies Mason, who reaches down and lifts the bear before handing it to Scotty.

Jack says, "Mason, really? Let's just leave it here."

"No way, Jack. Lucky is with us."

"Whatever, Mason. Then why don't you carry him?"

"Carnahan doesn't mind. Plus, I need my hands free just in case Clyde comes charging at us with a chainsaw."

"Give it a rest, Mason. That's getting old."

"I'm just sayin'."

"And I'm sayin' that we need to get to the next room—like now."

"Okay, okay, fearless leader. Your wish is our command," says Mason as he jokingly bows.

Looking back at Scotty, Jack cannot help but pity the boy, who's now lugging Mason's pet around.

After opening the next set of doors, the trio sees more trees.

"Whoever built this place spent a fortune on landscaping," Mason points out.

As Jack passes a particularly large trunk, he hears Mason yell, "Duck!" and sees a stick fly just above Scotty's head. Jack recoils and falls on his backside.

"Stop!" Scotty cries.

Jack looks up to see Amy breathing hard with wild eyes and holding a large stick in her left hand.

"Amy, what's going on?" Scotty asks. "You nearly took my head off."

The girl's shoulders ease after she recognizes who else is in the room with her.

"Are you okay, sis?" Scotty asks, trying to calm her.

"No, I'm not okay!" She carefully points and says, "He's—he's over there."

"Who's over there, Amy?" Mason asks. "There's nothing over there."

"Over there. He was just over there. When you came in, he ran. You weren't watching. He ran behind you. He's waiting for another chance, I'm sure. Waiting to get me. With his big teeth and his scary eyes and…." Tears begin to stream down her face.

Jack wants nothing more than to embrace Amy and to tell her how foolish he was, but instead he just says, "Amy, you have to tell us what happened."

"A creature attacked me. It's a giant man-wolf, Jack."

Mason looks at Jack with a disbelieving face and sees that even Jack is having a hard time with this revelation. Jack wants to believe but doesn't see the evidence. He thinks, *Is Amy losing her mind? Her imagination is running wild. Maybe she saw a shadow or something?* "Maybe we should have a look," Mason announces flippantly.

"No," begs Amy.

"Amy, I want to believe you. I really do. But you have to know how crazy this sounds," Jack explains. "I've got your back, Mason. Let's check it out."

Scotty sheepishly agrees. "We'll all go."

Amy is clearly hesitant, but there is strength in numbers. She continues to wield the stick as she follows the three older boys.

Carefully, they creep. A thought comes into Jack's mind: *What if she is telling the truth?*

The large tree gets closer, and Mason raises his fist mockingly and says, "Come out, come out wherever you are, Mr. Wolf." He peers around the tree and yells, "There he is!"

The other three immediately jump back in fear until they hear the uncontrollable laughter of Mason.

"I got you guys good! There's no wolf here. You should have seen the look—"

"I am not lying, Mason Chick! It was here."

"Oh, Amy, get over it," responds Mason, still chuckling. "I'm not buying."

"Okay. So, we have Amy. Let's go," says Scotty, who begins to walk back towards the doors they entered.

Just then, Amy cries out in alarm. "No! He's there!" She's pointing to a spot somewhere amongst the trees ahead of Scotty.

Jack glares in that direction and wonders, *Does she see him?* Before any of the boys can spot the predator, though, Amy bolts for the set of doors behind them.

"Amy!" Scotty calls. "No, we're leaving!"

But, she is already through the doors.

"Guess we'd better grab her," says Mason, who turns and pursues her.

Scotty reluctantly follows.

After peering in the direction that Amy pointed, Jack slowly decides to leave. However, just as he turns away, Jack catches a glimpse of two beady eyes glowing in the dark for a split second. He's convinced, now, that Amy had seen a wolf, and he runs to the doors following the others.

Chapter 31

Jack joins the others in the next room. Inside, there are more trees and a large wooden tub containing a small pool of water.

Amy is breathing hard.

"Calm down, sis," says Scotty. "We need to get out of here and go back."

In a panic, Amy waves her arms wildly, still frightened. "I'm not going back that way, bar the doors—bar the doors now."

Mason laughs and asks, "With what?"

Jack suggests, "Mason, let's move that trough thing in front of the doors."

"Jack, you don't believe—"

"Come on, Mason, just do it, please," Jack urges. The glowing green eyes haunt Jack. He knows Amy is telling the truth.

The boys struggle with the heavy object.

"Oh, that's cute. Look, a broken candle, a chef's hat, and an apron." Scotty is pointing at the three objects gathered in a corner of the room. "Three men in a tub—just like the nursery rhyme."

Jack observes Scotty's excitement and considers that all those years of reading fables are finally paying off.

Finally, the wooden trough is heaved in front of the door.

"That thing's a lot heavier than it looks," gasps Jack.

"Happy now, Amy? No wolf can get in here," says Mason, thick with irritation.

Jack, panting from the exertion, decides it's time for some clarity. Calmly, in as pleasant a voice as he can muster, he asks, "So what happened?"

Amy tells them about leaving the cart, entering the ride, and her run-in with the wolf. Mason's frustration with Amy spills out, and he says, "The wolf? Are you really sticking to that story?" Mason's voice drips with disbelief.

Jack sees red flush on Amy's face as she answers him, "Mason, he was real. He attacked me and said he wanted to get me. I thought it was just some dude in a costume, but when he opened his mouth, those terrible fangs—"

"He said? The wolf spoke to you? Oh, Amy, you're killing me." Raising his pointer finger to his head, Mason spins it, insinuating Amy is cuckoo.

"You have to believe me!"

"Sis, you do have to realize this is a little hard to swallow."

"Oh great. My own brother thinks I'm delusional."

"Remember when you broke my Barbie doll in two, Mason?"

"What does that have to do with anything?"

"Everything! You know what, Mason? I have no clue what my brother sees in you andwhy he follows you around like a puppy dog. For that matter, I have no idea what anyone sees in you. You're a selfish, arrogant snot who thinks he can bully whoever he chooses because his dad's a rich lawyer."

Jack intercedes by saying, "Amy, this is not helping."

"And what is it with you, Jack? Just because Mason steps out of the cart, you go running to him. You guys are the whole reason we are in this mess in the first place, and now I sit here and tell you what happened, and you all have the gall to think I am lying?"

"Amy, I believe you," says Jack, trying to relax her.

Mason throws his hands up in the air in disbelief. "Oh come on!"

"Mason, obviously something happened. Look at her. She's freaked out about something."

Even though Jack had seen the eyes, something in his head tells him not to mention it. Mason and Scotty would think he was loony if he told them.

"Mason," Scotty says and then carefully clears his throat. "My sister is not crazy. She would not be this upset. Jack's right, she had to have seen something."

The words of Jack and Scotty seem to have a calming effect on Mason.

"Okay, I'm sorry. Maybe you did see something, but I still don't believe you saw a wolf. Some dude in a really good costume, maybe, but not a wolf."

Although this is not much of a concession, Jack knows it is a big deal coming from Mason. He watches Amy, and she seems to ease, at least a little. She had been brutal with her words and perhaps had humbled Mason a bit. However, knowing Mason the way he did, Jack considered that it was more likely that the boy admired her little tirade. Now, possibly Mason is just trying to play nice and make up for some hurtful words of his own. At any rate, Mason decides to break the tension by saying, "We need to get outta here. Let's go back the way we came."

Jack is thankful for the change in Mason's tone and mentions, "Guys, there's another set of doors that way—just ahead. How big can this place be? We're sure to find the exit at some point."

Jack's rationale makes sense to them all, but no one wants to move.

All four teens begin to look around. They perceive that something has changed about the ride since they got stuck. It seems alive. The trees don't look plastic, the sounds effects are not crackling and buzzing, a gentle breeze flows through the room, and the leaves on the trees sway back and forth.

Mason spots a squirrel sitting amidst one of the branches above. It is looking directly at the teens, and he says, "Uh… Jack, that's a real squirrel."

"I see that," says Jack with an astonished look.

"Maybe he just wandered in here," Scotty offers. "Like through a vent."

"This whole place—it's alive," Amy says.

Jack thinks, *Time to take charge before anyone freaks out*. He chooses to temporarily ignore the new surroundings and muster the troops.

"Amy, you want to leave?" Jack asks.

"I didn't want to be here in the first place."

"Then let's go."

"And what about him?" she asks while pointing at Mason.

"Mason, you gonna play nice?"

"Is the squirrel gonna play nice?" Mason retorts.

"Look, let's just find a way out, okay? And from now on, we stay together—no matter what. Deal?" Jack asks.

Scotty's the first to jump in and says, "Yeah. I'm good."

"Mason?"

Jack's question diverts Mason's attention from aiming a rock at the squirrel. Mason turns to Jack and shrugs a yes. When he turns back around, the squirrel's gone. Mason throws the rock anyway, and it lands in the foliage of the tree and bounces off a limb or two before thumping to the grass-covered ground.

"Amy? We can't stay here." Jack declares.

"And what about the wolf?" Amy responds.

"Oh, geez, the wolf again," says Mason.

"Mason." Jack scolds. Then he addresses Amy. "We'll keep our eyes out for the wolf, okay? And we're not going back through there." He points to the set of doors securely impeded from opening by the large wooden tub.

Amy grips her stick, realizing that staying in the room isn't really an option. She moves next to Jack and nods.

Jack looks into Amy's eyes and tells her, "Look, we're all sorry. We should not have left you alone in the first place. You're mad at us; I get it. But what's happened has happened, and we can't change that now. If you'll help us get out of here, we can all go home."

After a pause, Amy gives a nod as well.

A gentle breeze blows across Jack's face, forcing him to wipe long bangs from his right eye. He wonders, *What is going on in here?*

Chapter 32

His paw presses firmly on the side of his head. He had not expected that. The girl is a fighter. He had not seen the stick in her hand until it was too late. He will not make the same mistake again. Removing his paw, he looks at the traces of blood, and says, "Blasted girl!"

After the others arrived, he had decided to retreat, to continue the hunt later. He considers whether he should bide his time until she is alone again or just take them all. At least he knows now that all the dreams he's had about the girl can now come true. He surmises that whatever he had tumbled into a few nights back had just been a decoy, someone's idea of a joke or a countermove intended to throw him off her track.

He enters a tiny wreck of a straw shack that had once been the home of a rather terrified pig and thinks, *This will not do. A slight wind could topple the hut. Reinforcement is in order—but that can wait.* Ripping the sheets from an inadequately small bed, he tears off a strip of fabric for a makeshift bandage. Looking at the bandage infuriates him further, and with a vicious howl of emotion, he slings the cloth to the floor and cries, "No weakness!"

Turning to a small wooden table, he looks longingly at an empty plate adorning its surface. The empty plate stares at him and mocks him while his stomach rumbles. The previous day's meal had done nothing to hamper the burning hunger within him. He realizes that only the girl will satisfy his appetite, and he slams his paw upon the table, causing the plate to rattle. He thinks, *Why do I want her? Why do I need her?* Looking at the plate as if it were his only ally in the world, the wolf says, "I know I promised that you would have her today."

He focuses on the plate and then states, "Today is not over!"

The plate seems to smirk at him.

"I said the day is not over!"

The wolf's paw slams the table once again, and the plate nearly flips in response to the force. He calms himself by breathing more slowly while he appears to be listening to the plate.

"True, I can simply circle around them and cut them off before they get to the bridge." Again, he seems to be listening.

"Who?"

The wolf nods and says, "I know he does not like me."

Starring at the plate, he slants his head as if hearing a verbal reply.

"I said I know he does not like me! I don't care who is with her. Next time will be different. Enough! You'll hold her soon enough. Then we will both be satisfied."

Chapter 33

Still contemplating their exit from the room with the tub, a temporary peace has stilled the restless teens.

Jack breaks the calm by suggesting, "So we press on? Hope there's an exit somewhere down the line?" He's ready to keep moving.

"I'm in," Mason declares.

Amy nods.

Scotty pulls out his cell phone. "Guys, what if I call my parents? They can get a hold of someone outside the ride. They can send someone in to get us."

"No!" Jack and Mason chime in unison.

"Why not?"

"Just no, Scotty," says Mason, who glares at him with heavy stern eyes.

"Scotty, if you call your parents, then we're totally busted. We can make this right."

Scotty considers Jack's words and looks at the phone.

"Oh, it doesn't matter anyways—it's dead. That's funny, I charged it last night."

"Well, that puts your latest brain surge to rest," Mason remarks in mock relief.

A low hum reverberates through the room.

> "The foursome argues and rues the day
> The time they choose to come and play.
> In the woods awake and full of dread,
> Perhaps a coffin would be their bed?
> Finish the story, words they will need
> Or the travelers will lose their lives, indeed."

The words of the narrator silence them and several seconds pass.

"Okay, were moving from bizarre to creepy," Mason admits.

"Let's get to the next room," Jack asserts. Inside his head the last rhyme resonates, and he thinks, *Finish the story…. Or lose their lives—what did that mean?* Mason and Scotty pass cautiously through the next set of doors.

Jack holds up, waiting for Amy. He desires some acknowledgement and hopes for a sign that things are still good between them. So he offers, "Amy?"

"You left me, Jack."

"Yeah, I'm really—"

"You left me," she repeats as she passes on by.

Jack realizes, *She's still mad,* and he feels dejected but tells himself, *I can't blame her.* As he passes the threshold to the next room, the words "the foursome argues and rues the day" haunt him. Somehow, Jack believes, the ride knows what they are doing.

Chapter 34

In a remote section of the woods, standing beside a great oak tree, a tall lady and an elegantly dressed man speak in hushed tones. During their conversation, a fat grey squirrel climbs down on the outstretched hand of the tall slender lady and starts chattering. After a moment, the lady beams excitement and exclaims, "They are here! This is wonderful!"

She lovingly stokes the squirrel's tail and asks, "Where are they now?"

The squirrel clicks into her ear.

"Excellent, the time is truly at hand. You must both watch them. Do not interfere, unless you have to. No harm must come to them. Their safety is of the upmost importance."

"Yes, milady," confirms the man in a polite English accent.

"Has the wolf behaved?" the lady asks.

"He has tormented a few of the subjects, and we lost a pig, but otherwise, all is in order," the man answers.

"What a vile creature. You must keep an eye on him. He must not actually get to the girl, only pursue her."

"Yes, milady," the man agrees.

"When the time comes, he cannot destroy all we have worked for. He must do his part for the common good, or we shall intervene. Do not fail me. Freedom for all is at stake."

The squirrel begins chirping away.

The lady responds, "Ah, my child, you have done well." Nodding her head, she says, "Now, off with you both, my children. Let me know of their progress."

The lady pauses and takes a deep breath, and says, "This is the day we have waited for. All of our dreams, all of our hopes rely on these noble children. If they succeed…. Imagine it—we can all be free."

Chapter 35

Jack is the last to enter the room and is taken aback by their new surroundings. He had grown accustomed to the outdoor scenery of the last few rooms. Now, to his surprise, they have entered into a creepy old laboratory, but it is simply incredible. Shelves line the walls, and all sorts of books, vials, and beakers adorn every corner of the room. On top of a waist high metal shelf sit three cages, including one with two live white mice. Also, behind a metal table stands a narrator mannequin holding his book, and next to the narrator is another set of doors.

"Jack, this is awesome! Look at these books," says Scotty as he pulls volume after volume from their resting places and reads the titles. "*Hexes and Curses, 101*; *New Uses for Newts*; *Undetectable Poisons*; *Batty about Bats*. Oh man, two giant books dedicated to love potions!"

Mason pulls back a sheet that covers a human skeleton lying upon a flat metal gurney. "Would you look at this? It's all so real."

Amy taps the top of the cage where the mice are imprisoned and says, "They're so cute! Maybe we should set them free."

"I don't think we should be messing with any of this stuff," Jack says. "Guys, aren't you forgetting about getting out of here? It's starting to get late. We are supposed to be meeting the Carnahan's by—"

There is a hum and a crackle.

"Enthralled by the lab, the travelers have stalled.
The danger ever present they have not recalled.
Move forward on through the wood
Through the doors ahead they should.
Curiosity peeked in the laboratory.
Their task, not to forget, is to finish the story."

For the second time, the same words have been uttered by the strange figure. "Finish the story."

"He's telling us what to do," says Jack, who walks to the mannequin and reads the words that were just proclaimed. A curious thought enters Jack's head: *What if I simply turn the page of the book? I could look ahead and see what's coming.* His hand shoots to the page corner, but the pages are stuck together and none of them will move.

Jack says, "The book, the narrator…. It's telling us to finish the story. I think it's trying to guide us, help us."

"Jack, you don't believe that those rhymes have anything to do with us, do you?" asks Mason, who turns his attention away from the skeleton and looks at Jack.

"Yes, I do. The last two times the voice has spoken, it's said to finish the story. It's obvious Mason. And this time, he's telling us to go through those doors ahead."

"It may be obvious to you, but how does that help us any?" asks Mason. "I mean, what does it mean? What story?"

"I don't know," Jack thinks for a second and then suggests, "Okay, what about this: In the ride, there are four characters, right? Well, you remember the ride ends when they chop down the beanstalk?"

"Yeah," Mason responds and nods.

"Well, maybe we're supposed to finish the story and the narrator is leading us back to the beanstalk."

"Are you kidding me, Jack? You think we're supposed to beat some Giant by chopping down some beanstalk? That is ridiculous."

The rebuke stings a little, but Jack knows that somehow he's right. Still, he adds, "At least it's a direction."

Mason considers, then counters, "For all we know, the voice is simply part of this undiscovered part of the ride. Maybe someone's watching us."

"Do you see any cameras in here, Mason?" Jack challenges.

"No," replies Mason, who looks anyway.

Jack takes the opportunity to make a point, "It can't be a coincidence. It's too spot-on."

Looking to Amy for support, Jack is disappointed as she once again turns her head away from his gaze.

"What story, Jack? Look you're getting carried away," Scotty declares, much to Jack's agitation. "I agree, though, that we need to move on."

"Scotty, get your head out of those books," Mason calls down at the boy.

After placing a book on the ground, Scotty grabs Lucky and begins to head for the exit, but then turns back to a shelf and fiddles with a couple of the brightly colored vials and a brown piece of paper. His eyes are spellbound by the different effects within his grasp.

"I said let's go," states Mason at the door motioning for the others.

Scotty ignores Mason, though, and reads the simple writing on a slip attached to a vial. It says, "Pour the contents of the yellow vial into the blue cylinder. Mix evenly by moving the cylinder clockwise."

Mason, who had already exited, returns to the room and asks, "Scotty, what on earth are you up to?"

"Hold on a second," responds Scotty. The boy's tongue is licking his bottom lip as he carefully pours the contents of the yellow vial into the cylinder. Slowly he swirls the contents.

Pop! A small explosion in the cylinder causes it to vibrate, and Scotty drops it to the floor. It shatters, and a small cloud of red smoke wafts into his face.

"Now you've done it. What were you trying to do?" Mason questions.

Scotty, slightly panicked, wipes his face with his shirt sleeve. "It said, 'Strength Potion.' I was just trying to—"

"Oh brother, Carnahan, leave this stuff alone and let's get outta here."

Mason once again attempts to leave the room, but Scotty remains standing while he re-reads the instructions.

Mason yells, "Scotty!"

Chapter 36

Clyde stumbles in the dark in the room where the tailor and his apprentice stand as he's in route to the fuse box. Another attempt to revive the radio fails. He thinks, "If Gwen is pulling my leg with some sort of prank, it's a good one." But, Clyde knows that Gwen is not a prankster.

The dim light of the room provides just enough clarity for his eyes to see that something is missing from the chest of the tailor, the badge.

"Great, why can't people just leave well enough alone?"

Scanning the room, Clyde peers from corner to corner looking for other missing pieces of the ride. After a sigh he leaves the room, and for the next few minutes he endures more stumbling from stepping around trees, rocks, and other various props that had been placed for the atmosphere and enjoyment of the riders. Finally, making his way into the room with the fuse box, he opens the lid. *Everything looks fine,* thinks Clyde, *but what's this…. A loose wire?* He jiggles the wire back and forth until the ride suddenly comes to life.

Clyde hears a faint noise from behind the doors ahead that sounds like voices. He wonders, *Are the kids coming back? Did they leave the ride? I told them to stay! Well, I can't blame them. All cooped up in this—*

The sound of more voices comes from behind him.

Okay, Clyde, get a hold of yourself. Someone's just coming in to check on you. Maybe it's Gwen.

The whispers grow louder and come from ahead of and behind Clyde, who experiences an unwelcome familiar feeling creeping up the back of his neck. Suddenly, he hears exactly what he had refused to recallcalliope music. Through the mental walls of his memory, the face of Douglas Finch appears. He realizes he must get back to the kids.

Chapter 37

Reluctantly leaving the lab behind, Scotty moves through the doors into the unknown. He is still wiping his eyes as he moves. The smoke had made his eyes itch. As soon as he takes one step into the new room, he is met with a cold blast. It feels like he has just stepped into a freezer. The pudgy boy is awestruck by the brilliance of the new landscape. The floors, walls, and small pine trees are all covered in a thick blanket of snow. After looking down at the white powdery substance, he cannot help himself and proceeds to roll up a snowball and throw it at Mason. The snowball aimlessly falls an inch short of its target.

Mason looks down and asks, "Oh, you want some of this, do you?" He quickly creates a large snowball himself, and Scotty begins to back up, playfully. Mason launches the ball, and it hits Scotty with a dull thud on the side of his neck.

"Owww," Scotty moans, holding his wet neck.

"You shouldn't play games you can't win, bud," Mason mocks.

"Guys, this is not the time for that," Amy scolds.

"What is that over there? Look," says Jack, pointing.

The others gaze firmly on what they perceive to be a green stick on the ground just under one of the four pine trees. After further observation, though, Scotty realizes that the stick is alive. It is actually a small green snake on top of the white mass. Scotty hates snakes, and it seems to him that this one is looking directly at them. It makes little difference to Scotty that the snake is only about one foot long.

"Don't move, guys. It's afraid of us," Mason cautions.

Scotty does not budge. Years ago, his father had cornered a snake under the hot water heater in the Carnahan garage. It was as small as this one, but his father had forced Scotty to join him in getting rid of the reptile. He was handed a rake while his father held a shovel. Following the instructions of his father, Scotty poked at the snake with the end of the rake: once, twice, three times. However, it only seemed to encourage the creature to stay put. When his father walked out of the garage to grab a trash bag, Scotty decided to try again. This time, as soon as the rake touched the body of the animal, it darted from its hiding place and made a straight line toward him. Lashing out in anger, the snake struck at Scotty's leg. Perhaps it was the hum of the heater, but Scotty had not noticed that the snake had been making a rattling sound; however, after it had sprung, the tail was visible. Luckily, because of the winter weather that day, Scotty was wearing jeans. The teeth had not penetrated his flesh, only the loose end of his pants. Scotty slung his left leg out and slammed the rake down on the reptile's back. The force of the well-aimed blow severed the snake in two, but the head kept its lock on Scotty's pant leg. At this point, his father returned and grasped the top half of the snake from Scotty's pant leg, threw it on the ground, and made another stab at it with the shovel. The snake's hideous eyes were still open, and ever since then, Scotty never wanted to look at any snake's eyes.

Scotty, though, now finds himself looking into similar reptilian eyes. He thinks, *This time, I don't even have a rake.* None of them dares to move, but they need to get away from the unwavering snake and move on to another room. This time, there are two new sets of double doors: one straight ahead and one to the left.

"Okay," says Jack. "When I count to three, let's cut to the right and make a dash to the door ahead."

"No, Jack, it would be easier to get to that door on the left," Mason retorts.

Scotty thinks, *Of course they are arguing. They have been doing it all night.* He is growing tired of it.

Amy shivers and yanks the hood of the borrowed red sweatshirt over her head while Jack and Mason debate the merits of their own plans without taking their eyes off the snake.

"Look, we need to keep going forward, Mason. If we deviate from the plan—"

"What plan? We're just trying to get out, so let's just go left."

"No, it's—"

"Guys, that's enough!" interjects Amy, a little more assertive than usual. "It's too cold to stand here shivering. Let's just go one way or the other."

"Okay, okay. We'll go to those doors," Mason concedes. "I just want to get out of the cold."

Satisfied with Mason's acquiesce, Jack moves to the right.

Suddenly, the snake jets out with astonishing speed, blocking Jack's path.

"That takes care of that," Scotty fearfully advises.

Mason moves to the left, but once again, the snake shoots in that direction and cuts off an escape to the door.

Shaken by the speed and menace of the reptile, Amy yells, "What do you want?"

Despite the harrowing situation, Scotty is struck by a sudden urge to laugh by contemplating the notion of his sister having a conversation with an animal.

The snake lifts its head from the ground, and, like a cobra, it hovers there swaying right and left. Then to their astonishment, it says, "Would you be interested in making a deal?" The snake's voice is ominous and foreboding, and it continues, "I merely want you to get me out of this cold room."

Scotty's jaw drops, and Mason looks to Jack in complete shock. Jack can only stare at the thing as Amy steps back in amazement.

Chapter 38

Scotty's dumbfounded. Moving behind the others, he says to his companions in a hushed voice, "I don't remember any nursery rhyme about snakes?"

The others ignore him. Jack is fixated on figuring a way out of this obstacle.

Mason, seeming to not be baffled by the situation, goes ahead and asks the snake, "What's your offer?"

It replies, "I know of a certain object, located here in the wood. It would prove useful to lost travelers like you."

"Okay, what object?" Jack, with curiosity piqued, asks.

"I will tell you… once I am out of this place," the snake replies.

"He's bluffing, Jack," Scotty warns.

"What makes you think that?" Jack replies.

Scotty looks at Jack, shakes his head, and offers, "It's a talking snake for crying out loud. Hello? Snake?"

"Oh, I assure you this is no bluff," the snake calmly hisses. "Why are you so distrustful?"

"Like I said, you're a snake!" answers Scotty, emphasizing the word "snake."

Jack continues to push for more information. "Tell us about the object, then, if we can trust you."

"Pick me up, and carry me out. You will not get one word from me until then."

"Why can't we just open the door and let you out? Why do we have to pick you up?" Mason asks suspiciously.

"Because there is a step I cannot navigate on my own," replies the snake, sounding disheartened.

"What do you think, Mason?" asks Jack.

Mason ponders for a moment and then says, "Well, I guess.... But who's gonna do it?" Mason looks around at the others.

"Not me," chimes Scotty. "I hate snakes."

"Don't look at me," Amy adds.

They stand staring at each other. Scotty waits for Mason to say something. This is his kind of thing, but there is an obvious hesitation. *This is strange*, Scotty thinks.

After twenty seconds of uncomfortable silence, Jack announces, "I'll do it."

Scotty sighs in relief.

"Oh, good gracious," announces Mason. "It's always me who has to do the dirty work. My uncle Charles had a snake once, and I held it a time or two."

"But Mason, Jack said—"

"I know, I heard him, but I'm the one who does the hard stuff. Just step aside. I'll do it."

Scotty, confused by the sudden change of heart, arrives at the conclusion that Mason did not like being one-upped by Jack.

"Excellent," encourages the snake. "You will not regret it, kind sir."

"You had better behave yourself," responds Mason.

The others stare at Mason as he approaches the snake. Slowly, carefully, Mason picks up the snake by its torso, and the snake dangles from his hand.

"No funny business," Mason commands.

"I am so cold. Please tuck me into your shirt—I am about to die."

"No way."

Scotty listens to the snake's hissing voice. And, suddenly, a thought pops into his head about a fable he read years ago.

Again, the reptile pleads, "Let me in your shirt, please. I will be forever grateful."

This time while Mason holds the snake aloft with one arm, he lifts his shirt with the other.

"No, Mason!" Scotty yells. "Remember about 'The Farmer and the Snake' from Aesop's Fables?"

Thinking fast, Scotty plunges his hands into his pockets, searching for something to hurl at the snake. Charging at Mason, he pulls the stolen scissors from his pocket and with unknown skill, he hurls them like a dagger. The shears strike, but, not the snake. They clip Mason's hand.

"Owww!" blurts Mason, who drops the snake and clasps the oozing cut with his other hand.

Shocked by the sudden eruption of activity, Jack ignores the snake and rushes to Mason while Scotty sees the result of his folly and moans in anguish.

The snake is confused by the activity and instinctively strikes at the nearest legMason's.

Chapter 39

Two things have happened that have encouraged Clyde. The music has stopped, and for some odd reason, the radio clinging to his belt has chirped back to life. On his way back to where he left the kids, he hears, "Clyde? Clyde? What's going on in there?"

Hoping the radio would not die, he quickly fumbles with the button on its side and says, "I'm here, Gwen. Radio is playing tricks on me."

Clyde finally reaches the place where he left the kids. He pauses, taking in the situation, and says to himself, *Nothing. No train, no kids. Blast! I told them to stay put.*

Pulling the radio back up to his mouth, he asks, "Gwen, have you seen the kids?"

"Clyde, what's the matter? No, the kids haven't gotten off the ride yet. They aren't with you?"

"No, long story."

"Well, they should be off any minute. I don't remember the ride taking that long."

"I told you the power is going off and on in here."

"Clyde, the power has been on the whole time you've been in there."

"Gwen, this is no time for joking. I can assure you the power is off in here."

"Okay, Clyde, whatever you say, but listen for yourself."

Through the receiver, Clyde hears the distinctive music from the outside of the ride.

"Hear that? The music is on."

It was proof, and Clyde realizes there is no disputing it now. He says, "Okay, the power is on... out there. But there is some kind of weird short in here that's making things go off and on."

However, even as he says this, he knows it doesn't make sense. He thinks, *Better get out there and have a look. Maybe those kids will be waiting for me when I get out there.... I hope.*

Chapter 40

Jack watches as the snake's wild eyes and frothing mouth lash out at Mason's leg.

"No!" Amy calls.

Just as the fangs are about to sink into Mason's unprotected leg, the hurtling body of Jack tackles Mason, sending both of them to the ground. The snake's fangs taste air as it flies past the two plummeting boys.

The snake settles back on the cold white floor and prepares for another lunge. This time it targets Scotty.

Jack screams at the reptile, "Get away!"

Eyeing the frozen figure of Scotty, the snake shoots forward at him.

Scotty, scared stiff, watches as the reptile advances. He throws up his hands and looks down at the floor. Jack is too far away to help.

Just as the snake is about to strike, Scotty reacts. The boy reaches down and maneuvers Lucky in front of him, like a shield.

The snake is charging with fangs poised for a deep strike, and it smashes into the plush toy, earning a mouth full of fluff.

The events seem to transpire in slow motion for Jack, and he realizes he must interfere. Rising to his feet and taking three lunging steps, Jack grabs the bear, complete with the snake's jaws locked onto the animal's soft insides, and slings it like a discus. The circling momentum of the bear shakes loose the fangs and sends the snake hurling into the opposite wall.

Amy rushes to Mason. She takes Mason's hand and looks at the gash that is now oozing blood from Scotty's wayward scissor throw, but she doesn't allow her complete attention to be taken away from the vile creature lurking on the floor.

"Let's go now!" Jack yells.

Through the doors to the left, they immediately jump up on a large step into the next room and into the unknown.

Chapter 41

"He was going to bite you, Mason, as soon as you put him under your shirt. I didn't mean to cut you. You know that, right?" asks Scotty. "When he asked to get in your shirt, that was the clue. 'The Farmer and the Snake'—I can't believe I didn't think of it sooner. In the fable, the snake convinces the farmer to put him in his coat due to the cold ground and snow, but he strikes the farmer all the way home."

As Scotty tries to explain away his actions, Amy kneels down to observe the gash. "Oh, this is quite a cut, Mason. Jack, can I cut a strip of your sweatshirt for a bandage?"

The sweatshirt had been a Christmas gift, but Jack knew he needed to help his friend. Plus, he figured this might help him be in better standing with Amy, reasoning that a little manipulation to get back in her good graces would be worth the loss of the hoodie.

"Of course," says Jack. "Go ahead."

Amy takes the scissors and gently cuts a long strip from the sagging sweatshirt.

"Let me see the cut, Mason," says Jack.

"It's not that bad," reassures Mason, but a grimace of discomfort reveals that the pain is worse than the proud boy is willing to let on.

Jack says, "I don't think you'll need stitches."

Scotty contributes, "You do know I was trying to help, right?"

"Yes, Scotty, yes!" Mason's tone makes it clear that despite the agreement, he is upset with Scotty.

Amy says, "Give me your hand."

She gently wraps the red bandage around the wound, and a curious sensation of jealousy intrudes upon Jack. He thinks, *She's being awful kind to him all of a sudden.* Jack is glad that Amy's attitude toward the boys has been calmed from the tirade of fury she had unleashed upon them—especially Mason—ten minutes ago. Still, Jack does not like this sudden display of kindness toward his friend.

"Thanks, Amy," Mason sheepishly mutters.

Jack tells himself, *Change the subject. Divert her attention.*

He says, in a particularly high volume, "Uh, Scotty, you came through for us back there."

Scotty sheepishly replies, "By cutting a gash into a chunk of Mason's flesh?"

"No—with your knowledge," Jack replies.

"Oh, that."

"If you hadn't known about that old fable, the snake could have sunk its teeth into Mason. I think your knowledge of these stories is really going to come in handy tonight. Isn't that right, Amy?"

"Uh… that's right. Good job, Scotty," says Amy, who stands to pat her brother on the shoulder.

Scotty finally changes his glum expression and smiles at Jack. Amy and Jack can see his pride well up inside.

"Well, I am glad it has finally come to good use. I'll try and think faster next time."

Mason stands and says, "But next time, hit the snake." This is a good-natured jab with an unmistakable tone of sincerity hidden underneath.

Mason flexes his hand and says, "Really, it's not that bad."

"So, do you think the snake was being truthful?" Jack questions.

"About what?" asks Mason, still looking at his wound.

Jack replies, "The item we would think was useful."

"No, he just wanted a snack," says Mason.

"Yeah, you're probably right," says Scotty, who is observing a stack of logs in one corner. "That seems to be a theme around herestrange creatures wanting to eat us."

"I don't think it's very funny," informs Amy as she folds her arms.

Mason rolls his eyes and says, "Oh great, cue wolf-phobia again."

"I don't get it, you guys. Why aren't you more concerned about it," she states frankly.

"Cause he ain't tryin' to eat *us*," Mason laughs.

"Very funny," Amy pouts.

The rigid line of her mouth pleases Jack. He hopes that the tenderness of nurse Amy toward Mason has already faded.

"Hey, guys, look!" says Scotty, who holds aloft a small hatchet in one hand while dragging Lucky behind with the other. "Now, this will come in handy! Just in case another predator tries to get a little tidbit."

"Here, give me that," says Mason as he snatches the hatchet away from Scotty. "Just so you don't go all *Last of the Mohicans* on me again."

A stiff breeze wisps across the room. Up until that point, none of them had even bothered looking around. Now that they do, they observe the walls of the room, itself. They are lined with rubble and large rocks. Brown hulking boulders lurk in every corner, and a particularly massive rock stands leaning against a door.

Pointing to the blocked exit, Jack declares, "Well, there is no use trying to get through there." After he says this, the breeze stiffens, and a whistling noise accompanies it. This time the teens look for the source of the wind. The breeze calls their attention to a large brown rock formation jutting out from the wall to their left. It looks like a cave opening. The brown rocks arch over a black hole, the source of the breeze.

"This doesn't look very inviting," Jack mutters. "I think I have had enough strangeness for one day."

His eyes peer at the rocky structure. It looks just like the entrance to a cave at the Bell Family State Park.

Just inside the opening, before the blackness shrouds everything from sight, lays a pile of bones.

Taking off his glasses, rubbing his eyes, and repositioning his glasses back on the bridge of his nose, Scotty remarks, "Is that a human scapula?"

"A what?" Mason questions.

"A scapula. I mean, a shoulder blade," Scotty explains.

They all take a closer look, but only close enough for them to verify.

"Can someone explain why there are human bones in here?" Jack offers.

No one speaks. The grim discovery mutes them until finally, after an extended period of silence, Mason ventures, "Twenty bucks, it's Douglas Finch."

Chapter 42

Mason doesn't like the look of the dark, foreboding cave mouth. He thinks that something about it whispers danger. A few seconds of straining stares into the pitch black mouth proves futilethere is no way any of them could see what lays waiting in the dark hole. The stack of bones serves as a grizzly welcome mat.

Mason walks over to the doors obstructed by the boulder and calls, "No use trying these doors. We couldn't move these rocks if we had a bulldozer."

His cut throbs, but he does his best to ignore the pain. He thinks he has to, believing that if he's not going to get them out of this mess, who would? He contemplates, *The wimpy Scotty? Amy, a girl—yeah right. Jack who seems distant and in la-la land since we got off the train? No! It's up to mighty Mason. I'm the only one thinking clearly and the only one strong enough to get us out of this mess.*

His noble thoughts of his own grandeur are interrupted by the whimpering tones of his glasses-clad lackey saying, "You think we have to go through there?"

"It's the only way out, I guess," confirms Jack grimly.

"We need to keep going," Amy agrees. "If only we had some sort of light."

Without warning, the speakers pipe the familiar voice through the room:

> "The viper was foiled in spite of his plot ill-conceived.
> His strikes narrowly missing the companions, now relieved.
> But the path waits, dismal and dreary.
> Of the cave waiting, four souls should be leery.
> Take up the axe handle with care,
> For who knows what foe will be waiting in there."

"You can't tell me that it's not talking about us now!" Jack concludes.

"All right, so someone is watching us. What good does that do? Unless the voice can produce a light for that entrance, everything it has said has been 'all the path this' and 'the end that,'" Mason declares.

"The voice said to bring the axe," Jack counters. "Sure would come in handy to cut a beanstalk with."

"That's right," Scotty affirms.

Mason stands thinking and considers, *Jack's right. There is no denying that the voice is talking to us. But how could that be?* In his head he looks for a reason, and he finds one.

Suddenly, Mason snaps up, and a thought pours from his mouth: "Guys, this is one of those reality shows! I bet we're on a hidden camera somewhere! They've got us going through all these hoops for someone's entertainment. I bet there's a secret room somewhere with a bunch of TV execs laughing their butts off at the way we are floundering and running."

"Mason, really?" asks Jack, who rolls his eyes at this new revelation of his friend.

"Yeah, really."

This time Amy decides to put the kibosh on the theory by saying, "Then explain the talking snake, the talking wolf, the—"

"Special effects. A guy in a costume. You know they can make anything in Hollywood these days."

"Mason, that ridiculous," says Amy with a sigh.

"No, think about it," counters Mason. He is not willing to let go of his idea, although the talking snake sure seemed real enough to him.

Mason wonders, *Maybe the reality show is a silly idea?* But, he thinks it is the best idea anyone has offered yet.

Peering carefully around the room, Mason clears is throat and announces, "Okay, I've been thinking about a plan."

Amy chimes, "Oh great… you thinking."

Mason, ignoring the sarcasm, continues, "No, listen. That squirrel, right? Remember him? Well, he got into this building, probably through some vent like Scotty said. Okay, so look right above your heads."

Above the teens is a large square vent covered by a metal grate.

Mason keeps going, "So far, we've just been, like, wandering from room to room. So when we got in here, I stared looking around. You see, I saw this movie just last week about a secret agent trapped in an old warehouse that was set to explode. He climbed up a stack of boxes and squeezed into a large vent in the ceiling. He made his way through the vents and got out of the building before it blew to bits. What if we found a shaft like that and made our way to the exit?"

A low laugh escapes from Amy's mouth. She says, "Oh, that's brilliant, Mason. We'll just climb right up. What are we going to do—move some of these rocks and scale them? Or, better yet, we could levitate."

"Hey, I'm not crazy. I saw one of these vents in the lab a couple of rooms back. And the table in there would be perfect to stand on."

"I'm not going back," Amy counters obstinately.

Mason chuckles to himself and then mutters, "Oh yeah, your wolf."

"And the snake, genius," retorts Amy.

"Amy, I think it's a great idea," declares Scotty.

"Of course you do," says Amy, frowning at her brother.

Scotty gives a terse look to his sister and asks, "What does that mean?"

Amy sighs and says, "You know exactly what I mean."

"I make my own decisions," defends Scotty. The boy crosses his arms in defiance.

Amy laughs and says, "Sure you do."

"Just shut up, Amy," attacks Scotty.

She continues the coaxing, "Is that you talking, or Mason?"

"I'm serious," Scotty moans.

"You wanna check with Mason first to see if he's gonna back your play here? 'Whatever you say, Mason.' 'Should I jump, Mason?' 'How high, Mason?'"

Just as he always does, Scotty withers.

Mason sees the tide turning away from his idea, so he presses Jack, "What do you think, Jack? It's worth a shot, right? I mean, if there is a wolf or something trying to get us…." Mason supplies a dramatic pause for Amy. "Then he can't get us up there," finishes Mason with a twinkle in his eye.

Jack looks to Amy and once again recalls the two glowing eyes. He responds, "Actually, it's not a bad idea."

"There you go, Jack!" affirms Mason. "Great, that settles it. The next time we see a vent, we try the plan."

"That is unless we find an exit first," adds Jack.

"Right," agrees Mason. "Now let's move on."

Amy dares a few steps toward the cave and says, "I don't like the idea of going in there, but looks like that's the only way out."

"Hey," Scotty says. "Remember the last room, the one with the snake? There was another set of doors."

"Yes, you're right," Amy agrees.

Mason says, "If *you* guys are too scared of that cave, why don't we go back into the snow room and make for those doors. Maybe we could go back to the lab and climb into the vents?"

"It's either the cave or the snake," Scotty concludes, clearly not liking either option.

Mason can tell Jack is thinking hard because he's chewing his upper lip.

"What do you think, Jack?" Amy asks.

Jack looks at Amy and smiles. He says, "I think we go back to the last room. I have to admit that stack of bones and the warning of the narrator settles it for me. We got past the snake once, we can do it again."

"Have you got an idea?" Scotty asks Jack.

"Yeah. I do."

Chapter 43

Clyde takes a hand towel from his waist and wipes his forehead.

"So you left them there in the Giant's lair?" Gwen asks.

"We've been over this. When I came back to the spot where I left them, they were gone. I just don't get it. Where are they? The ride does not take this long." He rubs his head. "You said the ride has not stopped working out here?"

"Yeah. You totally confused me when you said the power was off inside."

Another empty train exits the final set of black double doors.

"Clyde, don't worry, those kids probably got off the ride during one of the power outages you talked about. They don't strike me as trouble-makers. They'll come walking out any minute."

"I hope your right."

He isn't sure Gwen believes him about the power outage inside, and he can't blame her. He does not want to press the issue. It would only make things more complicated. Still he can't help but wonder if the strange power outages had a connection with all the other bizarre events that had unfolded in the Enchanted Forrest.

"Gwen, you remember that night when you...." Clyde stops himself before asking her about the strange calliope music, but he is tempted to ask her about it now.

"What night, Clyde?"

"Never mind. Just thinking aloud."

"Clyde, what are you not telling me?"

He wants to tell her. He wants to let someone else in on the dark secret of the ride he had kept hidden from all of the other employees. It would be nice to have someone share the burden. Still, when we had told the police all he knew about the Douglas Finch incident, they thought he was loony and dismissed the information way back then. However, tonight was the first time he had heard that ominous music for himself. In the end, never-theless, he decides not to pursue the matter with Gwen, although the guilt yanks at his already strained nerves from leaving the kids.

"Nothing. Just getting too old for this stuff, Gwen. It's getting late. Look, I am going to radio for some help. I'll get another employee to go back in with me. I think you should look for the parents. Not sure who brought them here tonight. The Braddock boy usually gets dropped off. Maybe all of them were, but we need to make sure just in case a parent is lurking around here somewhere. I don't want them coming after you or me because we didn't let them know what is going on."

"Good plan. Do you want me to call anyone else?"

By the girl's tone, Clyde knows the "anyone else" is Howard Snodgrass. He tells her, "No, not now. No reason to panic him, yet." But he knows this is a lie.

Although he doesn't want to, Clyde determines to go back into the Enchanted Forrest. His concern for the kids overcomes his reluctance to ever venture into the Dark Ride again.

Chapter 44

"So, we are all good with the plan?" Jack asks.

All three heads nod solemnly. For now, at least, they are on the same page.

Approaching the entrance to the snow-covered room, Amy cracks the door open with her long stick. A cold breeze engulfs the travelers.

"Mister Snake, we have a bargain for you. Are you in there?"

There is a period of silence, and Amy looks back to Jack and shrugs. Mason stands behind Jack's right shoulder, listening intently for any word from the viper while Scotty grips Lucky, who, for his part, is missing a chunk of his posterior and quite a bit of stuffing.

Then, with a feint hiss, the snake says, "I am listening."

Based on the sound of its words, the teens perceive that the reptile is clearly on the far side of the room.

"Okay, you, stay where you are. Do not move, or the deal is off," Mason warns.

"I am game. Enter. No one is stopping you."

Amy places one foot inside the door and tilts her head into the room. The snake is visibly coiled at the foot of the doors they intend to take.

"Stay where you are," she calls.

"I heard you the first time. I have not moved. What is this deal? Does it involve hurling sharp objects at me?"

With the coast clear, the three boys follow Amy into the room.

Jack chooses to ignore the mocking statement of the snake and coolly responds, "We know you want out. Scotty here was afraid you were going to betray us." As he says this, Jack starts to shiver and rub his hands together.

"He was the betrayer. Did I not offer you a prize of great value?"

"Look, that is in the past. We talked things over and are prepared to take you up on your offer. Let's just get out of the cold, okay?" Jack urges.

The reptile hisses, uncoils, and inches forward.

"Then I guess we have struck a bargain. One of you will take me to the next room, and I will show you the item."

"Right," says Jack. A look to Amy signals that the plan is under way.

Mason steps forward cautiously and says, "I will pick you up—just don't do anything stupid. Oh, and you're not getting in my shirt. I don't care how cold you are." To his left, Amy inches forward.

The snake's body ripples from side to side as he slithers towards them. Mason kneels down with his hand extended.

When the snake is only a couple of feet from his hand, Mason yells, "Now," pulls back his hand, and rolls to the right. With a lightning fast motion, Amy slams the stick down at the snake. Then a torrent of chaos breaks loose. The snake has suspected a rouse and darts hard to his left, avoiding the thundering strike, which results in Amy grimacing in pain as the stick reverberates on the hard frozen ground.

The viper is now full of rage. It hisses ferociously and, with mouth agape, lunges.

Jack is caught by surprise, and this time, he isn't able to prevent an attack.

Chapter 45

Scotty has no idea how the snake is able to hurl himself so high in the air. He can only watch as the viper shoots through the air and hits its target. The fangs sink deep into Jack's shoulder.

A look of intense shock washes over Jack's face.

"Jack!" Mason yells from his crouched position.

Amy prepares for another swing, but it is too late. The creature is dangling from the boy's body.

The pain in Jack's shoulder morphs into fury, and he reaches up and catches the snake just under its head. A loud violent yell erupts from him as he yanks the snake hard. It relinquishes its hold, but Jack's shirt rips and flesh tears away as fangs rip from the wound. Staggering, Jack steps back, and with his left arm, he shoves the door behind him open. Then he deposits the snake into the cave room and with a forceful slam shuts the door.

From its new abode, the viper hisses, "You'll never get out of the woods alive!"

All three rush to Jack.

"Oh, man!" screams Jack, "Ahhhh! It burns!"

"Are you okay, Jack?" Scotty asks but immediately chides himself for the foolish question.

"Yeah, it just…. Crud, did you see that? He just leaped up before I could…. Oh, man!"

"Jack, I'm sorry," consoles Amy. "He just moved so fast. After he bit you, I couldn't take the risk of hitting you."

"It's okay, Amy. You tried."

Stretching his shirt at the collar, Jack observes the wound. It's puffy and hot. Two small deep red holes circled in white are accompanied by streaks of torn flesh where Jack had ripped away the snake's head.

"Oh, Jack, it's nasty," says Amy.

Jack seems unfazed and says, "It will be okay."

Amy looks doubtfully at him, but he tells her, "No, really, it already feels better."

"I wonder what kind of snake that is?" asks Scotty, giving voice to the question none of the others want to address. "It could be poisonous, Jack. Should someone suck on the wound?"

Jack forces a smile in spite of the pain and says, "I don't think that will be necessary, Scotty. I'll pass. Look, it's not getting any warmer in here. Things didn't go exactly according to plan, but we're here and the snake is not blocking our way."

Another grimace from Jack

Chattering, Amy asks, "Are you sure you're okay, Jack? We can wait here a little longer."

"No," Jack states, "We are all freezing." Then after a pause and a deep breath, he adds, "Maybe once were in the next room, we can stop?"

Mason says, "As long as you're okay, all right then—let's go. I say we go back to the lab."

"No," counters Jack, "Let's just press on. If we don't find the exit soon, then we can head back."

Scotty prepares for an argument, so he is surprised to hear Mason say, "Okay." He thinks, *Wow, that was easy. I guess even Mason has a heart. He's letting Jack call the shots after the bite.*

Mason leads the group to the set of doors across the room.

As they pass over the frozen floor, Scotty decides to ask Jack about the snake. "Was it just me or did that snake seem to have a round head?"

Jack replies, "I don't know, Scotty, I wasn't thinking about that. I know what you are getting at, though. You want to know if the snake was poisonous or not."

Scotty continued, "Well that's not entirely true, you see there are a few poisonous snakes with rounded heads, but it is very uncommon in America."

"Not sure those rules apply to talking snakes," Jack responds.

"Jack, most American poisonous snakes have a triangular shaped head, and for the most part, the old story about all triangular-headed snakes being..."

Scotty stops talking as Jack crumples to a heap on the cold, snow-covered floor.

Chapter 46

Not more than ten seconds ago, Jack appeared fine. Now, his fragile body lies shivering on the frozen ground Only Scotty had suspected the worst, and now his suspicions are vindicated: the viper is obviously poisonous. If ever he has wanted to be wrong, it is now. Scotty arrives at the boy's side and calls, "Jack!" looking desperately for any sign of consciousness. Soon, Mason and Amy are there, too.

With anguish and fear in his voice, Scotty announces, "He's poisoned, I knew it."

"Jack, can you hear me? Please, Jack!" Amy cries.

There is no response.

Jack's eyes are rolled up into the back of his head. He is clearly oblivious to the world.

"What do we do?" Amy asks, looking at her brother and then to the panic-stricken face of Mason.

"I saw a bunch of books on healing back in that lab room," Scotty says in a rushed tone. "We can at least get him outta here and put him on that table."

Not waiting for help or confirmation of his idea, Scotty attempts to lift Jack's body. Mason leans down and quickly lends a hand. The boys struggle with the dead weight and drape Jack's arms over their shoulders. There is no time for delay.

Amy kicks open the doors to the strange laboratory. She sweeps the skeleton that had occupied the metal table off to the floor and says, "Set him on here."

The boys gently pick Jack up and hoist him onto the slab. Then Scotty quickly runs to the nearest shelf and begins cycling through the books. He is soon joined by Amy, who begins pulling book after book off the shelf.

Mason calls to Scotty, "Is it too late to suck out the poison?"

From over his shoulder, Scotty responds, "Maybe not, go ahead."

He peeks over his shoulder to see if Mason will follow through with it and sees him fumbling with Jack's shirt and then pausing over the wound.

Mason looks intently and then calls out, "Just find something, Scotty—I'm sure it's too late!" Then, looking gravely at the boy, he says, "It's going to be okay. We're going to figure something out. You stay with us, Jack—stay with us!"

Scotty re-focuses his efforts on finding something that can help. He thinks, *Where were those books on healing? Think, Scotty, think!*

His efforts thus far are fruitless. He has found nothing on healing. Searching his memory some more, Scotty rushes to the wall on his right and reads titles: *Clairvoyance*; *Modern Magic Uses for Toads*; *Zombies, Zombies and More Zombies*. He realizes this isn't the shelf and looks on the one below where he finds *Do It Yourself Love Potion Reversal Spells* and *Removal of Sleep Hexes*. He recognizes that he is getting closer.

Finally, he arrives at the books on healing. Scotty picks up one called *The Warlock's Book of Healing Potions*. He flips through it in a hurried motion but finds nothing on snake bites.

Mason, for his part, looks down at the festering wound and then covers it back up.

All of a sudden, Amy cries out, "Here, this!"

Scotty drops the potions book and runs to his sister.

Amy hands her brother a book called *Ancient Poison Remedies*. Looking at the index, he sees that Chapter 11 is titled "Snake Bites." *Here it is!* he thinks and turns to that part. The script is handwritten and hard to read, but it looks just like an entry he would have read from his mother's Rotary Club recipe book.

"Apply mixed ingredients directly to wound,
1 four-leaf clover
1 pinch of bat ashes
3 ounces of harpy spit
2 wings of moth
2 drops of viper poison
4 drops of dragon's milk"

While Scotty reads the words aloud, Amy searches through the vials, beakers, and drawers of the room for the ingredients. Hastily, she places a vial on the table and announces, "Harpy spit."

From the wall behind Scotty, Amy announces, "I've got bat ashes and a four-leaf clover!"

Scotty commits the following contents to memory and joins the frantic search. In a drawer just below a large glass jar containing a withered hand of some sort, Scotty finds another of the ingredients. He informs Amy, "Dragon's milk! We need wings of mouth and viper poison—hurry!"

By now Mason has also joined the search, but with reckless abandon is flipping discarded bottles behind him to the floor.

"Be careful, Mason." Scotty says. "You don't know what kind of havoc is in those vials!"

"Right."

"Moths' wings!" Amy calls.

The search is nearly complete as the three continue to ravage the lab looking for the last item. Amy pulls the final unchecked container from the back of a cabinet and reads out loud, "Crocodile tears."

Scotty concludes, "There's no viper poison!"

Mason approaches Jack and says, "Gonna have to take off his shirt."

Jack's deflated, helpless body twitches as Mason yanks at the garment. He shoots a glance toward Scotty and asks, "You sure you know what you're doing? Last time, you blew something up."

"I was screwing around," defends Scotty.

"And what about now? You know what you're doing?" asks Mason, emphasizing the question again.

"I can read a chemical mixture."

"I don't know, Scotty," Amy questions.

"If you got a better idea, let me know. Otherwise, I'm mixing this thing up or Jack's gonna die."

Mason and Amy look at each other. Then Amy gets in Scotty's face and demands, "You promise it's not going to make him worse."

"Worse than dead? No." More softly, Scotty adds, "He's my friend, too. Okay?"

This response is good enough for Amy. She hands over the ingredients, and Scotty goes to work. All of a sudden, a thought occurs to him. He calls out to Mason and Amy, "Two drops of viper poison. Viper! The viper—we have to get him. It's our only hope."

Mason stares at Amy and Scotty and then says, "You're right. I'll go."

Chapter 47

The radio call for help has been answered. The rotund Oliver Sparkman arrives first on the scene.

"What's up, Clyde? The Enchanted Forrest giving you fits?"

"Yep, it's been moody all night," Clyde answers.

He doesn't want to take the time to explain the entire story to the middle-aged public relations manager, nor does he have the time to be picky. Oliver Sparkman is a likable type but not the sort of guy you would call for any heavy lifting and possibly one of the last people Clyde would have called for in this situation

"I came as soon as I could. I was taking care of a kid who was puking his guts out on the roller coaster. Apparently, too much popcorn. That butter gets 'em every time. What amazed me is just how much—"

"Oliver, come with me. We're going into the ride," says Clyde. Although he likes Oliver well enough, his babbling sometimes gets on the old man's last nerve.

"What's this all about?"

"Four teens inside"

"Practical jokers, eh? Reminds me of that time that Bailey kid—"

"Oliver, we need to go now."

"Geez, Clyde, you sure are all hot and bothered."

Another employee ambles up to the duo.

"Oh good, Colton is here. I caught him trying to clock out. I told him you had called for backup and he would be staying for a while."

Colton Spurlock is obviously testy and says, "But I was supposed to get off 20 minutes ago."

"What, you got a date tonight kid?"

The older teen glares at the two men and says, "Yes."

More pleased with the athletic and younger arrival, Clyde declares, "You're with us now, captain. Let's get in there."

A voice from across the way calls, "Clyde!"

Now what? Clyde thinks.

Gwen walks deliberately up to the other employees accompanied by a large man with a black ponytail and flannel shirt, who is followed by a blonde lady in an aqua tank top and jogging pants with a small child clinging to each hand.

"These are the Carnahan's," informs Gwen. "I told them what's going on."

"Houston Carnahan," the large man announces. "My kids are stuck in there, huh?"

I don't have time for this, thinks Clyde. "Look, Mr. Carnahan, we're going in there to bring the kids out. There is no reason to be alarmed. We just wanted to make sure you knew—company policy. Now, if you'll excuse us."

This time the lady speaks and asks, "Our kids aren't causing any trouble, are they?"

In spite of Clyde's attempt at deadpanning the situation, she is obviously concerned.

"No, ma'am. Just stuck. This thing happens every day. We will go in and get them. Stay here, and I am sure they'll be out here in no time. Look, will you call the other parents? The Braddocks and, uh, the Chick kid's—"

"Father. Mason Chick lives with his father," says the Mrs. Carnahan, finishing Clyde's thought.

Clyde thinks, *Titus Chick—that's right. How could I forget him?* He tells Mrs. Carnahan, "Yeah, good," and then says, "Gwen, make sure the Carnahans are taken care of."

"I'll go in with you," Houston Carnahan declares.

"Sorry, Mr. Carnahan, I can't let you do that. Really, everything is fine."

Oh man, we're losing time, thinks Clyde.

This time, Oliver chimes in and says, "Company policy, Mr. Carnahan. Listen, if I had a nickel for every time we handled a situation like this, I'd have like fifty-eight dollars. Ha ha!"

Clyde thinks, *And if I had a dollar for every time I heard Oliver tell that anecdote....*In spite of the lame joke, Houston Carnahan seems appeased for now.

Why did you leave them in there by themselves? Clyde asks himself as he heads for the entrance.

Chapter 48

Amy is reading and re-reading the recipe to Scotty. Her brother carefully pinches a second moth wing and removes it from a glass bottle.

"You think Mason'll be okay?" Amy asks.

"It's Mason," says Scotty as he pours a blue liquid into the concoction he's brewing.

"Are you sure you got three ounces of harpy spit?"

116

"Amy, that's the fourth time you've asked that. I know what I'm doing."

Scotty is standing over a counter looking down at a wooden mixing bowl. Amy thinks, *This is the boy who cannot make a grilled cheese sandwich and now we are trusting Jack's life to him?*

"Does it matter which order you put them in?" Amy asks.

"We're mixing them together. What does that matter?"

"I don't know, it's just—"

"Maybe you should check on Jack?" Scotty asks, although it's not really a question.

Setting the book down, Amy walks over to the table where Jack lies. The boy is breathing deeply and doesn't show any movement aside from an occasional shudder. The wound has turned a hideous dark green with traces of purple lines circling around the fang punctures.

She had always liked Jack. Ever since her family had moved north from Louisiana when she was four, he had been kind. While Scotty's other friends, especially Mason, had tormented her, Jack was always gracious. One winter's day four years ago, she decided that she liked Jack Braddock. They had all been over at the Zuckermans' for a Christmas party, and the kids were down in the basement seated around a pea green card table, killing time playing Uno and eagerly awaiting the signal from upstairs that it was time for presents. The TV was playing the old black and white movie *It's a Wonderful Life*. None of the kids were paying much attention until a scene depicting a school dance played. The conversation that ensued became etched in her memory.

Mason was already oozing with confidence and announced, "When I'm in high school, I'm going to date every cheerleader in school. What do you think, Scotty?"

"Uh, I don't know. Girls are gross. You don't live with three of 'em," said Scotty as he placed a yellow card on the discard pile. "Draw two, Teddy."

"You may not like them yet, but just wait, Scotty boy," Mason continued. "I already have a girlfriend, and I even held her hand at the basketball game last week." He discarded a red card on the stack.

"Yuck," Teddy Zuckerman mocked.

From over a large fan of cards, Jack looked in awe of the bragging Mason and asked, "You held Ginger Lopez's hand?"

"Yep, I'm gonna kiss her, too. I'll be the first one of us to kiss a girl. I bet you're thirty years old before a girl will kiss you, Braddock."

In defense, Jack looked around the room and said, "Yeah right, I'll kiss a girl before you'll ever talk Ginger Lopez into that."

"Who you gonna kiss Jack, Blair?" Mason challenged.

The other three boys laughed mockingly. Scotty in particular snorted in violent laughter.

At this point, irritation was visible on Jack's face. He said, "Maybe I'll kiss your sister, Carnahan!"

Laugher erupted from the boys all around the table, and Amy blushed a dark hue of red.

"Boom! Oh, he got you good, Scotty. Nice one, Jack," Mason chuckled.

Embarrassed beyond belief, Amy looked at Jack.

He grinned wryly at her and winked as if to say, "Nothing personal."

But from that day on, the idea of being close to Jack Braddock made her heart beat faster. He had been joking, she thought for sure, but sometimes found herself wondering, "What if....?"

And now, here he is, fragile and suffering on the table. Earlier that night, she had, for the first time, felt like Jack had shown real interest. Something had been stirring in him, she is sure and thought he had even been close to taking her hand. *Things had been going so well,* she thought, *until that jerk, Mason, convinced them all to get out of the cart.*

All she can do is hope—hope that the jerk would come through and bring them the viper.

Chapter 49

"Cautious, very cautious. We don't want to end up like ol' Braddock back there, do we?" says Mason to himself.

He thinks it is only natural that "Mason the magnificent" would have to save the day again. However, previously it took all the courage he could muster to pick up the thing, and his bravado fades as he makes his way through the snow-filled room. He asks himself, *What was I thinking?* "Here, snakey-snakey," Mason says as he cracks open the door to the cave room slightly. "Okay, snake, you got one of us. Are you satisfied now?"

There is no response, and Mason wonders if he is in there.

"Look, we need your help," Mason says.

After another moment of silence, Mason hears a hiss from across the room.

"Why would I help you? You tried to kill me, twice?"

"You are the one who started the biting stuff."

"Only because your friend tried to smash me."

Sensing the snake is still far away from the doors, Mason steps into the room. The snake lays coiled in front of the woodpile.

"Look, you got what you wanted. You are here in the warmth, out of that cold room."

"You are right. I am perfectly content here. There is no reason for me to help the likes of you."

"Just listen, snake. Here's the deal. There is another warm room just back a ways. In it there are a couple of fat mice. I am sure you would like a little dinner."

The snake appears to consider this and then says, "This does interest me, but how do I know you have the mice? You tried to deceive me once." He hisses coolly and uncoils.

"Now, look, no funny business. I thought you might like a little proof."

With his right hand, Mason reaches into a pocket of his shorts and lifts one of the mice by the tail. He asks, "How's this for proof?"

The snake hisses in delight and says, "Yes, excellent."

"There are two more where this came from, but listen here," commands Mason. He then reveals an item that had been dangling behind his back. It is the silver head of the hatchet, which glistens under the low lights. Mason states, "Don't make me use this. You come with me peaceably, and I'll let you at the mice."

"No need to threaten, child. We have a deal," says the snake as it glides close to Mason. Summoning courage and thinking again of Jack, Mason picks the snake up again. Trying not to envision the snake's gaping jaws and the horrid strikes, Mason holds the snake away from his body. The hatchet is held with his other hand, poised tight in his grip ready for trouble at any moment.

After crossing back through the snow-covered floor Mason leans into the doors that lead to the lab. *This has to work....* he thinks, *for Jack's sake.*

Chapter 50

"Look who's here for dinner!" Mason announces their arrival.

He holds the snake out for Amy and Scotty to observe. Both teens seem relived that Mason has accomplished the first step of their plan. Although Mason is still far from feeling comfortable about holding the cold-blooded fiend, he is at least keeping up appearances while dangling the critter before them.

"How's Jack?"

"His wound is getting worse, and he's started to shake and wheeze," Amy informs.

"The mixture is ready, Mason," says Scotty as he pours the ingredients into a glass vial.

The snake looks at Jack, and says, "That was a good bite, near his heart. I venture he has less than ten minutes."

Amy growls lividly at the snake's remarks and says, "You, you horrible little creature! Does this make you happy?"

Mason resists the urge to chop the snake into bits with the hatchet. Instead, he tells the snake, "Okay, now you will do your part. We need some of your venom."

"What are you doing? What for?" The snake asks.

"I don't think it's any of your business," Amy fiercely retorts.

Mason keeps a cooler head and says, "You are going to help us make a potion that will cure our friend here."

"You're wasting your time."

"Do we have a deal or not?" asks Mason.

"Where are the mice? Let me see them."

Amy walks to a shelf and removes a cage from its perch. She sets it gently on the floor beside Mason. Two other small cages rest on the floor there as well.

Mason shoves the snake at the cage and says, "There they are. Satisfied?"

"Oh, yes—they look so delicious. It has been months since I have had a mouse."

Mason nods at Amy. He knows the girl does not like the idea of feeding the rodents to the predator.

"Venom for the mice. Okay?" Mason asks.

"Absolutely. I am at your service. But I must tell you there is no cure for my bite. If this concoction of yours does not work, I still get the tasty little morsels, right?"

"A deal is a deal," says Mason and then adds, while thumbing the axe head, "but any funny business…."

Scotty rounds the table and approaches the snake nervously.

Mason readjusts his grip on the snake and asks, "So how do we do this?"

"I saw this on Animal Planet," Scotty says. "Take your hand and push down on the top of his head. Uh, Mr. Snake, place your fangs over the rim of the vial." Scotty holds the vial out away from his body and up to the snake. "When the fangs are there, push down gently, Mason."

With his right hand Mason positions the axe under his arm. Then using both hands, he pushes down on the head of the reptile. Two small drops of clear liquid drip from the serpent's mouth into the vial and slide down the glass.

Mason moves the snake away from the vial.

The snake says, "There. You have your venom—now give me my food."

Before Mason relinquishes his grip, he asks, "Is that enough, Scotty?"

"I think so."

The group and the viper watch as the small drops blend with the red-colored potion. Scotty jiggles the vial to make sure the liquids combine. As he does, the ingredients turn a bright purple and a small puff of gray haze escapes from the vial.

Scotty nods, satisfied with his creation.

"Now, now! Let me have the mice," the snake hisses.

"First, we make sure Jack gets the potion. Then you get the mice, just in case we need more," Mason says and pulls the axe from under his arm and motions it in the air to remind the snake of just what could happen if he makes a sudden move.

Scotty walks over to the table where Jack, white-faced, sweating, and shivering lays.

Amy does not move from Jack's side, hoping and praying that the plan will work.

Watching with heightened anticipation, all parties look on as Scotty pulls at the bottom of Jack's jaw. With his other hand, he pours the contents down his friend's throat.

Chapter 51

Amy looks on, clinging to hope that Jack will respond to the potion.

Scotty, for good measure, clasps one hand over Jack's mouth, and with the other, he clasps Jack's nose, explaining, "My mom has to do this to the twins."

After seeing Jack swallow, Scotty relaxes his grip and removes his hands.

Coughing, Jack suddenly lurches and rolls off the table while shaking violently.

"It's making it worse!" Amy cries.

Scotty rushes down to Jack's side and tries to hold him still, but the pudgy boy is no match for the convulsions of Jack. He calls out, "Amy, a little help here!"

The girl had been in a daze from just looking at Jack suffering, but Scotty's urging wakes her. She grabs Jack's right arm and attempts to force it down, which turns out to be no small feat.

On the ground, on table in the corner of the room, three cages sit. Two of them are empty, and one is holding two mice. Setting down the hatchet, Mason quickly takes the mouse from his pocket and places it back into the cage with the other two mice.

He looks at the snake and says, "You better hope that venom of yours works." Then he quickly grabs the hatchet again.

Amy's level of discomfort rises as Jack's convulsions grow harder to contain. She decides to try a new tactic and starts whispering into his ear, "Jack, remember when we met? We had gone to the circus at the Falls Armory. My family had just moved to Tennessee, and your parents sat down next to us on the front row. You were laughing so hard at those clowns."

Jack's legs stop twitching.

Scotty notices that Jack's convulsing is slowing down. He tells his sister, "Whatever you're saying, whatever you're doing—keep doing it!" Then, while holding Jack's left leg, Scotty looks at the book again, searching for a possible mistake.

"And I remember you dressing like a clown for Halloween the next year. You had those huge red shoes and that bright green wig. You were so funny looking. You know, I hated clowns until that day."

With no warning, Jack's body goes limp.

Amy yells, "Scotty!"

Scotty, who had, until then, been pouring over the list of ingredients for the fifth time, abruptly looks at Jack and comments, "Oh no."

"Why isn't he moving?"

Deep lines of concern wrinkle Scotty's forehead. He shoves his glasses back up the bridge of his nose and declares, "Well... because... I don't know."

Amy takes Jack's hand and squeezes it. She glances at her brother, who has already moved to a shelf and is searching through various vials, most of which were broken during the previous search. He gives a look to Mason, who seems to be enjoying holding the hatchet over the snake's head.

"Jack Braddock," Amy whispers. Then, before she can talk herself out of it, she kisses him on the cheek.

Amy lifts her head once again to make sure no one is watching, and she hears the snake cry from across the room, "We had a deal! Let me have the mice!"

"Just be patient," Mason says and squeezes a little tighter on the snake.

"Put me in the cage now!"

"First, I want you to look at Jack and see what you did."

The snake glances over at the boy and says, "I know I bit him. If he dies—"

Mason drops the snake into the cage, but it's an empty cage. Quickly, he slams the lid down.

Faintly, Mason hears the snake crying, "Treachery! Traitors! Liars!"

Mason laughs and says, "Well, it seems like I dropped you in the wrong cage—oops."

"We had a deal. You cannot do this."

"I just did."

Chapter 52

Scotty leaves the shelf to scan Jack's shoulder. As he observes the wound, he remarks, "The color is coming back to him." Incredibly, the bright purple hue is fading before his eyes, and the pale face of the unconscious Jack begins to redden.

Frantically hoping, Amy asks, "Did it work?"

Scotty replies, "I think it may have. The wound already looks better."

All three circle around Jack, hoping the formula has worked. Finally, with a cough, a moan, and fluttering eyes, Jack comes to.

"What happened?" he asks.

"You were bit by a snake, and you nearly died," informs Scotty.

Jack blinks rapidly, and says, "I what?"

Amy blinks and smiles and responds, "We almost lost you. You don't remember?"

Jack glances up around the room. Mason stands to his right. In the corner are the three cages, and he sees that one of them holds a very upset snake that is crashing into the sides.

"You okay?" Scotty asks.

"Uh, yeah, I guess so."

Jack raises his torso by pushing up with his elbows. He continues to try to regain composure and says, "I don't remember hardly anything. I just had these weird dreams about clowns."

Amy represses a smile and asks, "Really?"

"Yeah, I kept seeing one with baggy polka dot pants and, like, these big floppy shoes. It was really funny."

"I bet."

"I think I can stand."

"You sure, Jack?" Scotty asks.

"Yeah, I'm a little woozy, but I'll be fine. Help me up."

Scotty and Amy help him to his feet.

"Oh man," Jack says as he grips his shoulder. "That's where it bit me, huh? Man, I'm a little dizzy." He motions to the snake held captive in the cage and asks, "Is that him?"

"Yep. Same one that took a swipe at me," Mason confirms.

"Okay. I remember that. What now?"

"You let me go!" the snake hisses violently.

"Nope," says Mason, "I think it's time you got what you deserved." He winks at the others and gestures for Scotty to open the doors to the cold room.

"What is this, what are you going to do?" asks the reptile.

Carefully, Mason eases his hand through the plastic handle that prevents the snake from coming too close. The snake wildly strikes at the top of the cage with no results. Mason maneuvers the cage out the door and into the cold.

"There is your reward, loser."

After the door shuts, they hear the snake's desperate cries, saying, "No, I helped you! You will pay for this betrayal. You kids have no chance in the woods! No chance! I am the smallest thing you have to worry about. You will all die!"

Amy cannot help but let a little humph of satisfaction escape from her mouth. With that, she turns her attention back to Jack.

Chapter 53

Wallace Braddock is sitting in the recliner of his living room. On the television, a man screams about the virtues of a new weight loss scheme. Wallace is only halfway paying attention to the tube while fingering through an issue of *Newsweek*.

The phone rings and Wallace thinks, *Stupid telemarketers. Why don't we get rid of that thing and just use our cell phones?* After two more rings, Brenna calls from the kitchen, "Are you going to get that, honey?"

"No, it's just somebody trying to sell us something."

An irritated humph floats through the air as Brenna Braddock marches into the living room.

She looks at the caller ID and announces, "It's the Carnahans," after which she shoots an irritated glance at her husband.

Once she picks up the phone, she changes her tone and gently says, "Hello. Oh, hey, Carol."

After Wallace hears his wife say, "The park wanted you to call us?" his interest is peaked and he uses the remote to turn down the television.

"Carol, Jack is asleep upstairs."

Wallace looks at his wife and sets down the magazine.

"That can't be right. Wallace, go upstairs and check on Jack."

Clearly hesitant to follow orders, Wallace makes an exaggerated effort to crawl out of his comfortable chair.

"You said they were stuck on the ride? How long?.... Ummm, Carol, let me call you back in a second.... Goodbye."

Brenna hangs up the phone and quickly proceeds up the steps to Jack's room where she had checked on him not more than thirty minutes ago. In spite of the call, she cannot believe that Jack would sneak out. She fully expects to see her boy lying asleep in his room.

"What's going on, mom?" Blair asks and removes the headphones from her ears.

"Stay in your room, Blair."

In spite of the warning, Blair follows her mother.

With one glance in the room, Brenna Braddock's fear is realized. Wallace stands above Jack's bed with sheets in hand. They all see the dummy lying still on the mattress.

"That little sneak," Blair muses.

"He snuck out, Brenna."

"I see that, Wallace. Carol said he's stuck in the Enchanted Forrest. She said he's been in there for an hour."

"He deceived us—I can't believe it."

Blair, dripping with vileness, says, "I can. I always said—"

"Go back to your room, Blair!" Brenna directs.

The girl complies.

Brenna exclaims, "He left the house in spite of being grounded!" There is unmistakable disappointment in her voice.

"Well, he sure went to a lot of trouble. He made a dummy. Look at this thing."

"Wallace, they've been in the Enchanted Forrest for an hour," Brenna informs. Her disappointment is giving way to a twinge of worry.

"What?"

"They're stuck in that, that dark ride."

Although Brenna has not been to the park in years, something about the ride triggers a memory from long ago. Finally, a name comes to her, and she asks, "Wallace, remember Douglas Finch?"

"Oh, honey, there you go. That was a bunch of silliness. Goodness, that was years ago. You're not actually suggesting…. Brenna, the kids are just stuck. This has nothing to do with that. Besides, that Finch boy ran away. He's probably living somewhere in Vegas."

In spite of his assurance, Brenna remains unconvinced. She says, "Wallace, we're going to Storybook Hollow."

Chapter 54

Jack's recovery quickens. He's still suffering from an occasional twinge of pain, but the dizziness is behind him. Whatever concoction Scotty put in the vial did the trick.

Jack tells the others, "I owe you, guys, big time."

Mason shrugs off the thanks by saying, "Hey, I wasn't going to lug you around this place any further than I had to."

His gift for turning a sincere moment into a laugh always amuses Jack, who grins at Mason's remark and says, "Of course not. You'd have made Scotty carry me."

"Ha ha, funny man," responds Mason. He then snatches Lucky back in defiance of Jack's insinuation.

Jack looks at Amy, and it seems she is obviously relieved. He wonders if things will be better now between them. Then he shifts his attention to the predicament that still exists for him and his friends.

Jack says, "Okay, I suggest we get back to the business of finding our way out. If this is what the ride is going to be like from here on out, the quicker we find the exit, the better."

"Funny you should say that, Jack," mentions Mason. "Remember how I told you there was an air vent in here?" He looks at the others, waiting for his moment, and goes on, "There's an air vent right above your head."

Sure enough, above Jack's head is a metal grate screwed into the ceiling. Jack thinks, *Looks like we will be going all "secret agent." But what about the narrator's words? What about finding the end of the story?* He is confident that the narrator is guiding them, pushing them through the ride, but he knows that he must now go along with this plan because of his previous negotiation with Mason. He thinks that if he reminds Mason about the narrator now, it will start a new quarrel, which would be no good for any of them, especially since the group now seems so cooperative.

Jack says, "Okay, Mason. I'm in. Scotty, Amy?"

Scotty, who is fumbling thumbing through a rather thick book on invisibility, ignores the question while Amy looks nervously up at the grate six feet above their heads.

She says, "I'm not sure. Can we even fit up there?"

"Won't know till we try. Come on, Amy, it's our best chance. We can avoid any danger up ahead. Just like the guy in the show. We escape before the bomb goes off," Mason urges.

The girl, still unsure, does not reply.

Mason ignores Amy and says, "It's settled then. Let's get outta here."

Jack, though, observes Amy closely, trying to read her thoughts. He knows that things are not, in fact, settled for her.

Mason, on the other hand, immediately begins moving the table that Jack had used during his sickness and says, "If we position the table under the grate, we should be tall enough to lift ourselves up there."

With Mason preoccupied with his project and Scotty engrossed with the vials, Jack takes the time to check on his status with Amy.

He tells her, "Sorry for giving you a scare back there."

Amy responds, "Jack, it wasn't your doing. It was scary, but I'm just glad you're okay."

Then she gently places her hand on his shoulder and gives it a light squeeze. The tenderness in her eyes provides Jack with renewed hope. He wants to hug her, or take her hand, something, anything to let her know that he really does have feelings for her. But, just as he considers the right path to take, Mason busts up the moment.

"Steady the table, will ya, Jack. That is if you're up to it. I'm getting on."

Jack thinks, *Amy will have to wait*" and says, "No problem."

He nods at Mason and grabs hold of the table while the he lifts himself to a standing position.

"Yep, this is good," says Mason. "Once we get this vent cover off, we can all climb up easily."

"How you gonna get that thing off?" Jack asks.

"Good question. There has to be something in here somewhere. Scotty get your head out of those vials and help us find a screwdriver or something."

Scotty is reading the label on a small container that looks like an Aspirin bottle. It says:

"Shrinking potion (results immediate, but temporary—
handle with extreme caution)
created by Dr. Thomas H. Thumb."

Standing to attention at Mason's call, Scotty places the small bottle in the right pocket of his shorts. He asks, "A screwdriver? What do you need one of those for?"

Jack realizes that Scotty has missed the entire vent discussion.

Mason says, "Pay attention for goodness sake. Do you want to get outta here, or do you want to camp out with your books and potions? Get me a screwdriver or something that will loosen these screws."

"Check. I'm on it," says Scotty.

His foray through the various vials is over. Amy and Jack join the search, but they find nothing.

"Come on, guys. Just find something with a thin edge."

They decide to try using a book cover, but it's too flimsy.

"There's not much in here," Jack announces. He is almost relieved. While Mason's idea is good, and he has committed himself to trying it, he would prefer to keep his feet on the ground.

"I've got it!" Mason announces. "It's been in my pocket the whole time." He produces the badge stolen from the Tailor's shirt. Lifting it in the air, he places it into the notch of one of the screws. "Excellent. Perfect fit."

With minimal effort, the first screw gives way followed by the second. As soon as the fourth screw gives way, the metal vent drops like a rock. Mason, clearly unprepared for the obvious result, has to duck his head.

The vent crashes to the metal table and bounces off onto the floor causing a series of crashing sounds.

"So much for stealth," Amy remarks as she nervously peers at the doors.

Jack stares at the doorways, unsettled as well and leery that perhaps the loud crash will somehow alert someone or something that wants to have them for dinner.

Mason pulls himself into the vent shaft and disappears for a moment. After a few seconds, he says, "Oh man, this is awesome! This is going to work."

Mason's head drops into view, and he looks down on the others and says, "Hand me Lucky."

"Are you serious, Mason? You're going to lug that thing around up there?" Jack asks and rolls his eyes.

"No, Scotty is," replies Mason. He laughs and winks over at Scotty, who is clearly not paying attention.

Amy bends down to pick up Lucky. Jack can swear he sees her whisper something into the animal's ear.

"Okay, who's next?" asks Mason. "Come on, Scotty."

Scotty gives the lab one last look. It's as if he will miss the place. With reserve and caution, Scotty scales the table and then nervously stands up and puts his arms in the vent.

He tries to join Mason but says, "I can't pull myself up."

"Too many tacos? Gee, Scotty, you really need to cut down on the calories," jabs Mason, who then shoots a hand down for Scotty to grab.

Scotty's body seems to levitate up through the hole, and then Jack says, "You're next, Amy."

The girl easily navigates the table and pulls herself up. Once inside the vent, she says, "Come on, Jack, there is plenty of room up here."

Jack then attempts to lift himself up into the black hole, but another twinge of pain shoots through his shoulder. After trying again and feeling another shot of pain, he says, "I'm gonna need some help."

Mason responds, "Nice, Jack, you and Scotty, both, huh? I don't suppose you saw how easily Amy did it?"

He thinks of reminding Mason about his shoulder, but decides not to. Mason is kidding anyways. He reaches down with both hands to help Jack up.

Inside the vent, Jack can barely make out the silhouettes of his three friends who are also on their hands and knees. The shaft is too narrow for anyone to even stoop. It's also quite dark since the only light comes from rooms below.

Before moving on, Jack looks back into the laboratory room and spies the vent cover. He wonders, *Maybe we should have grabbed it, replaced it somehow?*

Chapter 55

The group begins their trek through the vent. Mason is in the lead with Amy close behind. Scotty, who is now toting Lucky, is just ahead of Jack. The pass is narrow and they are hampered by the space constraints. Jack thinks, *When Mason said there was "plenty of space" he must have been trying to make everyone feel better about his plan.* Still, they make progress in the small tunnel.

Whenever Scotty's body dips, Jack can just make out the shape of Amy ahead. It has been a long night, but he is comforted by feeling that she seems interested again. He ponders, *How long have I known her? What is it about this night that has made me notice her in a different light? Is it just a crush? Is it the way she is wearing her hair? Is it her initial shyness that seemed so appealing? Or is it just the fact that Amy Carnahan is growing up?* Jack can't say for sure, but he does know that he is totally into her and that it feels right. Even with everything that is happening around him, he is constantly having to stop dwelling on her.

Jack senses that the slow progress of Scotty is putting him further behind the others. He knows they have to make this work—and quickly— because a new problem crosses his mind. He has no idea how long they have been in the ride. Up until this point, he had not thought about his parents and his escape from the house. They had been occupied with enough trouble, but now, the idea of being busted by his parents catches up with him.

Jack starts to imagine, *They will ground me for life. Blair will like that. Oh, I can see the smug look on her face now.*

These thoughts trouble Jack, but he decides he will gladly take the punishment if he can just get home in one piece and out of this crazy ride. He looks ahead as Scotty struggles with the cumbersome bear. He thinks, *Good ol' Scotty, loyal to a fault.*

The short chubby boy idolizes Mason Chick, who represents everything Scotty is not. Jack had often wondered how much longer Mason would allow Scotty to be his friend. They were about to hit high school, where the social order of things changes. Mason is worried about popularity, sports, and girls, though not necessarily in that order, whereas Scotty shows no signs of aptitude in any of those subjects. In line with this, Mason had been showing signs of being too cool for Scotty. Just last week, Mason had invited Jack over for a get together after a summer league baseball game. When Jack arrived, he was surprised by the number of girls hanging out at the Chick home, while there were plenty of people from the "in crowd," there was no Scotty.

When Jack quizzed Mason as to why Scotty was not there, he coldly responded, "Jack, I didn't invite Scotty. He would just get in the way. He would rather be reading some book anyways."

Jack notices that Amy and Mason are putting quite a bit of real estate between Scotty and him. So, in hushed tones, Jack says, "Scotty, hurry up."

Scotty pauses, looks back, and says, "I'm trying. It's just this bear—it's cumbersome."

"Let me take him."

"No, Mason asked me to do it."

"If Mason wanted to ride a flamingo, would you?"

"What?"

Jack knows the answer is yes, so he says, "Just keep going then."

The low glow of light provided by the rooms underneath seems to brighten, which means they are approaching another room. As he passes over the vent, Jack takes the opportunity to peer into the room below. However, he can't make out anything below: the gaps in the cover are too close together. He wonders, *Are we going the right way?*

Then Jack hears two voices from below and stops to place his ear to the cover. He asks himself, *Who is talking? Maybe they're people who can help?*

Chapter 56

With an ear pressed to the vent cover, Jack tries to make out the muffled voices below. A distinct, gravely male voice is addressing another person. It's clear to Jack that this is not Clyde.

"We have lost track of them."

"You what?"

"We cannot find them—donot worry—it is only temporary. They have to be close."

"This is not acceptable. Everything hinges on their progress. If anything happens to them…."

The second voice belongs to a female. She has a kind, gentle voice.

Jack thinks, *Are they talking about us?* He imagines that perhaps these people have been sent to get them out and that maybe he should try to contact them. But, he dismisses this idea because he doesn't recognize either voice and decides that even if he could somehow remove the vent cover, it would be better to make it out without official help.

The speaker of the first voice says, "Of course, milady…we will find them immediately."

"I do not need to tell you that…."

Jack's attention is taken away from their conversation when he notices the presence of another crawling toward him. Looking up, he sees that somehow Amy has made it around Scotty and is crawling back toward him.

"What is it, Jack?" she asks.

Jack lifts a finger in front of his lips, instructing Amy to be quiet.

She nods and mimics Jack, then places her ear to the vent as well. Jack is trying hard to listen, but he thinks, *She smells so nice.*

The woman's voice wafts up through the opening, saying, "There is considerable danger ahead. I am counting on you, Victor."

"Your trust is well placed, milady. We will locate the companions and keep watch."

"You must not allow them to see you, yet. They need to do this on their own."

"Yes, milady," responds the man. He then shuffles toward an exit, and Jack hears a door shut.

The cryptic conversation is over. In spite of this, Jack does not want to move. His face is inches apart from Amy's. Their noses are practically touching. Both remain still, ears to the vent, looking at each other.

A rush of heat floods Jack's face. He looks deeply into Amy's eyes, searching for any sign. The girl does not shy away from the gaze. She breaks into a grin and whispers, "This is cozy."

The woman's voice disrupts the moment. Jack breaks the stare and peers down into the vent, desperately trying to make out something, anything.

"We cannot make a mistake now. Follow Victor. Keep your eyes out for trouble. I am counting on you as well."

Jack wonders, *Who is she talking to?*

He turns his focus back to Amy, hoping to re-kindle the gaze they had shared, but the girl is obviously puzzled by the voices and no longer in the moment.

"What is this all about?" she whispers.

He simply shakes his head.

The lady speaks to the mysterious subject again and says, "The Troll, of course, might be a problem. He may not cooperate. You will have to be cunning."

This time Jack and Amy can barely make out a click and a squeak.

"Yes, I know you will do your best. Now, find the teens and Victor. Good fortune to you."

She has to be talking about us, thinks Jack.

He looks over Amy's shoulder in an effort to make eye contact with the other boys. However, they are out of sight. He thinks, *Time to move on, to catch up with Mason and Scotty.*

"Let's go, Amy. They are pretty far ahead, but not too far, knowing Scotty."

Amy nods, and with a little effort, turns in the narrow space. Jack has to duck to avoid her right leg swinging around.

Jack is now following Amy, but his attention on her crawling form is broken when he hears a faint thud from behind. However, after swiveling his head, he sees nothing and tells himself, "Just your imagination."

He continues his crawl, but then there is another thud, followed by another. Jack stops and thinks, *What is that?* The thuds are getting louder, and suddenly, Jack realizes they are being followed.

Chapter 57

Jack pumps his knees and hands up and down and catches up with Amy.

"Someone is behind us!"

"What?"

"Up here with us, chasing us. Go—fast!"

Amy picks up her pace, and Jack feels sweat starting to emerge on his brow. He wonders how far have the others have gotten. Even though he's moving as fast as his body will allow, the noise is growing louder. Up ahead, Jack sees the shape of Scotty, and he hears Amy alert the other boys.

"Mason, Scotty, someone is chasing us—go faster!"

The vent turns to the right at a tight, uncomfortable angle, and this slows the progress. Amy and Jack have now caught up with Scotty, and Mason is just ahead.

"Someone is up here?" Scotty asks while trying to maneuver the large stuffed bear around the turn. He seems confused.

"You heard her—now go," urges Jack.

They move along a straight path that leads to another twist, though it one is not as sharp as the previous one. After this, a fork in the path leads off in two directions.

"This way," Mason calls from the path to the right.

The group hears *thud, thud, thud,* and Amy begins pushing at Scotty, saying, "Scotty, come on, you're going too slow!"

"I can't help it!"

How far behind is the pursuer? wonders Jack. Daring to look back, Jack makes out two glowing green eyes about 20 yards behind. He feels outright terror and starts to sweat uncontrollably.

Another turn forces everyone to the left. There is no time for the teens to worry about where they are going, and while occasional vent covers provide lighting, no one is stopping for a look. It is a mad chase, and all four teens can now hear the dull thuds of the rapidly gaining antagonist.

Finally, Jack looks back again but sees no eyes. He is slightly relieved and eases his pace, thinking that they have put some distance between them and the pursuer Suddenly, though, he hears the thuds again, even more loudly this time.

He increases his speed again, and then he hears a faint exhale come from close behind him.

He yells, "Go, go, go!"

Chapter 58

The intensity of Jack's panicked yell provides more inspiration for Scotty. His knees slam hard against the flooring of the shaft. He's breathing hard, almost wheezing, but Scotty believes the work is paying off because he thinks he sees the exit up ahead. However, it turns out to be another vent cover.

Amy pushes her brother forward again. This, along with the cumbersome bear, has pushed Scotty's nerves to the breaking point.

He tells his sister, "You're not helping."

As Scotty approaches the vent cover, he focuses on the figure of Mason up ahead. In spite of all the negative reinforcement, he has managed to gain ground on his friend. This decreases, though, when his right knee slams down on the vent cover, which makes a slight give.

"Whoa!" says Scotty, and before he can calculate what will happen if his other knee strikes the cover, it gives out, unable to bear his weight.

Suddenly, there's nothing beneath him, so Scotty and the bear flail in midair and crash into the concrete below. Scotty lands squarely on his left shoulder and is overtaken by a feeling of intense pain. The agony tearing through his body makes him lose awareness of where he is or what has happened. The next thing he can make out is a figure dropping down from the open shaft above.

It's Mason, who asks, "Scotty, can you get up? Are you okay?"

"Owww! My shoulder—it's broken."

"You have to get up. We have to hide."

Scotty hears two other bodies landing on the floor, feet first.

"Is he okay?" Amy asks.

Mason roughly lifts Scotty by the right arm.

"My shoulder! Be careful—my shoulder!"

"I know, Scotty, but we have to move. Come on," Mason pleads.

The flurry of action is happening so fast, and Scotty's head feels like it's spinning.

Mason takes a look around and asks, "Is this the cave room?"

The four hear a familiar voice:

> "A poor choice they made, no shortcuts to take.
> It's left them in panic, their escape to make.
> Into the cave, they must proceed.
> The words of the narrator, they better heed."

"Quick—duck into the cave," Jack says.

The other three maneuver inside, and Scotty is ushered sharply to the left.

Amy is there at his side and tells him, "Duck down, Scotty." Then, she pushes on his injured shoulder.

"Ohhhhhh! My shoulder."

"So sorry, Scotty. I didn't mean to."

"Just don't touch it," Scotty moans.

Mason shushes the siblings and in a whispered yell, he says, "You have to be quiet. I know it hurts, Scotty, but you can't make a sound."

Suddenly, tall black boots on black legs emerge from the shaft. Then, with swift dexterity, the pursuer lunges down to the floor.

At first glance, Scotty perceives this hunter to be a man in a top hat and a long black coat. However, he soon realizes this is not a man but a wolf.

Still, he doubts himself and wonders if it can it's real or whether his bad vision is playing tricks. He can barely make out the figure, now holding his top hat in his hand, or paw. The creature is sniffing and looking while standing on two legs. At one point, he glances in the group's direction, and they duck lower.

Scotty is the only one who dares to look again. In spite of the intense, burning pain, he peaks through one eye, his good eye, and sees the wolf cautiously creeping around and bending to pick something up. Scotty realizes it's his glasses. The wolf sniffs them and promptly discards the spectacles to the floor. Although the predator is deliberate, with eyes roving up and down and to and fro like two green search lights scanning for prey, it seems to Scotty that there is something preventing the wolf from walking any closer.

Is something making him nervous? Scotty wonders.

The wolf bends down and sniffs at the pile of bones near the entrance. By this point, he is only a few feet away from them.

Scotty closes his eyes and squats more deeply against the interior cave wall. Then he prays.

Chapter 59

Amy has been vindicated. They have all seen the wolf. However, any temptation to express feelings of "I told you so" will have to wait. All four of them are now sharing in the anxiety she had been carrying alone. Huddled together and clinging to the side of the cave, the four companions hold their collective breath.

Amy is pressed against Jack's chest. She grabs his hand and looks up at him In spite of the precarious situation, his lips form a thin smile.

"He's gone," Scotty mumbles to the others.

No one else dares to speak in case Scotty is not correct. Then, after another minute of uneasy tension, Scotty lifts his body from its cower.

"He's moved on. Look, he's not there."

"Scotty, it may be a trick. Get back down," Jack urges.

"No, he won't be coming back…. at least for a while."

Amy breaks the hand lock between her and Jack and rises. She asks, "What makes you say that?"

"He's apprehensive. I watched him. He looked around and sniffed the bones. He was so close. I swear I could smell his breath—it reminded me of barbecue. I ducked back down and waited. When the breath was gone, I peeked."

"You could have gotten us killed," Mason expresses.

"No, he didn't see me. I'm sure of it. He walked backwards slowly."

"Don't you mean *it*?" Mason clarifies.

"No, I'm sure it's a man."

"How are you so sure?"Jack asks.

"Did you see the clothes? Definitely a man-wolf."

Unwilling to give in, Mason slyly remarks, "Scotty, clothes do not make the man."

"Oh Mason," says Amy, "that was terrible. I mean, really guys, who cares? We're going to argue the gender of a wolf? Go on, Scotty, what happened?"

"That's just it—nothing. He looked around, and I promise he looked worried. He backed up carefully like he was trying to be silent."

"Well, if he was doing it to drive us out of our hiding place, then mission accomplished," Jack points out.

Amy stares hard at the door where the wolf vanished. She doesn't like Jack's last point. He has no idea how terrifying her encounter with the wolf had been. The events between her and the wolf replay in her mind. She wonders, *What did he mean by "you are the one I have always wanted"?*Finally, Amy resigns herself to the fact that Scotty is right: the wolf is gone. Now, at last, Amy lets them have it. She says, "So, there is no wolf, huh?"

"You were right, Amy. Better now?" Mason smugly offers.

"Nice, Mason, great attitude," says Jack, who decides to speak for the others. "We really do owe you an apology for doubting you. But what we need to do now is move. We should either try and unblock that door or go through the cave. We are not going back into the cold room again."

"Agreed," says Mason. "I just don't know how we ended up right back here. We traveled a long way up in the vents. Should we take another stab up there?"

Scotty, whose injured shoulder has escaped their recollection, whimpers, "I don't think so."

Amy rushes to her brother and says, "Oh, Scotty, your shoulder. I was so scared with the wolf and all. Let me look at it. Can you move it at all?"

"Just a little," Scotty replies. A grimace of pain passes over his face, and he says, "I think it's broken."

Amy goes ahead and presses on his shoulder.

"Ahhhhh! Easy!"

"Nothing feels broken."

"Since when did you become a nurse?" Scotty questions.

Ignoring Mason, again, Amy mentions to her brother, "I separated my shoulder in fifth grade, remember?"

"Yeah, basketball camp," Scotty answers, grinding his teeth as Amy continues to prod the injured area.

"What do you want us to do, Scotty? It's probably a deep bruise or something, but if we need to rest…."

"No, I can walk. It just hurts. That's—"

A buzz and a crackle come from a sound system:

"Four have endured, all the frailer.
Thief, wanderer, apprentice, and tailor.
The companions are set to finish their role,
But no closer are they to achieving their goal.
Enter the cave, it is a must.
But prepare to defend those you trust."

"Oh, I am so sick of those rhymes," Scotty announces in pain.

"He's trying to tell us something," Jack suggests feebly. "The voice said to go into the cave. He's talking about the four of us. Can't you see?"

"If it's talking about us, who is he calling a thief?" Amy asks as she looks around at the boys. Still, she is starting to think that Jack is right about the narrator communicating with them. She looks at the stick in her hand and thinks, "Surely, he's not talking about a stick."

Mason announces, "Okay, gang, I know I'm right now. This is all a big game. Don't you think it's awful convenient that we're right back here in front of the cave? Those doors the wolf went out lead back to the snow room. Those doors over there are blocked by those rocks. Whoever is pushing us or leading us wants us to go in the cave. This is all one big joke. We're gonna walk right into a TV crew eventually."

"But," Amy retorts, "the snake bite? Remember not more than an hour ago Jack lying helplessly on that table? And, what about Scotty's shoulder? Do you think they planned that, too?"

"No, just casualties of the production. I bet we can sue the pants off these guys. Yeah, we'll all get filthy rich."

Amy thinks to herself, *You're already rich.*

Mason adds, "I guess we all owe Scotty a big thanks." He slaps Scotty's shoulder, totally oblivious to the effect of this action.

"Owww!"

"You are such an idiot," Amy chastises. "Scotty are you—"

"He forgot, Amy," Scotty says with a groan.

Amy thinks, *I wish you would stop making excuses for him.* "Yeah," says Mason. "I forgot. Sorry, Scotty. I got carried away. Anyways. let's move out. I want to be the first one to see their faces when we tell them they are liable for Scotty's injury. Onward, troops! No time for cowards!" And with this, Mason plunges deeper into the cave.

"Oh brother," Amy says. "He makes me so—"

"I know, Amy, I know," reassures Jack. "We better follow him anyways. He may be a little insensitive, but at least he's in a good mood. Scotty, you good to go?"

"Yep, I'll live," Scotty says and forces a smile. Then he points to his frames lying on the floor next to the pile of bones and says, "My glasses."

Amy retrieves them and tells him, "One of your lenses is cracked."

"Just what I need. Put them on for me anyways."

Amy lifts the frames to his head, and Scotty blinks and says, "Great. Just great. It's the lens over my good eye."

Commiserating with her older brother, Amy gently pats his good shoulder and says, "It has not been your day."

Scotty looks around the room in his new cracked glasses and discovers something. He calls out, "Guys, over there—beside the pile of bones. That was not there last time we were here."

Amy and Jack wander over to the creepy pile, and both see the object Scotty is pointing at.

Amy declares, "It's a work belt. My dad has one in the garage."

Jack scoops up the belt and starts to look inside. He comments, "Interesting. Wonder if there is anything in here that would come in handy?"

From ahead, Mason reappears and says, "Come on, guys. Up ahead, I smell something."

With interest piqued, Scotty and Amy follow Mason into the cave. Jack takes another look at the work belt and then slings it over his shoulder and follows.

Chapter 60

Jack sniffs the air and tries to catch the scent of what Mason was referring to.

"Come on guys," Mason beckons. "A few more steps. I started to smell it just up there."

Leaving the dim light of the room, the four delve deeper and deeper into the cave. The small passageway is unlike any other they had traversed thus far. The floor is rocky and jagged, and at times each one of them has to hold out a steadying hand against the cave wall.

All five of Jack's senses begin working overtime. His hands feel rocky crevices, he tries to smell the odor Mason had told him about, his ears are poised to listen for clues of whatever lurks ahead, he can taste the stale air of the cave, and his eyes are now transfixed on a very faint glow a good ways up ahead.

His mind is working on a completely different problem. There is something unsettling to Jack about Scotty's previous revelation. He contemplates, *The wolf was apprehensive? Was he afraid of something, or did he simply lose their scent?* Jack feels like the latter is highly unlikely, so his ears continue to strain, listening for anything. He replays the rhyme of the narrator, "Prepare to defend those you trust," in his mind and thinks, *He's telling us to be cautious. Well, duh, we really don't have a choice.*

Amy's hand brushes against Jack's. He grasps it and tells himself, *I could get used to this.* His other hand is tightly wrapped around the large blue stuffed bear, a burden he has decided not to endure for long. He had taken the bear despite the silent protest from Scotty. Jack plans to tell Mason at the next chance that if he wants Lucky, then he can carry him.

As the group approaches the faint glow, the cave tunnel opens up into a larger room—or at least Jack thinks it is a larger room. There is not enough light for him to really tell. However, there is now plenty of light for Mason and Scotty to be able to notice Jack holding Amy's hand, so he releases it and thinks, *Hope she understands. It's just too soon for the others to know.* In the middle of the room is a long, narrow wooden table. Adorning this is a flickering candle, which has been producing the dull glow. Also on the table are three small bowls with wooden spoons flanking them, and around the table are three wooden chairs.

Jack drops Lucky next to the table and picks up the candle. He walks toward one of the dark corners of the room looking for an exit. When he doesn't see one, he continues to make his way around the perimeter of the large room.

"That smell… it's coming from the bowls," Mason declares. "Jack, bring the candle back over here."

Jack doesn't comply, though, because he has found a short, brown door with a rounded top and a bronze handle in its center. It is well hidden on the right side of the room.

Jack calls to the others, "There's a door over here! Come on over! Let's just get out."

"No, come back over here, Braddock! I want to check this out," Mason urges.

Jack is irritated by the request and thinks, *We should just leave.* A tinge of something fowl flickers around his nose, but this smell dissipates as Jack makes his way back to Mason and the table.

Mason takes the candle from Jack and sets it back on the table. He looks into the containers and eyes the contents. "It's like oatmeal," he says and makes an exaggerated sniffing sound over the largest bowl.

Jack is confused by Mason's sudden nasal intoxication and comments, "You said it smells bad."

"No, I said it just smells."

"Well, which is it then?"

"It smells good—very good."

Jack walks over to the table and takes a whiff for himself. A waft of something insanely sweet tickles his nostrils. He thinks, "It's pumpkin, no maple, maybe ginger…."

He can't decide, but whatever it is smells heavenly. This reminds him that he has not eaten any supper. In fact, none of them have, Scotty's assault on the gingerbread house withstanding.

"Oh, that does smell inviting!" Jack says.

Mason picks up a spoon.

Overcoming the temptation, though, Jack says, "Mason, ignore it. We don't need to be screwing around in here. Let's just head out those doors." He points in the direction of the now hidden escape.

"Oh man, Jack, it smells so good. What's it going to hurt—just one bite?"

"I don't think you—"

Mason dips the wooden spoon into the large bowl and shoves a heaping pile of the brown mush into his mouth.

"Eoouwch! Hot, hot—too hot! This one's too hot!" exclaims Mason as he fans his mouth with his hand.

As soon as the words are out of his mouth, Scotty screams, "Spit it out Mason! Spit it out now!"

Jack is startled by Scotty's sudden vocal excretion and gives him a befuddled look. Then suddenly, as if he is finally catching on to the punch line of a joke, he understands. In fact, all of them understand and are not surprised when they hear a low, deep growl.

Chapter 61

Jack's hair stands up on the top of his head as all four teens turn to face the source of the growl.

As they do, Scotty chastises Mason by saying, "Oh no! No, no, no! Goldilocks, Mason, come on—don't you read at all? You tasted papa bear's porridge!"

Lumbering into the dull light, a massive brown bear rears up to full height, revealing itself to the gawking onlookers. The creature, a ferocious seven-foot monster, is now in full view. Another deep, guttural growl rumbles through the room.

The corners of the room had been so dark that none of them had seen the well-hidden giant. Jack had actually only been a few steps away from running into the beast during his search for the door until he stopped to come back to the table. Now, his eyes feel as if they will pop out of his head. He thinks, *This is unreal. It is so close. Could we outrun the animal? Do I play dead?* Backing up instinctively, Jack surveys the room. It is so dark. He asks himself, *Where was that door? Based on where the table is, that door is blocked by the bear.* He knows they have to either get around the bear to that door or find the way they had come in.

The horrible beast takes another step forward, hurls its head up to the sky and releases a fierce roar.

"I'm out," says Mason as he takes off running back the way they came. He disappears into a dark corner of the room.

Scotty and Amy both hit the ground and crawl under the table.

Jack thinks, *Oh great, we're playing hide and seek now—with a bear*, and then he makes his move. With one hand on the work belt over his shoulder, he takes four full steps away from the lunging bear. With the dexterity of an olympic hurdler, he leaps and clears the table of the candlestick.

Shocked at his jumping prowess, Jack turns back towards the table and says, "Come on, guys! You can't just hide under there."

"His shoulder!" Amy cries.

Scotty is hunkered down under the table, cradling Lucky with one arm and his injured shoulder with the other. His mouth is tensed, and his teeth are grinding as a result of the pain.

"Scotty," yells Jack "It's coming this way—move now!"

Looking back to the bear, Jack sees the behemoth approaching the table. He rushes toward the table, himself and blows out the candle creating complete darkness. After this, he ducks down and crawls under the table with Amy and Scotty.

The bear's charge is stalled, and it gurgles.

From the other side of the room, Mason calls, "What did you do that for?"

"Good idea, Jack," Amy whispers.

Jack beams in the darkness.

"Scotty, you think you can crawl?" Amy asks. "We should be able to get by that bear now."

"Yeah, I can crawl. I wish that bear didn't have a tapetum lucidum."

"What?"

The bear is sniffing, searching.

"That bear has a tapetum lucidum, so it can see better in the dark than us. His eyes will probably get used to this in a minute, but it will take us longer."

Amy asks, "Where's the exit, Jack?"

"It's too dark to tell," he replies.

After he hears a large growl, Jack wonders, *Has the creature's eyes grown accustomed to the light with his tapetum whatever?*

Jack motions a finger in front of his lips before he remembers Scotty and Amy can't see him.

They listen and try to gauge where the bear is. They can hear the heavy breathing of the animal and the sound of its paws striking the ground.

Jack's stomach starts doing backflips, and sweat starts to ooze from his pores. He can tell the bear is coming closer!

Suddenly, from the other side of the room, Mason calls, "I found where we came in. Just make a break for it. Come toward my voice."

Jack rolls from under the table and says, "Come on, guys."

He takes off running followed by Amy and Scotty.

Mason can hear their feet and yells, "Move it—this way!"

Jack's ears are on alert, and he hears shuffling behind them.

"Over here!" Mason calls.

Jack corrects his course a little and stops when he runs full into Mason. The collision causes a minor ruckus, but neither is hurt.

Jack asks, "Did the bear follow?"

"I don't hear him coming," Mason declares.

When Amy is halfway down the little cave, she sees a glow that lets her know the entrance is not far ahead. Amy quickly calculates. The exit, it's maybe only 20 yards ahead.

She says, "Scotty, you okay?" When there is no response, Amy asks again, "Scotty?"

But, Scotty doesn't answer because he isn't with them.

Chapter 62

Scotty nervously listens for the bear. When Jack and Amy ran, he had rolled to try and get to his feet, but as he did so, his shoulder throbbed and he wilted. The bear had not followed Mason's previous yell, and this made Scotty whimper in fear while wondering, *Can he see me?*

The bear's heavy breathing is close, and Scotty can hear it sniffing. He thinks, *He smells me. The bear is at the table.*

Then there's a growl.

"Help!" Scotty cries in fear.

Pushing with his legs, he attempts to stand and start running. However, something is pulling at his legs. Suddenly, Scotty feels a sharp pain as claws dig into his ankle.

"He's got me!"

Scotty reaches back for something to hold on to, but the bear gives a yank and Scotty's entire body rushes forward. He kicks in the air wildly and his foot strikes the bear, whose grip relaxes, allowing Scotty to back away quickly.

Then he feels an arm pulling him up. The pain in his shoulder aches.

"Come on, Scotty," says Jack while holding onto him.

The bear is now standing at full height. It grunts while assessing the best way to get at its dinner.

Mason rushes into the fray. He fumbles in the dark and with a surge of effort flips the table to its side. The table topples over, forming a small wall of temporary protection for the group, who crash down behind the makeshift barrier.

They hear another growl, followed by banging. They are rocked by the force of the bear slamming against the table. At this point, Mason grips his axe and flings it at the bear. It misses horribly, and as Mason ducks down behind the barrier, a slashing paw just misses his head.

Amy, who is pressing all of her weight against the defense while sitting, uses her stick to wildly flail up over the wall, hoping to strike the bear. However, the bear dismisses the strikes like they are obnoxious flies and continues to bash against the wooden table.

If the bear were just a little more intelligent, it would easily have realized it has the strength to hurl the table out of the way, but the animal is apparently content to bash against the opposite side.

Just then, Jack reaches to his shoulder where the work belt is draped. Reaching inside, he finds that it contains an assortment of tools. Desperately, he pilfers through the items within, looking for anything that can be of use. Scotty watches as Jack pulls a small flashlight from the belt and then reaches in to find something else.

"Jackpot," says Jack. "A small can of mace!"

From his seated position, Scotty looks up to see the bear staring directly into his face as it peers over the table. Saliva is dripping from its mouth, signaling dinner time. The bear swipes at Jack's head, and a whoosh of air causes his hair to shuffle.

"Here goes nothing," says Jack. "Cover your faces."

"What?" Mason yells.

"Just do it," Jack replies as he holds out the can of mace for the others to see.

Without another moment of hesitation, Jack scrambles to his feet and sprays the contents of the can up into the beast's face.

The effects of the spray are immediate. A wail of pain erupts from the animal, and a paw lashes out and strikes the can out of Jack's hand. It flies 20 feet to the other side of the cave and into the darkness. The impact of the strike evokes a jolting pain in Jack's hand.

With his weapon detached, Jack retreats, cowering down behind the barrier. The dazed, lumbering giant makes a wild lunge at the table. With horrible pain scorching its eyes, it puts its entire body weight into its last desperate attack. The entire table spins, swinging the teens around in a complete 180-degree revolution. Jack shines the flashlight toward the dark wall and sees that their path to the door, their original goal, is now clear.

"The door!" he cries. "Scotty, you have to come with us now!"

All four sprint to the exit.

On the way out, Mason kicks an object, sending it spinning forward along the floor. He stops to pick it up and feels the wooden handle of the axe. Mason hears another growl and realizes that the bear, in spite of its blindness, is just behind him. He takes off sprinting for the exit with axe in hand.

Chapter 63

Jack is the first one through the doors. Then Amy and Scotty emerge behind him.

After a few more seconds, Mason finally lunges through the door and yells, "Close the doors! That thing is not giving up!"

Jack slams the doors shut and says, "Look for something heavy we can put against these doors!"

After a quick survey of the room, they see a black cauldron with green slimy liquid in it. It would require the strength of all four of them to move it, but they soon manage to move it against the doors.

They are all frightened beyond belief as they scan the room further.

The lighting is dim but not as dark as the cave. Fluorescent white tube lights dully glow in the ceiling, and these reveal some trees and a stump or two.

"Are you okay, Scotty?" Amy asks.

"Craving some Junior Mints," he replies in between gasps for air.

"There's a gingerbread house a few rooms back, but that's it," Amy replies.

"I'll pass."

Once he's confident that the cauldron will hold, Jack looks up at Mason, who's right beside him and sees him peering down into the cauldron's contents.

He asks, "Mason, what are you doing?"

Mason breaks his gaze from the cauldron temporarily. He approaches Amy and says, "Let me see your stick."

Amy jerks her prized weapon behind her back and demands, "Why?"

"Umm, Mason? How 'bout we not stir the cauldron full of probably creepy things," Jack suggests.

Mason rolls his eyes and says, "Whatever."

He proceeds to store the axe in the waist of his shorts, and the head sticks out like the butt of a revolver.

Looking across the room, Jack sees two more sets of doors, one to the right and one to the left.

They hear a familiar humming sound:

"The teens prove clever, avoiding the beast.
One false move and they would have been its feast.
To survive in the story, their wits must be keen,
For in this wood there's far worse yet unseen.
Two doors, on either side, to continue your flight.
Go to the left in order to make things right."

"There's worse?" Amy responds to the voice in dismay.

"I don't like the sound of that," Jack states grimly. "But it clearly told us to go through the door on the left."

"Hey," says Mason. "Let me see that flashlight and the belt."

"Here," Jack says as he flips the flashlight to his friend and then hands him the belt.

Mason holds the light, assessing its weight and says, "Looks like we didn't come out of there empty handed."

"Yeah, I guess that mace can really saved our bacon," Scotty adds.

They are all quiet for a moment, still gathering themselves after the encounter with the bear. Then Scotty asks in a feeble voice, "Are we all going to die?"

"We're okay, aren't we?" Jack replies.

"Come on, Jack," says Mason. "This is bad—really bad. Who knows what's going to happen in this place?"

"Yeah. It's not my favorite ride anymore," Jack muses.

Scotty strolls over to Mason and peers over his left shoulder as he rifles through the various pouches in the work belt. From one of them, he pulls out a small notebook, and after looking at it, he says, "Hey, guys? Um... you should look at this."

"So, it's a notebook," Amy sighs. "What's so big about that?"

"Look at the cover."

Jack can't read the expression on Mason's face, but something is troubling him to be sure. Jack takes the small memo-sized notebook and stares at the cover. A name has been written on it in cursive lettering:

Douglas Finch

Jack thinks, *Can this be real? Is this the actual work belt of Douglas Finch?*

Chapter 64

"Unbelievable, huh?" Mason asks.

Jack hands the notebook to Amy, so she can look at the writing herself.

"You've got to be kidding me?" She says. "No, this can't be real. Mason, you wrote this while we weren't looking." She passes the notebook to her brother.

"What?" Mason counters, looking incredulous.

"No, Amy," Scotty confirms. "I've seen Mason's handwriting—or that scribble he calls handwriting—and he didn't write this."

As Amy thinks, she bites off a corner of her index fingernail nervously. She muses, "So it's not just an urban myth? There really is, or was, a Douglas Finch?"

"Well, it's either that or we're falling right into the mother of all practical jokes," Mason declares, still unwilling to give up on his reality TV angle.

Scotty shoves his ever-sliding glasses back up the bridge of his nose with his pointer finger and says, "Okay, let's just assume this is his work belt. I guess the next logical question is what happened to him?"

When no one responds, Mason is quick to supply an answer, "Hello? The bones outside the cave?"

Jack, though, doesn't want to consider that question. He takes the work belt from Mason and asks, "Did you see anything else in here of use?"

"Well, there's a small hammer. But I havn't checked the last pocket."

Rifling quickly through the undiscovered pouch, Jack lifts out a folded piece of yellowed paper. "What's this?" he asks, but after unfolding the old document, Jack asserts, "It's a map."

"A map of what?" Scotty asks excitedly.

"It's a map of the ride, I think."

As the boys gather around the yellowed parchment, Amy opens the red notebook.

"Do you think he got trapped in here, too?" Scotty questions.

Mason shoots Scotty a scowl and says, "Uh, hello, knucklehead. Of course he did. We found the notebook in this crazy part of the building, didn't we?"

"Guys," Amy breaks in, "I guess none of you bothered to actually open the notebook. Get a load of this. There is a lot of writing here."

If you found this notebook, it means my fate has been sealed. It also means that you share in my predicament. I have penned some brief notes in the hope that others like me trapped in this strange ride will be able to find their way out. Take the map I have made. It should help you find your bearings. Beware, there are dozens of passageways and doors and a great many of them lead to danger. During my wanderings, I encountered a rhyme written in a stone wall. I believe it is the key to finding the way out. However, after days of endless thoughts and unanswered questions, I still don't know what it means. Perhaps it will make sense to you. It said:"

> *Keys will cry to you, to a valued room.*
> *Many perils you will face. Avoid your doom.*
> *Within its walls a volume resides.*
> *This is what I now confide.*
> *The treasure is gold, and the lady will be true.*
> *The gingerbread house is home, and that is what you must do."*

Perhaps whoever recovers my notebook and map will find this useful in getting help. You are trapped in a crazy world. I wish you all the luck that I apparently did not have.

Yours,
Douglas Jay Finch

P.S. Do not cross the bridge.

Chapter 65

All four stand silent. Jack is speechless at this newest bombshell of a discovery. The grim reality that Finch did not make it out alive is the prevailing thought on his mind.

Breaking the silence, Scotty whimpers while holding his shoulder, "More rhymes…. just what we need."

"No, Scotty, this is exactly what we need," Mason declares excitedly. "This is real help, this map, the rhyme on this paper; this is a gold mine of information. And when I say gold mine, did any of you catch that bit about gold? I bet there is some kind of treasure in here."

The bit about "real help" is what sounds most appealing to Jack.

Mason quips, "Okay, Scotty, you're the fairy tale king around here. Take a shot at deciphering this rhyme."

Once again adjusting his damaged glasses, Scotty seizes the notebook from Amy. His beady eyes glance back and forth over the page while the other teens wait for the guru to uncover the hidden mystery.

A minute passes. Then another. Finally, an impatient Mason cannot hold his tongue and asks, "Okay, what are you thinking?"

"Well, I guess…. Well, we are in some fantasy world, so I bet there will be, like, talking keys, and they will be crying. It says the gingerbread house is home. I bet the keys will tell us how to get back there through some hidden door. There will be some gold lady there—"

"Or, there will be lots of gold in the gingerbread room," Mason says. "Remember, the doors to that house were locked. That's what we're supposed to do—find the talking keys and unlock the gingerbread house. Then we get the gold and go home! How about it, Jack? Easy, right?"

"Well, that does make some sense, but you're leaving out some of the rhyme. Let's see here," Jack says as he takes the notebook from Scotty. "Um… okay, so keys will cry to us. That means we will probably encounter some sort of magical keys. These will give us access to some hidden room. That seems clear." Jack looks up at the others. All three are hanging on his every thought.

"Yeah, better. That makes a lot of sense—keep going," Mason says.

"There must be something valuable inside the room."

"Something gold, right?" Mason inquires.

"Yes, that's what it says, but 'the lady will be true' line…. I bet there's some gold statue of a lady hidden in the room. We know there are dangers. We've encountered a few already. 'Many perils you will face. Avoid your doom. Within its walls, a volume resides'….. Maybe we are supposed to find some liquid of some sort once we get the statue and take it to the gingerbread house?"

"Jack, you're brilliant! That's it. All we have to do is find the keys, enter the hidden room, grab the statue, avoid danger, find the volume or whatever and get to the gingerbread house—great!" Mason announces.

Jack responds, "Well, guys, listen, this is great and all, and it does make sense, but what about the narrator's rhymes?"

"What about them, Jack?" Amy questions.

"So, I think the narrator is telling us we have to finish some story. We have taken the roles of the characters in the ride. I think he's trying to tell us that we have to find the exit ourselves. He told us to take the left door. I think the narrator is telling us we have to go that way to finish the story. Don't you remember he said 'go left to make things right'? I mean a lot the rhymes have been about completing this or—"

"Hogwash, Jack," Mason cuts Jack off. "You said it yourself this makes sense."

"No, listen, the narrator said a thief, a wanderer, a tailor, and an apprentice will have to finish the story. Guys, it's all clear. Amy is the wanderer. Remember she got separated? Mason, you're the tailor. I mean the tailor was bold and brave, just like you, and you do have that badge. And the apprentice is Scotty. It's so obvious." Conveniently skipping the role of the thief, he continues, "We are the characters, this ride is our story, and for some reason we have to make things right."

"Okay, Jack, you've lost me there. Why can't we do what we are supposed to by finding this clue?" Scotty counters.

Jack has to admit he has a point. But he stands firm because he believes the narrator is trying to help them.

He says, "Maybe Douglas Finch didn't listen to the narrator. He just kept going deeper and deeper until he finally—"

"Jack, we need to follow the clues here. You deciphered the rhyme as far as I'm concerned. All that narrator has done is scare the pants off us and give us cryptic rhymes. Every time we've gone in a direction that voice told us to go, well, bad things have happened. He led us straight into the cave with the bear," Mason argues.

"But what other choice did we have?" asks Jack.

Mason responds, "Jack, we have a choice now. This is real direction. I, for one, say we check out the map and look for the keys. What do you say, apprentice?" There is dripping sarcasm in the last few words.

"I agree with Mason, Jack. Let's just follow the map," Scotty announces.

Of course you do, thinks Jack, who looks to Amy for support.

Looking down at the floor and avoiding eye contact with Jack, Amy starts, "Jack, um, well, you were bitten by a snake, and Scotty has injured his shoulder. A bear almost killed us all. The map, well, it's something real. It's not some mysterious clue. I just want to get out of here, now. Let's just follow the map."

"'Atta girl," Mason crows, taking the map in his hands and spreading it out on the floor.

Jack could understand why Scotty backed Mason, but he's disappointed that Amy does too. *Since when did she start siding with Mason?* he thinks. A twinge of jealousy firmly takes a seat in Jack's head. However, he knows he can't blame her for siding with Mason. After all, she made a good point. Regretfully, he gives in and joins Scotty and Mason in studying the yellowed map.

A series of boxes representing rooms are scattered across the parchment.

"Look here! This says 'The Vault.' There's even an X on it. X marks the spot, right? I would bet a thousand dollars that this is where we find the treasure. We look for the key in one of these other rooms, open the door to the vault, take whatever is there, and go to the gingerbread house. See, here is the cave. That means we are here, and we need to take the doors to the right. It seems like we have a few rooms to navigate before we get there," Mason declares.

"The narrator said go left," Jack argues.

"Look, Jack, we have already decided. We're following the map. If you want to follow the mysterious voice that has almost gotten us killed, be my guest."

Jack gives no response. He knows he has lost this battle. Looking at the map, Jack feels a little lump develop in his chest, for he is certain there will be danger lurking in each of those rooms, possibly trying to stop them—or eat them. Dismissing these thoughts, he continues to scan the paper. The rooms are labeled with names that describe them, such as garden, grove, vault, chasm, and clearing. The gingerbread house is even labeled. Other cryptic notes are written in some of the squares, too. They say things like, "Beware golden orbs," "fiery lass," "whimsical tune," and in the square labeled "the grove," there are the words "grandfather rodents." None of these notes are clear enough for them to decipher, at least not now, but each seems to spell out some awaiting danger.

"Okay, so we just left the cave. The room we are in leads to the 'garden.' We take that door," says Mason, ignoring the other set of doors to the left. "It looks like each of these rooms has two or three sets of doors. Man, I can see how someone could get lost. From the 'grove' we have, depending on the route we take, about six or seven rooms to clear before we hit the vault."

Suddenly, the cauldron rattles, and from behind the doors, a growl erupts.

"Okay, gang, time to move on," Scotty nervously asserts.

Chapter 66

Outside the ride, Gwen and Clyde are doing their best to keep the Carnahans at bay. Time was wasting, he and his companions were ready to enter the ride when Houston Carnahan started getting really loud, he decided to help keep things calm before re-entering. At one point Clyde thinks he is going to have to physically restrain Mr. Carnahan. The man is younger and much stouter than Clyde, and he is relieved Gwen is with him for support. He wonders if he might be making things worse by not going in now, thinking, *Gwen is much better at this type of stuff. Let her do her thing. The other parents are on their way. Maybe their arrival will give the Carnahan man somebody to gripe with?*He steps away from the parents to join Oliver and Colton, who await his arrival at the front of the ride. Just then, from the corner of his eye, the figure of a dumpy, football-shaped man saunters around a corner. "Great. Just great," thinks Clyde, "Snodgrass is here." The squat little man is tugging up on his pants with every step, only stopping to occasionally wisp the dozen or so remaining long hairs on the top of his head down over the rest of his balding scalp.

Ignoring the parents and Gwen, Howard Snodgrass, grim-faced, makes a beeline for Clyde, who fires a pre-emptive strike over the bow by saying, "You told me to not disturb you."

"Clyde, that was a stolen prop. These are missing kids. Completely different. I might need to call the lawyers. If Sparkman there hadn't called me—"

"They're just lost in the ride," Clyde says while shooting a look of irritation at Oliver.

"I don't care if they're playing hide-n-seek. This place is already a sieve with money, and I'm not getting sued 'cause some kids decide to pull a prank that gets their parents' panties in a wad."

Pulling out a cell phone the size of a brick from who knows where, Snodgrass types a message by bashing away at the keys with pudgy fingers. Before he finishes, he asks, "Are you sure they have not gotten out? They are not having a good laugh drinking some milkshakes over at Sonic or something?"

"No sir, Gwen's been standing here all night."

"Just find the kids, Clyde. Do your job."

Snodgrass pauses, waiting for some voice on the other end of the phone. Then he says, "Pritchard? We got a problem at the park. No, no, no, not that again. It's with the Enchanted Forrest… the Dark Ride. For crying out loud, Henry, haven't you ever even been here? Never mind. Look…."

Things have gone from bad to worse for Clyde. His only escape is to get back inside the ride. With a nod and a gesture, Clyde leads his crew through the front gate into the ride.

Chapter 67

The laboratory, the sight of Jack's near-death experience, is disheveled. Dozens of broken vials and books are toppled over, and the vent shaft is flush with the cement floor, which is awash with liquids from the broken bottles and vials. A slender lady looks over the room in a pleased manner.

She states, "Well, I cannot say much for their housekeeping skills. They made a complete mess of the study." This good-natured observation is followed by a pleasant laugh from her.

The grey squirrel is resting gently on her folded arm and begins clicking and squeaking.

"These brave children, bless them," says the lady. "I see they have tried to make their own way."

The squirrel makes more clicks and squeaks.

"We were lucky. I had forgotten about the viper."

The lady listens to more noises by the squirrel.

"Yes, the bear. I knew that would be, shall we say, hairy?" says the lady, laughing at her own quip. "But they overcame, and neither you nor Victor had to interfere. Did they receive the gift?"

She pauses for another brief response.

"Excellent, we are in luck. The whole ordeal was too close of a call. Perhaps Victor will need to be more assertive. What?... Perhaps another gift? The danger will only grow. It is a fine line we walk. They need to do this on their own. They must fulfill the prophecy for the good of all. If we interfere beyond what we have already done, then all could be lost."

Squeak, squeak, click, squeak, pause, and *squeak.*

"Any sign of the wolf?"

More clicks and squeaks.

"They have outwitted him thus far, yes. He will not give up."

Again, more squeaks and clicks.

"Yes, dear, in the end I am certain he will get his due."

More chatter in the squirrel dialect.

"Yes, they are. They are truly the ones of whom the prophecy speaks. Now go. Be my eyes, kind one. Gently push when needed, and give Victor my thanks yet again."

Pleased with the events thus far, the lady is encouraged. *There is hope,* she thinks.

Chapter 68

A gentle push of the door reveals the most massive garden any of the teens has ever seen. From the bottom of the ruddy floor grow wild green clusters of plants. Exotic looking flowers reach toward a yellow ceiling. The colors are almost dizzying in their splendor. This is the brightest room they had encountered since entering what they had, until now, known as the Dark Ride. The density of the growth gives little room for walking.

"Well, at least we know we are on the right path. The map is accurate. This must be the granddaddy of all gardens!" exclaims Mason.

"It appears to me that the plants are actually lined up by species," Scotty states as he squints his eyes at a particularly verdant plant.

"Chalk another one up for the guy who listens in school," Mason muses. "So just ahead should be a room called 'The Grove.'"

Ignoring the dripping sarcasm, Scotty continues, "If every room inside this place has a theme, or is based on some sort of tale, then my guess would be this is Mary's garden."

"'Mary, Mary, quite contrary, how does your garden grow?'" Amy absently calls as she runs her hand along the stem of a tall tulip.

"I would say a little too well," Jack answers.

Mason, who is investigating a little further ahead, calls back, "I can barely make out a path through these weeds. There should be a door straight ahead. It will lead us closer to the vault!"

Scotty rushes up to Mason's side.

"Come on, Jack, let's catch up," Amy encourages.

Jack thinks, *What's her hurry? Mason had gotten them into this mess in the first place: he had left the ride, he had tried to play snake handler, he had tasted the porridge.* Mason looks at the map and then back at the foliage. He uses one of his arms to push a tall plant to the side and says, "It's got to be—"

"Filthy, filthy hands!" cries the voice of a female from somewhere behind the foliage.

"Filthy, filthy little hands!" reverberates the female voice through the garden. And then, in measured beats, it oozes, "Do... not... touch... my... pets."

Scotty whispers in hushed tones to the others, "I'm gonna guess that's Mary."

Taking a stab at diplomacy, Jack answers the strange new voice. "Uh, we are trying to move on. Just tell us where the door is, and we will *kindly* be out of your way," emphasizing the word "kindly" in an overt attempt at graciousness.

"A door? A door? They want to find a door?" says the voice in almost a sing-song fashion.

Jack answers, "Uh, yes ma'am, if we could find the door, we will be out of your hair."

"Well, if you simply want to get out as you say, kindly desist from touching my plants and take a right at the cockle shells."

"What is a cockle shell, Scotty?" Amy asks, looking for direction from her trivia-enriched brother.

"Honestly, I don't know. I guess we just have to make a guess."

There is a bustle in the plants to their left. All four turn at once to face the cause of the commotion. A lady with long red hair steps into a small clearing just ten yards behind them.

She asks, "What are you waiting for? Leave. Be on your way."

"We don't know what a cockle shell is," Jack admits.

"You don't know what a cockle shell is?"

She snickers a self-righteous laugh and steps back into the foliage. Once she is out of sight, she calls, "Then I suppose you had better find out quickly." Her sinister laugh fills the air.

"Is that a warning?" wonders Jack. Turning around, he sees the gaping jaws of a very large Venus Flytrap opening just above Amy's head.

"Amy!" he shouts.

The girl looks at Jack innocently, not aware of the danger.

Jack leaps at her, tackling her and, thus, saving her from the two jaws that slam closed at the exact spot where Amy's head had been.

Another set of enormous Venus Flytrap jaws bound down toward the toppled bodies of Amy and Jack, but Mason rushes in like a linebacker and knocks them clear with his shoulder.

"This way," commands Mason.

Scurrying to their feet, Amy and Jack look over at Mason, who has found a path of some sort. Jack backs away from the carnivorous plant, takes Amy by the hand, and makes a wide swath over to Scotty. Another plant bends down to block their path, but this time, Mason raises his axe at the plant. With his point made, the plant moves out of their way.

"Stop that, you vile brute, you will hurt her!" the hidden voice cries.

"Those have to be cockle shells!" Scotty calls, pointing towards several plants with what look to be oysters on top.

They head to the right, and just as promised, a door looms ahead. Although the maze of plants prevents them from running, they move as fast as they can toward the exit.

While they do, the voice makes one last ominous declaration: "If you come back into my garden again, you will be plant food. Plant food!"

Chapter 69

In the icy room, the wolf hovers over the caged snake.

The reptile says, "If you will simply take me out of this frigid room, I will tell you where the children went."

The wolf is craving food. His hunger gnaws at his rumbling stomach. Unfortunately for him, the small viper will not make much of a meal, more like a snack.

The wolf asks, "So, you want to make a deal?"

The viper lifts its head above the cage floor with excitement and answers, "Yes, that's it—a deal! Perhaps you would kindly remove me from this cage and let me rest inside that warm coat of yours?"

"Well, I could… but how 'bout this instead: you just tell me where the children went, and I will not make a soup out of you."

"There is no need for hostility, friend. Simply take me out, and I will give you the information you want."

The wolf considers this, but time is passing quickly. Every minute wasted is precious.

Finally, a wild smile lights up the wolf's face, and he says, "Okay then, snake."

The wolf lifts the cage cover from its base. The snake remains still and says, "The coat, please. It is very co—"

But, before the snake can finish the sentence, a paw has him by the throat. The wolf picks the viper up in mid-air and snarls, "Where are they?"

The snake gasps for air.

"Tell me, snake, do you prefer to be souped or skewered?"

"Um, neither."

The wolf lowers his head, allowing his saliva to drip freely, and says, "Then tell me which way they went."

The snake considers his options. There aren't many. He tries to swallow but has cotton mouth. Finally, he says, "The cave. They must have gone into the cave because they didn't come through here."

"Thank you," says the wolf, but he doesn't let go.

"You can let go now. I told you where they went."

The wolf starts to let the snake go, but stops when his stomach rumbles. He thinks that perhaps a snack is in order.

"No. No, no. Please. I told you where they went."

The wolf is already licking his lips for a bite.

Chapter 70

After he's clear of the garden, Mason looks around confused. While taking out the map, he scans the new surroundings.

This room is a return to the darker rooms they had grown used to. There is just enough light for them to make out toys scattered every-where on the floor: bikes, scooters, a hula hoop, tin soldiers, dolls, and little model cars. In one corner of the room, casting a rather formidable shadow, is a gigantic shoe.

"Looks like a school yard. I don't think this is a grove," Scotty points out.

Mason retorts, "Ya think?"

Jack looks at Scotty, expecting the all-knowing declaration that this scene is in fact from the "Old Woman Who Lives in a Shoe." However, it does not come. Jack thinks, *Maybe Scotty is giving us a little credit to figure this one out on our own? But where are the kids?*Amy walks over to inspect the shoe from a short distance while the three boys, feeling no immediate threat, take a seat for a brief rest on the floor amongst the scattered toys. Scotty picks up a tin solider and examines it, and Mason quietly scans the map. Seeing the others occupied, Jack subtly removes the backpack from his shoulder and unzips it. He reaches in and runs his hand over the smooth shape of the goose. It is his prize. A thought crosses his mind: *If I had not gotten off of the ride to grab it, we would not be here now?*

The thought troubles him for a second. He glances nervously over to Amy, who is still staring the shoe up and down. Jack thinks, *What if*

Amy finds out? That would be bad, way bad. Maybe I should get rid of it"
He peers into the backpack and looks down at the golden statuette. The small goose glimmers in the dull light, and Jack marvels at his prop. A feeling of satisfaction overtakes the guilt. He contemplates, *No, this is quite a souvenir now. If we make it out of here alive, I'll at least have something to show for it.* He quickly zips up the backpack and steals a glimpse back at Amy, who turns and begins walking to the where the others sit. Jack hastily lifts the pack back over his shoulder.

With his evaluation of the map finished, Mason says to the others, "So here we are." He points out for all to see the small box labeled "The Shoe" on the map and adds, "I wonder who that shoe belongs to? What is it, a size 212?"

"It's from a story," Scotty advises.

"I know, Scotty, just making a joke, okay? Anyways…"

Mason looks at the map again and says, "Guys, we should have gone straight just like I thought, but we followed Scotty and we took a right."

"Wait a minute, I went the way you said," Scotty argues.

Jack can't help but be irritated at Mason, thinking, *Another reason we should not be following you.* He says, "Well, you have the map. Couldn't you tell we were going the wrong way?"

"Jack, we were kind of fighting off an attack from 12-foot tall plants, and I went the way she told us to go. I was only trying to get us outta there."

"*He's right,* thinks Jack. In spite of this, though, he can't help himself and says, "Well, maybe you should give me the map? Or better yet, let's just toss the thing and do this on our own."

Mason responds, "What's your deal, Braddock?" and stands up.

Scotty also stands, but he is uncomfortable by the rising tension and starts drifting toward the shoe.

Jack tells Mason, "My deal is that you're the one who decided that this map was legit, that if we followed—"

"Jack, you're just mad because we did what I wanted. You've been out of your head all night. You want to just settle this now?"

Mason drops the map to the floor and, clenching a fist in front of Jack's face, says, "Maybe if I beat some sense into you this—"

"Okay, that's enough!" interrupts Amy, who steps in between the two boys. She looks for backup from her older brother and spots him just as he is reaching for a small door on the side of the shoe.

Amy yells, "Scotty, get away from the door!"

Scotty stops. Temporarily, the actions of Scotty have restored order for Jack and Mason, who break their mutual glare. Mason gives one last scowl at Jack before turning fully toward Scotty.

"Geez, Scotty, what are you thinking? Who knows what's in there?"

"Well, I was thinking that since you two were arguing like babies, maybe there is an old woman in there, or some kids who could help us."

Both Mason and Jack are shocked by the scolding.

Amy says, "Like anyone in this crazy place has been helpful."

Scotty shrugs and backs away from the door. As he does so, a small golden handle begins to turn downward. He yells, "Someone is coming out!"

Mason raises the axe, Amy clutches the stick, and Scotty shuffles back behind the others, lifting Lucky like a shield. Jack, with no weapon in hand, slings his backpack from his shoulder and prepares to fling it.

The door opens slowly, and a large black boot emerges accompanied by a voice saying, "Greetings, travelers."

A man steps into the room. He is clad in a purple frock coat and red leggings, the kind of outfit Jack remembers from school trips to Shakespeare-type plays. His black hair is slicked back with some oily substance, and a pencil-thin mustache rests like an inchworm above his lip.

He proclaims, "You are most welcome here!"

Jack thinks, *That voice is familiar.* The stranger continues, "I bring you greetings from the Queen of the Wood. She is most pleased that you have finally arrived. We have all been waiting for you."

Jack realizes that this man is the one he heard in the vents talking to the woman.

"Have I startled you?" the man asks.

The group relax their weapons.

"No—well, yes," Jack confesses. "Uh, sir, who are you?"

"Oh, yes, let me introduce myself. My name is Victor. I am but a humble shoemaker, but I also serve our benevolent majesty, the Queen. I have been sent to give you aid on your journey."

"Our journey?" Amy questions.

"Yes, your journey. Your journey through the wood. The Queen has interest in seeing that you make it out unharmed."

Too late for that, Mason thinks.

"Because of that interest, I have been instructed to give you something that may help." Victor reaches into his purple frock coat and pulls out a velvet bag the size and shape of a baseball.

Mason cuts an angry eye toward Jack, places the axe back in his waist-line, and steps forward to take the pouch.

He asks, "What is this for?"

"All in good time."

"Are you going to lead us out?" Amy questions.

Victor gives a high-pitched laugh and then says, "Lead you out? I am afraid I cannot do that. The prophecy prevents…. But perhaps I have said too much."

"The prophecy?" Jack inquires.

"All in good time."

Mason asks, "Can we meet the Queen?"

"All in good—"

"Yes, *time*—I get it," Amy curtly says while fiddling with the end of her stick.

"Oh, such spunk—delightful! It is that kind of spunk that will aid you in your quest."

"We have a map," states Mason, a little too smug for Jack's liking, and offers up the map before the man.

"Oh, how wonderful! This will be a help indeed," informs Victor. With one of his white-gloved hands, he lifts it in front of his face, and after a brief examination, declares, "Excellent, excellent indeed. Why, I never knew a map of the wood existed."

The look on the man's face and his remark about the map strike Jack as a little dishonest. He thinks the man has seen the map before but wonders why he would lie about it.

Mason says, "We seem to have taken a wrong turn, in the garden, you see." Like a tourist holding up a map before a gas station attendant, Mason continues, "We are heading to this vault room."

"Splendid!"

"So that is where we should go?" Mason asks to confirm.

"All in good time."

Amy raises her hands in total frustration.

Mason goes on, "Yeah, okay, well we took a wrong turn here," pointing to the block marked "Garden."

"Ah, yes, Mary's garden. She steered you here? Well, that's simple. Merely do the opposite of what she says."

Scotty snaps his fingers and says, "Right, she is quite contrary. That's so obvious now."

Jack sees some hope and asks Victor, "Well, are you coming with us at least?"

"Mary does not hold me in high esteem. It seems during my last foray into the garden she claims I broke the stem of a dandelion."

"But that's a weed," Scotty declares.

"Oh yes, I know, but not to Mary. They are precious, living things. And to cut a long story short, because I did not do as she indicted, I agreed to never enter her garden again. Take courage, my friends. You are doing wonderful for yourselves. Think of how far you have come. You will be out of this place before you know it."

Mason raises his eyebrows and asks, "Uh, Victor, is there some treasure or something we have—"

"I have said too much. Simply take the pouch, conquer, and prevail, brave travelers! Luck to you all."

Before any of them can offer another question, the man disappears into the shoe.

"Okay, that was strange," Scotty declares.

Frustrated with the cryptic words of the man, Jack says, "I'm not done getting answers," and marches to the shoe and tugs on the handle.

It is locked.

Chapter 71

Mason holds the pouch in his hands, eyeing the purple bag and testing its weight. He likes the smooth velvety texture, and he rubs it between his hands while thinking, *There is certainly something in here.* "So what's in the bag?" Scotty asks as he saunters up alongside Mason.

"I don't know. Let's take a look," replies Mason, who hastily pulls a golden string that gathers the pouch together.

The binding loosens, and Mason, instead of emptying the contents into his palm for all to see, lifts the pouch up to his eye. He likes this effect, this mystery, this showmanship. After all, being the center of attention is in his blood. A wry smile emerges in the corners of his mouth. Holding his palm aloft, he makes a theatrical production out of emptying three small golden coins into his hand.

"Is that real gold?" Scotty asks.

"It has to be. Look at it—it's real." Mason responds.

He then lifts one of the coins to his mouth and bites it. He is not sure what he is supposed to find out from doing this, but he has seen it in the movies. The cold metal gives a little under the weight of his bite, and Mason is satisfied that the coin reacted exactly like the genuine article.

He continues, "I'll tell you another thing. This proves that there is treasure out there… lots of it. You heard that guy, uh, Victor. When I asked him about the treasure, he got all zipper-lipped."

"He did that with just about every question we asked, Mason," Amy reminds him.

Jack says, "I have to admit, it does feel good to actually meet someone or something not wanting to eat us for a change. I wonder what he meant with all of that prophecy stuff."

Mason cocks his head to one side, and in his best Victor voice, he states, "All in good time."

Amy rolls her eyes and feigns a gagging sound, but Scotty pays no attention to the quip because he has taken a coin from Mason and is admiring it. However, the joke actually makes Jack grin. Mason and Jack had been so close to a brawl not five minutes ago, but this was not unusual for the boys' relationship. Like five-year-old kids, they could hate each other one minute and then be friends the next. Still, Mason remains a little vexed at Jack's odd behavior, but he is willing to let it slide. That is, as long as Jack complies with his wishes.

"He said that those coins would help us. What did he mean by that?" Jack quizzes the others.

"All in good—"

"Give it a rest, Mason," Amy says and grabs the second coin from midair as Mason flips it. She asks, "Is there any writing on them or anything?"

Upon hearing the subject of coins, Scotty rejoins the conversation by saying, "No, not on mine. What about yours?"

"No," Amy responds.

"Well, if Victor said they would come in handy, I guess we should keep them safe." Mason concludes. Scotty and Amy agree and hand their coins back to Mason.

"Jack, you carry it," urges Mason. "You're the responsible one."

Mason knows the group will gel better if Jack is on board. So, for selfish reasons, Mason wants to make friends with Jack. His earlier attempt at humor was only the first salvo in the attempt to get things right. He offers the bag to Jack and wonders, *Will he take the bait?* "Sure, let's get moving," Jack says as he takes the velvet pouch.

Good, thinks Mason, *maybe he will get back to 'normal Jack.'*

Chapter 72

Jack wouldn't be able to explain why, but he can never stay mad at Mason Chick for very long. In sixth grade, Mason had written Jack a note from "Lauren Van Wormer." It read:

> *Hey! I like you. I would like to kiss you.*
> *Be my boyfriend. Meet me behind Bell Tower at recess.*
> *Wait for me there, no matter*
> *how long it takes me to get there.*

Of course, looking back on it now, Jack sees the complete and utter idiocy of his failure to realize it was a joke. He should have known based on the caveman-like dialect. Yet, he did fall for it and stayed standing behind the Bell Tower for two hours after recess. Mr. Darby, the computer teacher, found him after the entire Polk Middle School faculty had been on a "Jack search." Jack missed a pop quiz, and because he would not tell the teachers why he was there, he got a zero. The zero subsequently cost him TV and Xbox for one week. His mom doesn't mind an occasional "C," but a zero is out of the question.

His classmates of course knew exactly where Jack had been after Mason shared the brilliance of his plan with just about the entire school in the bus line. Jack was so mad at Mason that he did not speak to him for all of 20 hours. In spite of the brutal punishment, and the embarrassment, Jack could not possibly stay mad at Mason. All it took was Mason handing him a powdered donut as he walked onto the bus the next morning and all had been forgiven. In fact, Jack congratulated Mason on the prank. Jack does love a well-played prank.

Despite their disagreement on the validity of following the map, the encounter with Victor is the encouragement Jack needs to go along with his friend for now. Victor had made a big deal about the map.

"All right," Jack declares. "Time to visit our friend Mary. You guys know what to do."

"Yep, remember, go the opposite of whichever way she says," Scotty reminds the crew.

The door gently opens as Mason gives it a careful shove. Amy, who is last, has not even fully entered the room when a squealing, yelling, panic-stricken voice yelps, "Intruders, hostiles, interlopers! Get out, get out, get out! You will ruin my garden. Ruin it, ruin it, ruin it!"

Before they had entered the room, the group had rehearsed what they would say to Mary. This time, Mason, speaking in a monotone voice all together unlike anything Jack had ever heard before, says, "Mary, we are leaving."

In spite of the tension, Jack can't help but chuckle at Mason. He is possibly the worst actor in the history of the art. His voice sounds like he is reading straight from a cue card.

Mason goes on, "You had better tell us where 'The Grove' is, or I will take this axe—"

"Not sure if she can see us, dude," Jack whispers.

"I'm holding an axe! With this axe—that I am holding—I will chop down your precious little plants."

Mason looks to the others for approval. Scotty gives him a thumbs-up, Jack nods, and Amy giggles silently with a hand over her mouth.

Suddenly, there is a shriek followed by a howling, "Noooooooooooooo oooooooooooooooooooo!"

From their immediate right, the woman—now wild and red-faced—runs at them fullsteam ahead at a pace that could compete with the bear and the snake's. She is the complete picture of fury, charging from behind the foliage with a large shovel in hand while screaming a battle cry. Mason is forced to lift up the axe in defense as her shovel swings down. The collision of the two instruments produces a dull thud.

Although she is shocked and stunned at the charge of the woman, Amy swivels her head just in time to see a giant Venus Flytrap lunging at her. Amy ducks and leafy jaws crack shut above her head. Another Flytrap wraps a green stem around the legs of Scotty. The boy loses balance and slams down hard on the floor, giving a yelp of pain because of his shoulder. Jack is dizzy by the sudden chaos all around him, but is able to focus enough to help Amy.

"You will not harm my garden!" the woman howls in rage.

"Lady, we don't want to. We just…." leaves off Mason, who has to stop speaking and back away in order to avoid impact from another swing of Mary's shovel.

Meanwhile, Scotty has been lifted high in the air, and the boy's body is dangling over an open-mouthed carnivorous plant. At the same time, another Venus Flytrap lashes out and succeeds in closing around the legs of Jack, who has pushed Amy out of the way.

"Jack, no!" Amy cries.

"The stick! Hit it with the stick, Amy!" Jack yells.

Another green stem reaches out to capture Mason from behind. As the vine wraps around his chest, Mason reaches out and grabs it.

Mary is rearing back her arms, preparing for another swing at Mason. He tells her, "I'll chop it in half, if you make another move."

She stops. The shovel lowers.

Mason orders, "Make your plants back off!"

The woman looks at Mason with a hate so intense that Jack thinks her eyes might actually shoot fire. Then, in an instant, a smile crosses her face, and she whistles.

Scotty is gently lowered to the ground, and Jack's enclosed legs are free. The plants, in obedience, shrink back to their original positions.

"Now, you tell us where to go, and we will leave. It's that easy," explains Mason.

"Why didn't you simply ask, my darling children?"

"We did," Mason reminds her.

"Oh, sure you did, sweetie," says Mary in a tone that sounds like a southern belle. However, this change in demeanor has made Mary seem no less creepy to the group as the shovel-swinging lady they encountered earlier.

Mary continues, "Listen, when you get over to the tulip poplars, turn right."

"No funny business, lady!" Scotty cries while holding his aching shoulder. "Or my associate goes choppy-choppy."

Jack is a little surprised by the intensity of Scotty's tone.

"Of course," Mary says. "Why would I ever harm any of you precious pumpkins? Just do as I say and you will be out lickety-split."

Amy grabs onto Jack's hand and says, "Let's go."

He had temporarily forgotten how nice it felt to have her fingers interlocked with his.

The group heads for the tulip poplars and then left.

"I said 'right!'" yells Mary.

Vines suddenly begin to trail toward them.

"Run!" Jack cries.

With the door in sight, the four race toward it, dancing around vines and dodging shooting darts from a bamboo plant. Finally, they smash through the door it into another room.

Chapter 73

The group is now in the Grove. The room is dark except for a dull glowing light that exudes from the windows of a small little cabin tucked away in the corner.

The well-studied map has shown the travelers that they are now on the right path. They should take a door that is straight ahead, although the path there may not be a straight one since trees and stumps are littered around the room. Jack thinks that, if not for the danger lurking around every corner, this might have made a nice romantic spot for Amy and him, whose hands are still clasped while they deliberately trail behind the others. As horrifying as things have been, Amy and Jack feel that at least this part of the experience is exciting and fun. Still, every time Mason or Scotty turns to speak to either of them, they separate their hands as if they had been caught in the cookie jar.

Although the cabin looks interesting, Jack realizes there is no reason to check it out. All he wants to do now is simply follow the map, get to the doors, and finish this deal.

"Maybe we should check out the cabin," Mason says.

Jack thinks, *Oh, just great. I am in no mood to argue anymore.* He clinches Amy's hand and gives her a look, trying to encourage her to take up his argument for him.

Getting the hint, she asks, "Shouldn't we just get through the next set of doors?"

"Amy, if we get to the vault and don't have the key, what good is that going to do?" Mason counters.

Jack realizes, *That's true. Mason is making some really good arguments. Perhaps he's right? Maybe the narrator is not helping us? Bedsides how long had it been since—*

> "Perilous trails and plants that bite.
> Two friends that avoid a fight.
> Voices want their way, they shout.
> Only the end will see them out.
> A foolish choice has been made.
> Retrace their steps for the price must be paid.
> But, for now, keep eyes set on high.
> Danger, which lurks, their success to deny."

Did I just will that to happen? wonders Jack.

"Hey, the marrator. More gobbledygook," calls Mason.

After scanning the room, Jack spots a narrator robot beside the doors on the opposite wall, but he asks himself, *Was that there before?*

"Okay, Mason, you have to know he's talking about us now for sure," Jack says casually, trying his best not to sound argumentative. "'Two friends that avoid a fight'? It said we made a poor choice; he wants us to follow his direction. Maybe we should go back?"

This last question has pushed too far, though. Mason glowers at Jack and states, "We are not going back."

Quickly retreating from the confrontation, Jack flippantly asks, "What do you think he meant with that last part?"

"I don't know, Jack? I get it—whatever it is, whoever he is—it's talking about us. I give in. But he can talk about us all he wants, that doesn't change the fact that we need a key, a treasure, and an exit. And I am willing to bet if we are going to find the key, it will be somewhere like that," says Mason while pointing to the cabin. He begins making a direct path toward it.

Jack thinks, *No use arguing any further. It would only spoil the peace.* Scotty sees Mason heading toward the shack and follows initially, but then stops.

Amy and Jack, who are just behind Scotty and enjoying the lack of attention, walk up behind him.

"What are you looking at?" Amy asks her brother.

"You guys gonna join me?" Mason inquires. He is already at the porch of the cabin.

"Hold on, Mason. Scotty sees something," Jack calls.

Scotty says, "Look at that stump, or mushroom. Whatever it is, it looks…. Wait a minute. It's pretty dark over there. Jack, shine the flashlight over."

Scotty walks toward the object of his attention and says, "Looks like someone's thrown out a little bowl here on the ground."

The flashlight clicks on, and Jack swings it over to Scotty.

"Oh man, guys, this one's easy. This is curds and whey!" Scotty announces proudly.

Scotty walks back over to Jack and hands him the bowl. Jack does not look at the contents but flashes his light around the room instead. After arching the flashlight up and down, he finally sees something near the ceiling: eight little glowing orbs descending from above the mushroom-like stool.

168

Chapter 74

Jack drops the bowl to the ground and yells, "Let's get out of here!" as the giant spider is lowering itself towards him.

From the steps of the shack, Mason runs towards the commotion and sees the spider for himself. He takes out the axe and heaves it at the eight-legged monster. However, He misses badly, and the axe crashes into the far wall.

"The door—get to the door!" Jack yells.

Without wasting any more time, all four of them make a quick dash for the door on the far side of the room.

The spider is slow and deliberate as if it knows something the others do not.

Amy reaches the door first, but is unable to open it. She announces, "It's locked."

"What?" questions Jack. He frantically shoves at the door before confirming that Amy is right.

Jack feels a wisp of air above his head and hears a dull thud against the door. He realizes that the spider is shooting webbing at them.

"What do we do?" Scotty asks while looking at Mason.

The spider is now on the floor inching toward them. Jack notices that the bowl is a few feet in front of the menace, and he decides to run and grab it.

"Jack!" Amy calls as she watches him run right at the spider.

Before the spider can reach it, Jack picks it up and hurls the dish and its contents at the spider. It is a direct hit, and the thick curds and whey blankets several of the glowing eyes.

"To the shack! If it's locked, we'll bust through the window—come on!" Jack commands.

As they sprint to the porch of the shack, a shot of webbing just misses Amy's feet.

Jack grips the doorknob and turns it while crashing his shoulder into the door, praying that it will give. It does, and all four move into the protection of the cabin.

Chapter 75

Five frustrated parents, some kids, one sulking teenager, and a handful of park employees stand outside the Dark Ride. All of them are looking intently at Howard Snodgrass.

Why me? thinks Snodgrass. It is a question he has asked himself multiple times over the last seven years. He wonders, *How many worthless nights have I spent babysitting this worthless park?*

Facing the crowd, he says, "Look, my employees are doing everything in their power to see that the kids get safely outside."

He feels he has already answered the same 20 questions multiple times: first from the Carnahans, then from the Chick guy in his tailored business suit, followed by the Braddock couple, who arrived last with their silent, brooding teenage daughter.

Howard reassures everyone again, saying, "Just stay calm. There is no need for panic. This kind of thing happens all the time." He has already said that same line six times tonight. This time, he adds, "Your little darlings are totally safe."

"Look, Howard," says Titus Chick while sending a menacing look his way. "These *things,* as you say, may happen all the time, but not to my son. I don't think you realize who you are dealing with."

Actually, Howard knows exactly whom he is dealing with. Everyone in Cassidy Falls is well aware of the Chick law firm.

The lawyer continues, "How do you lose track of four teenagers for well over two hours in a ride? You are aware that this has lawsuit written all over it—especially if this happens all the time? I'll tack on negligence for fun."

The other parents all nod in agreement.

Howard wonders why he had ever been sent to this forsaken place. He recalls that one day he was working as supervisor of the mailroom at the Newcastle Group home office in Annapolis when his father, the CEO, had promised great things, telling him, "Howard, we've got a special assignment for you. We've purchased an amusement park in Tennessee. We would like you to oversee the operations."

What Howard did not know was that the assignment was simply a way for his dad to ship off his spoiled deadbeat son.

The happiest day of Howard Snodgrass's life had been the day he heard that they were tearing down Storybook Hollow. He had badgered his father on the phone nearly every day since the announcement of the park's closing, and he had been promised another assignment once the faltering park closed its doors for good.

"Have you called the police?" Wallace Braddock asks.

"The police? Are you not listening to me? Your kids are going to be out any minute. It's a building—where could they have gone?"

"I don't know," replies a combative Houston Carnahan, raising his voice. "Isn't that your job to figure out?"

My job? thinks Snodgrass. This is all the frustrated man can take. He declares, "My job is not to play mama bird to some reckless teenagers. Have you considered that they are the ones who are sneaking around there in my ride unattended? Do you know what unsupervised teenagerss do? And I'm happy to counter-sue for any damages inside the ride and anything that's missing."

A whirlwind of escalating voices erupt from the mouths of each and every one of the parents. Seeing that his last comment pushed too far, Howard nervously grabs his phone, pretending to get a phone call.

"Sorry, excuse me, uh, I have to get this. Gwen, see that the parents get some free popcorn or something. Back in a flash."

Snodgrass marches back behind a food stand a few steps away. He can hear the incredulous cries and has no intention of rushing the pretend phone call.

"Can I get anyone some popcorn?" Gwen asks, but the offer goes over like a resounding belch at a funeral.

A red-faced Titus Chick reaches for his phone while the Braddocks and Carnahans begin talking to Gwen, grilling her with the same set of questions they had asked Snodgrass.

Meanwhile, Howard thinks, *Safe for now. Geez, Clyde, hurry up and get those teenagers outta there.*

Chapter 76

Inside the cabin, the four teens are panting in relief. Amy senses tears welling up inside her. The outward toughness she has shone all night is beginning to unravel. At this point, she does not care who leads them, nor does she care what advice they follow. All she wants to do is get out of this place alive. It has been one thing after another, and on top of everything else, she's nervous about a giant spider that's wanting to eat them.

Nervous, on edge, and pushed beyond the limits that anyone can expect of a thirteen-year-old girl, she begins to cry.

Scotty sees his sister with her head lowered in her hands and attempts to calm her.

"Amy, we're okay. We made it past. We are safe."

"Yeah. For now, we're safe… until someone comes out of the kitchen with a knife or something to chop us into little bits. What then?"

She looks up. Jack and Mason are staring at her. Each is looking as dumfounded as the other. Wiping the tears from her face, she straightens a bit.

Jack places a reassuring hand on her shoulder and says, "Come on, Amy. None of us is going to let anything happen to you. Now let's figure out what's in this shack and come up with a plan on how to get through the doors out there and past that spider."

Amy nods, appreciating Jack's reassurance, even though she remains no more comforted about their situation. She simply does not want to cry anymore in front of Jack.

"Guys, I know some of you…" Jack says, looking at Mason but keeping his voice very non-combative, "are not really wanting to listen to the narrator, but we really need to pay attention. I mean he did say something like, 'eyes set on high.' He was warning us about the spider."

Amy sees Mason nod. Even he must relent that Jack is right. Her eyes readjust to the light of the room. It is well lit, and to the mutual shock of all of the party, it is elegant. Judging by the looks of the outside of the cabin, Amy had expected to find a litany of taxidermy deer heads and fishing trophies. Instead, a fine oriental rug covers a shiny hardwood floor, a grand piano in the corner, and a chandelier hangs down above an elaborate dining room set in the middle of the floor. In the back of the room, there is a door.

If she didn't know any better, Amy could have believed she was standing in her own grandmother's house—squarely in the center of the room that no child was ever permitted to play.

Oddly, her thoughts take her back to a day when Scotty had gotten the only spanking she had ever seen her grandmother dole out. They were playing hide-and-seek that day. Scotty was eight, and she was seven. The kids' Grammy was known for second helpings, surprise gifts, doting wet kisses, and free access to the pantry, but she also had one rule in her house for her grandchildren: do not step foot in the china room. Up until this particular day, Amy actually couldn't recall ever having seen anyone inside the room except for her grandmother, who would tediously vacuum the room with ritualistic precision. However, on this day, Scotty ignored the rules and hid under the glass-topped coffee table, which sat beside an old grandfather clock that chimed hauntingly every 15 minutes. Because the room was indeed off-limits, Amy did not bother to look there. After being unable to find him, she asked her grandpa if he had seen the boy, and, apparently, Grammy overheard the question. Like a cop on patrol, her face grew rigid and suspicious. She stomped over to her china room and called out, "Scotty Hubert Carnahan! Show yourself this instant."

Amy had never heard this tone from Grammy. It was disturbing, but not nearly as disturbing as what happened next. The little boy crept from under the coffee table, and as he did so, a plate on display was jolted by one of his flailing arms. With a crash, the plate shattered. In an instant, the frail and loving Grammy transformed into a frightening persona, like the Grim Reaper. With lightning-fast reflexes, far beyond Amy's imagination for the 60-plus-year-old woman, she vaulted into the room, lifted Scotty by the ear, dragged him out into the den, and carried out corporal punishment.

Amy remembers feeling a mixture of comedy, from seeing Scotty splayed out over her Grammy's knees, and terror, from seeing the old woman deliver the punishment.

As soon as it was over, smiling, good-natured Grammy returned and said, "Now, you kiddos stay out of the china room."

There was no need to tell either of them, ever again.

The room in the shack, complete with a grandfather clock that ticks and tocks, reminds Amy of the china room. However, there is one difference: the hands on this clock seem to be moving around the face with rapid speed.

Chapter 77

Jack desperately wants to console Amy further. He wants to wrap his arms around her and teleport them away from all this. When looking at her face, still glistening with tears, he has to keep himself from rushing to her. Jack focuses on her eyes, and he wonders, *What is she staring at?* His eyes follow hers to the face of the grandfather clock. The arms are rapidly turning around the face.

Scotty and Mason are examining the table setting.

Scotty inquires, "Think there's something to eat in here?"

Mason responds, "How can you think of eating at a time like this? Oh, I guess you always think of eating," and jabs at Scotty's belly. Scotty feigns a smile.

"Guys, look at the clock," Jack says.

Mason looks and says, "Great, looks like it's 12:30. Man, we've been in here a long time."

Jack corrects, "It's not 12:30 or 12:40. No, the hands—look."

As the small hand clicks over to the Roman numeral one, a long chime strikes. From the top of the clock, three mice run down the side of the frame to the floor.

"The clock strikes one! Hickory, dickory, dock," Scotty announces and lets a small laugh escape.

"Well, unless they have guns that we can't see or razor-sharp piranha teeth, maybe they won't come after us," Mason jokes.

Jack watches the mice carefully. There was a small amount of ominous truth in Mason's words, although he half expects the mice to grow into monstrous carnivores. To his relief, the mice scamper away from them, but something is odd. The small rodents keep bouncing into walls and crashing into each other it is as if they can't see.

Then Jack realizes, *Three blind mice, of course.*Suddenly, the back door swings open. A large woman with a white apron storms into the room. Mason and Scotty run back to Jack and Amy, expecting the worst. Wild-eyed and open-mouthed, the large woman wields a knife in her hand. Ignoring the teenagers, the robust woman scurries around the room after the mice. Like the world's largest cat, she nimbly catches each mouse by the tail. Holding the mice with one beefy hand and brandishing the knife in the other, she turns to the back door.

As she opens it to leave she stops, looks back, and says, "You need to leave now." And with that, the door closes behind her.

"Oh man, I would hate to be one of those mice," Mason remarks. "She was not messing around."

"Well, I guess we need to leave," Jack declares.

Amy's in total shock. She declares, "See? I told you. Someone would come out of the kitchen with a knife."

"But she wasn't after us," Scotty points out.

However, his words don't really calm Amy.

Nervously, Jack spies the clock. The hands are moving rapidlyit's already 3:00. He thinks, *If the clock strikes one again with us in here, who knows what will happen.*

In response to Jack's earlier suggestion, Mason states, "But what about the spider? I think we should stay. I would rather deal with her than that thing."

Jack counters, "We're going to have to get past him somehow. Let's go out the back door and try to sneak around it."

Mason retorts, "But the door is locked, and the only other exit is back to that garden."

Jack thinks, *Why won't he listen to me? Tick, tick, tick.*

Scotty and Mason decide to make a sweep of the room. Before long, they are engaged in another conversation about Scotty's weight. Meanwhile, Jack notices that the butcher knife is still on the table and thinks, *Now that's just plain crazy. What kind of bizarre magic is this? That could come in handy.* He broods over the knife, evaluating whether he should take it or not. Then he grabs it.

Looking up, he sees the disapproving face of Amy. She has been watching him.

"You can't take it," she utters.

"Why not?"

"She has to have it… or she'll come looking for you, don't you think? We've already got a wolf and now a spider after us, but we were warned in the map, about the glowing orbs and the fiery lass. She looked pretty fiery to me. You steal her knife, and it could be trouble."

Looking back at the knife, Jack is torn. He has already stolen something tonight, and the guilt has been gnawing at him. However, he also feels that the knife could come in handy.

Chapter 78

His conscience gets the best of him, and Jack somewhat reluctantly places the knife back down on the table. He tells Amy, "You're right, we don't need another enemy. There's enough to go around in this place." Then, interrupting Scotty and Mason's discussion, he calls out, "Okay, you guys ready to roll?"

"Not with that eight-legged creature out there," Mason says.

"Maybe if we can sneak around the spider, then we can work the door open? We've got the hammer. Mason, we can't be in here when she comes back; you saw her."

Even though Jack's solution is far from ideal, the group, including Mason, knows it may be their only hope.

"Okay, Jack, I'm game," Mason says and pulls the hammer from the work belt now tied around his waist.

"Good. Finally, he sees something my way," Jack says to himself.

Mason continues, "Maybe I can grab the axe if I see it? Amy, keep that stick handy. If the spider sees us, you may have to go all Ted Williams on him."

"Who's Tim Williams?" Scotty asks.

Mason rolls his eyes and says, "A baseball legend. Played for Boston back in… oh, never mind."

Tick, tick, tick. The hands on the clock are at 11.

Jack announces, "Time to move, guys. Out the door, go. But be quiet."

The last to walk back out into the Grove is Jack, but before he does so, he decides to take another look at the knife. However, it's gone. He thinks this is odd, but he goes ahead and walks out of the cabin and quietly closes the door.

The group is behind the cabin, and there is no sign of the spider. With his back leaning against the cabin and taking one small step after another, Mason peeks around the corner.

"Any sign of anything?" Jack whispers.

"Nope. No woman, no spider."

"Good, just take your time—"

A pebble lands next to Jack. Not a muscle in Jack's body moves at first. He has no desire to look up, but he knows he must. Taking a quick glance to the roof, Jack yells, "Spider!"

Everyone looks up and sees the spider looking down on them with those eight glowing orbs.

Without a moment to lose, they bolt for the door, caution and silence being thrown out the window. Jack avoids a giant spider web that is draped from a tree. Then he looks back and sees the enormous spider that has a body so large it makes the cabin look like a play toy.

Mason makes it to the door but declares, "It won't budge!"

Pulling on Mason's arms, the two boys use all their strength in a desperate attempt at forcing the door open. Jack turns to get a gauge on the spider's location, and his eyes are met by a terrifying sight: Amy is caught in the large web. She had not seen it during their flight to the door.

Forgetting the door, Jack instinctively runs to her. He thinks, *That knife! I If only I had that knife!*The spider is drawing closer to the door. A shot of liquid flies past Jack's head and hits the door just above Mason.

"Get me out of here Jack!" Amy cries.

Jack lunges toward her. He tries to pull her away and calls out, "Help, Scotty, she's stuck! Help me!"

The web is so sticky thatJack's arm gets caught in it. Another volley of webbing then strikes Jack, and he has only one arm free. His flailing only gets him more tangled. Scotty has not come to assist Jack, and, now, the spider is almost upon them. Jack takes the flashlight and flings it at the monster. It makes a dull thud but has no effect. The creature continues to lumber forward toward its prey.

Jack says, "Your stick, Amy! Can you give me the stick?"

"No, it's stuck, too."

"Maybe I can fight him off," Jack says. He looks at the menacing giant, and just over its head, Jack sees a ray of light enter the room. He realizes that someone is coming through the door and hopes that maybe it will be someone who can help.

Struggling, Jack arches his neck to see the possible rescuer. He realizes it's the wolf and that the situation has just gone from bad to horrible.

Chapter 79

Scotty has heard Jack's cry, and he sees his sister caught in the web. His body wants to respond, but his legs are frozen to the floor. Even as the ominous hulking spider draws closer to Amy and Jack, fear deprives Scotty of his will. And as if a gigantic arachnid were not enough, a new player has entered the mix: a six-foot-tall wolf.

"Scotty, snap out of it!" Mason cries.

Scotty stutters, "Ma-Ma-Ma-Mason—the wolf!"

Mason, who has been working on the door, turns around and sees the wolf. He doubles his efforts with the door and says, "Scotty, help the others! Now—go!"

Scotty thinks to himself, *You coward. You can do this, Scotty. You have to do this.* He knows he must do something, but he's praying that somehow Jack can free his sister.

"Scotty, for crying out loud!" Mason screams.

The wolf rushes through the room, heading for Amy, and the scene before Scotty is amplified terror. In an instant, the spider turns away from its prey in the web after it becomes aware of the pounding footsteps from behind. A jutting spray of the sticky webbing hits the wolf in the chest, ensnaring both of his arms, and he falls to the ground due to the impact. Then another shot of webbing wraps around his legs.

Upon seeing the distracted spider, whatever mental chains once held Scotty to the floor unshackle. He runs to Amy and Jack. However, the spider whirls again, this time toward Scotty. Unaware that he has been marked, Scotty falls face-first to the ground after a thin rope of the webbing encircles his ankles.

"Oww!" yells Scotty.

His shoulder throbs. Scotty turns to see the spider slowly approaching him. It is making low clicking and gurgling noises while frothy white bubbles seep from its horrid mouth. Scotty knows that after it makes a few more steps, he'll be done for.

Then he remembers, *The scissors!* Scotty rolls onto his side and reaches into his shorts' pocket, searching desperately for the scissors, but his fingers tickle a small vial instead. He had forgotten about the vial.

Scotty yanks the vial from his pocket and attempts to hurl the vial, but it's no use. The pain in his shoulder will not allow him to make a good throw with his right arm. He considers throwing with his left, but he realizes that he has not thrown anything with his left arm since shattering Mr. Turner's windshield in third grade. Scotty tries again with his right arm, but the pain is too intense. He knows he will have to do it left-handed, but for greater accuracy, he decides to wait until the spider is closer.

Scotty thinks, *A little further. A little further.* Amy screams, "Scotty, move!"

The spider picks up speed toward Scotty, and just before it strikes, Scotty throws the vial.

Chapter 80

It's a direct hit. The vial breaks into a dozen tiny shards, and the contents of the potion spill onto the spider. Immediately, an orange vapor emits around the head of the spider. As the orange mist wraps and shifts around the entire body of the monster, a stunning transformation occurs. The giant spider begins to shrink. Jack watches in jubilation as the spider reduces, becoming smaller and smaller. But, he begins to get nervous when the cloud inches closer to Scotty. Before the orange mist can shroud him, though, Scotty rolls away. Then he pulls out his scissors and goes to work on the webbing.

"Jack—the spider! Scotty did—uh, Scotty threw—uh, Scotty shrank the spider!" Amy calls to Jack.

He glances at Amy, grinning at Scotty's heroics, and says, "I saw it."

Jack turns back to the spider and can now barely make out the eight-legged fiend. In spite of its rapidly dissipating size, the spider makes a final lunge at Scotty, who gets the webbing off his feet just in time to kick the creature, now about the size of a football, across the room.

It lands near the wolf.

"Look guys, this way!" Mason calls. He is standing with hammer in hand before an open door. However, the others cannot join him yet because Amy is still tied up.

At the same time, the wolf, who has managed to free an arm, is now crawling toward Amy.

"Jack—the wolf!" Amy screams as the predator inches towards her.

Scotty hurries over to Jack and Amy and begins snipping away at their bindings with his scissors. Mason also joins them to lend his support while being careful to avoid becoming ensnared in the same webbing.

Still, the wolf continues his desperate crawl. His green eyes are burning, remaining focused on Amy.

Mason and Scotty manage to free Jack and Amy, and Jack utters, "Thanks guys" as they rush toward the door.

None of them want to spend one more second in the Grove.

Chapter 81

In the next room, the four teens squat with hands on hips, sucking in whatever oxygen they can.

"Is every room going to be a trial like that?" Jack moans to himself.

"Did you see the size of his teeth?" Scotty asks in a gasping voice.

"Whose teeth, wolf or spider?" Jack answers.

Amy proudly hugs her brother and says, "Scotty, thank you. You really saved us back there."

In agreement, Jack extends a hand to Scotty and says, "Thanks, man."

Jack and Amy turn to Mason, waiting for his show of thanks to Scotty. Instead, the older boy asks, "What took you so long back there, man? Amy and Jack could have been toast, or eggs. Well, actually, probably bacon. I'm hungry. We need to get out of here or find some food."

Mason trudges off, and Scotty's once-beaming face falls.

Jack comes to Scotty's defense by saying, "Come on, Mason, we got out of there didn't we?"

Scotty takes of his glasses and fiddles with them. His mouth is tight, and his eyes are squinting. Jack realizes that he's thinking about something and says to himself, *Come on, Scotty, give Mason a piece of your mind.* "He's right. Sorry, guys, I really froze," Scotty apologizes.

Amy gives Mason a scolding look and says, "Are you forgetting that he did not let us die. If it wasn't for whatever he did to that spider…. Of all the nerve, Mason Chick…."

Waving his arms in the air, Jack interrupts, "Okay, okay. Scotty, how did you do that to the spider? It just, like, shrunk."

After relating the story of how he found the shrinking potion, Scotty's confidence is restored.

"We're not out of the woods yet, guys," Mason points out.

Although the pun was not intentional, Mason's point is valid, and Jack knows it. With every new room, new danger awaits.

Jack looks around at their current surroundings while Mason whips out the map from the work belt.

"Looks like we are back on track," Mason informs. "We need to go left, through those doors at the end of the room."

The room is, of course, dark. The walls are almost black and the center is not much lighter. Still, the group can tell that more stumps litter this room and another set of doors to the right is barely visible.

"Looks as if a lumberjack went to town in here," Jack notes.

"Either that or eight-foot-tall beavers," Mason quips.

From the far end of the room, the group begins to hear a humming noise. It's not a mechanical noise, but an actual human sound. Jack eventually recognizes the tune as "Frère Jacques." After turning his eyes to the dark corner of the room, he barely makes out two small legs, which are just visible below the knees. The rest of the body is shrouded in the shadows.

"Hello?" Jack calls. By this point, the others also see the focus of Jack's call.

There is no answer, but the humming continues.

"Excuse us, but…." Scotty beckons.

The humming continues.

"Let's just go," Amy says while pushing at Jack's side.

Jack, Amy, and Scotty prepare to simply avoid the person and walk out the door at the left end of the room. Mason, however, does not move an inch because he is obviously curious.

All of a sudden, the humming stops, and the legs start to move.

The three who are leaving stop their momentum. Even their breathing seems to halt.

Then, from the shadows, a small girl emerges. She is clad in a tattered smock dress, which at one point must have been white, although large brown streaks and yellowing stains have overtaken the garment. The girl's face is ruddy, smeared with what appears to be dried mud, and medium-length tangled brown hair hangs from her head. The entire package is creepy, but none of her unkempt features can take the group's attention away from the empty look on her expressionless face or her pair of haunting blue eyes.

The girl takes another step toward them and stops. She levels her hands at her chest and fiddles with a small brown box the size of a domino, but she never takes her eyes off them as she begins to hum another bar of her haunting tune. With one hand, she pulls a match across the box. Fire begins to sizzle at the end of the stick and casts a flickering shadow across her face. The effect is beyond disturbing.

The humming stops, as if the flame provides a solace for her. The girl now watches the fire burn, and no one is sure whether to move or not.

Just before the light burns out, she asks, "Would you like to buy some matches?"

The light fades out. She begins humming again, "Frère Jacques, frère Jacques...."

Chapter 82

Although Amy feels this is the creepiest display the group has seen in any of the rooms, she can't help but feel some empathy for the girl and wonders, *Is she trapped in here, too?* Amy begins walking toward the girl, but is halted by the extended arm of Jack. Amy shoots Jack a quizzical look, but there is no sternness in Jack's face. Amy understands his intent and rethinks her decision to go to the girl.

Instead, she calls to her, "Um, little girl, what are you doing here?"

There is no verbal response or even a hint of recognition that she has been spoken to. The creepy little girl simply strikes another match and waits as the light flickers out.

"Are you trapped?" Scotty asks.

Again, she stands motionless. Here pale blue eyes are staring not at the teens but at some empty void.

"So, this is interesting," Scotty says, breaking the tension. "Maybe we should be moving on then, right guys?"

"Right," Jack confirms.

"No, not yet," Mason retorts. "What's she doing? Why is she here?"

Amy wants so desperately for the girl to say something else, thinking it would be nice to converse with another female after being cooped up in the building with boys all night. Also, for all Amy knows, this seemingly frail little girl could have wandered into this world just like they had and is now defenseless in this horrible place.

Amy urges, "Please, talk to us. Are you lost?"

Again, nothing.

"All righty then. That settles it. Scotty, shall we?" Jack asks and takes a large, deliberate step to the left side of the room.

The girl strikes a match. Then a blink of something in her registers. In a tiny, breathy voice, she whispers from her chapped lips, "No, just waiting."

All four of them are startled at the sudden eerie voice of the girl.

"Uh, waiting? Waiting for who?" Amy asks in the sweetest voice she can muster.

"My grandmother."

"On, no," Scotty utters in a flash of recognition.

"What?" Jack asks with more than a little trepidation.

Scotty grabs his friends by their arms and starts dragging them toward the door. He says, "We gotta leave right now."

Chapter 83

Mason fights off Scotty's hold on him and says, "What're you talking about? It's a little girl."

"Hans Christian Anderson," Scotty whispers.

"Hands, wrist, and who?" Mason asks.

This time, Scotty enunciates, "Hans Christian Anderson."

Mason blows through his lips, making a dismissive sound, and says, "So what?"

"Well," Scotty says, "if you knew anything about children's literature, which you don't, you would know that in most of Anderson's tales somebody ends up dead."

Jack likes Scotty's verbal jab against Mason, although this information is unsettling.

Up to this point in the group's conversation, the girl has continued humming. Then suddenly, she strikes a match and goes quiet until it burns out. Afterward, she resumes humming again.

"Um, I'm with Scotty," Amy states.

Jack gulps and looks around the room, suspecting an attack from some unknown assailant. For the first time, he notices that the ground appears scorched. Also, in clusters around various stumps near the darkened corners of the room, blackened bones are visible.

Jack looks at Scotty, points to the charred remains, and infers, "She burned them, huh?"

Scotty solemnly nods his head until the flick of a match is lit, at which point the group looks over at the girl.

Once again, she asks, "Would you like to buy some matches?"

Jack, wide-eyed, looks at Amy.

"Why would we want to buy matches?" Mason asks dismissively.

Amy and Scotty start backing toward the door, and Amy asks, "Jack? Leaving?"

"Yes, like now," Jack answers.

"Would you like to buy some matches?" the girl repeats, but this time there is a little more vigor in her voice.

"Uh, no," Mason replies firmly.

The girl takes a step toward Mason.

"Give her some money. Give her money!" Scotty chirps.

Jack whips his backpack around a digs through its contents for a dollar bill. Holding it out to the girl, he says, "Here, yes, sold!"

However, the girl's mouth turns down at the corners, and her brow creases in apparent anger.

Jack grabs another dollar and asks, "Is this enough?"

The girl takes another step, and her pale face begins to show a tint of red.

There is obvious rage building inside the girl, and she says, "You should buy some matches."

Mason demands, "What do you want? He gave you like—"

"The pouch!" Amy says and jabs her hand into Jack's pocket to retrieve what Victor had given to them.

"Hey!" Jack objects, but the small girl is directly in front of him now with her hand on another match. She has started humming again, and her tune sounds forced and foreboding.

The girl strikes a match and raises it before Jack, who lifts a hand instinctively. The flickering flame licks the base of his palm, and he cries out, "Hey! What do you think...?" Jack pulls his stinging palm back and raises it to his mouth.

Amy raises three small coins from the pouch in front of the girl's face and says, "Here."

The girl takes her other hand and places her thumb and index finger over the burning match end, snuffing the flame. Then, after lowering both hands, she turns to face Amy and takes the coins. From an unseen pouch in her dress, she produces a small matchbox and hands it to Amy, who in turn gives it to Scotty to place in his cavernous pockets.

In a zombie-like trance, the girl walks over to a stump, sits down, and stares into an empty void.

Jack looks at the bewildered face of Mason and questions, "Now we go?"

"Now we go," Mason confirms.

The group heads for the doors on the left end of the room. As they pass through them, Amy pauses and looks back at the girl on the stump. She sees the now placid girl strike another match and stare blankly into the flickering flame. Once it burns out, the humming commences again.

"Frère Jacques...."

Chapter 84

Three flashlights spray rays of light across the silent rooms of the Enchanted Forrest. Clyde directs Oliver to go to his right and Colton to his left. Thus far, the search has been fruitless. Within the walls of each room, the search party is met by the same silent rooms with odd shadows caused by the emergency lighting.

As the three park employees enter the room with the giant tables and fireplace, Clyde utters, "This is where I left them." He recalls that his last words to the teens had been, "Stay in the cart," but he sees that there is no cart in this room. Sweat pours from his brow, and he looks at the doors that lead to the next room where he last saw Douglas Finch all those years ago.

Clyde glowers intently; his mind is full of dread. He thinks, *Through those doors.... Where had he gone? Where were those kids? This cannot be happening again.*

A hand on his shoulder interrupts the old man's thoughts. "What do you think these kids are up to?" asks Oliver.

"I don't know. Let's get moving. Colton, come on."

Colton is looking at the fireplace. He calls out, "Hey, Clyde, Mr. Sparkman, something is missing here."

"What is it, kid?"

"Well, there's usually a golden goose on this fireplace."

"What do you make of that, Clyde?" Oliver questions.

"Just another missing prop. A lot of stuff has been disappearing here lately." Inside his head, he tries to recall if he had seen the goose earlier that night, but he just cannot remember. *It's probably nothing*, he thinks.

"Come on," he calls and walks toward the next room.

As soon as he enters, there is an empty cart sitting still in the middle of the room.

"Well," Oliver notes, "we know they were here at least. Number 732: this is the cart you guys were in."

Colton swings his light around the tent and says, "I guess they moved on."

Oliver states, "Either they are in one of the rooms ahead having a laugh from playing some kind of twisted game of hide and seek, or they can't get out. Maybe the power outage caused a door ahead to prevent them from exiting."

"Yep, you're probably right, Oliver," Clyde says, but he knows in his heart that Oliver's wrong about either possibility.

A faint muffled sound comes from behind the wall over Clyde's right shoulder. Colton hears it and straightens up, stopping his search of the tent. Also in response, Oliver spins his light to the wall.

The old man walks over to the source and puts his ear to the wall. He hears another muffled shout. This time it is distinctly a boy's voice.

"It's them, it's got to be them," Colton asserts.

"Where are they?" Oliver asks. "Is there anything behind that wall, Clyde?"

"Ten feet of weeds, a fence, then the highway."

Colton theorizes, "Maybe it's just reverberating from somewhere else, like the sound is coming from here but it is really coming from one of the rooms ahead?"

"I don't know much about acoustics, Colton," Oliver says.

Clyde waves a hand at the others, signaling them to be quiet. However, no more sounds are heard.

Colton begins running his hands against the smooth wall of the room and says, "Maybe there's, like, a secret passage or something."

"You watch too much television, kid. I am banking on your first theory. Let's move on," Oliver says as he begins to walk to the next set of doors.

Colton shrugs and joins Sparkman.

Clyde, however, remains at the wall, peering at it.

After a few more seconds, Oliver asks, "You coming, Clyde?" while standing with one foot out of the room.

"Yeah," Clyde says. He rubs his eyes and takes a step to catch up with Oliver, who has disappeared through the doorway.

The others have no idea about the old ghosts Clyde is fighting in his mind.

Meanwhile, music begins to play in the room, but the three-man search party is already out of earshot.

Chapter 85

The disturbing encounter with the girl has left the group a little more cautious as they enter the next room. Before any of them says a word, Jack makes a complete sweep of the area with his flashlight. No one wants to be surprised by creepy girls or bears this time. Thus far, though, they are relived to find that the only visible object in the room is a large four-foot brick wall that spans about six feet in length with a forest scene painted on it. After spying this, Jack signals to the others, and they creep up to the wall on one side. Amy is wielding her stick; Mason, his axe; Jack, his backpack; and Scotty's picked up a rock.

As they creep to the wall, Jack whispers to Scotty, "You can't throw left-handed."

"I can, too."

"Remember Mrs. Turner?"

"Remember the spider?"

Jack shrugs an okay. They get close the edge, and Mason solemnly signals with his hands counting down: three… two… one. All four jump out, ready to tackle any unseen assailant that's behind the wall.

In front of them is one completely freaked-out deer. The fawn takes off hopping around the room looking for solace. Then, all of a sudden, to the group's shock, the deer jumps headfirst into the wall. Jack waits for the impact. However, the deer merely fades into the wall. Suddenly, the picturesque forest scene on the wall has a new fawn in the mural, just standing there placidly.

"Now that beats everything," Mason declares.

Amy offers, "Bambi?"

"Bambi," Jack confirms. Walking over to the wall, Amy taps it with her stick. It appears solid.

Even though all four of them are spellbound by the event, they have to admit that the spectacle does not seem all that unusual in the confines of this bizarre place. Eventually, they mentally return to the present situation.

Jack slowly walks around the wall, and once he's assured that nothing is hiding behind it, he breaks the silence and says, "Let me see the map, Mason."

Mason opens up the map, but holds onto one side of it. Jack picks up the other side and examines the map for a second. Then he says, "There are two sets of doors in here. One dead center, the other to the right."

Jack wishes Mason would relinquish his death grip on the map, so he tries a diversion by asking, "So what's the story with the little pyromaniac back there?"

Mason turns to hear what Scotty will say and drops his end of the map.

"She's the Little Match Girl," Scotty replies.

"That was obvious," Mason adds.

"I didn't make up her name."

"Yeah, I know, it was hands, wrist, and mandible-er-son guy."

"Anyways, in her story, she is supposed to sell a bunch of matchboxes, and if she does not, her father gets very angry at her."

Amy asks, "Angry, how?"

Scotty gives her a glance but says nothing.

"What did she mean by waiting for her grandmother?" Amy asks.

Again, Scotty says nothing and only gives her an uncomfortable look.

"So, she doesn't get a happily-ever-after?" Amy asks with obvious concern.

"Nuh-uh."

"What kind of fairy tale is that?" Mason jokes.

"The kind that doesn't have a happily-ever-after," Scotty grimly relates. "Most of the old tales don't actually have happily-ever-afters."

Jack suddenly holds the map closer to his face, ignoring the last few seconds of conversation, and calls out, "Mason!"

"What?"

"We took the wrong door. We were supposed to turn right."

"Garbage. Let me see."

Mason snatches the map and says, "I looked at this thing and...."

"It's pretty obvious, we blew it," Jack points out over his shoulder.

All four are assembled around the map now. Jack is upset, for the thought of having to re-enter the matchstick girl's room is not high on his bucket list. However, a thought pops into his sometimes-devious head: *This could play in my favor. Maybe the others will listen to me now. How do I play this?* Clearing his voice with too much vigor, Jack proclaims, "That's okay, Mason. So you blew it. We were all distracted by the girl. It's not your fault completely."

Unaware of the passive-aggressive verbal barrage, Mason folds the map into the work belt.

"We have another problem," Amy confesses.

The boys look at her expecting the worst.

"We gave her all the coins."

Chapter 86

A sinking feeling rushes through all four of them. Scotty suggests they run by the girl if they can't sneak past her, and the others agree.

Gearing up for the trip back through the previous room, Jack casually scans the present room again on last time and says, "Nothing has happened since we've been in here. Kind of odd."

"Come on, Jack, don't jinx us," Amy teases while shooting a playful elbow into his ribs.

Then, in the far right corner of the room, Jack sees a figure of a man and jumps back in alarm. However, after holding his flashlight before him, he sees that it's another narrator. Jack asks himself, *Has he been there the whole time? No way.*

After seeing Jack's temporary distress, the others spot the robotic mannequin themselves.

"Well, is it going to speak?" Mason grunts.

As if waiting for the invitation, the familiar crackling sound signaling the begging of another rhyme vibrates through an unseen spot in the ceiling.

> "Every step taken away from the goal,
> The price they pay will take its toll.
> The help they received
> May lead them to believe,
> But...."

Waiting for the finish of the rhyme, they hold still. After ten seconds, Mason finally comments, "But what? That's it?"

"I think it's broken," Scotty suggests.

"The rhymes are not coming from the narrator himself, genius. It's piped in from the speakers," Amy points out.

"Then the speakers are broken," Scotty clarifies.

Jack is sorely disappointed. He had been delighted that another clue was going to be delivered. Luckily, though, he remembers that the narrator's words had always been written down in the books the mannequins held.

Walking past the brick wall he approaches the figure and sees that the large book is opened in its hand. Looking down on the words that fill the page, he reads, "The help they received may lead them to believe, but…."

Jack thinks, *Now this is downright bizarre.* The "But" is written as the last word at the bottom of the page, and the next page is torn out. In fact, several pages are missing. Little jagged edges of paper give away the fact that someone had actually ripped them out. Now, only one page is left in the book at the end. Looking down at the last page, Jack sees more words.

The others join him around the mannequin. He points out the interrupted words and the torn pages and then points to the last page of the book, which reads:

"And the three of them lived happily ever after."

"Who lived happily ever after?" Amy asks.

"I don't know," Scotty answers.

Jack determines, "It's talking about us. We live happily ever after! Look, the narrator has been trying to give us clues all night. We've just been ignoring him. We need to go back. He is trying to lead us to some end. Maybe these missing pages—"

"But it said 'the three of them,'" Amy skeptically interjects.

"Right," Mason speaks. "It can't be us. There are four of us. It says here that only three lived happily ever after."

And then, no one speaks, for the gravity hits them at the same time.

Amy manages, "Does that mean one of us?"

"No," Jack adamantly replies. "That can't be what it means."

Mason goes for the jugular and says, "But Jack, if we just do what the narrator says, like you've been itching to do all night, one of us is gonna die."

"No, we're not," Jack defends.

Mason retorts, "It's right there in black and white, Jack. Oh, so wait, you wanna listen to the narrator as long as it fits in your little fantasy world, is that it?"

"No," Jack says. He is frustrated with the reasoning.

"Then we follow the narrator and one of us dies, or we follow the map and live. You pick."

Mason holds his ground. However, Jack is ready to make his stand. He is confident that he is right and says, "I think we should find the missing pages of this book. That's what we should be doing now. He's trying to get us to go somewhere, but we keep ignoring him."

It makes complete sense to Jack that if they are supposed to finish the story, then all they need to do is find the pages and follow the advice of the narrator. Still, the idea about someone won't be getting a happily-everafter is confusing to him.

"What about the map and the vault?" Scotty asks, looking to Mason.

"What good has following that map done for us?" Jack counters.

Jack and Mason are at a stalemate. As far as the others, Scotty seems to be wavering a little while holding Lucky to his chest, and Amy is keeping her thoughts to herself. Jack wonders what she could be thinking.

Jack says, "I think the happily ever after depends on us finishing the story."

"What story, Jack?" Amy responds.

"Can't you guys see? The story of this ride. We are the characters now; this is our—"

"Jack, the only thing I know is that this map is real. And that dude Victor was real. Your little theory is just thattheory," Mason argues.

Jack suggests, "Well, let's vote then. Who's for finding the pages?"

None of the others reply. Jack says, "Come on, are you serious? Scotty?"

"Sorry, Jack," Scotty replies. "I'm for getting out of here as quick as possible. I think maybe the map is the only real option we have."

Amy must now pick a side.

Jack looks at her, who for the first time since their earlier troubles does not look him in the eyes.

She says, "Jack, I'm sorry, it's just—"

"Fine. Just fine. We'll follow the map, then, and keep getting lost. Go ahead, Mason, lead us out of here. Need I remind you all that we are currently standing in a room we could have avoided according to your precious map."

Jack huffs off. He's aggravated, frustrated, and tired of fighting an uphill battle.

From behind him, he hears Mason say, "Great. Now he's gonna pout."

"I'm not gonna pout."

Mason turns to Scotty and says, "Yep. He's pouting."

Jack responds, "When we first came in the ride, the narrator said we—"

"The narrator said this. The narrator said that. Give it up, Jack. We may have made a wrong turn or two based on the map, but it's something I can touch, and I know if we're getting close or not. At least with this map, we know when we're lost. What about with the narrator? How do you even know where you're supposed to go? Huh?" Mason asks.

"Forget it. Do whatever you want," Jack replies. He's out of arguments, although he knows he's right even if he can't prove it.

Mason and Scotty exchange a look, and Scotty says, "It's not like we can't keep an eye out for the missing pages, right? Maybe there'll be something useful on them."

This is some semblance of a peace offering, and it at least acts to calm the situation a little. Nonetheless, they still have to get by the matchstick girl.

"So are we gonna be on the same page with that lunatic girl and her matches?" Mason asks.

Jack feels that Mason is trying to take over, but Jack doesn't see a point in arguing anymore, so he says, "Okay. Same page."

"Good," Mason grins.

Amy expresses, "What if the wolf got free of his webs and is in there by now?"

"Well, that puts a damper on things," Mason says. "But that's a chance we're just going to have to take. Scotty, you got any more of that magic shrinking potion?"

"Nope. You wanna go back to the lab?"

Just then one of the doors behind them swings open. Bracing for danger, they turn toward the door. They see a peculiar looking man in the shape of an egg waltzing into the room and carrying a short stepladder.

"Really?" Mason laughs.

Scotty snickers at the harmless looking man. He playfully calls out, "How are you today?"

The egg shaped man ignores them and simply places the ladder against the brick wall. He begins to climb.

Not wanting to wait any longer, Mason turns to the exit and says, "Let's go, guys."

Grudgingly, Jack follows with Amy close behind. Scotty is the last one to approach the doors, and before he enters the next room, he turns back to the odd man and says, "I would not go up there if I were you." Then he giggles and passes through the doorway.

Chapter 87

Jack and the others make their way into the wasteland that is the Match Girl Room. Knowing what to expect does not take the creepy factor down for them one single notch. She's still humming, and for now, at least, there's no sign of the wolf. The girl is sitting in the corner, starring with a blank expression. The teens avoid the area she's gazing at by taking exaggerated, almost cartoonish, steps away from her line of sight. They try to hide behind what they can in order to pass unnoticed.

When they are halfway across the room, a genuine sense of hope delights Jack. As they are nearing the door on the opposite side, though, suddenly the girl stands in front of them and blocks their path. Any plan to make a break for it has been crushed.

"Won't you buy some matches?"

"We already bought some matches, just let us by, okay?" Mason pleads.

The match the girl is holding burns out, and she starts humming. The kids decide to use the elusiveness of the darkness to skirt around her and make their way toward the door. But then, immediately in front of them, the girl strikes yet another match and repeats her eerie ritual.

"Look, we gave you all the coins we had," Amy tries to reason.

The girl seems to pay no attention to their efforts and says, "Won't you buy some matches?"

"Stop saying that! We already told you we have no more money," Mason says.

The girl's appearance steadily changes. Her clandestine features begin to sour. Her mouth turns to a scowl.

"Oh, for heaven's sake. Here we go again," Scotty whines.

Then, before any of the teens can object to his actions, Mason takes the escape into his own hands: he reaches out and pushes the girl.

The match girl is astonished by the sudden action and falls down.

"Mason!" Amy cries.

"No time for argument! Just get through that door," Mason commands.

Jack wastes no time in following Mason to the door, and Scotty is right behind them.

"Amy! Come on. No time for sympathy," Jack calls.

This instruction isn't heeded by Amy, though. She looks down at the girl and says, "I'm sorry."

The matchstick girl cradles up into a ball on the floor and begins rocking back and forth.

Seeing the odd reaction, Amy begins to apologize again by saying, "Sorry we—"

"Now!" Mason says, stepping in front of Jack and grabbing Amy's arm.

Mason, almost dragging Amy behind him, and the others arrive into the new room. But with one look, they are met with the last thing they expected. To their mutual astonishment, they are right back in the room with the brick wall.

Chapter 88

None of them can believe what they are seeing. Jack is equally heartbroken and confused. "Are you kidding me?" he howls in anger.

"Maybe it's a different room with a brick wall?" Scotty suggests hopefully.

Just like before, the ladder is propped against the brick wall, and now the odd egg-shaped man is sitting on top. Also, the narrator mannequin is sitting in the corner.

"Nope, this is the same room." Scotty points out.

"For crying out loud. How is this possible?" Mason sulks.

"How is anything possible in here?" Jack answers sharply.

Jack looks to Amy who is standing with her stick close to her chest. She is obviously agitated, but Jack is unsure of the exact cause for her displeasure. He figures that either she's mad about the room or she's upset with Mason for pushing the girl. He decides, though, not to ask.

Jack walks over to Mason and, while holding out his arm, says, "Let me see the map, Mason."

"What, so you can correct my mistake again?" he snarls.

"Fine. Lead on, O Master of the Map," Jack responds with an equal amount of irritation.

Mason raises his voice and says, "You looked at the map yourself. You said we needed to take this route."

"You're the one so attached to that thing, not me. Maybe if we would just put the thing up and look—"

"Three... lived happily ever after. *Three.* Remember? Time to drop it."

An unfamiliar voice calls down from atop the brick wall, "Keep it down! What is all the fuss about?"

Mason looks up and jabs, "Stay out of this, Humpty!"

"Okay, guys—enough!" Scotty declares. Both Jack and Mason are startled by the emotion in his voice.

Scotty nervously fiddles with Lucky and continues, "I'm just saying that you guys are driving me crazy. I don't think Amy or I...." Scotty looks over at Amy to see if she will support what he's saying, but he gets no response from her. He continues, "Um... we don't really care who is right or who is wrong. We just want to get out of this place."

Jack, breathing hard with his face flushed, waves his arm dramatically and says, "Okay, Scotty. I think we can all agree that going back through that door will lead us right back to the girl. Why don't we just take one of those other doors at the back of the room. Then our great leader here can look at the precious map, and we can move on from there."

Jack expects some degree of sarcastic reply because of his combative tone.

Mason retorts, "Finally. Some common sense, from you."

"Then it's agreed," Scotty says, playing the middle ground.

"I don't want to see that girl back there again," Mason grumbles.

Now Amy speaks and asks, "Why is that Mason? Because you shoved her down?"

"I had too."

"You're a bully," Amy accuses.

"Amy, she tried to set me on fire. She's dangerous."

"She's a little girl. A little girl, who's trapped in here just like us. Why don't you twist the head off some of her toys if we see her again?"

"What?" Mason asks. He genuinely has no recollection of the torment he used to cause Amy.

"You know what, Mason? You're just scared."

"I am not. I just think—"

"You're scared you're the one who won't live happily ever after."

Amy moves quick, gets right in Mason's face, and says, "Mason Chick, all you think about is yourself. You don't care about anyone else, and if someone gets in your way, no matter who they are, you shove them down."

Amy makes a final jab by saying, "A pathetic bully," and then backs off.

Jack's still angry at Mason, and although he enjoyed Amy's verbal attack, it's over. He knows that if they are ever going to get out of the ride, they'll have to stay together.

Turning to Mason, he says, "Look, I don't agree with following the map, okay? But I'll go along if that's what everyone else wants to do. The only way we're gonna get out of this is if we stay together. So, which door are we gonna take this time? The one straight ahead or the one to the left?"

On the outside, at least, nothing seems to faze Mason Chick. While considering Jack's question, he runs his fingers through his hair and seems to almost brush off all the hostility toward him.

Mason says, "I don't know, let's flip a coin. Amy, can I borrow a coin?"

"Yeah. Funny. Ha ha."

"Fine. We go left," Mason gruffly decides.

Amy stomps off toward the door, and Scotty follows. Mason and Jack, however, remain for a minute. Their friendship has taken a severe hit in the last few moments. Mason glowers at Jack, wanting to make sure that Jack recognizes him as the better man. Then he gestures for Jack to go first through the door, which he does after giving a shrug. This hacks Mason off way past his boiling point, and after entering the next room, Mason slams the door behind him.

From the other side of the now closed door, the group hears a yell and then a dull thud.

Mason looks at Scotty and asks, "Did he just...?"

"Yep."

Chapter 89

Howard Snodgrass is hiding. It doesn't look like he's hiding, but he's definitely hiding. He's standing just outside of the concession stand, far enough out of range to be out of view from the parents who have camped out in front of the Enchanted Forrest. Snodgrass peers out to the parking lot and sees flashing blue lights. He thinks, *Great. Just great. Who called the police? This is turning into one heck of a night.* He hears multiple car doors slam shut and wonders, *What? Did they bring the whole department?*

Three police officers waltz up to the Enchanted Forrest with their walkie talkies blaring. From his vantage point, he can see Titus Chick extending a hand to one of them. He tells himself, *Better get out there, Howard. Be calm, relax.* A tall mustached policeman in his Smokey the Bear-looking hat calls out, "Who's in charge here?"

"I am. Howard Snodgrass, General Manger."

The policeman looks at him, apparently sizing him up, which doesn't take long.

"So you've got some AWOL kids, huh?"

Mr. Carnahan calls out, "They've been in there for over two hours, and they won't let us go in."

Looking over at Carnahan, the policeman speaks to the assembly saying, "Looks like we've got quite a crowd. My officers and I will speak to each of you. Just hold your horses, and let us do our job. We will do everything—"

"We know. Everything in your power. We've heard that plenty tonight," Wallace Braddock retorts.

Brenna elbows him in the stomach and hushes him with, "Wallace!"

The cop glowers at Wallace. Taking out a notebook from his belt, the policeman, with pencil ready, responds to the rebuke by asking, "Sir, what is your name?"

"Wallace Braddock. That's two d's," Wallace asserts.

"Oh, *the* Wallace Braddock," responds the policeman. Then he turns to his officers and says, "We've got Speed Trap Wally over here, gents." This creates some muffled laughter from the police squad.

Brenna shoots a second elbow into Wallace's ribs and tells him, "You see, Wallace, I knew—"

"Look, Officer Howdy Duty," Wallace says, stepping over to the officer. "I don't care what you call me as long as you do your job. My boy's in there, and you don't want to deal with me if you don't bring him out."

"Are you threatening an officer, Mr. Braddock?"

"You mean Mr. Speed Trap?"

The two men size each other up. Neither is bluffing.

"Just do your job," Wallace voices and then backs off, dragging Brenna with him.

The Officer tries to restore his command of the situation by saying, "Look, I know everyone is on edge here. But I expect everyone to keep cool and keep your less-than-helpful-comments to yourself." He gives another look at Wallace.

Then the tall cop motions to a female officer and orders, "Quinn, take down the parents' names and statements."

Then, to another, "Markham, talk to these employees."

Finally, he turns to Howard and says, "Mr. Snodgrass, I'd like to have a word with you."

Howard thinks, *Great—just great! Why did I ever take this job?*Chapter 90The scene before Mason Chick sends his head spinning. To the left of him sits the little match girl on a stump, and he hears, "Frère Jacques, Frère Jacques," being hummed lightly. Using both of his hands, he scratches his face in frustration.

Never in his entire life has he felt this lost. In his mind, this even trumps the time when he was seven and lost track of his father inside a Nashville Wal-Mart for 30 traumatizing minutes.

Fortunately, the match girl has not noticed their arrival, in spite of the slamming door. So, although expecting some self-righteous comment from Jack or Amy, Mason takes out the map for what seems to him like the fiftieth look at the room.

Jack approaches him and Mason thinks, *Here we go.*

"Look, there has got to be something we're missing," Jack says. "It makes no sense. I suggest we search the room for another way out."

Pacified that Jack has not suited up for another round, he agrees but adds, "What about the girl?"

"I don't know," Jack says and shrugs. "Maybe she will leave us alone now."

"Maybe," says Mason, but then he sees Amy and utters, "No, no, no."

Jack wheels around in the direction Mason is now pointing and sees Amy walking up to the girl.

"Here, Braddock," says Mason, "you take the map. I'll take care of Amy."

"No," Jack responds, "I'll take care of Amy." There is a hardened look on Jack's face.

"What is your deal? Just take the stinking map. A moment ago you were all hot and bothered about having the thing. I'll take care of Amy."

Mason thinks that something about the look on Jack's face is weird.

"Fine," Jack says with a flash of irritation. "Scotty and I will look for another door."

Mason issues a guttural noise under his breath and says, "Okay then." He stomps off toward Amy.

The matchstick girl is rocking back and forth. Her face is red, and her eyes are closed. Amy speaks to the girl in a tender, caring voice and says, "Hey there."

"Amy, get back over here. We need to find a door," Mason calls.

Upon hearing Mason's voice, the girl's eyes flash open. This time the pale blue eyes are replaced by fiery red ovals. Immediately, she lights a match and hurls it at Mason.

"Would you like to buy some matches!" she screams.

The match strikes Mason in the forearm. It stings.

"Hey! Stop that you little—," Mason says and takes an aggressive step toward the girl.

Amy grabs his arm and tells him, "No you don't. Not again."

"What? Are you crazy? She—"

Another match strikes Mason, who is unable to shield himself in time. The burning stick hits him in square in the jaw.

"Ouch!" Mason exclaims and brings his right arm to his face immediately.

Amy turns to the girl and says, "Stop that! We just want to leave. We can help you."

"Over here!" Scotty yells.

Mason turns to see Scotty struggling to lift a brown wooden circle from a spot in the floor. Jack is helping him.

The girl strikes another match and flings it at Mason, whose attention has been drawn away from her. Amy steps in front of the match to deflect it with her hand, but she doesn't make contact and the match lands somewhere behind Amy.

"Look, we can help you," Amy pleads with the girl who is busying herself lighting more matches.

Suddenly, a small puff of smoke begins to envelope Amy's head. She screams, "No!"

To his horror, Mason watches as a fire begins to ignite behind Amy's head. The match had landed in her hood.

Mason rushes to Amy and starts patting at the flames.

In the meantime, the little matchstick girl gives a sinister snarl because she has lit Mason's shirt on fire from behind.

The burning sensation flashes across his back. Mason drops to the floor and rolls vigorously.

The girl starts humming again and continues to light even more matches.

Scotty and Jack see the chaos and drop the wooden hatch. Thinking fast, Jack grabs Lucky from Scotty and slams the bear on top of the fire in Amy's hoodie. The flame smolders from the lack of oxygen, and Amy whimpers in fear. After removing the bear from atop her head, Jack sees a large black burn in the bear's fur, just a few inches down from where the viper had gotten a mouth full of fluff. Jack then joins Scotty in trying to put out Mason's burning shirt.

The matchstick girl continues flinging burning matches at Mason. "Won't you buy some matches?" she says as she flings each one. "Won't you buy some matches?"

As Mason rolls on the ground, he suddenly feels a crippling weight. Scotty has jumped on him. The tubby boy muffles the fire, while Jack, with Lucky in his hands, is suffocates the visible flames that Scotty has not stifled.

After a brief struggle, the fire is out.

"You okay, Mason?" Scotty asks, looking directly in the face of his friend.

Mason is a little taken aback by the proximity of Scotty's face above his own and says, "Get off me."

"Guess that's a yes." Scotty confirms.

The boys hear a scream and look over at the matchstick girl, who is now smiling, lighting match after match, and slinging them at the dodging figure of Amy while repeating, "Won't you buy some matches? Won't you buy some matches?"

Another match lands on Amy's face. She's now had enough. Amy beelines right toward the matchstick girl, flinging the flying matches away. "I wanted to help you!" Amy tells her.

The matchstick girl lights another match and flings it at Amy, who knocks it away in midair. Getting to the girl and using a wicked backhand, Amy slaps the matchbox from the girl's hand. Matches fly from the box, littering the floor. The girl then bends down and begins to pick up each one as if each was a valuable treasure.

"No, no, no," the little girl says.

Amy's face switches to one of tenderness and of remorse for knocking the matches out of the girl's hands. She says, "Look, I'm sorry I...."

The matchstick girl is now talking to herself, saying, "I tried to sell the matches, I did, but they wouldn't buy them. Please don't be mad. Please don't be mad."

Amy feels a hand on her arm, and she spins around to face her brother. Scotty tells her, "As soon as she gets them picked up, she's gonna start again. We need to go."

"But Scotty, she—"

"You can't fix her, Amy. We need to go."

Scotty heads off toward the wooden hatch. He passes Mason, who's getting up off the ground without accepting Jack's offered help.

The group manages to get the hatch open, and they see a ladder leading down.

The humming starts again, and they all freeze.

"Get in the hole!" Scotty yells.

The little girl is moving toward them with her matches in hand.

The group scrambles to get down the hatch. Mason goes first and then Amy. Scotty starts to descend and then sees Lucky. He calls out, "Jack, get Lucky!"

"Leave him," Jack says.

"No, he's getting out of here with us."

Jack snatches the bear as Scotty disappears into the hole. Jack tosses the bear in and climbs down, pulling the wooden cover over him. From above, he hears a horrible scream. This causes them all to pause and listen for what will come next.

"Father. No, I tried to sell them. I did. But they wouldn't buy them. Please don't be mad. Please don't be mad."

Chapter 91

Jack has been descending the ladder for at least five minutes. So far, the teens have all climbed in silence, dwelling on the fate of the match girl. As Jack climbs, he's taking inventory of this whole ordeal, which he realizes has probably been the most agonizing thing in his life. He snuck out of his house, stole a goose, was nearly killed by a poisonous snake, was almost eaten by a bear, was chased by a wolf and a venomous spider, and came close to being set aflame by a little girl. Plus, his relationship with Mason is on thin ice, although the ordeal with the girl had at least brought them a little closer to the same team. On top of it all, the one positive aspect about the night has been a budding relationship with Amy, but Jack senses that things have cooled off a bit, and those first forays of flirtation back at the roller coaster seem like a long time ago to him. In fact, he even thinks about how this new "thing" he and Amy have going has been like a roller coaster itself with her taking his hand one minute and siding with Mason the next.

Breaking the silence, Mason informs, "I can see the bottom."

The climbers let out a sigh of relief.

Jack takes a peek, himself, and he, too, can see the bottom. He doesn't hurry up and eventually arrives on a smooth concrete slab of a floor. They are in a long narrow room, and lit torches adorn the walls. Two lengthy walkways are visible on either side of a large trough of water that has been etched out in the concrete floor. Black water spills down from an opening at the top of the wall on the far end of the trough. It ripples and splashes until it disappears through a metal grate at the end closest to them.

Amy and Scotty are looking around, and Scotty offers, "Some kind of sewer, I think."

Mason is also surveying the tunnel-like room and says, "Hey, that thing about crocodiles in sewers... that a fairy tale, right?"

"A myth," Scotty responds. "Different thing."

"So, no crocodiles?" confirms Mason.

"I dunno. I haven't ever been here before," answers Scotty.

"Let's just stay alert, okay?" Jack advises. "In this place anything is likely to happen."

Everyone nods in agreement.

Jack asks, "So where to now?"

"Looks like there's another ladder up ahead," Scotty points out.

A black ladder is at the other end of the room on the same side of the trough that the group is on.

"You okay, Amy?" Jack asks.

She simply nods, looking dazed and bewildered. Her hair has been singed, and it is tussled from the constant scratching she has been doing since the incident. Still, in this moment, Jack thinks Amy is as pretty as ever.

Amy offers Jack a little smile and motions to her hair, asking, "Is it bad?"

"Looks fine to me."

"Yeah, ha ha."

"'Course we are about a thousand feet underground in the dark on the banks of a sewer with black, nasty water, so I am not sure there's any sort of fashion code down here to abide by."

She laughs a little and Jack smiles. He thinks how "the roller coaster" just went on the up.

"Not sure what we would have done if you guys hadn't found that hatch," Mason confides. "Finch did not do a very good job with that little detail in his map. He should have written wooden hatch or something like that. It sure could have saved us time."

Jack bristles at the mention of the map. Even though all is clearly not settled between them, a temporary truce is understood, and none of them wants to restart the bitter infighting they had experienced over the last hour or so.

A rumble of hunger rips through Jack's stomach, but right now he's too exhausted to care.

"Sure could use a rest," he says.

"You can say that again," Mason responds. He ruffles with the work belt adjusting it around his waist.

Meanwhile, Scotty has found Lucky on the bank of the nasty water. He picks him up and declares, "At least he didn't go for a swim."

Noticing Lucky enveloped in Scotty's embrace, Mason confidently says to the others, "You see, my prize has been a hero more than once. Here, Scotty, no need to carry him all the way."

"No, I've got him, Mason," Scotty answers. He appears to be almost jealously guarding the bear.

"Give me the bear, Scotty. I don't want you getting too attached. Lucky here deserves a place of honor in my room."

Scotty begrudgingly hands the bear over.

And with that, the group begins to move toward the other ladder. Jack is walking next to Amy. Their hands brush and then clasp. This causes Jack to stand a little taller.

As they continue to the ladder, Jack looks around more at their surroundings. He is particularly confused by the room and wonders, *Why a sewer? Every other room in this place has related to some fairy tale or nursery rhyme? What's this all about?* After they walk a little further, Scotty hunches over and confesses, "I'm not sure how much more of this I can take."

Amy, still messing with the top of her head, says, "We have to keep moving, Scotty. We're all tired, but we can't just stay here."

The long walk to the exit is tedious and the tuckered-out group gazes right and left, expecting something to emerge from shadow.

Then, just as they are a few feet from the ladder, Jack sees movement from a small crack in the stone wall to his right.

Amy shrieks, "Rats!"

A procession of more than 50 rats spills out onto the floor and begins running around and in between four sets of legs.

Chapter 92

As they dance and weave to avoid the rats, Scotty looks at the crack in the wall and sees 20 more grey and black rats scurrying out. These repulsive looking rodents aren't anything like the pleasant lab mice they had seen earlier in the night. Some of the larger ones could pass for small dogs.

Sniffing and squeaking, the rats fill the space below their feet. One hideous rat scampers over Scotty's right foot. He kicks the varmint, and it lands on top of another but scurries around again.

"Just get up the ladder," Jack proposes.

"I can't move! These things are swarming!" Amy cries.

"They're just rats. Keep going," Mason demands.

The flowing water accompanied by the loud squeaking and clicking of hundreds of tiny feet is almost deafening. Nonetheless, from somewhere in the room, the teens are just able to make out the faint sound of music. It is soothing music, the kind you hear from an Irish wooden flute. The music begins to rise in volume, eventually eclipsing the sound of the rats, and it seems to have an effect on the rodents, for they start to line up in two single-file rows, standing on their hind legs and facing the end of the tunnel. Then they slowly edge forward in a bizarre trance, almost marching in time with the music.

The group is mystified by the vermin parade and have halted their progress toward the ladder while staring at the marching rats. Something, though, causes Scotty to look to his left, and he sees a man walk into the tunnel from a hidden passage. He's wearing a long green cloak that flows over his body and drapes over the top of his head like a cowl. Scotty can't make out any features of the man's face except for two bright yellow circles, which seem less like eyes than two beams of light, but he does notice that the man is playing a wooden pan flute. The instrument glides across where Scotty suspects his mouth would be if he could see it. The tune it produces is simply enthralling.

A sense of peace envelopes Scotty and his body longs to join the mice in following this elf-like individual back to the ladder they had originally descended. He is unable to resist, and he, too, beings to march.

Suddenly, Scotty realizes that he knows who this is, the Pied Piper. He tries to say something, but he can't. He's caught in the Piper's hypnotic music.

Chapter 94

Jack is also lured by the piper's tune. He can't stop his feet from moving toward the ladder he doesn't want to ascend. He tells himself to step right, but the order isn't followed. One foot at a time, he follows the procession. As the line turns, he catches a glimpse of the strange cloaked figure playing the wooden flute. Jack tries to pivot his foot again, but he can't. He wants to call out, but his mouth feels full of cotton. Amy, Mason, and Scotty walk before him in the same hypnotic shuffle.

Jack tries to will his mind to free himself from the trance, telling himself, *Wake up!* But this has no effect. The piper's music is controlling his actions, and he also realizes that it's having an effect on his emotions, too, for when he looks at Mason, he has no more feelings of enmity for his friend. Strange remorse for his actions fill Jack's thoughts: *Why did I sneak out in the first place? Why did I force Clyde to let us on? Why did I get out of the ride? Why did I steal that goose? Why was I such a jerk tonight to Mason?* Soon, though, all feelings of regret also begin to wash away. Jack is having a hard time thinking. The music is soothing him.

The beat of the music quickens, and his feet begin to march faster. Jack tries to speak again, but his lips and tongue do not move. In another attempt to fight the music-induced haze, he blinks. This makes his eyelids grow heavy, but Jack is comforted a bit in knowing that he retains some control over his body.

The group passes the ladder they climbed down. Jack thinks, *Now we're really going the wrong way.* Up ahead, he can hear the sounds of pouring water. He wonders is this is a drainage system. He hopes it is and that it has lots of pipes, one of which he may be able grab on to.

Before his eyes shut, he sees the rats at the front of the procession begin to dive into the water ahead to their left. Jack remembers that rats are able to swim, but these are sinking because they remain stiff in a trance.

Suddenly, Jack realizes, *He intends to drown us!*

The gravity hits Jack, knowing he won't be able to swim in this state. He watches in despair, on the brink of unconsciousness as the rats continue to file into the trough of water. His last thoughts before blacking out are of Amy.

Chapter 94

The march continues, and all of them are caught in the midst of the bizarre parade of rats. The stark realization that the piper is intending to drown them all has hit Mason as well. However, like Jack, he cannot fight the march to his doom. A feeling of genuine regret passes over him as well, and he wonders why he had been so argumentative with Jack. He asks himself, *Did Jack have a point about the narrator and the map? But if he* was and if only three of them get a happy-ever-after, what if I'm not one of the three? He also thinks about Scotty, and when he considers the way he has treated him, his feelings soften. Finally, he acknowledges the way he had always tormented Amy by picking on her. Now he wishes everything had been different.

Weary and dazed, Mason fights to stay coherent. While he lumbers forward, he feels an odd sensation near his right ankle and realizes that something is tugging at his shoe. This gentle tugging breaks the daze just long enough for Mason to slightly tilt his head to the right and down. Is that a squirrel? he thinks. The creature has now hopped onto Mason's foot, and his first reaction is to shoot his leg out and send the rodent flying; however, the trance prevents this from happening. His mind clouds again, and Mason simply chooses to ignore the foul thing. After a few more steps, though, more odd sensations break the fog. This time odd pricks scratch up his leg, and Mason thinks, "Oh, just great, that thing is climbing up my leg. This is not getting any better."

With blurry eyes, Mason notices that the rodent has climbed out to where Lucky rests in his grip. Then he sees a curious thing: the squirrel is chewing at the scorched plot on Lucky's stomach. It looks up at Mason and displays a large clump of fluff in its mouth. Mason tries to communicate, Get off me, you varmint!

The destination of the parade looms closer, and more rats are flinging themselves into the water. No, no, no, thinks Mason. Meanwhile, the squirrel climbs up Mason's neck. In order to shake off the rodent, Mason tries to lurch his head forward, but he cannot. The squirrel then latches onto his hair and drags himself to the top of his head. At this point, while it looks like Mason is wearing the rodent like a hat, the most curious thing happens. He feels the squirrel shoving fluff into his right ear.

Chapter 95

Could this be? wonders Mason, Is the squirrel helping me? The sudden real-ization startles him but also encourages him. He feels the tiny feet tickling him as they scamper around the base of his neck in order to place fluff into his left ear. Then, just like that, the music dulls to Mason and then dissi-pates. He can no longer hear the piper, and the dreamlike trance wears off quickly. Meanwhile, the squirrel has scampered down Mason's leg and retreated out of sight.

Mason is able to stop marching now under his own power, and he does so, pausing to think quickly. He realizes his best plan to save his friends is to catch the piper off guard. Resuming the march, he fakes a stupefied expression. Just ahead, he sees the others approaching the water. *Think, Mason, think,* he tells himself. *Should I charge the piper?* he wonders. He decides there is not enough time since the piper is about 20 yards away and by the time he would get there, the others would be in the pool. Mason turns to get a gauge on the piper and risks blowing his cover. Fortunately, though, the green-clad little man continues to skip while playing and doesn't appear to notice anything unusual. Currently, the piper is approximately six feet from the edge of the pool, and an idea springs into Mason's head. Of the group, he knows that only he would be capable of pulling this off. Readying his body for the motion to come, he tenses his legs, envisions his actions, and thinks, *It's now or never.*

With reckless abandon, Mason runs in a short arc, looping around a section of the pool, and then heads straight toward the piper. Mason then launches himself in the air toward the pool with the piper exactly opposite him. The adrenaline rushing through his limbs sends him higher than he ever dreamed. In midair, he tucks his legs under his arms in preparation for what will perhaps be the greatest cannonball splash of his life. At the apex of his jump, he watches as the piper catches a glimpse of the famous "Chick cannonball." There is nothing the odd little imp can do now but await the coming splash.

Chapter 96

The impact of the cannonball sends a titanic wave up, part of it is headed toward the piper. The oncoming wall of water forces the enchanter into a defensive position. He ducks but loses his balance as he tries to avoid the avalanche of water. With arms flailing, the flute flies from his grasp and the Piper is knocked to his back. The wall of water then crashes down on the sprawling man.

The music has stopped, and rats scamper in every direction.

Jack shakes off the trance. From the corner of his right eye, Jack sees Amy and Scotty shaking off the effects, as well, near the edge of the pool. Mason's jump into the pool happened just in time. Breaking away from the daze, he turns to see the piper, disheveled and drenched, lying on the ground and fighting his own soaked robes in search of the flute. Jack spots the instrument on the ground a few feet from the piper. *Time to act,* Jack thinks and bolts forward, free from any trace of a trance. By this point, the piper, too, has spotted the instrument and starts crawling on the ground toward it. As he runs, Jack spots Mason crawling up the side of the trench, and to Jack's adulation, Mason grabs the man's foot, preventing him from a final lunge to retrieve the instrument.

Jack runs past the man to the flute and slams his right foot down on the wooden instrument, splintering it into a dozen scattering pieces.

A scream of rage erupts from the iper.

"Time for a new flute!" Jack hollers victoriously at the man.

The hideous yellow oval eyes of the piper turn away from Jack and scan down to where Mason is clinging to his legs. Raising a knee, the man unleashes a furious kick toward Mason. Jack watches in alarm as a black boot thunders across Mason's jaw. Mason's eyes roll up into the back of his head, and his limp body crashes into the water.

Chapter 97

While shaking off her own effects from the music, Amy is slow to react to the whirlwind of activity. However, the crack of the piper's boot against Mason's defenseless jaw is a visual jolt of caffeine. Upon the subsequent fall of Mason's limp body into the water, she throws caution to the wind and knows what she has to do. Ignoring the now obvious fowl stench of the sewer water, she lunges into the water herself.

A splash of cold seizes her muscles. Amy has never been a strong swimmer; the three summers of swim lessons had been in vain. But now, with Mason's life on the line, her legs kick and arms carve a swath against the flowing current. Several dozen rats, who have returned to consciousness themselves, begin to paddle all around her. Her arms clip a rat, then another. One rat attempts to cling to her like a human life preserver. *No time to worry about them now*, thinks Amy. She sees Mason's back floating to the middle of the pool just ahead. The current aids her efforts by bringing him closer to her. As she continues to swim in his direction, Amy swats away several rats, no longer able to ignore the vermin whose sharp claws dig into her clothes and flesh. Suddenly, she experiences a shot of pain on her tender head from a rat that has crawled on top. While swatting at the rat, she tries not to lose track of Mason. Finally, she succeeds in yanking the rat off and flinging him away, and then she reaches Mason and turns him upright so he can get a breath.

Dozens of rats begin to swim toward Mason and her.

Amy cries, "Help me, Scotty!" but there is no reply. She looks to the path and sees that Scotty is just standing there looking at the enraged piper.

She yells, "Scotty!" hoping to draw his attention to her.

Scotty, however, continues to stand motionless.

In the midst of fighting away the rats while holding Mason's head above water, Amy checks for a vital sign from Mason.

She calls out, "Jack! He's not breathing!"

Chapter 98

Amy slaps Mason's cheek, trying desperately to snap him back to life.

She yells, "Mason, wake up!"

She is fighting to stay afloat, and her legs are beginning to tire from the constant kicking. Soon, her head dips below the water.

Underneath the surface of the nasty black liquid, Amy sees the rats and realizes that Mason is not the only one fighting for his life in that pool. Also, even while submerged, Amy still isn't able to touch the bottom. Summoning a burst of energy, she lunges with both legs and accelerates upward again, projecting Mason and her above the surface. Then a large charcoal colored rat scampers up her outstretched arm, and a black rat climbs on top of Mason, who remains unresponsive.

"Mason!" Amy yells again and makes a brisk downward swipe with her hand over the boy's chin.

She continues making clumsy swipes, hitting his check, his forehead, his nose, and his ears. However, these do not seem to be having any effect, and Amy thinks, *I have to get to the side of the trench, or we'll both drown.*

Although it's less than five yards away, she's not strong enough to reach the side. Instead she steadies Mason and checks for vital signs again. She thinks he has a pulse but can't be sure. He's still not breathing, so Amy wonders, *Should I give him mouth to mouth? I don't know mouth to mouth. Just do something. Mason's gonna die, if it's not too late already.*

Having no clue what to do, she decides to blow in his mouth. Even with the desperation of the moment, though, she still hesitates a little before she does and thinks, *I should have taken a class on this.* Nonetheless, she manages to place Mason's floating form upward with his face inches below hers. She takes her hand and pinches Mason's nose, recalling that she had seen this done somewhere. Then, lowering her mouth to Mason's, she prepares for the attempt and tells herself, *Mason is dead if I don't do this.*

Amy places her mouth on Mason's, and as soon as she does so, water gushes into her open mouth. This surprises Amy, and she doesn't notice a gurgling "What" sound coming from Mason's throat. Then, in her arms, she feels Mason stir. He begins coughing, fluttering his eyelashes, and shaking his head.

Mason gasps, "What…. Where?" with his arms flailing and legs kicking.

Amy says, "Stop, Mason—stop! You have to help me."

He gives another cough before calm breaks over his face at recognition of the familiar voice.

"Can you stay above the water on your own?"

"Did I get her good?"

"Her?"

"The lifeguard."

Great, thinks Amy. *He's out of his mind.* However, instead of trying to explain everything, Amy simply plays along and says, "You sure did, but we have to get to the side."

"Cool."

It is obvious to Amy that she will still have to guide him to the bank. So, with one arm under his, Amy kicks, along with Mason, to the side of the pool. Although Mason's kicks are quite weak, the extra push is just what Amy needs to succeed in getting them to the side of the trough. And, while Amy is relieved, she isn't able to let go of the idea that Mason had spit in her mouth.

Finally, they reach the side of the pool, and Amy takes one of Mason's arms and drapes it onto the concrete. He is now safe, and Amy asks, "You gonna be okay there?"

"I think so, but I am like so dizzy."

"Just stay put."

Amy lifts herself onto the bank and then pauses to see what is going on ashore.

Chapter 99

The enraged piper is on his feet now, and with lightning-fast reflexes, he charges at Jack. Overwhelmed by the sudden attack, Jack steps back. The piper is on him in an instant. A searing pain jerks his entire head forward. The piper grips a handful of Jack's hair, and shoves him to the ground face first.

Scotty watches in bewilderment. Even though he is no longer under the music's curse, he is now frozen in terror. He sees the yellow eyes of the piper turn toward him, and he responds by raising his hands in fear and ducking his head. As the piper advances toward him, Scotty wants to run, but, instead, he cowers and shakes as the man approaches.

"Sorry.... I'm sorry," Scotty stutters.

Then Scotty sees Jack behind the piper. He's back on his feet and makes a haphazard rush into the back of the piper, crashing into the small of the man's back. Scotty ducks in fear as the piper jolts forward. The mad musician, though, recovers quickly from the blow and turns and lifts Jack off the ground by his throat. Then, with an epic motion of his arm, he launches Jack into the wall of stone to the left. With Jack out of the way, the piper resumes his deliberate march toward Scotty.

"No, we didn't mean to," Scotty spits out in fear.

The instant the piper is upon him, Scotty tries to duck, but it's too late. The piper has him in a painful headlock. In this fashion, the piper drags Scotty back to the spot of the shattered flute and reaches down with his one free hand and picks up a piece of his prized instrument. He slams it down in disgust and emits another blood-curdling cry from his hidden mouth. Then, while continuing to hold Scotty under one arm, the piper reaches underneath his wet cloak to his belt and draws out a pistol. It is the kind of pistol that Scotty had only seen in pirate movies. The frightened boy tries to turn his head around, looking for any possibility of rescue, but the only other person he sees is Jack, who's lying on the ground motionless.

The piper throws Scotty to the ground and places one of his large black boots on Scotty's chest. Then he lowers the gun to Scotty's face.

"No, don't!" Scotty cries and waits for the explosion.

Chapter 100

Fresh from the water, Amy sees her brother in trouble, and, without hesitation, sprints toward him and launches her entire body into the right side of the mysterious foe just above his hip. The piper is not ready for the new assault, and the blow to his defenseless side sends the piper reeling. At the same time, he relinquishes his hold on the pistol, and it flies through the air and splashes into the pool. The piper tries to recover by wheeling around, but his right foot steps too close to the edge, and with his balance lost, he tumbles toward the water. As he does so, the piper manages to grab Amy by the hoodie. His attempt to drag her into the water with him is stymied, however, by Scotty, who grabs her waist and secures her. The piper then loses his grip and splashes into the black water.

Amy hopes the man is a worse swimmer than she. She anxiously watches as he flails about within his soaked garment. Then she sees an army of rats paddling toward him and witnesses no less than 20 large rodents climb onto the piper's body. He lashes out at them, but the piper is unable to fend off the oncoming rush while ensnared amongst his soaked cloak. It is poetic justice. The very rats that he had tried to drown are now the executors of one horrendous punishment.

Confident that she and her friends are now safe from the rat-covered maniac, Amy turns to aid her fallen brother.

She asks, "You okay, Scotty?"

"I'm fine. What about Mason?"

"He's okay... a little delusional—but what's new?"

The good-natured rib triggers a mutual grin.

"What about Jack, he took some nasty blows?"

Jack! What about Jack? Amy thinks and then says, "Scotty, get Mason out of the pool."

Amy rushes away from her brother toward the wall where Jack is leaning and holding the back of his head. Amy thinks he looks so fragile, so broken, and her heart flutters. She bends down beside him and hopes he is cognizant. To her relief, his bright blue eyes are open.

"Is it bad?" he asks.

"Looks fine to me. 'Course we are about a thousand feet underground in the dark on the banks of a sewer with black, nasty water, so it's easy to beat that."

The two share a smile. Then, half-joking, Jack asks, "Wanna kiss it and make it better?"

Amy gives him a serious look and asks, "You want me to?"

"No, I, uh.... I mean.... What I meant to say...."

She leans over and kisses his head and then leans back and smiles. "Better?"

"Yeah. But my lips hurt, too—you think you could—"

"Don't press your luck, Braddock," Amy teases.

They smile at each other.

Amy asks, "You ready to stand up?"

Before Jack can answer, though, Amy is already pulling him to his feet. He's woozy, and he braces himself on the wall for support.

Scotty approaches the two with Mason staggering alongside. Scotty is holding Lucky while Mason is looking around the room trying to register what just happened.

"What happened to the lifeguard?" Mason lazily utters.

The others exchange a look of concern, but Mason adds, "I'm kidding. There was a squirrel, though."

"Mason, we may need to see you to a doctor or something," Scotty says.

"I'm serious."

"Of course you are." Mason agrees.

The companions, all worse for the wear, shuffle one by one back to the ladder they were originally heading toward. Scotty and Amy take turns steadying the other boys. Amy, for one, has never been more thankful to get out of a room in her life. She is the last one to the ladder, and before she starts climbing, she gives one more glance in the direction of the piper. Then as she turns her gaze back to the ladder, something strange catches her eyes. She sees, midway down the tunnel, a squirrel, standing on two legs, watching her.

Chapter 101

Jack is the first one up the ladder. The cobwebs are starting to clear from his mind as he waits at the top of the exit for the other three. He sits giving no care to any dangers that may be lurking in this new room. He notices some grass and a tree or two then closes his eyes, just for a second. He thinks about obstacles he and his friends had encountered during the night. In comparison with the last 20 minutes of combat with the Pied Piper, Jack considers his group's overcoming of the other nemeses, such as the viper, the bear, the spider, and the matchstick girl, to have been a breeze. *It's like every situation escalates in sheer terror,* he thinks.

Jack reaches down to help Amy rise out of the hole while Mason grumbles, "My head feels like a washing machine."

"You think you might have a concussion?" Jack asks.

"Possibly." Then Mason thinks for a second and adds, "If I collapse, just roll my body to some corner and come back for me."

The others are glad that Mason's sense of humor has not been lost. And, even though an hour ago Jack might have taken Mason up on this offer to leave him, things have now changed because of the mutual experience they shared down in the tunnel.

They all take turns recounting the events in the sewer. Mason talks about the squirrel and his heroic cannonball. Jack speaks of his combat with the piper, and Amy retells her rescue of Mason, although she leaves out the part where Mason coughed up water into her mouth, and her final conflict with the piper.

Scotty, however, has taken a seat on the floor and remained silent during the storytelling.

Jack notices this and asks, "Okay, what gives, Scotty? You're being awful quiet."

Scotty briefly looks up at Jack and then buries his chin into his chest.

As Amy goes through the episode with the piper again for Mason, Jack approaches Scotty and places a hand on his head.

"Scotty? What's wrong?"

Shaking off the gesture, a red-faced, crying Scotty whimpers, "I just could not move. I stood there watching."

Tears are flowing from his face as he pushes his glasses back up the bridge of his nose.

Scotty says, "Mason was drowning, Amy jumped in to help, you were fighting, and all I could do was... nothing."

"We made it out, didn't we?" Jack notes, trying to encourage him.

"No thanks to me. I was too scared. I was... I'm a coward."

Jack responds, "You're not a coward, Scotty, so quit thinking you are. We need you in here. You shrunk that spider."

"Yeah, but only after I sat there watching you and Amy about to get eaten. What about next time? Am I simply going to watch my friends die?"

"No, you're not. It was you who mixed that potion that saved my life. You did that, Scotty. Not Mason or Amy, but you."

"But what about—"

"No, I don't want to hear it, Scotty."

Jack's assertive tone surprises himself, but he continues, "Okay, so you froze a couple of times. The three of us, well, we picked up your slack. Look, you are going to have to get up off your can and help us tonight. We can't make it out of here without you."

Jack's authoritative tone catches the attention of Amy and Mason, who join them.

"You okay, Scotty?" his sister asks.

"Yeah. I just needed a few seconds."

Scotty rises to his feet.

"Good," Jack confirms. "We've all had a rough night. I'm not sure how much longer we have to go before we finally get out of here, but we are all on the same page now. All the bickering needs to stop."

He shoots a look of confirmation at Mason, whose demeanor has changed to something weaker and less volatile. Mason nods.

"Okay, now let me see the map," Jack requests and holds a hand out to Mason, testing the newfound peace.

Quickly, with no hesitation, Mason hands the parcel over and says, "I think that if the room we are in now is The Chasm, then we are only three rooms away from the vault. But we still have not found any keys."

"We can worry about that when we get there," Jack asserts.

"All right, let's get back to business," Scotty affirms.

Jack holds out a fist to Scotty, who reaches forward and gives it a bump with his.

"So if we're in The Chasm, where's the chasm?" Scotty asks.

All of a sudden, they hear "mah-ah-ah-ah" to their right. They now pay attention to the environment of the room and realize that they are standing in a lush green field, complete with goats.

"Huh? Goats?" Jack mumbles.

Chapter 102

The wolf enters the sewer from a secret passageway. He looks around for any sign of the teenagers and sees the body of the piper pressed up against the side of the drain, almost entirely covered by rats.

He infers that the kids had been here and that he is too late. They seem more resourceful than he had considered, and a disturbing thought enters his mind: *What if they are too clever for even me? Nonsense, remember who you are. You are the wolf; they are your prey. Perhaps you will have a four-course meal?* After reassuring himself, the wolf straightens and sniffs the air. He surmises that the kids had not been gone long and wonders if he should take the ladder up behind them. However, he decides that the resourceful group will be able to keep moving, so he determines to travel further into the tunnels to the next ladder where he can take another passage and ambush them on the other side.

Chapter 103

So far, none of the goats have made a violent gesture towards the teen, but Mason's worried and asks, "What if they charge at Amy?"

"Um, charge Amy?" Jack responds.

"She's wearing red. Oh wait—that's bulls. My bad," Mason recalls.

"Sure you're okay?" Jack asks.

"I can still count by twos: three, six, nine, twelve.... Kidding."

Jack shakes his head. After their encounter with the piper, he is not sure whether or not the foursome could endure yet another close call. Although the break from danger had given the group time to heal mentally and physically, none of them had come through the journey unscathed. He had been bitten and apparently had nearly died; Mason was kicked in the jaw and nearly drowned; Scotty fell onto his shoulder through the vent and then was almost shot; and in addition to her hoodie catching on fire, Amy is being hunted by a wolf who wants to eat her. All in all, it has been a rough go for them.

"Great last trip to Enchanted Forrest, huh?" Jack muses cynically.

Still, Jack thinks the green field of this room is stunning. It's a plush verdant carpet of turf that supplies the goats with their sustenance.

None of the group appears to be in any great rush to start navigating this huge room, the largest one thus far. There is an unspoken pause of activity as if someone had called a timeout in this new room. But Jack soon starts getting antsy when he considers that another nefarious character could sneak up behind them. He determines that it's time to break the timeout.

He clears his throat and announces, "So, let's have a look around, right?"

"I'm not going anywhere near those goats," Mason answers.

"They're a third your size," Amy counters. "And you aren't wearing red."

Mason shakes his head and says, "But who knows in this place? They could shoot lasers out of their eyes."

Ignoring the last comment and walking over to the center of the room, Amy says, "I think it's safe to say I know why this room is called the chasm."

She ushers the other boys toward her, and soon Jack and Mason realize why, too, after arriving at Amy's side. From this vantage point, they can see a large deep canyon that runs the entire length of the room, splitting it into two equal parts. The two sides of the cliffs are roughly 25 feet apart.

"Over here," calls Scotty, who had wandered off a bit from the others. He's standing by a wooden bridge that spans the width of the gorge. "It's a bit rickety, but I think it will hold," Scotty estimates.

Jack figures that the verbal berating he had given himself has possibly motivated Scotty to take some more initiative.

"Lookout Mountain," Jack utters.

He and his family made annual trips to Lookout Mountain in Chattanooga, Tennessee, and there, just before you made it to the zenith of the mountain, you had to cross a bridge similar to this one, a swinging rope bridge. Jack, who has never been a fan of heights, hated every step. And, to make things worse, Blair has no such fear. She liked to hop up and down on the bridge and cause Jack to cower down on his hands and knees and grip the nearest available adult. This caused a bit of embarrassment when he was ten and accidentally grabbed hold of a particularly large, tobacco-chewing tourist from Austin, Texas, instead of one of his parents..

This bridge stretched over this present chasm is nowhere near as long as the Lookout Mountain one, but it is just as imposing to Jack, whose nerves are already worn thin.

"What's up, Jack?" Amy asks, noticing the sweat beading on his forehead.

"Oh, nothing," he lies. "Mason, you going first?" Jack asks, assuming Mason would jump at the chance to be the alpha male again.

"Nope, I think Scotty should go," Mason answers.

Jack is perplexed and thinks, *Something is just not right with him. Is he trying to make Scotty man-up? No, that's not like Mason. Something must be wrong.*

"Okay, I'll go," Scotty says and gulps.

He slowly extends a foot over the first planks of the wooden bridge and presses down on it. A relieved expression crosses his face, and he declares, "It's pretty solid."

After being assured that the bridge will hold, Mason follows Scotty onto it.

"Ladies first," Jack says and extends his arm out over the bridge while bowing to Amy.

"Why, thank you, kind sir, but I insist, you first," Amy tells him and gives a curtsy in return.

Jack considers how it seems odd to be having fun and flirting in this place. But, he figures, they're teenagers, and that's what they do.

Although it is not a far walk from one side of the chasm to the other, for Mason, Jack, and Amy, it seems like crossing the bridge is taking forever. This is because Scotty, ever cautious, is taking deliberate steps. Jack imagines that he could count "ten Mississippi" in the time it takes Scotty to move one step.

Jack extends his hand back to Amy, and she reaches out and clasps it. The boy looks back and she returns his gaze with a wry smile. It's exactly what the doctor ordered for Jack. He now realizes that all his previous worrying about whether or not Amy was agreeing with him or someone else didn't matter; It's obvious they like each other, and a disagreement here or there wasn't going to change that. His excitement about being in the throes of his first true crush makes Jack forget about fearing the chasm. In fact, the deep plunge to the unseen bottom of the cliff seems to hold no danger to Jack now. He is clearly under the protection of Cupid.

The travelers are halfway across the chasm, when Jack suddenly remembers the words of the P.S. in Douglas Finch's notebook: "P.S. Do not cross the bridge."

Unfortunately, it is too late, for from below they hear a menacing growl, "Arrrggghhh."

"Great. Just great. What now?" Mason cries.

Then, as if it had been shot upwards from a cannon, a huge horrible olive green creature flies from below the bridge to up above the bridge before landing on it with a thud, causing the entire structure to bounce. Looking up, Jack sees a massive troll blocking their path.

Chapter 104

Jack admonishes himself, thinking, *I should have known from the first moment I saw the goats. It is so obvious, now. What was I thinking? And Scotty—Scotty of all people—should have known this bridge would be straight out of the "Three Billy Goats Gruff."*

This troll is at least six-foot-five and is standing directly in front of Scotty. Jack thinks that it may be the most grotesque sight he has ever born witness to. It has green leathery skin, a bulbous nose with multiple black moles, and a mangy mess of a red beard that drapes down its bare chest.

The beast roars, "Who dares cross my bridge?"

Its teeth show no signs of dental care, and its breath, Jack thinks, is bad enough to kill small land-dwelling mammals.

Jack is suddenly aware that someone has grabbed him around the knees. He looks down and sees that it's Mason. *Wait a minute... Mason?* he questions. Jack would have predicted that Mason would have been the one to act first in this situation by speaking or doing something else. However, he's about as far from fulfilling that role as possible at the moment. The kick to his jaw and the subsequent spell of blackness had apparently triggered something within him. Jack wonders if his trauma surfaced some deep fear that Mason had not considered before or if it's a matter of Mason being confronted with the reality that he could in fact die.

"Answer me! Who dares cross my bridge!?"

Scotty says, "Uh... We do?"

"'We do?' Who are 'we'?" the troll rumbles.

"Uh, sir, we just want to pass, that's all. We're trying to go home," Scotty utters.

Mason releases his grip on Jack and stands up.

Jack stammers, "Uh, sir—Mr. Troll—uh, we would love to stay and chat, but we are very late for an important meeting."

"A meeting, you say?"

"Yes sir."

"Well, I have meeting as well. I am tired of eating goat. I think you might have a meeting with my stomach—har har har! Of course, the Queen has told me to let you pass."

Jack had forgotten about the Queen and is comforted in being reminded that they do have allies.

"But she's not my boss," says the troll. "She thinks she can tell me what to do. Sends her henchman to give me orders—bah! I will do as I please. I am hungry. Goat, goat, goat. That's all I eat. She will not deprive me of a little human flesh here and there."

Jack looks at the large club extending from the monster's hand to the bridge floor and calls out, "Mr. Troll, sir, you don't want to eat us. We are scrawny compared to the next group of kids."

"Next group?"

"Yeah, there is another group of travelers."

"There are more of you coming?"

"About eight, that's twice as many as us. And from what I saw, they are much larger."

The troll looks at the rather robust size of Scotty and drools. A line of spit drops from his mouth to the bridge.

"You do not lie?"

"Uh, no, I mean, yes, I am not lying. Big kids coming this way.... Go check for yourself," Jack lies.

He has not pegged the troll as a bright one and watches while it thinks. Then he sees the massive green monster grab Scotty and lift him up and place him on his other side.

Jack thinks, *He's bought the story. How ironic: just like the real tale.*

In order to avoid being touched by the troll, Mason scoots to one side of the bridge. There is little room for both the troll and him. Then the troll passes from Mason to Jack, who almost hurls at the wafting scent. The stench reminds him of a combination of road kill, bologna, and his Aunt Helen's sock drawer.

The troll passes Amy over and they are almost completely off the bridge, when the bridge starts bouncing up and down violently. The troll turns around and sees Scotty bolting to the other side of the bridge. It growls and charges back toward them.

Chapter 105

They all see the troll barreling toward them, and they flee to the other side of the bridge. Jack looks to the front of the structure and sees that the ropes of the bridge are tied to a large wooden stake at the end. He thinks that if they could just untie the rope before the troll gets to the other side, then it would fall into the ravine.

When Jack sees that Scotty and Mason are clear of the bridge, he yells, "Untie the rope!"

However, Scotty ignores the call and just keeps running toward the door. Mason also ignores Jack's plea and follows Scotty.

Jack realizes he will have to untie the rope. The boy hastily reaches to the thick rope knotted around the post. He strains to undo it, but it's too tight. Jack looks back and sees that the troll has almost caught up to them. He wonders how such a large beast could move so quickly.

The troll reaches out, grabs Amy, and turns her around. Then, as if she were a child's play doll, he lifts her with one of his trunk-like arms and holds her over the ravine.

Amy screams in terror, and this stops Scotty in his tracks. He turns around, and after seeing his sister in a helpless condition, he fumbles in his pants for the scissors while racing to stand beside Jack on the bridge.

Scotty yanks out the shears and, holding them like a knife, demands, "Put her down!"

The troll recognizes the false bravado of the pudgy boy with his shaking scissors and simply laughs.

Then he grunts, "You want me to drop her?"

Chapter 106

In an elegant room somewhere within the ride, the Queen, who's now wearing a regal dress, is sitting upon a throne made entirely of candy. The rest of the room is also splendored in tasty treats, such as a fountain of chocolate and tall arches of gumdrops. The squirrel is there, too, perched upon the arm of the chair.

"Well done!" says the lady. "It seems to me you have done nothing to interfere with the conditions of the prophecy. I must admit, I was fearful they would falter once they came into contact of some of our less hospitable residents."

Chirps and squeaks emit from the squirrel.

"Yes, Victor should have been there."

Then, as if summoned by her voice, the man enters.

"Victor, where have you been?"

"Uh, I have been following the travelers just as you asked."

"Is that so?"

"Yes, milady. They are doing a splendid job. Everything is going according to plan."

"Victor, then why is it that our friend here tells me that the travelers have encountered some trouble along their way."

The man bows and replies, "Yes, milady, I am truly sorry. I have been following them, but it has been a might bit tricky. Some of your less gracious subjects have not given me pass."

"Of course. But Victor, I asked you to aid them when you saw fit. I understand that they had some trouble in The Grove as well?"

"I was there watching from the shadows. It was a bit touch-and–go, as they say, but these four, these teens, they are resilient. I am doing just as you asked. I am only going so far as to keep them safe."

"And the sewer?"

"Milady, you know I can't deal with that match girl. They made it through all right. In fact, I think they did-in the piper."

"There are worse things here than the piper. If they fail, we will all die here. You must help them no matter your personal feelings, are we clear?"

"Yes, milady."

"And the bridge keeper understands my orders?"

"Given to him by myself, milady. He understands and will allow them passage."

"He had better. I am a bit unsettled. All of us, the entire community, depend on their success. Perhaps you should take a more active role? I fear for their survival, in spite of the prophecy."

"Of course, my Queen. I will hasten to them at once."

"Good. You are lucky that my pet here," she says while stroking the fur of the squirrel, "was less apprehensive about helping."

"I apologize. I will go. I did give them the coins, and they do have the map."

"Yes, I know. Thank you, Victor. What of the wolf?"

"He is pursuing them just as we planned. If he gets too close, I will take action."

"Excellent. All is well, although I cannot say it has been smooth."

"Yes, again I am sorry, my Queen."

"Go now, and push them gently."

With another low bow, the man rushes to a spot in the wall where two large, red-striped, candy canes hang suspended by a rope of taffy. He quickly grabs and lowers the one on the right, and an exit appears from nowhere in the wall, which the man scampers through.

The Queen then gently whispers to the squirrel, "He means well, my pet. Thank you for your brave action. Continue monitoring the situation."

The squirrel runs off after Victor, and the Queen eases back into her throne, closes her eyes, and dreams of freedom.

Chapter 107

They have searched every room in the ride, from the very first room to the last. After back-tracking to make one last check, they stand in the center of the ominous room where the empty cart sits.

"How could we have missed them?" Oliver asks. "Clyde, is there some escape route or somewhere we have not checked?"

"No, not as far as I know," he answers.

"There has to be some secret passage in here. Either that, or the kids gave us the slip," Colton suggests while placing one foot in the direction of the nearest exit.

"Should we go back and check the first few rooms again?" Oliver suggests.

"Maybe," Clyde replies. He is weary and flustered.

Neither Oliver nor Colton had been working when Douglas Finch disappeared. If they had, they would have the same sinking feeling as Clyde right now.

The radio at Clyde's side squeaks with Gwen's voice: "Clyde, the police are here."

Oh boy, Snodgrass will love that, thinks Clyde.

Gwen asks, "You found them yet?"

"Don't you think I'd have...." Clyde starts but cuts himself off, realizing he sounds a bit testy. After a pause, he says, "Nope, no sign of them. Are the cops coming in?"

"Yeah, I think. They're done questioning everyone out here."

Clyde looks at Colton and Oliver and motions to them as he tells Gwen, "I am sending Oliver and Colton back outside. Tell the cops I will meet them about halfway into the ride."

Oliver asks, "Are you sure, Clyde? We can stay if you would like."

He looks back to Colton for agreement, but he is gone. He left the room as soon as he heard the old man's reply to Gwen.

"No, Oliver, go on. We've searched the building; that's all we can do. Let's let the boys in blue take it from here."

"Okay," affirms Oliver, who then heads out of the room.

As soon as Oliver is gone, Clyde hears the calliope music, which produces a complete feeling of dread in him. He peers over his shoulder to the space in the wall that seems to be the source of the sound, and despite having examined this spot at least three times before, he sees something different now. This time there's a neon green sign with the word "Enter" glowing ominously.

Huh, thinks Clyde, *That's new.*Chapter 108The troll makes the boys stand together, threatening to drop Amy into the ravine if they don't comply. Scotty knows the situation is hopeless. Amy joins them, and now all four are prisoners of the troll, who nimbly ties a rope around his newfound detainees and forces them to sit with their backs facing each other.

While standing over them and licking his crusty lips, the troll relishes in his victory.

It says, "This is splendid indeed. I woke up this morning with the dry taste of goat still in my mouth. Little did I know I would have a much more enjoyable meal today!"

"But you did tell the Queen you would let us pass," Jack implores, looking for some way out.

"Yes, I did. But how is she going to know? I think I will simply tell her you all stumbled into the ravine. She will almost certainly fall for that."

Wicked laughter bursts forth from the creature. It is pleased with this play on words so much that it repeats the phrase: "Get it, fall for that?"

The troll looks back toward the bridge and wonders aloud, "Now, where exactly did I put my blade?" It walks away, searching the ground with a lowered head.

Scotty tries to free himself by wiggling, but this isn't working. However, an idea springs into his head.

He whispers, "Pssst! The rope is only tied in one spot. If we all squeeze together as tight as possible, it will relax. Then there might just be enough slack in the rope to get out."

"What good will that do?" Mason utters while eyeing the troll. "If we make a break for the door, the troll will catch us. It's not like we could all get away. I think we would only make him mad."

With a lowered voice, Jack declares, "We have to at least try. Just keep thinking. And, consider what we would do next if we can get out." He turns his head to spy on the troll and asks, "Scotty, what have you read about trolls? Do they have a weakness?"

Scotty thinks, mentally scanning through the pages of dozens of books.

He says, "Well, in the Tolkien books, they turn to stone in sunlight. But there is no sun in here. In a book I read called *Three Kings and Three Lions*, they were scared of fire. They are usually dim-witted, but this one seems at least a little smarter, although his rope tying skills are lacking."

Amy hurries her brother by saying, "Come on, Scotty, this is not the time for a lecture."

"Okay, I'm trying.... Um, in another book, I can't recall the name of, the trolls are extremely ticklish."

"Oh great—trolls are ticklish! Even if he is, what good will that do?" Mason comments, dismayed at the hopeless situation.

"I don't know," Scotty admits.

"It's a start," Jack encourages. "Scotty, which weaknesses does this troll have?"

"It is impossible to know, but maybe—just maybe...."

Scotty's face brightens, and he says, "That's it! It's a crazy idea but one that might just work."

Chapter 109

"This is our only chance. You're going to have to trust me," Scotty declares.

"Whatever," Mason says.

"We have no other choice," Jack points out.

Scotty continues, "When I count to three, squeeze together, push back against each other, and stand. Then, just follow my lead."

The troll is several yards away searching for his blade. It turns back for a second and says, "I hear you talking. Keep your mouths shut."

Lowering his tune to a faint whisper, Jack asserts, "Okay, Scotty, I'm game."

"Me, too," Amy adds.

Mason chimes in, "What else am I gonna do?"

"Just count, Scotty," Jack asserts.

"I told you kids to be quiet!" the troll bellows.

"One," starts Scotty as he fumbles at the outside of his pocket, checking for some item.

"Two."

Scotty is sweating, concentrating on his exact moves. He's telling himself, *I will not freeze, I will not freeze.*

"Three."

All four press together, and just as Scotty predicted, the rope goes slack and drops from their chests to their waists. After another shift, the rope falls to the ground.

With its back to the kids, the troll leans down and says, "Here you are."

It stands brandishing a rough looking goat antler sharpened at the end to a sinister point. Then it turns and sees the teens standing free from the rope.

"Making me work for my supper, I see. Well, I'll fix that!" says the troll, and it charges toward them.

Mason shouts, "Run for it!" but before any of them begin their flight, Scotty steps boldly out toward the troll.

"Stop right there, troll! I am a powerful magician and can create fire."

The lie provides just enough absurdity to make the troll stop and laugh.

Still, Scotty continues his farce, saying, "I am the Great Scott, and I will summon fire! You will burn to a crisp if you come any closer."

The others are astonished by the sudden bravery of Scotty and watch as he pulls the matchbox from his pocket and lights one of the matches they had "purchased" from the girl.

Scotty sees a look of surprise in the troll's face and thinks, *Excellent! This troll is afraid of fire.*

However, in spite of the obvious hesitance in the beast's face, the troll yells, "Think you're going to scare me off with a little flame, huh?"

"Stay where you are, foolish troll. This is just a mere taste of my power. Let us go and I will not incinerate you."

The troll stands its ground and thinks for a second.

This is actually going to work, thinks Scotty, but his confidence in the plan is dashed as the troll's face breaks into a devious grin.

"Then why didn't you already burn me, oh great magician?"

Jack, the quicker thinker, breaks in and says, "We were simply testing you to see if you would follow the Queen's orders."

The troll stops grinning and says, "A test, huh?"

Just then, Scotty's match begins to burn out, and he immediately tries to light another from the matchbox.

The Troll's hideous grin returns, and it says, "This is just some childish trick. You ain't no wizard."

Then, like a ball shot from a cannon, the troll springs at Scotty. He knocks the matchbox to the ground and lifts Scotty up by the legs.

There is nothing any of the others can do but watch since they have no hope of overpowering the giant troll.

"So here we are again," the troll says and laughs while walking over to the bridge. It lifts Scotty's helpless body over the top of the ropes and dangles him down over the chasm. Then, he adds, "You young ones sure are causing me a bit of a headache. Maybe I'll just drop you. No, you're too tasty of a morsel."

Although he is helpless, Scotty is unusually calm. He does the only thing he knows he can do as a last resort. He has spied the enormous bare feet of the troll, partially hanging off of the bridge, and he begins tickling them.

Chapter 110

Jack watches as Scotty begins to tickle the bare feet of the troll. To his astonishment, the troll starts laughing—not just giggling, but bursting out with howls of laughter.

"Stop that," the troll mutters between breaths. All of a sudden, the troll drops the antler. Then he also drops Scotty.

"No!" Amy screams.

"Scotty!" Mason yells from behind Jack.

Jack does not want to look, but before he turns away, he sees Scotty grab onto the ropes on the side of the bridge. However, he's barely hanging on.

Jack charges to the matchbox on the ground and declares, "Now you're in for it!"

He attempts to strike a match as quickly as he can, but the first one breaks. Quickly, Jack nimbly retrieves another, and this time it lights. Then, with a gallant charge, he throws the burning match at the troll, who recoils in fear. It's a near miss.

Amy calls, "Mason, come on!" and runs toward Scotty.

Mason is standing with a look of fear that none of them has ever seen before. He watches, eyes fixed on Scotty ahead of him, just beyond is the next set of doors. Eventually, he moves and begins to rush in the direction of Scotty. But he does not stop to help his friend. Instead, he's headed for the door.

Amy is shocked by this sudden retreat of Mason. She struggles to pull Scotty from his tenuous hold.

Scotty cries, "I can't hold on much longer—my shoulder!" The pain is obvious in his wide eyes.

Amy drapes her arms underneath her brother's and falls back with all of her might. The desperate heave allows Scotty to lift one of his legs onto the floor of the bridge. Amy is then able to help roll the rest of him to safety.

Jack is slowly advancing toward the troll. With confidence beaming, he calls out, "Woe to you, troll. I am the true magician; the others are merely my apprentices."

He is laying it on thick and enjoying the ruse, but then he thinks, *Time to go for the jugular*. Once he is less than five feet away from the vile creature, Jack lights the rest of the matches at once including the matchbox. This begins to burn his hand, but Jack ignores the pain for a second and throws the burning box at the troll.

The fiend cries in absolute fear and runs in full sprint back to the bridge. Then, with a fluent leaping motion, he vaults himself over both Amy and Scotty and plunges into the chasm. It is a full five seconds before they hear a crashing sound, followed by a cry of pain.

A sense of relief pervades the group. They hear another agonizing howl of pain waft up from the darkness below. The creature is alive but in no shape to pursue them.

Jack calls down into the abyss, "Do not bother us again, fowl creature."

Then, looking back to his comrades, Jack motions them towards the door. The three remaining teens bolt to the exit, and as they run, Scotty lifts Lucky from the ground.

Just before Jack spills into the next room, he looks back. A goat has wandered onto the bridge and is peering over the edge. It turns its head to Jack, and he's taken aback by the expression on its face. He asks himself, *Can goats actually smile?*

Chapter 111

In the next room, the four relieved teens spend a few moments in silent recovery.

Then Jack approaches Scotty and says, "That was brilliant, just brilliant," while clasping his shoulder.

"Ouch!" the boy responds.

"Oh, sorry," Jack apologizes.

In spite of the throb in his shoulder, though, Scotty is beaming, for he feels that his shortcomings from the previous encounters have been redeemed.

"Hey, big brother, you totally saved us back there," Amy encourages.

Mason utters, "Thanks."

Jack is confused by Mason's dour gratefulness. He shakes his head and asks, "What is it with you? You're totally acting weird."

"I am not," a defensive Mason counters.

"Sure you're not," Jack gently responds in a sarcastic manner.

Mason takes out the map and quietly studies it.

Meanwhile, Scotty looks over all of Lucky's wounds, and Amy leans over to Jack and asks, "What's gotten into Mason?"

"I think he's scared."

Their conversation is stopped, though, by Mason announcing, "I just don't get it. We should be in the vault."

Jack scans the new room. There are some small trees, and a small pond, where three dark-brown ducks are gliding through the water here and there. A large goose mimics their swimming motion.

"We still don't have the key either," Amy points out.

Scotty walks toward the pond.

"Not too close, bro," Amy calls.

"I know, I'm just looking around, taking a gander."

None of the others acknowledges this pun, but Jack knows that the witty comment indicates that Scotty is feeling better.

Scotty continues, "Don't worry, I'm just checking things out. Remember the matchstick girl room? Maybe the vault is behind another hidden passage."

"Makes sense," Jack responds. "Let's all have a... gander then."

Mason folds the map and walks toward the other end of the room. There are once again two sets of doors located to the left and right.

He sulks and says, "But the map shows that The Vault is here."

Amy and Jack spread out in different directions for more inspection of the room.

As Jack moves to one of the corners, he contemplates some of the unanswered questions: *Why did the words stop in the story? Does it mean something? Where are the missing pages? If there is no more story, how are we going to finish it? How do we get to the happily-ever-after?*

"Found it!" Scotty exclaims.

Jack turns to see Scotty standing before a cleverly concealed ladder, which has been made in the image of a tree. This time, the ladder leads up instead of down. They reason that this must lead to the vault.

"Good going, Scotty! You are on fire," says Jack.

None of them, not even Scotty, attempts to make a joke of Jack's last words.

Chapter 112

Rung by rung, Jack ascends the ladder with the others below him. He encounters a small wooden door that easily flips upward and reveals a new tunnel. Jack lifts himself up onto a wooden floor and glances around at the new path. To his right is a clay wall, and to his left is a long tunnel lit by several torches evenly spaced along the hall. It is an intimidating sight. Shadows flicker along the walls, which cause the room to feel alive and foreboding. He realizes they will have to walk down that path.

"Come on up," Jack calls to the others.

Instantly, Amy's head pops up.

"The others are right behind."

As Scotty enters the tunnel, he remarks, "This is the vault?"

Mason is the last up the ladder.

Jack asserts, "I'm going to assume that the vault is at the end of this path. I can't really see that far, but I'm guessing there will be a set of doors down there."

"Good, then we can get a hold of that treasure," Mason adds.

"More importantly, we can get out," Amy responds.

"But we still don't have the keys," Scotty notes.

Jack says, "We will cross that bridge when we get there. For now, let's just get down there and see what's ahead."

Jack takes the first step forward. There is no need for the flashlight with the torches lighting up the tunnel. It's a slow walk. Occasionally, a harmless bat flies from the dark ceiling and zooms down the hall. Due to all they've experienced so far, these bats, which at one time would have inspired a feeling of mutual panic, especially in Amy, do not even cause a shudder amongst the four hardened teens.

Soon, the group is able to make out a large door at the end of the hall. It's solid with no handle, and Jack can see writing etched into the wall just above the frame.

He says, "Look at that," and points this out to the others.

All four look at the writing, and Scotty begins to read the obviously ancient script:

"Four will enter the wood one day
With one chance to free all along their way.
All those trapped in their place can be freed,
A thief, wanderer, apprentice and tailor indeed.

The four must overcome on their own,
For this path they cannot be shown.
During their journey they will collect the keys,
Only the four, to enter as they please."

Scotty pauses then declares, "I think Jack is right." Defensively, Mason answers, "About what? It sounds like another bunch of the narrator's gobbledigook to me."

"We are the four," Scotty affirms. "The thief, the wanderer, the apprentice, and the tailor."

"Oh great, now you're going to go all narrator-crazy on me, too?" Mason whines.

"No, I am just saying that maybe there is some merit in these rhymes after all," Scotty carefully answers.

Jack grins in justification, but his enjoyment is cut short because Amy questions, "So who is who? Who's the thief?" giving another disapproving glare at Mason.

Jack's heart sinks, and he tells himself, *Oh man, I'm in trouble.* He decides to change the line of discussion and asks, "But what about the keys?"

"It said we would have them," Scotty confidently declares.

Jack looks at Amy, who is still surveying everyone else, trying to determine the identities of the four.

"What if the keys are like a mental thing? It never said what kind of keys they are," Scotty thinks aloud.

"Well if the treasure is behind the door and we have the keys, then let's just shove the thing open," Mason states.

He marches up to the door and pushes on it, but the door does not budge. However, at that very moment, the sound of stone grinding against stone rumbles to the right of the door, and a small chevron-shaped opening appears at the place in the wall where the sound was coming from.

"What is that?" Mason asks.

All four approach the indentation to observe it more closely. The opening is small.

"Mason!" Scotty hollers.

"Geez, Carnahan, I am right beside you!"

"Oh, sorry, Mason. Listen, you are the one who pushed on the door."

"So?"

"Look at the shape, it's like a chevron."

"A what?" Mason asks.

"A chevron is like, never mind. It's the shape of something you have, just look."

"The badge!" Mason yells, matching the previous volume of his friend.

Hurriedly, he pulls out the badge and places it into the groove. It's a perfect fit, but nothing changes.

"Now what," Mason, who's a little dejected, asks.

"I don't know," Scotty says. "I just assumed something would happen." He pushes his sliding glasses back up his nose.

They take a few seconds to consider the question before them. Then Jack breaks the silence by saying, "Keys—get it! Keys plural—not key. Amy, touch the door."

She gives Jack a quizzical look, but shrugs and walks over to the door. As soon as her hands touch it, the same stone lurching sound begins but to the left of the door this time. Then a long narrow indention appears in the rock.

"The stick, Amy, it's the stick! We do have the keys!" Scotty exclaims.

Amy places her stick into the space. It's another perfect fit.

Jack says, "It's just like the Douglas Finch thing said."

At this point, a sudden thought disturbs him and keeps him from saying another word. He has just vindicated Mason. Jack wonders if he had put his faith in the wrong thing after all. This realization disturbs him. In his mind, he remembers the statement "Keys will cry out to you" and realizes that each of them had instinctively grabbed something from the ride. Jack thinks, *Perhaps the narrator was wrong.*

"More proof, guys. The Finch stuff is legit," Mason crows.

"Okay, my turn," a confident Scotty declares. He touches the door, and another shape appears in the wall, this time just to the left of the badge. The shape is clearly the formation of a pair of scissors.

"Just as I suspected," says Scotty. "After all, I am the tailor's apprentice. Your turn, Jack."

Jack knows what his key is and knows that he must reveal it, but he's concerned that doing so will disappoint Amy. He touches the wall slowly while looking warily at the girl, praying that she will not figure out that he's the thief. He gulps, and a gap appears in the wall.

Jack reaches slowly into his backpack, and then he hesitates and says, "Uh, Amy, why don't you and Mason look for a... uh...."

Amy's face shows that she will not take the bait for what Jack is obviously intending to be a distraction.

"Oh, never mind," says Jack.

He searches his pockets for something else, hoping against hope that perhaps something else could be the key besides the goose. Then he has another idea: *What if I place my entire backpack into the hole?* He shapes the pack around its articles and places it into the crevice, but nothing happens. *Who am I kidding?* Jack thinks.

He resigns himself to the fact that the gig is up and opens the backpack. Slowly, he removes the goose for all to see. Immediately he looks at Amy, who is staring at him in disapproval.

Chapter 113

Amy is stunned. She thinks, *Of all the people who might've stolen that goose.... How could it be Jack? But it is. When could he have taken it, though?*

Her mind is racing, and she asks, "Jack? You're the thief?" Her surprise is obvious to all.

"But, Amy, we all took something from the ride. Mason took the badge, Scotty took the scissors, and you took the stick. This is what we were supposed to do," Jack tries to reason.

"I took the stick because I was alone and scared. Are you saying you took the goose 'cause you were scared, Jack?"

"No."

"I would expect this from Mason, but I thought you were better than that."

The whole night begins to clear up in front of her eyes.

She says, "Wait a minute. You left me in the train so you could steal the goose, didn't you?"

Jack doesn't answer, but his body language says all she needs to know.

"So all this time, I thought it was Mason's fault that you abandoned me, but it wasn't. It was yours."

"Lighten up, Amy. It's clear that—"

"Mason, stop talking, or I'm gonna retrieve my stick and swing for the fences, you get it?"

Mason returns to his more recent sheepish self and only nods.

Now the venom is filling Amy, and she turns all her wrath, all her anger, and all her frustration that have been building up throughout the night at Jack.

She says, "Listen here, Jack, you had me fooled. I fell for it hook, line, and sinker. You tried to pass yourself off as some knight in shining armor, but I see through that now. You're really just a thief. A thief who has risked all of our lives just to steal some dime store goose. Jack, we've nearly been killed time and time again all because of that, that thing."

Amy pauses a second catching her breath and then with misty eyes, she delivers the final blow. "And there I was thinking that something was happening between us. Was that all a game, too?"

Furious and unrelenting, Amy reaches out and snatches the goose from the startled hands of Jack.

Jack is speechless and motionless as Amy shoves the goose into the opening.

At once a clicking sound emits from the door, and the large barrier creaks open.

For their part, Scotty and Mason are dumbfounded at the outburst. Neither of them grasps the full weight of what is happening between Amy and Jack.

A few more silent seconds pass before Mason shakes off his bewilderment. He rubs his hands together and heads for the newly opened door, saying, "Golden treasure, here we come."

The four keys fall to the floor, and Mason greedily retrieves his badge while Scotty snags the scissors. Amy watches Jack to see if he will actually pick up the goose again. She wonders if he could possibly be that selfish.

Jack looks at Amy, and their eyes meet. It is as if he is trying to apologize for what he is about to do. Calmly, he turns his gaze away, takes a short step, bends down, and picks up the goose.

The thief can't let his treasure go, thinks Jack.

Amy sighs and picks up the stick.

Mason moves through the door first, and Scotty follows close behind.

Amy looks at Jack and tries to penetrate his heart with a deadeye glare. Jack shrugs, and she turns to face the door. The vault, the destination they have been seeking, is before them.

Chapter 114

Things with Amy have taken a horrible turn for the worse for Jack. His brain is quivering with the realization that he has just blown his chance. Up to this point, all he wanted was to be near her. He had focused so much on the "thing" that was going on between them that the hardships they had mutually faced had been regarded by Jack as simply a shared experience, the most bizarre first date of all time. But now, the wanderlust for the prop, and the revelation of his theft, have left things broken. In Jack's mind, after seeing the morbid face of Amy, things feel irreparable.

He thinks, *Why is she so mad?* He wants to blame her, to explain it all away, thinking, *She's the one who's taking this way out of context.* But the fact is that Amy had put it together that he had actually been the reason they were all in this mess. Jack considers that this new revelation would almost certainly trump all the hand-holding and flirting of the past few hours. Even though the door to the vault hangs open, it does little to make Jack feel one bit better. In spite of the victory of reaching their goal, he can take no joy in it. He thinks, *It's my fault we are here. She is right.*

Amy walks past him without giving him the slightest acknowledgement. Then Jack puts the goose back into his backpack and drearily follows the others into the next room. After taking three steps through the door, Jack halts quickly. The others are standing with their backs to him, simply gazing around the room.

"Would you look at this place," Scotty admires.

"I don't see any treasure," Mason remarks. "Looks like nerd heaven."

What Mason is referring to is evident to Jack immediately. The room is circular, and rows and rows of shelves circle the room from the floor to the very high ceiling, roughly some 30 feet above their heads. Each of the shelves is stacked with books. He surmises that there must be hundreds of thousands of books.

"Some vault this turned out to be," a dejected Mason broods. "What are we supposed to get here? Aren't we supposed to get some treasure outta here and take it to the gingerbread house?"

"That's what we guessed, Mason," Amy adds. "I think we guessed wrong."

Just hearing Amy's voice makes Jack rub his temple in memory of how their relationship had gone bad so quickly. He wonders, *What can I say? What do I do?* He contemplates initiating an attempt at recompense with the girl, but before he has time to do so, he's interrupted by the sound of a man clearing his throat.

A voice utters, "And so they came to see the man, who tried reveal to them a plan."

Spinning quickly away from the shelf-covered walls and toward the center of the room where the voice came from, Jack spots a desk he did not notice before. He thinks, *That voice... it's so familiar.* The man at the desk is sitting in a large black chair with his back toward them. Then, slowly, the chair turns to face them.

All four have the same jaw-dropping reaction. There seated before them, living and breathing, is the narrator.

Chapter 115

Jack is hit by a mixture of confusion and, at the same time, comfort. He realizes that this is not a robot or a mannequin, or else, Jack thinks, if it is, it's the coolest one ever. But, Jack has to believe this really is a man—*the* man, there before them all.

He can only manage to squeak out the words, "What? How?"

"Greetings, travelers."

Just like his plastic counterparts, the man's head is covered in a white tussle of hair, white facial hair adorns his chin and carpets his upper lip, and a wrinkled white suit clings to his barrel-like chest. Jack thinks these characteristics make him look like Mark Twain.

The man says, "So I see the time has come after all these years."

Mason is the first to put together a sensible question and asks, "Who are you?" with a hint of confrontation in his voice.

"Me? Well, I guess you can call me Sam. Some of the employees here in the ride have taken to calling me that. They think I look like this Samuel fellow."

Jack waits for the man to continue, to tell them something else and ease the confusion each of them is experiencing, but the man does not continue. He simply fiddles with a pencil on his desk and stares flippantly at the teens.

"Uh, Mr. Narrator, uh, Sam," Jack asks sheepishly, "Could you tell us where we are?"

"Lost, a little lost."

"Yes, we know that. How do we get out? That's all we want," Jack explains.

"Yes, my young friend, that is what they all want."

"Who do you mean by 'they'?" Scotty asks.

"Why everyone—everyone here at least."

"So, do you know how to get out?" Mason inquires, his voice now tinged with frustration.

"The manner of your leaving, my dear tailor, is up to you. You determine the outcome of this story."

The man winks at them and continues to fiddle with his pencil.

Jack has heard this before. Just like in the rhymes throughout the ride, this narrator, this Mr. Sam, is telling them to finish the story.

Jack asks the man, "So we're supposed to finish the story, just like you said, I mean those models of you said?"

"Exactly."

Jack feels a sense of vindication and continues, "So you've been trying to tell us what to do, right? Giving us hints along the way?"

"You could say that."

Mason quickly asks, "So I am the tailor, right? And Jack, here, is the thief?"

Jack winces at the proclamation.

"Amy is the wanderer, and Scotty is the apprentice?" Mason adds.

"That is correct," The man affirms.

"So, what does that mean?" Mason asks.

"These are simply the roles you are playing," Sam answers.

Amy says, "Look, I don't care who is playing who. I just want to get out of this place and go home. Can you help us or not?"

Jack is a little startled by the tone of her voice.

"My dear girl, like I said, it is all up to you."

At this point even Jack is growing weary of the cryptic responses. He attempts to change course and asks, "So, Mr. Sam, what are the books for?"

"To record stories, of course. I am the keeper of stories. I protect them here in my library—a vast treasure."

"Whose stories, exactly?" Amy asks.

"Like I said, everyone here," the narrator replies.

Scotty nods and says, "I get it; this is The Vault."

Jack begins to connect some dots in his own head and asks, "By 'everyone,' you mean these books are the stories of everyone who has entered the ride?"

"Anyone who enters the woods has their story written here," Sam states.

It is becoming clearer, at least to Jack, and he rushes another question, "So you're saying my story is written here?"

"Your story is in a book," Sam affirms.

Jack feels like he is on a roll but now decides to ask the question that has bothered him for much of the night.

He says, "Okay, I understand. So you were talking to us through those books, trying to help us get somewhere." Jack gives a confident look to Mason and continues, "But we got to a point, and then there were these missing pages?"

"Yes, well, the answer is simple. Your story is not yet complete," Sam says and grins.

Before Jack can ask another question, Mason bursts out, "Look, we are tired of the riddles and the games, the unfinished story garbage. Where is the gold? We need to get the gold."

The man rises to his feet, still smiling. He sets the pencil down on the desk and walks by them. Stopping beside the door, he remarks, "Ah, so you seek the gold. Well, I cannot help you. It is for you to choose the path you take. Thus far, you have chosen to ignore my words. Jack, I have told you all along you must finish the story, you must make things right. That is all I can say."

With that, the mysterious Sam leaves.

Jack is angry at Mason's impetuousness and wonders, *Did he drive the narrator away?* He has so many questions, and he calls out, "Wait! Sam! What do you mean make things right?"

Instead of answering, though, the man walks into the tunnel and disappears into the dark.

Jack rushes to follow him; however, it seems to him that the man has vanished into thin air.

"Mason, you made him leave!" Jack cries back at the others. "He was here in the flesh. He could have helped us."

Mason leads the others into the hall and responds, "He was not telling us anything. He was just giving us more riddles. We want to know how to get out, not play games. All he told us was what we already knew. What did he tell us that will help one bit?"

Jack looks to Scotty for support, but he shrugs in agreement with Mason. Then he looks to Amy. However, she does not look his way.

Rubbing salt into the wounds, Mason adds, "Yeah, listen to your narrator. Some help."

Jack is crushed.

Chapter 116

An undeniable cloud of misery floats around Jack's head as the others march back into the vault. Not only has Amy spurned him, but the narrator has disappeared just as he thought the secrets of the ride were so close to being revealed. His depression strikes him as a counter-balance to the wild enthusiasm and exuberance now coming from Mason.

"Look for the gold!" Mason exclaims. "The clue in the notebook clearly said there would be gold. There might be a secret stash in a wall panel or something."

The inspired Mason immediately heads for the desk. He scatters papers and opens drawers.

For her part, Amy stands to the left of Jack with her back to him. She sifts through the books on a lower shelf.

Just let her cool off, Jack tells himself. However, the tension is killing him. He can't resist the urge to make things right as soon as possible. He goes ahead and says, "Amy, I'm sorry. I had no idea that—"

"Scotty, none of these books will open," Amy states, completely ignoring Jack.

"You're right," Scotty says as he fumbles with another book on the far side of the room. "These things are, like, sealed up."

Jack stares at Amy. His frustration is rising. He says, "At least talk to me."

Oblivious to the rising conflict, Mason shouts, as he knocks over a large stack of paper, "Don't worry about the books! Look for the gold!"

Jack's hurt is starting to shift towards anger, and he's reaching a boiling point. He cries, "Amy, this is not fair! How would I have known that any of this would happen?"

The sudden outburst from Jack startles Scotty and Mason. Both boys turn to look at him. Suddenly, Jack is very aware that he has made a mistake. He is cautious not to continue in his outburst and risk giving his pals a clue that there has been something between Amy and him. Also, his urgent plea has not achieved the desired effect on Amy; she simply walks away and starts fiddling with more books next to her brother.

"Mason, Jack, look at this!" Scotty calls.

"What?" Mason asks as he looks up from behind the desk.

Jack does not move but looks in the direction Scotty is pointing. Above Scotty's extended finger on the fourth shelf up is a book with a gold spine. It is the only one like it in the entire room.

In spite of all the drama, even Jack realizes that they have found the gold.

Chapter 117

Mason is clearly disappointed that the gold is not an actual treasure, but he is undeterred after realizing this book is the item they have been seeking. Mason takes pride in concluding that the narrator is just a senile man full of riddles and that now Jack has to conform with his wishes. It is a relief for Mason to know that all they have left to do is get it to the gingerbread room in order to get out of this bizarre world.

The teens jump into action to retrieve the book. The desk slides with ease with Scotty and Jack on one end and Amy and Mason on the other. They place it right below the book, and Scotty places Lucky on the ground and then climbs on top of the desk. Mason notices that Scotty does not even grimace when using his hurt shoulder to lift himself up.

With Scotty atop the desk, Mason looks to Jack in eager anticipation of the victory and notices that Jack looks sullen and angry. He's guessing this attitude is a result of Amy's words, but he wonders why Jack should be so affected by them. After pondering this a moment, Mason thinks, *Wait a minute! How could I have missed it? Jack and Amy like each other, or at least they did like each other.* The pieces are fitting together for Mason like a finished puzzle. Now he understands why Jack faked the trip back at the Hall of Mirrors, and he can see why Amy would feel so betrayed. *It is so painfully obvious now,* Mason thinks, *but what in the world did Jack see in her? I mean she's no Lauren Van Wormer. She's Scotty's little sister for crying out loud.*

The epiphany brings Mason to a drastic conclusion. He tells himself, *Mason, old boy, it's everyone for themselves. Jack and Amy... well, they aren't worth the effort. Not if your efforts mean getting kicked in the face by some elf wearing green tights and playing a sissy instrument like a flute. No, Mason, you're going to have to take care of yourself first. Let the lovebirds quarrel.*

Mason looks at Scotty steadying himself on the table and entertains thoughts about isolating himself from his old friend. *Things have changed. What do the two of us have in common? I'm going to walk out of here alive and rich. If the others make it, so be it. But from now on, it's up to me to get outta here with or without them.*

Mason says, "Come on, Carnahan, reach. Do I have to come up there?"

Scotty is standing with his right arm in the air. The book is tantalizingly just beyond his reach.

He replies, "No, I've got this—just give me a second."

Scotty extends to his tip toes and taps the base of the golden book. It's not enough, and Scotty relaxes back on his feet. However, he doesn't give up but, instead, makes a sudden lunge upward. This time, he grasps the top of the spine and yanks at it with his fingers in a claw-like maneuver. The book tumbles from its notch in the shelf, and at the same time, Scotty tumbles and crashes to the floor.

Amy starts to move toward her brother, but he's quickly back on his feet and tells her, "I'm okay," while grinning from ear to ear.

"Your shoulder!" Amy says.

"It's okay. I fell on my butt," Scotty informs and laughs.

The book has fallen directly in front of Jack, but he just stares at it on the floor before him.

"Well, Jack, pick it up," Mason urges.

Jack reaches down, and with a sour look he hands it to Mason, who has closed in on him eager to see the prize.

Mason declares, "It's just a gold book. Won't even open." There is a twinge of disappointment in his voice.

"I don't care if it were made of diamonds," Amy announces. "Let's just get it and get outta here."

"Here, Jack, you carry it," Mason commands, keeping with his nasty habit of letting others carry anything burdensome to him. He shoves the book into Jack's arms and says, "Now, off to the gingerbread house!"

Jack responds, "Mason, who do you think you are ordering me around like you're some sort of king?"

"I'm the one who's trying to get us all out alive," Mason retorts.

"Yeah, sure, and you sure tried to get us out alive by helping us get past the troll. You know, I'm not sure why I ever liked you in the first place. You've always been more concerned with yourself than anyone else."

Mason stares at Jack with a look of shock on his face. He doesn't understand what has brought on this verbal barrage. As a result, his anger kicks in. He turns his head and says, "Come on, Scotty."

The two of them start marching to the door. As they do, they hear Amy call out, "Don't you think I should carry the book? Wouldn't want someone to steal it, would we?"

Amy takes the book.

Mason thinks, *Ouch! Man, he's really burning his bridges.* Mason looks back for Jack's response and sees him bite his lip.

Standing there ostracized and clearly defeated, Jack offers a simple comment about the book in Amy's hands, "Why that book out of all of the books here? Why this one?"

Mason responds, "Braddock, you have to get out of your funk. Who cares? If it's our ticket out, then let's take it and go."

"But isn't it curious to you at all?" Jack asks.

"I'm going home, Jack. You coming?" Mason replies.

Chapter 118

Clyde stands in silent bewilderment, looking at the glowing "Enter" sign humming just above the illuminated door, which has suddenly appeared, while continuing to hear the toots of the eerie organ music.

What is going on here? he wonders. His thoughts trail back to that night years ago when Douglas Finch disappeared, and he ponders about a connection to this occurrence. *Did Douglas Finch walk through this door?* he asks himself. This thought unsettles him, but, still, he contemplates what might be waiting beyond the portal.

"Oliver!" he calls, but there is no response. The others are long gone. *Just how long have I been standing here?* Clyde wonders. Suddenly, a new, equally unsettling thought crosses his mind: *Did the kids walk through this door?*

Before his mind calculates any further, his hand reaches out to open the door. But, he stops short, thinking, *Whoa, hold on there, partner. What if Finch went through this door and that's why he never returned? Could that happen to me, too?* He stands at the door for a long time, tossing scenarios through his head. He asks himself, *Where else could the kids have gone? We've searched every inch of the ride. They had to have gone through this mysterious door.* All of a sudden, a memory of Edna enters his consciousness. He remembers a time when they were in their twenties and a thunderstorm raged outside their home. They were huddled together, listening to the radio, and they began to hear the howling of their neighbor's dog.

"The Ferguson's are gone for the night, dear," said Edna.

The memory is so vivid that Clyde's heart jumps at the mental sound of his wife's voice. He recalls that she asked him to get the dog and bring him in.

She had said, "Clyde, if you don't help that dog, who will?" In Clyde's mind, he sees the hesitation in his younger self.

Just like that, the memory fades.

Now Clyde wonders, *What would Edna think if I just stood here? I have to go through, for their sake. It's all up to me.* Emboldened with newfound courage, Clyde firmly places his hand on the door.

"Clyde!" a gruff voice calls out.

The old man is alarmed by the voice and turns to see three people with flashlights making their way into the room. He realizes it's the police and is somewhat relieved.

Clyde calls back, "I think they're in here."

One of the policemen, Jimmy Dockins, knows Clyde, as most people in town do, and he walks closer followed by a female cop and Houston Carnahan.

Clyde turns back to the door, but it's gone.

"They're in where?" Dockins asks.

Clyde is taken aback by the disappearance of the door and is speechless to answer. He wonders, *Should I tell them about the door? They'll think I'm crazy?*

"What kind of game are you playing?" Mr. Carnahan shouts. "You said they were in here. Well, where are they? I don't see my kids anywhere."

Dockins spins to the angry parent and says, "Mr. Carnahan, cool down. Your inclusion, coming in here, was on the condition that you would not be a nuisance."

"Sure, right, but it's not your kids who are missing, now is it? All I know is my son and daughter went into that ride with this man and—"

Clyde's heart sinks. He clearly knows where this is going.

"—he comes out without them. 'They've disappeared,' he says. Can't you see?"

The officer is obviously growing irritated, too, and responds, "Mr. Carnahan, I am warning you, this is no time—"

"No, you listen to me," Carnahan says. He points at Clyde and states, "He knows something. For all we know, he's the one who took them." Houston takes a step toward Clyde and tells him, "Look, old man, tell me where the kids—"

"Honestly, I don't know what happened," Clyde protests.

"Officer Quinn, I think it's time Mr. Carnahan goes back outside."

"You're kidding me, right?" Carnahan defiantly exclaims.

"No, I'm not. Quinn, get him outta here."

"No way! I'm not moving!" Carnahan insists.

"Yes, you are now. Don't make this any uglier."

"How can you tell me to leave? Can't you see, he's your only suspect."

"Look, I've known Clyde my whole life. If he's guilty of any of this, I'm a monkey's uncle. Now go with Quinn here before I tell her to cart you off to the station."

To Clyde's relief, the man finally relents and Quinn leads him out of the room.

A few seconds pass. Both men are standing quietly. Finally, Officer Dockins breaks the silence, "Tell me I'm not a monkey's uncle, Clyde. Convince me."

Clyde starts and stops several times, and then finally admits, "I don't know if I can, Jimmy. All I know is that I left the kids in the room before this one. When I came back, they were gone. Simple as that."

"You're gonna have to do better than that, Clyde."

Chapter 119

The group has made their way back down the tunnel. Three of them are moving quickly with the prospect of escape rejuvenating them. Then there's Jack. As far as he's concerned, the night's events could not be going worse. Aside from the situation with Amy, he's puzzled about the mystery of the book. It bothers him, and he's been thinking about it all the way down the tunnel. *Something is not right,* he tells himself.

Amy has already descended the ladder. Jack looks over to Scotty and nods. The heavier boy lowers himself down.

Before Scotty takes more than a couple of steps down, Jack says, "Scotty, the narrator said these books contained stories. What is it about this one that's so important? What if we are not supposed to take it?"

Although he is asking Scotty, it is Mason who responds, initially with a long moan and then, "Give it a rest, Jack. For all we know, someone in the gingerbread house wants something to read."

Scotty wants no part of this and speeds his descent down the ladder.

Defeated again, Jack resigns himself to dropping the subject. He lowers himself onto the ladder and descends. After hitting the ground, he looks for Amy. However, after looking left and right, he doesn't see her.

Once Scotty is on the ground, he asks, "Where's Amy?"

"I don't know," replies Jack.

"What's going on?" Mason asks after jumping down from midway on the ladder. "Where's Amy?"

"We don't know," Scotty answers.

Mason looks around the room and asks, "Did she leave?"

"No way," Scotty declares. "She wouldn't have left without us."

Jack's stomach begins doing cart wheels, for he knows Scotty is right.

"Amy!" they all call.

There is no response.

Jack can't fight the feeling that something bad has happened. He even perceives that the room has seemed to darken and close in.

Then from the corner of his eye, Jack spies a new door that has been opened at the far side of the room.

"That door wasn't there when we were here before," Jack announces.

The three boys dash to the new opening. On the ground is a black piece of cloth. Jack looks grimly at the others.

He says the two words none of them wanted to hear: "The wolf."

"Guys, this is bad," Scotty moans. "Do you think he took her?"

"Yeah, he's probably been following us waiting for the right time to strike," Jack confirms. "At least she was level-headed enough to leave a clue."

"What's worse is Amy has the book," Mason remarks. "We have to get it back!"

Jack is appalled and asks Mason, "What about Amy?"

"Yeah. Of course, her, too, duh. Let's go."

Mason takes off down the new tunnel with Scotty right behind him. Jack brings up the rear, hoping it's not too late.

Chapter 120

The wolf shuffles off to his base with Amy draped over his shoulder. He is elated, and even though the girl is resisting by kicking and hitting, this only adds to the joy of the moment for him. In fact, for the wolf, Amy's fear is exhilarating.

He had waited patiently at the bottom of the ladder, and his patience had paid off. The wolf had fully expected to have to fight off one or two of the others, but the girl descended right into his arms by being the first one down the ladder. Now, the creature is imagining that the payoff is going to be delicious. He can't wait for his stomach to finally stop growling, and he even ponders the idea of returning for one or two of the boys, thinking that they would make a nice follow-up meal and the plump one could even be devoured as a sweet dessert.

"Why are you doing this to me?" The girl yells as she kicks, grabs, and yanks at anything she can reach. This doesn't seem to be having an effect on the wolf's overwhelming strength.

Still, she asks, "What do you want from me?"

The girl's questions and aggression strike the wolf as odd. He thinks, *She doesn't seem afraid. In fact, she seems downright angry.* The girl continues to scratch and claw, and the wolf could swear he feels his coat being ripped apart at the seams, yet he carries on.

Through the narrow passageways, the wolf navigates his way back to his hut. It takes a few minutes longer than usual with the furious girl over his shoulder, but his acute sense of smell easily directs him through the intricate system of passages.

Finally, they reach the hut, and the wolf begins his preparations. He manages to tie up the girl to a spit, and Amy soon finds herself suspended over a pile of sticks. The wolf examines the situation and moves an empty plate from one side of the table to the other while thinking, i He wants everything to be perfect.

"Why are you doing this? You, you beast!"

At last, the wolf addresses the girl, "Because I am the wolf. This is what wolves do! It is all I have ever wanted. For years I have longed for this moment. For years all I have wanted was you."

"I am not going to be your supper," Amy declares indignantly. "I don't care if you're the wolf or not. This is ridiculous. I am not from this place. How could you have wanted me? My friends and I only got lost in here today."

The wolf cannot help but respect her moxie, and he halts his activity.

"I have a family; you can't do this. I am going home."

Suddenly, the empty plate speaks to the wolf, *What are you doing? Do not let her fool you! She's lying to you. I need the girl to fill my void. You want the girl. Do it. Do it now!*

The wolf starts to question the girl, but before he speaks again, the low powerful rumble in his stomach quakes and the pain almost doubles him over.

Then he says, "You're lying to me. Yes, you should be eaten. That is your destiny."

The wolf snatches two flint stones and begins clanging them together over the fire pit. The dry embers start to smoke.

Chapter 121

As the boys enter a completely new area, they ignore the trees and barrels that are scattered around the room. Instead, they focus on a small gap in the wall to their left. On the floor in front of the gap is a piece of black cloth.

"She's ripped off another piece of his clothing," Jack confirms.

"That means they went this way," Mason declares.

"Let's go," Scotty says and lunges into the gap.

The boys find themselves in a small passage and begin running. Jack is determined to find Amy. His recent issues with her make him even more desperate. He has no intention of letting things end as they are. More importantly, he wants Amy to be safe, to have here happily-ever-after. The thought of Amy being the one.... Jack stops thinking.

At several points, the passage splits in different directions, but whenever this occurs, Jack's flashlight finds a small piece of cloth, which lets the boys know which way to go. He assumes correctly that Amy had been tearing at the wolf's coat on purpose.

The boys finally arrive at a door. With no effort to hide their entrance, Mason shoves it open. There before them is a small room, in the corner of which is an even smaller hut—no larger than a child's fort. It is made entirely of straw.

Whispering, Jack addresses the others, "He's taken her in there."

"How do you know that?" Mason questions.

"Well, there are no more scraps of cloth on the ground," Jack says as he surveys the well-lit floor.

"What do we do?" Scotty frantically asks.

Mason turns to Scotty, "Do you have any matches left?"

"What for?" the boy answers.

"Mason, we can't burn down the shack. Amy is in there," Jack explains. "We have to get in there; no time for talk."

Mason's face looks surprised, almost fearful, and he says, "We have to get that book."

This shocks Jack. He wonders what's happened to his cavalier, hard-charging companion.

"Okay, Jack, let's go," Scotty says. "There are three of us, one of him."

After he makes this proclamation, Scotty pulls out his scissors and holds them in front of him as a weapon. The bear, Lucky, has been discarded at his feet.

Marveling at this new bold attitude from Scotty and the strange reversal of roles his friends have undergone, Jack responds, "Scotty, we can't physically take on that wolf. We'll have to focus on getting Amy and getting out."

Jack looks at Mason, who stands dumbfounded at the situation, and walks up to him, places a hand on his shoulder, and with grim determination states, "Mason, we're going in now, with or without you."

Mason says, "Yeah, okay. I'll hold the door to the exit open. Good plan, Braddock."

As he moves toward the exit in a completely serious fashion, Jack and Scotty exchange a glance, and Jack says, "Guess it's just the two of us."

"Yep."

"Got any ideas?"

"How 'bout don't get eaten?"

Jack considers this and then replies, "That'll work."

The two move quickly toward the hut, but then Jack stops and says, "You know, that's not really much of a plan."

"I know."

"How long you think we got?"

Scotty shakes his head and says, "Not long."

"We need a plan."

Both think for a second. Then Scotty snaps his fingers, and announces, "Okay, here's what we're gonna do."

Chapter 122

Inside the hut, Amy hangs in terror. Held firmly in place by rope, she hovers just above a smoldering fire. She is completely mortified by the terrible reality that the wolf plans on eating her.

"This is a dream. You're just a figment of my imagination," she states emphatically.

"Yes, this is only a dream, and you are about to make my dream come true!" the wolf responds and laughs.

"You can't be serious about this! I haven't done anything to you. Come on, let me go. I'm just a girl."

The wolf strolls over to his empty dinner plate as it says, *Now would you listen to this. She thinks she can talk us out of it, she does.* Lifting the dinner plate to his ear he pauses, as if listening for the response and then he speaks, "What you think she needs? Some salt?"

Amy thinks, *He's mad. He's talking to the plate.*

"Maybe just a little salt then," the wolf says and takes out a shaker from a little cupboard in the paltry hut.

A series of thoughts rifle through Amy's confused mind: *This cannot be happening. Why did I walk down the ladder first? If I had come down second....* Then she thinks about Scotty, her mom and dad, and the twins. Each face brings on more pain, as she wonders if she'll ever see them again. Then she contemplates, *Where are the boys now? Are they looking for me? Did they see the pieces I ripped from the coat?*Granulates sprinkle over her body, and Amy realizes that the creature is dashing salt on her.

She hollers, "Stop that! I am not your dinner!"

"Did you hear that?" the wolf asks the plate. He lets out a sinister laugh and then theatrically announces, "I do believe this girl is in denial."

Amy looks at the plate and half expects it to talk, but as she does so, she notices that there on the table is the book. She thinks, *No! Now the boys will never escape!*

As the seconds roll by, the fire gains hold of the wood and the heat intensifies. Amy's lungs begin to fill with the lifting smoke, and her bare forearms start to burn with pain. Soon, every inch of her body feels as if it is on fire. Now, the full reality of the situation sinks in for Amy. She understands that her body is roasting.

"You can't do this!" Amy screams in anger. "Just let me go, now!"

She can no longer see the wolf, for the smoke has blurred her vision.

"Enough! Time for you to keep quiet," the wolf says. Then he pulls out a long white bandage from his coat, shoves the cloth into Amy's mouth, and ties it around the back of her head.

This is it, Amy thinks. Then a thought pops into her head: *"Three of them lived happily ever after."* She begins to cry.

Chapter 123

Amy feels a sudden rush of air and notices that the smoke begins to streak toward some new destination. She strains her neck to see what the source of this change is, and as she does so, she sees Jack running toward her. In no time at all, he kicks over the spit, and, now, Amy is on the floor a couple of inches away from the fire. She has been saved, at least for the moment, and the burning sensation that had been simmering every inch of her body starts to wane.

Amy is dazed from the fall, but when she looks up, she can make out the shape of Scotty. Unfortunately, the wolf is on him quickly and swings a large paw into the chest of her brother. The boy drops like rock to the ground, and the scissors fall from his hand just in front of Amy.

While keeping her eyes on the Wolf, Amy starts rolling ever so slightly toward the scissors. As she does so, she sees Jack fling his backpack like a mace against the back of the beast's neck. The force of the blow sends the wolf forward, and he collapses on the ground.

Jack rushes to Amy, grabs the scissors, and begins to saw at the thick rope.

Meanwhile, the wolf is regaining his composure. Amy notices this and tries desperately through the gag to communicate it to Jack. She blinks her eyes quickly and tries to kick her legs and move her head. However, he pays no heed.

Only a few strands of rope have flayed under the sawing motion of the shears. Amy realizes this is taking too long.

The wolf, who is now standing, howls a hideous bellowing sound. Then, in an instant, the creature launches himself at Jack, and the two bodies crash into the side of the makeshift fire, resulting in sticks and flames being scattered on the floor. The wolf positions himself to corner Jack.

Just then, Scotty, looking disheveled and weak, begins sawing at the rope. Soon the last thread snaps and Amy's hands are free. She pulls the gag from her mouth and tells Scotty to go help Jack.

As he does so, Amy begins the slow process of unfurling the rope wrapped around her torso.

Just as the wolf is preparing to deliver a violent blow across Jack's face, Scotty grabs the plate from the table and breaks it over the back of the fiend's head. But, this only seems to agitate the wolf, who turns back to Scotty and snarls, "I will kill you all!"

By this point, flames have started to lick two sides of the hut. The thatch has provided ample kindling for the now raging fire.

Amidst this chaos, Amy is surprised by the clarity of her thoughts. After freeing herself entirely from the rope, she picks up the metal pole that had once held her up above the fire, and makes her way into the fray with the boys.

She sees the wolf, who's holding Scotty by his collar, fling him to the ground and then give Jack, before he can get back on his feet, a solid kick to the gut.

Amy swings the pole at the wolf, like she had done earlier with the stick. This time, though, the Wolf spins just in time to grab the pole from her hands before it makes contact with his head.

"Not this time, little girl," the wolf mocks and slings the pole to the ground. The creature gives Amy a snarl and says, "You will not win."

He grabs a paw-full of Amy's hair and drags her over to the table. At the same time, flames are engulfing the hut, and Amy doesn't see a way to escape.

Then suddenly, there's a dull ping, and Amy feels the grip on her hair relax and eventually let go. The wolf drops to the ground unconscious. Standing above the fallen creature is Jack with the pole in his hands.

"Let's get out of here," Jack says while trying to catch his breath in the smoky room.

Amy nods and asks, "Where is Scotty?"

"Just get yourself out of here!" Jack responds.

He then rushes over to Scotty, who is curled up on the floor. Jack says, "Come on, Scotty, you've got to get up."

Nearby, Jack sees his backpack on the ground and slings it over his shoulder.

Scotty moans, "Is Amy okay?"

Jack answers, "Yes, can you walk?"

"Sure," Scotty says and grimaces in pain. "The book. Where is the book?"

"Don't worry about the book. This whole place is going to burn to the ground!"

"We can't leave it!" Scotty cries.

"Yes we can!" Jack declares firmly.

Amy's voice calls out. She is standing by them now. An odd tinge of compassion fills her heart, and she asks, "What about the wolf? He'll burn—we can't leave him!"

"Are you crazy?" Scotty curtly replies.

"Help me, Jack!" she pleads.

Without further discussion, Amy's rushes to the fallen body of the wolf. She tries to drag the beast to the door, but she can't do it by herself. She turns to look for help and sees that Jack is already close by.

He grabs hold of the wolf, too, and says, "On three. One, two, three."

As they pull, they hear Scotty call, "The book! It's over there!"

Scotty jumps through the smoke and haze to the table, which is starting to catch fire, too.

After dragging the wolf to the door, Amy watches in horror as a large chunk of the flimsy roof collapses just in front of her brother.

"Forget the book! Come on!" Jack calls.

"Scotty!" Amy cries.

Jack and Amy succeed in getting the predator's limp body through the door, and as soon as they relinquish their hold on the monster, both of them rush back to the entrance of the hut. However, neither can see anything because of the thick smoke.

"No!" Amy screams. In her mind, all hope for her brother's safety is lost.

Just then, a body crashes into them, sending all three to the floor outside the hut. Scotty has made it out the door. Never in her entire life had Amy been so relieved.

Scotty is lying on his side away from Jack and Amy. He's breathing hard, gasping for fresh air amidst the smoke. Then he turns toward his companions, and they see that he's holding the book.

Chapter 124

All three teens are still gasping for air. The burning hut now looks like a pep rally bonfire in the corner of the larger room. Luckily, the stone walls of the room are impervious to the flames.

Jack can't believe what they've just done. Not only did he and Scotty rescue Amy, knock out the monstrous wolf, and escape the burning hut, but Scotty also recovered the book.

Mason walks over to the black-faced teens and stands slack-jawed. He is holding Lucky like a comfort blanket to his chest and asks, "You get it?"

Jack is still troubled that Mason had not helped them, and he ignores the question and instead says, "We had better just get out of here."

"What about that?" Mason asks, pointing at the wolf. "Is it alive?"

"I think so," Amy replies.

"We have to kill him, or he'll just come to kill us. What inspired you to drag him out?"

"Because it was the right thing to do," Amy says defensively.

"The right thing?" questions Mason.

"Yeah. The right thing, Mason."

Suddenly, Mason seems to find his boldness again and stares at Amy. Earlier in the evening, she might have backed down and agreed with Mason, but now she stands her ground. For the next several seconds, the only sound is provided by the crackling, burning hut, which has now been reduced to a couple of small rapidly dissipating walls.

"I'll do it," Mason announces. He drops Lucky to the feet of Scotty and searches the room until he finds a large rock, which he picks up. Then, walking over to the collapsed body of the wolf, he uses both hands to lift the heavy weapon above his head, ready to deliver the deathblow.

Chapter 125

"Stop!" Amy calls.

She has a violent look in her eyes, which stuns Jack.

"You are not going to kill him," Amy adds.

While Mason is holding the rock, Amy puts herself between him and the wolf. A standoff between them ensues and lasts for nearly a minute with Jack and Scotty watching as the two parties glare at each other.

"Are you serious?" Mason exclaims. "You have to be kidding. He was going to kill you."

Amy does not reply, but Jack knows Amy will not be dissuaded.

Scotty walks to his sister's side and says, "Amy, what if—"

"Stay out of this, Scotty," his sister directs.

Mason says, "Listen to your brother, Amy. This wolf, this killer, he's not going to leave us alone. He will wake up, and when he does, well, it's you he's after."

"Then you, Mason Chick, have nothing to worry about. It's my life on the line then, right? Leave him be!"

Mason drops the rock to the floor and utters, "Okay, then, but if he catches you, I am not going to stop him."

"Fine!" Amy staunchly exclaims.

Suddenly, from the door to the left, Victor enters the room.

Jack is startled at first by the sudden appearance of the man.

"Excellent!" proclaims Victor. "You have defeated the vile creature. You are truly the ones we were expecting."

Jack says, "Uh, Victor, we have the golden book."

"Wonderful! That is the most excellent of news! Marvelous, truly marvelous! May I see it?"

Scotty lifts the book in front of the man.

"I can't believe it! The Queen will be pleased! You have truly earned your freedom!" asserts Victor, whose eyes are shining brightly, beaming with satisfaction and pleasure.

"Where have you been?" asks Mason. "We could have used a little help tonight."

Jack is struck by the fact that Mason, the boy who had just left him and Scotty to rescue Amy on their own, is asking this question.

"I could not interfere: it is the prophecy. But I was confident you would come out unscathed. You are the chosen ones, after all."

"What do you mean *chosen ones*?" Jack asks.

"Well, the prophecy, of course."

"What about it?" Jack responds.

Victor is reluctant to share, but does so anyway and says, "Long ago, the Queen discovered a prophecy about four teens who would enter this world. They, and only they, would have the power to find four keys, which would unlock the door to the vault. Then they would retrieve the very thing that has the power to restore freedom to all who are trapped in the woods, and everyone would be free."

After hearing this, Jack considers how the prophecy might relate to the strange rhyme in the Finch notebook.

Meanwhile, Scotty asks, "And we are the four teens?"

"Of course you are," says Victor. "And believe you me, the Queen is eager to get a hold of that book. We are all indebted to you."

"So if we give her the book, we can go home?" Amy asks.

"I don't see why not. We simply need to take the book to the Queen," responds Victor.

A rush of excitement floods over Jack, who thinks, *Well what are we waiting for?* But as his hope escalates, a tinge of skepticism still gnaws at him, and he wonders, *But what about the narrator? Why is he guarding the vault?*

Mason gestures to the book nestled in Scotty's hands and says, "I told you, Jack, this here is our golden ticket."

Ignoring Mason, Jack asks another question, "Then why didn't you show us the tunnels so we could avoid all the danger? If you wanted us to survive, why couldn't you help us?"

Instead of answering him, the odd man says, "Come along, travelers. Let's make our way to the Queen."

An alarm rings in Jack's head, but none of the others seem to care whether or not the man has any answers for them.

Victor continues, "I don't think that wolf will be out forever. We should be moving along now."

"Agreed," says Scotty.

The four teens follow the man back to the entrance of the secret passage.

Just before they cross into the tunnel, Jack looks behind him at the fallen wolf and notices that one of its eyes is open.

Chapter 126

Jack walks farther and farther away from the smoky room. Amy is right in front of him, and he wonders if the events in the hut had softened her anger at him.

At a volume that only she can hear, Jack says, "Hey, Amy, about the goose and—"

Amy stops and turns around to face Jack. In a quiet but matter-of-fact tone, she says, "Look, Jack, I appreciate you saving me and all—that was great, and I owe you one—but you lied to me, so whatever else might have been going on between us is done now, okay?"

Jack blinks. He's not sure how to respond, but before he even has a chance to do so, Amy heads off quickly to catch up with the rest of the group.

Great, just great, thinks Jack. Still, in spite of the obvious rejection, his thoughts continue swirling around the book. Primarily, while passing through the dimly lit passages, Jack is bothered by one nagging question, and as they descend down a slight incline and take a right at a fork, Jack finally asks, "Victor, what is so important about this book?"

Victor stops, looks back towards Jack and replies, "Ah, excellent question, my boy. Well, you have recovered the Queen's story."

"Her story?" inquires Jack.

"Well, put simply, we are all controlled by the stories. That is what the Queen wants to end. That has been her goal from the moment I met her. She truly is a kind woman. Her noble aim is to see everyone free. She is the only one who cares about everyone who has been brought here against their will. The ultimate goal is freedom for all. And, as the Queen, once she is freed from her prison, she has the power to free the rest of us."

"And you, Victor?" Jack asks. "Were you brought here against your will, like us?"

Victor looks off for a moment. His mind is adrift in memories. He says, "A long time ago," but then suddenly snaps himself out of the remembrance and states, "We must be going."

Victor's explanation is puzzling to Jack, and he asks, "Then why was the narrator holding the book in the first place?"

Mason, clearly with agitation in his voice, chimes in and says, "Jack, give it a rest. We are going to get out. Didn't you hear the man? We won already."

"Oh no, good lad, it is a fair question. I am certain the Queen will explain it fully, but the narrator, well he, the narrator that is, is trying to keep those books to himself. Jack, he does not want anyone to have the freedom to leave."

This explanation troubles Jack, and as the party continues its march down the tunnels, he expresses the conclusion he's drawn: "So we basically stole her book from the narrator."

Victor stops and looks at Jack in the eyes. With a kind expression that exudes faith, he says, "Jack, it was foretold long ago that you four would arrive and grant all who live here freedom. You four... you are heroes."

Jack considers this a moment while starting the walk again. Then he asks, "So what about our stories? What about our books? Were they in that library, too?"

This time Victor does not stop. He simply calls back, "Patience, Jack. I assure you, the Queen only wants what is best. We are about to arrive. All of your questions will be answered."

The dim passageway dips, rises, turns, and straightens, at which point Victor finally proclaims, "We are here."

However, this doesn't make sense to the teens because in front of them is a bare stone wall. Then Victor raps on a particular spot on the wall, and a whirling sound begins. Soon afterward, from above the teens' heads, a rope ladder drops to the floor, barely missing Scotty.

Victor announces, "We will simply climb the ladder to our destination."

One by one, the teens scale the ladder up into an opening in the roof. At one point, only Victor and Jack remain in the tunnel, and Jack sees this as an opportunity to ask another question, this time without Mason's disapproval: "If the Queen is in charge of the woods, then how is she held against her will?"

Victor responds, "You should just climb the ladder, little thief." The tone is spiteful. It is as if Victor is telling Jack he has had enough.

Jack glares at the man but decides it would be a good idea to comply. So, he begins to climb.

The ladder is sturdy and easy for Jack to navigate. Once he's at the top, the light of a new larger room burns his eyes for a moment. He rubs them fervently for a second or two, and then his vision finally assimilates to the light of the room.

The scene is familiar. This is the room where the group had initially seen the gingerbread house. Jack takes himself back hours ago to when they had first been in this exact spot and realizes, *This is where everything had gone crazy.*

Mason bellows, "This is it—just like the notebook said. Take the gold to the gingerbread house."

Victor walks to the house and pulls a key from his pocket. Then with grand pomp and flair, he fumbles with the key in opening the door.

Jack asks, "So why is the door locked?"

Victor replies, "Because, my boy, well, you have seen for yourself. Some of our cohabitants can be a little, shall we say, testy?"

The door to the house opens. Victor bows to the side of the door and says, "After you."

They enter the house, and within five steps they stand and stare at the unbelievable sight. The entire room is made up of candy decorations: peppermint spirals, a fountain of chocolate, and long tassels of licorice stretching from ceiling to floor. The smell is intoxicating—a mix of cinnamon, chocolate, vanilla, and mint wafting here and there. There is too much to take in all at once. Everything about the room is truly amazing.

Victor declares, "Welcome to the Queen's palace."

Mason says, "Uh, Victor, how can this be? That little gingerbread house is tiny on the outside, but this room—it's so large."

The man lets out a chuckle, clearly enjoying the teen's astonishment and says, "Things are not always how they appear on the outside, my friend. Let's just say there is more than a little magic in this place."

Jack, too, is in awe. He wonders if this is one of those space-time-dimension kind of things like in a science fiction story, for even though it had looked like they were walking into a small cottage, it is a massive mansion inside.

"Where is the Queen?" Amy asks.

By the tone of her voice Jack guesses that the room's wonder is wearing thin on her, and she simply wants to get on with it.

"She will be here shortly. Relax and enjoy the beauty of the palace. In fact, take a bite if you would like. Everything here is edible and easily replaced," Victor explains and waves his arms with an exaggerated gesture across the room. "Perhaps you like cake? The mantle there is made completely of red velvet. Or, maybe you prefer shortbread? The lattice work over there is awaiting your arrival."

"Oh man, I am hungry," Scotty remarks and immediately heads for the chocolate fountain.

"No, thank you, we will just wait here," Amy replies, casting an admonishing look at her brother.

Dejected, Scotty breaks off his momentum for the fountain.

Jack, meanwhile, is looking for anyone to share his concern. However, Mason is drunk with victory and Amy is unapproachable for him, so he pegs Scotty.

The tailor's apprentice returns to the group and rubs his stomach in hunger. Jack walks over to him and whispers, "Don't you think that guy is a bit weird?" motioning toward Victor.

"Well, maybe," responds Scotty "But he seems nice enough."

"He's too nice if you ask me."

"Come on, Jack, things are finally starting to go our way. Please, let's just do as he says."

"But—"

Just as Jack is about to press the issue, Victor calls out, "I now present to you the Queen of the Wood."

From a corner of the room, through an entrance Jack had not seen, an elegant, beautiful woman appears. It is the Queen.

Chapter 127

Officer Dockins does not want to believe the old man has anything to do with the disappearance, but the facts are hard to ignore. Clyde was the last person to see the kids, who had not left the ride, and the building had been thoroughly searched. Add to this that nearly the same thing had happened years ago in the Finch case, again with Clyde being the last one to see him.

For the tenth time, outside the ride the senior officer and Quinn go through the events of the night with Clyde. The other policeman on site is busy holding the perimeter, constantly being barraged by questioning parents. Dockins feels a little pity for the young cop having to deal with the hostile parents, but he tells himself that everyone has a job to do, and at the moment, his happens to be getting to the bottom of Clyde's story.

Quinn asks, "So you just left the kids in the room and went to the fuse box."

"Right, that's what I did. I've told you that already. Look, I feel horrible about this."

"I know, Clyde, I know," Dockins says. "But you have to look at this from our perspective. You are the only connection. You have to be patient with us. Are you sure you are telling us everything?"

The old man nods slowly, but there is something in his eyes. With over 20 years on the job, Dockins can tell Clyde is holding back, and that bothers him.

"Clyde, you can trust us," assures Dockins.

"I know, Jimmy, I know."

Officer Dockins had spent most of the last hour trying to affirm his trust to the old man by playing good cop, but it had accomplished nothing. At the present, things do not look good for Clyde. Soon, the Crime Scene Investigation guys would be here, and they would make another thorough sweep.

From the corner of his eye, Dockins can see the shabby form of Howard Snodgrass stalking around the perimeter, easing his way by the young cop and making a path toward him.

"Oh brother," the officer moans.

"Can I speak with you, sir?" the tubby man demands more than asks.

"Sure."

Snodgrass looks accusingly at Clyde and says, "I mean away from the others."

"Okay, just for a second."

The two men take 20 steps toward the ice cream stand.

Snodgrass begins, "Look, Officer, I just want to know one thing. If you find out that Spahn has something to do with this ugly mess... well...."

Dockins can tell Snodgrass is uncomfortable but tells him, "Spit it out."

"Okay, I just want to know, is the park liable?"

Dockins smirks. He has known Howard Snodgrass for all of an hour and a half, but he's

already got him figured out.

Jimmy says, "Well, Mr. Snodgrass, he is your employee. But, as long as you do background checks on everyone, then you're probably not liable. You do perform background checks on all your employees, right?"

The look on Snodgrass's face reveals that he doesn't, and Dockins smiles to himself as he heads back over to Clyde.

Chapter 128

Jack's breath is completely taken away. As impressive as the interior of the palace is, it has nothing on the sheer beauty of the Queen. With a fluid grace that enhances her all the more, she almost glides over in front of where the four kids and Victor stand. Long blonde hair cascades down her shoulders, and a golden dress flows over her figure. On her shoulder, perched and eating a nut, is a squirrel. Jack wonders, *Was this the squirrel from the Pied Piper Room, the one Mason told him about? The same squirrel he had seen watching them way back at the beginning of the ordeal? Yes, of course, he had been helping them along the way.*

The Queen says, "Finally, you have come. We have waited for so long. I see you are no worse for the wear. None of you were harmed?"

However, before any of the teens can answer, she continues, "You are most welcome here. I assume that Victor has allowed you to enjoy my home?"

Again, before waiting for a response, she looks Jack square in the eyes and says, "Oh, my dear, you are even more handsome than I imagined."

Jack's face is hot with embarrassment, but the compliment still makes him beam. His shoulders relax to a shrug and his backpack crashes to the floor.

Then the Queen turns to Mason and says, "Brave tailor, so valiant, so cunning. I am certain by the looks of you, that you are a gallant warrior. How else could the four of you vanquish some of our more unpleasant residents?"

Jack sees Mason gush as well. In fact, he slightly bows before the Queen and responds, "Thank you, uh... your majesty."

The charm and pleasant aura of the Queen is unmistakable. She is clearly nice, but it seems so theatrical, like she's reading from a script and this begins to bother Jack.

"The wanderer," she proclaims while petting the grey squirrel on her shoulder. "I could not have imagined such a cute little girl to be a part of our redemption. Thank you, my dear."

Jack turns to Amy and sees a look of pride on her face.

At last the Queen turns to Scotty and says, "And we have here our apprentice—what a noble young lad. And there in your hands, the prize. You have truly saved us all. The prophecy is fulfilled. You are all to be rewarded."

Amy quickly asks, "Then will you please get us out of here?"

Mildly irritated by the frankness of Amy, Jack speaks quickly before the Queen can take offense, "What she means is that for our reward, we only want to go home, your majesty."

The hope of escape dangles before them. Jack thinks, *Is this it? Will we soon be free?* His excitement grows, but a voice inside his head tells him, *This is too good to be true. What about the book, the narrator?*Scotty and Mason look intently at the face of the Queen, hanging on her every word. Amy is still glowing from the compliments that the Queen paid her.

At this point, the Queen gently extends her arm toward Scotty and asks, "Noble apprentice, may I have the book? I shall take the proper steps for your departure."

Without hesitation, Scotty hands the book to the Queen, who gives him a reverent nod and then says, "Victor?"

"Yes, milady."

"Accompany our guests outside. I will finish the preparations so they can have their reward. I will be out soon to join you."

Victor then gestures to his left and waltzes to the entrance. He bows to Amy and says, "Ladies first."

As Jack walks through the doors he thinks. "We are finally going home!"

Chapter 129

Once the teens are outside, Jack is once again mystified by the contrast in size between the Queen's enormous sanctum and the quaint little ginger-bread house. The room looks exactly as it had when they had first entered with two notable exceptions. Jack notices when he looks over to the corner that there is no longer a narrator robot standing where it once had been. Instead, something else catches his eye on the ground where the manne-quin had once stood. The book the narrator had held lies upon the floor. To their left, Jack takes notice of a small camp fire. Who had prepared the fire and where it had come from is a mystery.

"We will stay here and await the Queen," Victor states.

None of them says a word, but Jack can see the giddiness rising in each of them. Still, something is troubling Jack. His own expression is actually more confused than jubilant, and when he sees the doors on the other side of the room, more questions gnaw at Jack in his head: *What was all this about making preparations? Why could they not just walk through the door?*

After all, it had been through those doors that they had entered this crazy place. The real ride, the real world is just beyond those doors.

"What is that for?" Amy asks, pointing to the fire.

"You will see," Victor replies.

"More unanswered questions," Jack responds.

"Leave it to Braddock to suck the life out of this moment," Mason groans while elbowing Scotty.

Ignoring the typical Mason cut and looking back at the doorway to the original part of the ride, Jack thinks, *The door is so close. What is preventing me from going home? I should leave now.* His own thought surprises him but his instinct encourages him and the path is clear. Without saying anything to the others, he begins to step toward the door, one foot at a time.

"My little thief, you cannot go that way," Victor advises.

"Why not?" Jack replies.

"Just be patient, Jack," Amy coolly states.

Her voice stops him for a second. *Does she want me to stay?* he wonders. He replays her tone in his head. Nonetheless, Amy had been so cold and unresponsive earlier that not even her words could persuade him now, so he continues.

Victor smiles dismissively and says, "Go ahead and try, but unless the Queen changes the story, none of us can leave through that door."

In spite of Victor's confident reproach, Jack saunters up to the door and attempts to push the bar and leave.

It's locked.

"I told you, there is no use," Victor politely reminds Jack.

Undeterred, Jack turns to the others and asks, "Mason, do you still have the hammer?"

The other teens remain standing like mindless lemmings awaiting their leader.

Mason responds, "Braddock, what are you doing?"

"Just tell me, Mason. The hammer, please."

Jack sees the wary Mason roll his eyes. Then, only to appease Jack, he answers, "Yes, it's here in the work belt, but, Jack, just chill out, okay. You're not going to screw this up for us. The Queen will show us the way out."

"I'm not waiting for the Queen. Can't you see something is not right here? It's all too easy. "

Walking back to them, Jack holds his palm out to Mason and says, "Look, you can stay and wait, but I'm trying to get out that door."

Victor rubs his forehead as if suffering some vicious headache and attempts to reason with Jack, saying, "Come now, the end is so near."

"What is wrong with you, Jack?" Amy questions.

"Here, Jack," Mason says, extending the tool. "Take the stupid hammer. We're staying. Right, Scotty?"

Victor slowly walks toward the door.

Scotty replies, "Jack, I don't want you to leave without us."

"Then come with me—now."

And with hammer in hand, Jack marches back to the door. He ignores Victor who is standing beside the door and goes to work on the first hinge. Suddenly, he feels a hand firmly press down on his shoulder with the fingers burying themselves deep into his flesh. Then he is spun around away from the door.

Amy yells, "Victor, what are you doing?"

"My dear child, you have to wait for the Queen," responds Victor. His voice is oozing with kindness in stark contrast to the firmness of his grip.

Jack reaches for the hand and tries to pry it off.

Victor says to Jack, "No matter what you do, the door will not open. Show some manners, boy. You are now an honored guest of the Queen. What will she think if you are over here trying to pry the door apart? No, please, just take a spot next to the others."

Jack is in pain. In spite of the words, Victor's grip confides no politeness. The man forces Jack back toward the line with the others, and Jack sees Mason give a smug grin.

Should I fight? wonders Jack. He considers his options for doing so. *Strike Victor? Slam my foot onto his? Elbow him hard in the ribs? The elbow, that will be my best shot. But then what?*

All of a sudden, a commotion erupts from a passage in the wall. Then a vicious snarl bellows out from the space, and a voice says, "The girl is mine!"

As everyone's lock onto the passage, Victor releases his grip, and Jack thinks to run. However, the shock of what he sees freezes him. Now limping into the room is the wolf, who is breathing hard. His coat has been singed from flames, black soot covers his fur, and his top hat is tilted to one side on his head. In between breaths, he growls, and his eyes are fixed on Victor as he slowly steps toward the party while dragging his left leg.

The wolf says, "The girl, you will give me the girl now!"

"Stay back, vile creature!" Victor commands and steps briskly in front of Amy to shield her.

Jack is slightly impressed by the man's courage. However, all signs of bravado are erased as Victor's authoritative voice changes into a cowering snivel when he says, "Please, you must not interfere... the Queen."

"I told you, I will have the girl. If you value your life, you will leave."

Closer and closer, the wolf limps toward Amy.

Jack decides he had better act. Still, even though the wolf is clearly hurt, Jack knows he won't be able to overpower him by himself. He considers that Victor might actually be of some use and that Scotty would help as well, although he cannot count on Mason.

Time to act, thinks Jack. Swiftly, he charges at the wolf from behind and jumps on the creature's back. His body clamps upon the surprised foe, and he clings his arms tight around the wolf's neck.

Although injured, the wolf is still too powerful and rocks Jack's body from side to side. Soon, Jack's arm lock is broken by the monster's massive paws. Then, the wolf bites Jack's hand.

Jack immediately drops to the floor, holding his injured hand. He sees blood pouring from the wound. Then, looking up, he watches as Scotty, with scissors in hand held out before him, charges at the wolf. However, the boy is easily swept aside. His sister also decides to attack and Amy steps around Victor to take a wild swing at the wolf with her stick. It seems, though, that the wolf was somehow prepared for the strike. The blow to his ribs doesn't seem to faze him, and the wolf simply clamps his arm down over the weapon.

Jack begins to stand back up in preparation for a second attack, and as he does so, he notices that Mason is just standing and watching the spectacle.

At this point, Victor grabs Amy and jerks her behind him. In a nervous voice, he tells the wolf, "You... you... must stay, sir, stay... back."

Jack has determined a new plan of attack. He intends to plow forward aiming a shoulder at the beast's bad leg.

All of sudden, though, the skirmish is stopped by the sound of another voice.

"What is happening? Please, my friends, quarreling is so childish!" admonishes the Queen.

Chapter 130

All eyes turn to the authoritative voice, and Jack is once again stunned at the appearance of the radiant Queen, thinking, *Could she possibly be even more beautiful?* She seems to almost be glowing as she stands at the door of the house. His gaze is broken, though, by the pain in his hand, and as he looks down at it, he notices that blood is dripping onto the floor beneath him.

"What has happened here?" the Queen asks. Her attention turns to Jack, who is pressing hard on his bleeding hand. She moves, seeming to float across the room toward him, and says, "Oh, my poor child, let me see."

Her voice is just as sweet as it had been before, and she adds, "I beg you, there needs to be no quarrel among us."

The Queen takes Jack's back pack and sets it down on the ground. Then taking Jack's injured hand in her soft hands, she can see that four fang marks had punctured the soft spot between his index finger and thumb on both sides.

The Queen gives the wolf a stare, admonishing the creature like a scolding teacher and says, "My dear wolf, this is not proper behavior. It will not be tolerated. You will back away. Back away from the girl."

The wolf is apparently compelled to obey and moves back and stands still. However, his mannerism does not suggest that he is as enamored with the Queen as the others are.

"Thank you," says the Queen. Then she looks down at the wound again and begins to whisper something. They are words that Jack cannot discern, but instantly the pain in his hand subsides. Then, to his amazement, the fang marks dissolve into clear pink skin. She drops Jack's hand, turns to Victor, and says, "Now, Victor, I am not sure what has happened, but I am sure there is no need for any hasty action."

Victor bows yet again and says, "Sorry, milady."

"We shall put the whole nasty scene behind us," declares the Queen. She shoots the wolf another disdaining look and adds, "All of us."

Then, looking back at Victor, she continues, "The fire is prepared I see, but I must say, it is lacking a little."

The Queen then turns to the small fire and begins to mutter more of the unintelligible words under her breath. Suddenly, the small little fire grows. The once red flickering flames lengthen several feet, and a green light appears around the fire.

The Queen's sudden mastery of the wolf, the healing spell, and whatever she had just done to the fire is enough proof for Jack to believe that she truly is as powerful as she is radiant.

"Now, brave travelers, I have made final arrangements. I have what you need," informs the Queen, who holds aloft a stack of papers for all to see. Triumphantly, she beams and says, "I have the missing pages of your story!"

This is a bombshell for Jack. He feels vindicated that the narrator had been right, that the missing pages were the key, and that they had to finish the story. Now, in addition to being relieved, Jack is downright excited.

Mason asks, "So what do we do?"

"Well, I shall read them, of course. Once the story is finished, we can all live happily ever after. Should I begin now?"

A low growl exudes from the wolf, "No."

"What was that, my dear friend? Is there a reason you are interrupting? Oh, I see, you want the girl. Of course, you are upset now that you see she shall escape?"

The wolf responds, "No." Something about the Queen has humbled him.

"Well brave ones, shall I begin?"

Jack looks at Amy, who is still on the floor and grasping her shoulder. Then he asks, "Uh, could we have a moment, your majesty?"

"Of course, my child."

"Guys, can we talk about this first?" Jack begs.

Amy and Scotty begin to walk toward him, but Mason, for his part, glowers at Jack.

Then he makes an exaggerated disgusted step toward the meeting and says, "I've had about enough of this, Braddock. Why do we need a pow-wow now? The woman just healed your hand, and you're still going on with this suspicious routine? Let's get this over with and go home."

Scotty adds, "I have to agree with Mason, Jack. We're so close now."

Jack responds, "I don't know. I just don't want to rush into this. There is something not right here."

Mason declares, "The only thing not right here is you, Jack."

"Let him speak his mind," Amy retorts.

Jack sighs for a moment, realizing she had actually defended him.

"But this better be good," Amy continues.

The warning from Amy stings, but he starts to make his case by saying, "Look, I know you guys want to go through with this. I'm just saying that it does not feel right. I know she's nice and all, but why won't they let us out the door? Why do we need to have our stories read?"

Amy replies, "But isn't this what the narrator told us to do—finish the story? Isn't that right, Jack? It's what you've been wanting all night."

Her face looks five years older, more mature and prettier than Jack remembered.

"Yes, that's right," Jack says. "But he was trying to lead us somewhere else. We didn't really do what he wanted."

"Jack, we are going to finish the story. We are doing what is right. The Queen, she's going to reward us," explains Amy with an expression so pleasant that it puts Jack at ease. If Mason had offered the very same point, Jack would surely have countered it, but coming from Amy, Jack gives consideration to the reasoning.

He thinks, *The narrator told us to go another way, but the Queen has been so kind. She healed my hand and staved off the wolf. I want to finish, but still... it seems... too easy.* Soon enough, though, Jack succumbs to the collective will of the others. He tells them, "I guess you're right. But I'm just saying—"

"Enough with the buts, Jack," offers Mason. "It's time we got out of here—all of us! We all know what we need to do."

Then he looks at the wolf and continues in a softer tone, "We could try and walk out, but who's to say that wolf's not going to follow? He's pretty determined to kill Amy."

Jack admits to himself that this is a good point.

Before the huddle breaks and before Jack can object, Mason announces to the Queen, "Okay, we're ready!"

The Queen gently nods and gracefully lifts the papers. Then she says, "Young apprentice, I shall read yours first."

Chapter 131

Jack thinks, *This is it, the moment of truth. It is the moment we have labored all night for.* In spite of his uneasiness about the situation, Jack is looking forward to hearing what the Queen will read.

"Please step forward, noble one," she says.

Jack watches as Scotty takes a deep breath and steps toward the Queen. He is grinning happily, awaiting whatever the story has in store.

Everyone in the room is smiling, with two exceptions: Jack, who is obviously still a little concerned, and the wolf, who is now looking totally flustered, which Jack dismisses as the look of a sore loser.

The Queen clears her throat with an exaggerated cough and begins.

"The apprentice presented the key he had taken,
A gift for the Queen long since forsaken.
The boy had lived with little will of his own.
He left it up to the tailor which way to be shown.
Until one day when the tailor left him alone in spite of his pleas.
Abandoned in the wood, the apprentice fell to his knees
Lost in the dark forest with no one to lead,
For he could not live for himself in his hour of need.
Resigned to his fate, lonely and cold,
His vision left him as he grew old,
A blind lonely beggar, hopeless in the deep dark wood,
A sightless follower with no leader, his fate far from good."

The words of the Queen were joyous and spoken with a great amount of celebration. But the script is far from what any of them expected, and Scotty stands with an expression of disbelief.

Before any of them can speak, Scotty, as if in a trance, pulls the scissors from his pocket, waltzes woozily to the Queen, and hands her the key.

He then saunters back over to the side of the others and says, "What was that? I don't want to go blind!" as tears begin to stream down his face.

"Wait a minute, what is going on here?" cries Jack.

"Isn't it obvious? This is his story. Are you disappointed?" the Queen smirks.

"Is this some kind of a joke?" Amy declares. "That is not a happy ending."

"Oh, but it is, pretty girl. A happy ending for me, and that is all that matters. Let us be clear about this. You have agreed to have the stories read. Now, I will read them one by one. It is your reward for bringing me the book, and, equally important, you will each give me your key!"

The Queen turns the scissors over in her hands while eyeing them and says, "A simple pair of scissors? This is a key? Here in plain view the whole time. How plain."

Jack turns his head to Mason, who is staring in disbelief. Then he tells the Queen, "But that's not a reward, that's terrible. We helped you." His voice trails off and then rises again, saying, "You are supposed to let us go!"

"Of course you helped me! And now, I will help myself—to your keys."

The Queen cackles in laughter.

Jack is defeated. The hope he had once had, the hope they had all had, is now gone. He has been betrayed. Now, as Jack observes the Queen, he notices a bizarre change that has come over her. The Queen, once radiant with kindness, looks sinister, dark, and ominous. She still smiles, but it is a terrible smirk. *Had she grown taller?* Jack wonders.

Instead of appearing welcoming, the Queen looks imposing, and her entire body is glowing with some sort of green light, the same green light that surrounds the fire.

"That cannot be the story. Change it now!" Amy challenges.

"Silence!" commands the Queen. Then she gives an exaggerated wave of a hand, and, suddenly, none of them can move. Jack's arms and legs are frozen in place. His muscles strain to move, but they can't.

The reality of what has happened hits Jack square between the eyes. This queen, this once glamorous beauty, is nothing more than a witch! *Of course,* thinks Jack. *The witch in the fairytale.* He realizes they are at her mercy and that the whole ordeal was a setup in order for her to acquire the book and the keys.

In spite of his frozen limbs, Jack can still turn his head, and he sees Victor standing triumphantly to his left with his arms folded in front of him in self-satisfaction. The man says, "A great day, my Queen!"

"Victor, yes, we have finally won, but this is not just our victory. This is a great day for all who are trapped in the woods. That selfish narrator, who has imprisoned us, will no longer be able to keep us from making this world a better place!"

The chilling words send Scotty into a gush of panic. He looks at Jack and then at his sister.

Trying to speak between sobs, he mutters, "No, I want to go home. Please, someone, help me!"

Suddenly Scotty's expression turns dull. Tears still gush from his eyes, but they turn void of any light.

The Queen shoots an evil eye at Scotty and barks, "I said *enough!*" Then she clears her throat and waves her arm, making each of their mouths slam shut.

"And now, young tailor, learn your fate."

We've made a terrible mistake, Jack thinks.

Chapter 132

Mason awaits the Queen's words, praying that somehow, someway his story will turn out better than Scotty's.

The Queen turns to face him and says, "Come forward, tailor."

Her hand shoots out in front of her, and a long finger points to Mason, whose legs begin to move in an awkward motion toward the Queen. No amount of effort can prevent his legs from moving closer to the evil woman.

"Shall we continue?" the Queen muses. Then she looks down and, with a twisted grin, reads.

> "The tailor extends the key to the Queen,
> The item that until now she had been unable to glean.
> His pride and vanity had led him astray.
> His own arrogance, for that he would pay.
> Selfish and vain he cared little for his friends,
> His life in his old world he could never mend.
> So the Queen offered life to the miserable boy:
> Serving her was the only way he could obtain such joy.
> A tailor he would be in her fitting room now.
> Loyalty to her, forever his vow."

"This is a fitting story. Proud boy, so full of himself. We must cure you of this, my child," says the Queen, whose self-righteous confidence fills the room.

"Simply wonderful, milady!" Victor exclaims.

Now Mason, too, is crying. He cannot help but grab the badge from his chest and place it into the waiting hand of the Queen, who looks down at the badge and cocks her head, studying the trinket.

The tough exterior Mason had long protected crashes down as he ambles back to the side of the others. As his body continues to move by no will of his own, he ponders, *Serve the Queen? Never see my dad again?* A thick knot balls up in his throat and more tears follow. Mason can still turn his head, and he looks back to see Amy with her eyes puffy and red, Jack standing with his mouth twisted and obviously furious, and Scotty weeping because of his own sentence.

Mason tells himself, *You can fight this! Move!* However, the spell that the witch has conjured keeps him still.

A sudden question crosses Mason's mind: *Is this my fault?* He realizes that he had insisted that the Queen proceed, but he reassures himself that they had all agreed. Plus, he thinks, *It was Jack who insisted we finish the story. He's the one who beat us over the heads with those words.*

As he wrestles with these thoughts in his need to blame someone else for the predicament, Mason is called back to the grim situation at hand as the Queen begins to speak again.

Chapter 133

"And now for our pretty little wanderer," says the Queen with words full of fake kindness.

More than anything, Amy wants to reach out to Scotty and somehow comfort him. She tries desperately to say something, but the Queen's spell won't allow it, and her body moves toward the enchantress. Never in all her life has she been so scared, so terrified. Her sentence is next.

> "Little Red, our wanderer, our damsel in distress
> Tried so hard her own sins to confess.
> Taking her key, she gives it away.
> The key, now the witch's item to display.
> She could not stand the sight of her own face,
> For other women were beautiful, she longed to take their place.
> She stayed in the wood to serve the lovely Queen,
> Serving her daily, her palace to clean."

A feeling of despair washes over Amy. Somehow, the Queen had known about her insecurity, and as if reinforcing the words, the Queen, in spite of her wickedness, seems to appear more beautiful to Amy. No other emotion can trump Amy's own feeling of worthlessness. The words the Queen had read seem to control the girl's actions.

Amy proceeds to set the stick before the Queen.

"What an excellent story, my Queen!" Victor exclaims, beaming with delight.

The Queen sets the stick down to her side after observing the item and says, "Amazing... such dull items, these keys."

After her sentence has been read, Amy returns to her spot with the others. Her story is just as terrible as Mason's and her brother's, and her heart is hurting for them just as much as she feels hopeless for herself. Jack's story is next, and the thought of the boy makes things eternally worse for Amy. In spite of his deception, Amy's heart aches for Jack, and she asks herself, *Why have I been so cruel to him?* She wishes he could forgive her, and if she could speak, she would yell, "I'm sorry, Jack! Forgive me!"

Amy considers how after all these years she has let one mistake ruin everything and that now she will never have the chance to make things right.

Chapter 134

Jack knows his story is next, and his stomach does cartwheels.

The Queen examines all of the teens briefly and says, "To think we have been waiting all these years for these children. It is absolutely delicious."

She is clearly savoring the moment. Then she suddenly stops and displays another wicked grin, adding, "Why, with all of the excitement I had not even noticed it before. Look, Victor. It seems the tailor has kept your belt safe."

Jack is confused. He contemplates, *Victor's belt? Wait... it's not Douglas Finch's bag?*

Victor says, "I am glad they have kept it safe. It is my only reminder of the world I left behind before that glorious day I met you, my Queen."

Jack realizes, *Victor is Douglas Finch—the Douglas Finch!* This truth makes Jack feel even sicker to his stomach. He considers how the whole night had been a trap, a game. The work belt they found had been deliberately placed, and the map with the note had been an elaborate hoax in order for these villains to get the book from the narrator. *But why?* Jack wonders.

As he's thinking hard about this, the haze begins to clear, and he angrily tries to yell.

"Ahh," the Queen remarks, "the thief has some words for us, Victor. Perhaps he would like to thank us no doubt? Feel free. Speak."

"You moved us through this world like pawns," asserts Jack. Then he looks at Victor and says, "You're Douglas Finch. Why did you do this to us? Why are you helping her?"

The man does not answer. He simply breaks into a joyous chuckle, obviously pleased that at least one of them had solved the riddle.

Jack turns back to the Queen and tells her, "You couldn't find the keys yourself, but now you have your stupid keys, so let us go!"

"This child thinks he is wise beyond his years," the Queen states proudly.

"You wanted access to the vault. Was that your goal? You want to control everyone; you want to change all of the stories!"

"Excellent! What a truly ingenious child. You see, my young thief, I am going to change this world for the better. For far too long we have been trapped here. I will burn the book, my book, and take control of this world. The narrator will no longer control my story, for the book will burn. Its existence will be wiped from memory. Then, those people represented in that vault will have no will of their own, for they do not know what is best for them. I will change their stories one at a time. Thank you—all of you! For years I have waited for you, and now I have won."

The reality of the grand scheme hits Jack. They had done everything for her. They had shown her the way. They had taken the bait hook, line, and sinker.

He attempts to speak again, but a gentle wave of the Queen's hand forces his mouth to shut tight. Then his legs move forward under no power of his own. With her long finger, the Queen is begging him forward.

Jack thinks, "If only we had not taken the book from the narrator...."

The Queen clears her throat and then begins.

> "The desperate thief would grow full of wrath.
> He had been so sure he had taken the right path.
> The key he had was useless to the boy,
> So he adorned his Queen with her latest new toy.
> Now lost in the wood, the boy had to survive.
> Only his talent of theft would allow him to thrive.
> Caught and imprisoned, convicted and tried
> For his many sins that he choose to try and hide,
> Imprisoned to pay for his life full of strife,
> He died bitter and angry at his choices in life."

Somehow, Jack knows that whatever the Queen had read would come true, but, still, he wonders, *Is this my fate?* His thoughts start to become cloudy and he can't think straight. He tells himself, *Fight it, Jack! Stay here!"* However, his body starts toward the backpack in order to retrieve the goose for the Queen. Unexpectedly, though, he suddenly stops as if his own will is confused, and he thinks, *What is happening to me?*

Chapter 135

From his vantage point, the wolf is engrossed in the events unfolding before him. One by one as the Queen reads the stories, he notices that the teens seem to fall under some sort of spell. A gnawing emotion eats at him, something he had not expected at all. It had hit him just as the Queen summoned Amy forward. Her fear, her obvious regret, and the emotions on her face—they drew out something that had long laid dormant in his soul. To his utter shock, he feels actual remorse, even sympathy, for the girl he had hunted with such vigor.

However, the sympathy is not exclusive to the girl. He feels guilt for the others as well. He knows the kids had actually saved him from the fire. When he had been inside the burning hut, he had blacked out, and when he woke, all he saw was the procession of kids leaving. The wolf recognizes that these brave kids had outwitted him. He considers how they had fought him with such tenacity, even here in this room, and in the room with the spider, one of them had actually taken care of the spider for him by using the shrinking potion. So, although it seems strange, he respects them, as a hero respects his rival. Now, as these kids are being imprisoned by the Queen, a realization hits him: they are prisoners now just like him.

Suddenly, it is all very clear to the wolf. Once he had awoken that night in the ride, it was the Queen who had instructed him to get the girl. *How had he been so foolish?* he thinks. She was using him to drive the teens to her. Also, while he had longed to eat the girl, his actions were being manipulated by the Queen.

He wonders, *Did I act foolishly? Now that the Queen has deceived the teens, will she deceive me again? Will she truly give me the girl? No, probably not. But what can I do? The Queen can simply hex me. Still, now that the Queen no longer needs my services, she will dispose of me anyways.*

The wolf decides that whatever he is going to do, he must do it quickly. He tells himself, *It's now or never,* and then springs into action. The wolf, in spite of his bad leg, launches himself at the Queen. The distance closes, and just as he is about to plow into her body, she turns. A look of disbelief flashes across the Queen's face. Then she slides to her left. In mid-jump, the wolf attempts to re-position his charge but can't properly manipulate himself with his injured leg.

"What are you doing?" screams the Queen. Just as the wolf passes her by, she mutters a spell.

The wolf howls, and all of his joints start becoming stiff. Before he loses complete control, though, he slings a wild paw into the air in an effort to scratch, maim, or inflict some injury. This misses the Queen, but one of his sharp claws does manage to spear a piece of paper, which rips away from the raised hand of the Queen. Then, after another moment, the paper is dislodged from the wolf's nail and wafts into the air.

The wolf lands with a thud inches from the crackling fire.

The Queen cries out in rage, "You fool!"

From the hard ground, the wolf watches as the paper, gently floating, comes to rest in the fire.

Chapter 136

As the entire bizarre scene plays out before Jack, who moments ago had been lulled into a dream like stupor, he is revived by the sudden action taking place and watches as the paper falls into the fire.

The Queen furiously screams at the wolf, "Vile creature! You will pay for your insolence!" Then she turns to her accomplice and says, "Victor, once we have disposed of the book, perhaps you can find an interesting method of repaying the beast?"

"With pleasure, your excellence!" replies Victor, standing behind the fire, a catlike grin across his face.

Jack is just able to make out his friends who are standing to his right. All of them are staring blankly at the wolf, who is lying on the floor, immobilized by a spell. Then an odd thing happens. As the paper, now in the fire, quickly wrinkles to ash, Jack finds that he is able to move his arm. So, he also attempts to wiggle a foot, and it responds.

The page, he thinks, *it had to be the page! That's my story the wolf knocked free into the fire. Of course! The Queen said she would burn her book and be free from the words that bind her. This must be happening to me. But, what do I do now?*

Acting cautiously, Jack decides to remain still for the moment, surmising that it will be better if the Queen doesn't realize he can move. He then waits for his chance to strike.

The Queen turns her attention to the agitated kids and confidently addresses the assembly, appearing to have regained her composure.

She says, "A page has been burnt. One of you should be free. Are you playing games with me, children? The time for games is over." In a low voice, the Queen, without taking the time to cycle through the pages, begins another incantation in an effort to quickly imprison whoever was set free by the burning page.

Jack knows he has to act. He thinks, *If only it was not solely up to me. I wish the narrator were here to help.* Suddenly, the Queen's incantations stop. She seems distracted.

"I see I'm a little late for the party," Jack hears someone say. He recognizes the voice and realizes it's the narrator's.

Chapter 137

The narrator approaches the witch, who is looking much more hideous than glamorous. She takes a few steps toward the man, erasing most of the distance between them. Her face is blood red, and the green aura surrounding her is burning brightly.

The Queen says, "You are too late! The prophecy is fulfilled. I have read the words of their stories! And I hold the book—my book!"

The narrator responds in a hushed voice, "You have no clue, my dear. You never did. You cannot change what has been set in motion."

"But you are wrong. I hold the book! My book!" the Queen says with a cackle.

"When you entered the woods long ago, you thought you could change things then, but—"

"You will no longer control me," the Queen admonishes.

"I never decided your fate. You made your own choices," the narrator responds.

While trying to pay close attention to the words being exchanged, Jack can feel the rising heat from the fire. He's working on connecting the dots of their conversation with the information he already knows. Jack looks over behind the fire at Victor, or Douglas Finch, who is looking very concerned. A thought pops into Jack's head: *Was the Queen just someone else who entered the woods?*

"Quit trying to trick me, old man! I won't let you do that again. Your time has passed."

Jack notices the witch has relaxed a little and figures she must feel confident that she has finally won.

Then the narrator's voice increases in volume, and he says, "You decided that your story would be about controlling others, so that is why you are trapped. You are no longer welcome here. Your last attempt at controlling your pawns has failed. I will take the book now."

Like a child protecting a toy from another, she pulls the book to her side and holds it tightly with both hands.

The witch says, "No, you will not have it! It is mine. The prophecy foretold of this day, the day of my victory!"

Then, turning to the fire just a few yards away, she deliberately walks toward the flames.

Chapter 138

The Queen picks up her pace toward the fire, and the narrator is doing nothing to stop her.

Jack wonders what is going to happen and questions why the narrator isn't taking action. The fire is just to his left, and as the Queen nears it, Jack decides it's up to him and that he must get the book away from her. He hopes that as a result of her squabble with the narrator, the Queen has forgotten that one of them is free.

The Queen draws dangerously close to the fire. She casts a malicious look at the Narrator and then holds the book out in front of her with one hand while keeping the three remaining papers in the other.

"The book will burn," the witch says. "You cannot stop—"

Jack launches into action. He grabs the book with both hands and pulls with all of his might. Alarmed by the sudden movement and attack of the boy, the Queen flails, and the papers containing the stories of the other teens fly upward. The inertia makes the Queen lunge forward, and she loses her grip on the book, which Jack now has in his clutches as he spins to the floor.

Off balance, the Queen trips into the fire. Immediately, she hops back out but not before the flames have licked at her robes. Before long, she is overpowered by her fiery attire: the green light that had once enveloped her is now a violent orange, red, and yellow blaze. A sudden rush of activity and chaos fills the room as Victor rushes to her aid.

"My Queen!" he calls out while wildly patting at flames with his hands. The Queen is now a picture of panic—dancing, rolling, and jumping as the man beats at her body.

As a result of the chaotic situation, the Queen's holding spell is broken. Immediately, the wolf regains his feet, begins snarling, and looks wildly around the room: first at Amy, then at the narrator, and then at the Queen and Victor.

Meanwhile, the fire is still wrapped around the Queen, who cries out in pain as Victor continues his efforts to stifle it.

Jack was watching this from his vantage point on the ground, but his attention has been redirected to the snarling wolf with drooling teeth barred, and Jack sees that the creature is staring at Amy.

Chapter 139

In spite of his attempt to save the kids, the wolf still wants the girl. In fact, the impulse for her is actually stronger now than it had been earlier. Before, he had stood in obedience to the Queen, respecting her power, but with her presently being occupied by her predicament, he considers going after the girl. At the same time, though, he cannot resist the urge to feel empathy for the teens.

A voice in the wolf's head tells him, *You could still have her.* It is the shattered plate that he has reformed in his imagination.

The plate calls to him, *You need her—I need her.*

But the Queen, she was using us... it was she who—"

Forget that! You have no time for this. Do it now!

During this period of indecision, it is Jack who acts first. The wolf is surprised as the boy stands up, collects the papers in the air, and delivers them to the fire. The wolf watches him warily and realizes that he must strike now before the pages burn and the girl can run.

"You must fight the desire within you," says the narrator to the wolf. "You, too, can start anew."

"I must have the girl," responds the wolf, instinctively barring his fangs for the old man to see.

"No, you must control the urge. This is not who you are."

The authority of the man's voice surprises the wolf.

"But she is all I have ever wanted."

"No, she is not. You once made a foolish choice, and you ended up here in this world. You were imprisoned by the Queen."

With the mention of her, the wolf redirects his gaze from Amy to the hapless witch. He sees that the flames have subsided and she is being assisted by Victor, who is cradling her fallen body.

"You were trapped in the ride," continues the narrator. "You were a simple attraction for people to fear, until the day she could use you as a pawn. Then, when she sensed the time was near, you were released to help the Queen realize her schemes. She wanted them to fear you and run to her, to fear you and embrace her."

The wolf knows this is true, but in spite of the new reality, he still wants the girl. He considers that he can wait a little longer and see how things play out.

His attention turns to the Queen and Victor, who is helping her to her feet, and he beholds a ghastly sight. The Queen's face is scorched. One of her cheekbones is exposed, the flesh devoured by the licking flames. The wolf is not sure what is more surprising: the fact that the Queen is still alive and now on her feet or the hideous state of her body.

Chapter 140

Jack watches as Douglas Finch assists the Queen to the door of the ginger-bread house. In spite of her pitiful state, Jack feels little sympathy for the woman who had attempted to enslave them all. He wonders, *Is she going to get away? Is the narrator just going to let her walk?*

As the Queen and Victor proceed to the door of the palace, a mutilated jaw lowers from the witch's mouth, and she weakly says in a low raspy voice, "This is not over yet. I will have revenge."

Then she coughs and gives a moan of pain. Her gnarled body is assisted by Victor as they proceed toward the door, but once they arrive at the threshold, she stops and turns back with a wild look that's apparent even through her horrid features. It appears as if she is muttering something, and she painfully straightens herself and attempts to lift an arm.

"We have had enough of that," the narrator speaks coldly. "Leave us."

Resigned to defeat, she sags back down into a pitiful hunch and disappears through the door of her palace.

However, before Victor can pass into the house as well, the narrator calls out, "Douglas Finch."

The duplicitous man stops halfway through the door.

"It is not too late for you," the narrator asserts. "Your story is far from finished. She does not have to control you any longer."

Douglas looks at the narrator and also at the kids. Then for a second, the man looks into the house at the Queen before looking back at the narrator. With a frown of resolve, he turns and shuffles through the door to rejoin the witch.

Next, turning to the wolf, the narrator reminds the beast, "This also applies to you."

The wolf does not react. He simply stands there with his eyes on the man.

Thus far, Jack had been fixated on the grim scene so much so that he had forgotten to check on his friends. Now, he sees Mason doubled over and holding his stomach, and Scotty looking around and waving his arms, apparently delighted at his ability to move. Then his eyes rest on Amy. He doesn't go to her immediately but simply watches her.

Amy says, "Mr. Wolf?"

Jack is shocked by this but not as surprised as the wolf, who, wide-eyed, is obviously taken off guard so much so that he takes a step back.

Amy continues, "I just wanted to thank you for helping us."

The wolf quietly examines her, then looks to the others, and rests his eyes on the old man.

Chapter 141

The wolf appears unable to move, though the witch's binding spell is no longer affecting him.

Now Amy walks toward Jack. She starts crying.

There is a lump in Jack's throat that feels to him to be the size of a bowling ball. He stands his ground, not knowing exactly what is to come.

The girl's arms wrap around his waist, and her head nuzzles into his chest. "I'm sorry," she sobs.

He wants to scream, "No!" but holding back this urge, he simply whispers, with his mouth close to her ear, "No, I'm sorry."

For the first time since entering the ride, he embraces her in full view of the others. Immediately, he quickly looks over to Scotty and Mason, but then chides himself for caring what they think about it. With unabashed freedom, he kisses her on the forehead. Together, the couple stands in silence as the others watch for what seems like an eternity.

Amy looks up into Jack's eyes and says, "I'm sorry I treated you like that tonight."

Jack quickly responds, not wanting her to feel any blame, "No, I'm sorry. It's my fault, remember? I got you into this mess."

Amy knows this is a sincere apology, and her tears dampen his badly torn shirt.

The embrace continues in silence until Mason cannot hide his disdain any longer, "Barf, are you serious? All that mushy kiss-and-make-up stuff right in front of us?"

Scotty's eyes are the size of saucers, indicating that he's finally in on the secret.

The narrator approaches the couple and says, "Well, you acted very bravely, Jack."

The boy relinquishes his embrace of the girl and takes her hand. Then Jack looks up at the narrator and says, "Thank you. If you had not come when you did—"

"Well, you asked me to come."

Jack is confused, thinking, *When did I ask for help?*

Scotty approaches the narrator now, holds out a hand, and says, "Thanks, uh, Sam, right?"

"Yes, and thank you, brave apprentice. You all have truly done something marvelous here today."

"But we were the ones who stole your book," Jack admits while glancing over at Mason, who is still standing awkwardly just a few steps away from the others.

"Yes, that . . . well . . . ," the Narrator acknowledges.

Jack proudly hands the book to the narrator and says, "Here, we are giving it back now. I am truly sorry."

Jack waits for the response. The narrator simply looks at the book and then lowers it in one hand to his side. No words follow.

From the corner of his eye, Jack watches Mason, and he wonders, *Is he going to say anything? Thank the man? Anything?*

Mason sees Jack watching him and finally speaks, as if he has to, asking, "So do we get out now?"

How can he be so ungrateful? Jack thinks. He shakes his head at Mason, letting him see the disappointment.

The narrator responds, "Well, the story is not finished yet."

Jack asks, "The story is not finished?"

"Why, yes, you still have a little way to go."

The narrator, with book in hand, turns to leave.

This new revelation crushes Jack, and he can tell the other teens are exasperated as well. He asks himself, *Is he really leaving us? What more do we have to do? Is this because we didn't follow his rhymes?* Jack looks at the wolf, whose eyes still remain focused on Amy, and the boy wonders, *If the narrator leaves, what will this beast do?*

Nervously, Jack begs the narrator, "Don't leave. Stay with us; help us."

"Well, Jack, I would, but you still have some things to do on your own."

"Like what? You've never really come out and told us what you wanted us to do?"

The narrator looks into Jack's eyes and says, "You have to make things right."

"But how? Just tell us, please."

"Jack, just think about it. You need to make amends. I cannot do it for you."

The tone of the narrator makes it clear to Jack that the conversation is over.

Amy clasps Jack's hand and tells him, "We can finish this, Jack."

A little frustrated by the last few words of the Narrator, Jack watches as the old man approaches the entrance to the passageway from which the wolf had emerged.

Then, just as the man is about to disappear, a loud *crash* echoes through the room. All four teens, the wolf, and the narrator are jolted by the sound.

Soon, another *crash* is heard, and then, another. Each time, the floor shakes and the walls vibrate.

"What is going on?" Jack yells.

Amy cries, "What now?"

A thunderous voice says, "Fee fi fo fum!"

Chapter 142

The echo of the booming voice reverberates through the room and shakes Jack's nerves.

"What is that?" Mason cries.

"That's trouble, big trouble," growls the wolf. He scurries behind the gingerbread house.

For a moment, everything is silent.

Amy clings to Jack. Scotty holds his place. The narrator, who had seconds ago been on his way out of the room, is now standing fast.

Mason, on the other hand, makes a dash to the door. Upon reaching it, he pulls at the handle wildly.

"It's still locked!" he calls out. Then he tells the narrator, "Open this thing, come on, man! Do something. We've got to get out."

Showing no emotion at all, the narrator simply replies, "It's too late."

As soon as the narrator utters those words, the wall to their right collapses in piles of dry wall and stones. Jack ducks down and tries to shield his face and Amy from flying fragments as white dust fills the air.

After the initial implosion, Jack stares into the gaping hole in the wall. He can make out a very large hairy arm that's holding a club the size of Jack's entire body.

"Fe fi fo fum!"

Jack coughs from the powdered air but holds his gaze at the hole as the dust begins to settle. Now, he sees a giant bare foot breaking through the haze. More of the wall implodes as the remainder of the leg flings through the expanse. The Giant is clearly visible now. He has a thick black beard that reaches down to his chest, and a similar black mane of hair hangs down from his head to his shoulders. He's wearing a ragged green shirt and ripped brown pants, both of which cling to his enormous frame. One of his feet, which are roughly the size of canoes, is in a boot, and this comes to rest inches away from Jack.

Then as the Giant slings his club out of the gap, it crashes into the side of the small gingerbread house, which collapses like a stack of cards. The Giant forces the rest of his body through the gap and appears to fill up nearly half of the room. Even as he is hunched over, his head brushes the ceiling.

"I am here for the thief!" the Giant exclaims.

Jack's terror is now on overload.

"Which one of you stole my goose?"

Panic eclipses every other emotion in Jack's mind. He clings even tighter to Amy who is still plastered to his chest. The tension is unbearable. Jack looks desperately to the narrator, who is watching the scene with no expression on his face.

"It's him. He's the one who stole your goose," Mason cries while pointing at Jack as he walks toward his friend.

Tearing her head away from its nesting spot in Jack's chest, Amy angrily cries, "Mason!"

Scotty, also outraged by the decree, joins his sister, asking, "What are you doing, Mason?"

So much for anonymity, thinks Jack. *The gig is up.* His only outward reaction is to simply shake his head in disbelief at Mason's betrayal.

"Well, boy," the Giant says as he casts his enormous yellow eyes down at Jack. "You shall return what you have stolen."

The stare of the Giant shakes Jack. In fact, he is so utterly terrified that he cannot speak, and only a ramble of guttural noises escapes his lips.

"Jack, come on, just give him the goose," Mason implores.

The backpack. Where is it? Jack thinks. He contemplates if the Giant would simply accept the goose and leave them alone.

Jack gently separates himself from Amy's embrace and begins scanning the floor. He tells the Giant, "Uh... hold on just a second. I have it here somewhere."

The boy tells himself, *Think, Jack, think. Where is it?* He recalls that the Queen sat it down somewhere when she healed his hand, and he walks a few feet behind him to locate the spot. Unfortunately, the area has been covered by fragments of the crumbled wall. Still, Jack knows he must try to recover the backpack, so he begins digging around in the debris. Scotty and Amy soon join him in the search, but Mason only watches as does the wolf, who has moved to not be in the way of the excavation.

Jack quietly says, "It was here. I remember the Queen set it down."

After a few more seconds of rummaging, Scotty announces, "Got it." He lifts the pack above his head as if it were a treasure of great value unearthed for the world to see. Then Scotty steps over a large piece of dry wall and hands the pack to his friend.

To Jack, it is indeed priceless. "Thank you, Scotty," he says.

Jack is relieved, but he's still unsure whether or not the Giant will take the goose and leave.

Immediately, Jack unzips the pack, and as he does so, he tells the Giant, "Uh... sir, I do have the goose. I didn't know it was yours."

"Give it to me," the Giant bellows.

Jack reaches into the pack and rifles through its contents. However, Jack is unable to feel the smooth object he's looking for. He opens the pack wider and looks inside. A mortifying fear emerges in him when he realizes the goose is missing.

"It's not here!" he cries.

With a panicked reply, Amy questions, "It's not there?"

Jack spills the contents of the bag on the ground. There are the cups he won earlier along with the small red ball and, also, the package of

Twizzlers he had totally forgotten about, but there is no goose. *Where is it?* Jack wonders. He replays the events of the last few hours and thinks, *How could I have lost the goose? Did I leave it in the key slot? No, I remember I grabbed it out.*

"Jack, did you ever lose sight of it?" Scotty asks.

"No," he declares. But, even as he says this, he remembers the Queen setting it down at his feet as she was about to heal his hand. He had been inside the gingerbread house when he had dropped the backpack on the floor.

"The Queen took it," Jack states. The blood in his veins goes cold.

The Giant responds, "You lost it? Someone stole it from you!"

This time, Amy attempts to come to the rescue. She says, "That's right; the Queen took it. Maybe you can find her still. She went into that—"

"Enough!" the Giant declares.

Amy cowers backwards.

"So the burglar has been... burgled—ha—how fitting," says the Giant, whose cold glare is replaced with a grim smile revealing a jagged row of stubby brown teeth. "If the Queen has it, perhaps I will never see it again."

Jack sees the hand of the Giant tighten around his club.

"Well, I shall have to have compensation for my loss," the Giant thoughtfully announces.

In spite of the grim reality of the moment, Jack cannot help but be amused by a Giant using the word "compensation." All of Jack's stereotypes of Giants have been busted.

The narrator now addresses the Giant, "What would you like as repayment?"

"Well, I think I will take the boy, of course."

"What?" Jack catches himself yelling.

"You heard me. You will be my compensation."

Amy rushes to Jack and wraps her arms around him. She shakes her head in defiance and says, "No, Jack can't go; he belongs with us. Find the Queen. She is the one—"

"I will hear no more from you, little lady," the Giant states while lifting his club and lowering the end just inches from Amy's face.

This silences Amy, and she begins to tear up again.

All of a sudden, Jack is pushed from behind, causing him to move forward a couple of steps.

"Take him, and you will let us go, right?" asks Mason, who glares sheepishly at Jack.

"Mason!" Amy yells.

"Mason, you coward!" exclaims Scotty.

Defensively, Mason retorts, "Don't you remember? This is what it said: three of them will have happily-ever-after. I have to get home."

"Of course all I want is repayment. I am not that unreasonable." explains the Giant, whose voice has changed and now sounds unnaturally pleasant. "Something was stolen from me. I take the boy in return. He pays his debt to me, and we are square. It is only fair. Look here—"

"But that does not seem fair," Scotty declares. "It was a statue."

"Fair? I am the one to determine what is fair. After all, I am not the one who stole something from you."

Jack's head is spinning. He looks at the narrator for help, but the old man simply continues to twirl the end of his white mustache. Then Jack looks to Mason, who seems eager about betraying him. Jack knows he should feel malice toward him, but when Jack sees Mason looking frail and scared, he knows Mason is just doing what he does best, looking out for himself. Instead of malice, Jack feels pity for him.

"Jack, let's run," Amy urges in his ear.

Where? Jack thinks. He considers that even if they could escape right now, the Giant would continue to hunt them, so they'd never be at peace until the debt was paid. All of sudden, a strange feeling of accountability flashes in Jack's mind: *I took the goose. I am the one who got us into this mess. If I leave with the Giant, the others will go free.*

Wrestling in his mind with the reality of his guilt, he slowly lifts Amy's chin, looks into her eyes, and whispers, "I'm not running from my mistakes anymore, Amy. The time for running is over. This is all my fault."

Then, he turns to the Giant and says, "I'll go."

Chapter 143

Scotty is downright mortified by what's just happened: the Giant's demand, Mason's betrayal, and Jack's acceptance. After everything they had been through during the night, he can't believe that Jack's just going to accept this.

"You're not serious, Jack?" Scotty exclaims.

"No! You can't," Amy cries. Her face is full of desperation.

The wolf simply shakes his head in disbelief.

Mason, looking at the door, nervously asks, "Okay, so now we can leave?"

Before the Giant can reply, Scotty attempts to reason with the behemoth again. He says, "Sir, we all know the Queen has the goose. What if we were to get it from her and bring it back to you?"

"Well, I am afraid I cannot just let this criminal walk away unpunished. Besides how can I trust a thief and his companions to bring it back?"

"We will bring it back," Amy asserts.

"No, I'm afraid I cannot trust you," the Giant says.

Scotty responds, "Yes, I get that, but...."

He tries to remember everything he can about giants about fairytales, considering how this strategy had worked with the troll.

"But what?" asks the Giant while looking quizzically at Scotty.

Stories flood into Scotty's mind. He stammers, "Uh, well, uh, let's say...."

Then he looks down at the floor and sees the contents of Jack's backpack spilled among the debris. He thinks, *That's it! It might work, if the Giant would just bite.*

"I don't have time for your delays, boy," the Giant states.

"What about a game?" Scotty asks.

The Giant looks puzzled and replies, "What do you mean?"

"I mean you and Jack here play a game," Scotty announces.

"Scotty, what are you doing?" Jack inquires.

"Trust me, okay."

The Giant seems to be listening, and Scotty continues, "You two play a game. After all, Jack doesn't have the goose. Let fate decide if he should be punished. If Jack wins, he is free; if Jack loses, he goes with you."

Mason pulls Scotty's arm and mutters into his ear, "You can't trick him like you did the troll. What if you make him mad? He will kill us all."

Scotty replies confidently, "At least Jack will have a chance. Of course we can't trick him, but it's the best shot we have."

Mason turns away from Scotty and addresses the Giant, "Whatever happens, win or lose, we can go, right?"

"Of course. I said I would let you go, right?"

There is a moment of pause while the Giant is obviously considering Scotty's query. Then he chuckles and says, "Yes, splendid idea. I like games."

Scotty beams with hope.

"So, what will it be?" the Giant asks.

Scotty winks at Jack and says, "The shell game."

Chapter 144

Wallace Braddock watches Clyde sitting with a cup of coffee in his hand and talking to two of the police officers. He looks at his watch and sees that it's 12:27 a.m.

When Houston Carnahan came out of the ride earlier, he was fuming mad. Now, he tells Wallace, "The old man has something to do with this, and the cops are over there treating him like a teddy bear."

For the last hour, Wallace has put up with this smoldering anger. Houston had also worked up other parents, so much, in fact, that when Clyde had exited the ride, Mr. Chick screamed, "We want our kids back, you liar!"

The crowd around the parents has swelled. Several reporters have joined the throng, probably clued in to the event from their police scanners. About a dozen park employees are there, too, in addition to some curious park attendees who were drawn in by the activity despite the late hour. Also in this mix of people is the Crime Scene Unit from another county, which had arrived, entered the ride, and returned without the children.

Wallace, in spite of the accusations from Mr. Carnahan, is still apprehensive about accusing the old man. At this point, he sees the two officers with Clyde stand up and begin talking to some new arrivals, three grim-looking men in dark blue suits. The five of them move away from Clyde, leaving him sitting alone.

Wallace decides to take this opportunity to speak to Clyde one-on-one and tells his wife, "I'll be back."

"Where are you going?" Brenna asks, looking at him with eyes red from a night of worry.

"Just stay here," Wallace responds.

Houston sees Wallace pull back from the crowd of onlookers and starts following him. "I see that look in your eye, Wallace. What are you up to?" Houston calls.

Wallace grimaces, thinking that Houston could ruin everything.

He says, "I'm going to talk to Clyde."

"Then I'm going with you."

"That may not be a good idea," Wallace argues, but he knows he won't be able to stop Houston from coming along.

Houston grins and assures Wallace, "Don't worry, I'll be good."

The two men realize that sneaking around without being noticed by the police isn't easy. Wallace and Houston loop widely around the snack bar and walk through the carnival games. Then as they near the ice cream shack, they spy Clyde sitting alone and sipping his coffee. While trying to keep just out of sight of the nearby officers, Wallace crouches while Houston stands back flush against the wall peering nervously from left to right and back again.

With the old man less than ten feet away, Wallace whispers, "Clyde, over here."

The old man turns and blinks. Lines of worry clutter his eyes and forehead. He leans back and moves his head around the back of the stand. He rises to his feet cautiously and erases the distance between him and the two men.

Clyde asks, "What are you doing, Mr. Braddock?" Then when he sees Houston, he looks visibly disturbed.

"Look, we just want to ask you a question or two. I promise Houston won't bite—right, Houston?"

The large man nods, but it is clear he is not happy with Clyde.

Wallace begins, "Look, Clyde, when you left the kids, did you hear any of them say anything about sneaking off?"

Clyde sighs and says, "No. Uh, Wallace, I don't think you should be—"

"I know, Clyde, it's just, I mean, we're worried to death out here and no one will talk to us. Could they have left the ride and the park without you knowing?"

The old man nervously looks over at the cops who are speaking in their huddle about ten yards away.

Then he whispers back, "No. Even if they went out the fire escape exit, the only path loops them back to the front of the ride. And Gwen was out here the whole time." He pauses, sighs again, and continues, "Look, Wallace, I promise I don't know what happened. I had nothing to do with this."

Wallace feels a hand squeeze his shoulder hard and knows it's Houston, but he ignores him and says, "I believe you, Clyde." He needs Clyde to feel unthreatened, even though Wallace still has his doubts. He is hoping for some kind of a breakthrough.

Wallace goes on to ask, "Did you see anything unusual in the ride?"

The old man hesitates and then sets down his coffee mug on the concrete ground below. It is obvious that something is troubling him.

He replies, "Well, uh, not really."

Houston can't keep quiet. "What are you not telling us?" he exclaims.

Wallace bristles and shushes the large man. He quickly looks around the corner at the huddle of officers and is relieved to see that none of them seem to be aware of this conversation. Then he gives another critical look at Houston, who's hovering right over his shoulder.

Suddenly, footsteps click on the pavement behind them.

"What are you gentlemen doing back here?" asks Officer Quinn.

Wallace responds, "Look, we just want some answers. You're not telling us—"

"What's going on here!?" Officer Dockins yells from the huddle of police.

Then he begins walking toward the group around Clyde and says, "Carnahan, Braddock—what on God's green earth are you doing? You were told to stay—"

"I know what we were told," Wallace asserts. "But our kids—"

Dockins waves his hand in front of Wallace's face, signaling him to be quiet. The officer says, "You two are obstructing a police investigation. I'm not sure what's gotten into you, but this is a serious offense. Quinn, take these two back to the—"

"Wait, Jimmy," Clyde interjects. "Let them stay for a second."

Dockins is surprised, as are Wallace and Houston.

"There is something I haven't told you," the old man says.

"Well, spit it out!" exclaims Houston.

"When I was in there earlier... when we first started searching for them... well, I saw this door."

For the next five minutes, Clyde explains in detail the strange events he had kept hidden. He recounts in detail the music, the glowing sign, and the door.

Then he mentions, "In fact, the same thing happened back when the other kid, Finch, disappeared years ago."

"Why are you just now telling us this, Clyde?" Dockins asks.

"I told the cops about the door back when Finch disappeared. They checked it out and found nothing. They said I was crazy and made me go see a doctor for months until I had to make a formal statement that I had concocted the whole thing about the door. But I know what I saw, and no shrink's gonna tell me different."

One of the Crime Scene guys who had joined the party comments, "It does sound crazy."

Quinn snickers until she sees the disapproving face of her superior. Then she coughs and regains composure.

"Clyde, you're telling me this crazy music starts and this mysterious door just appears out of nowhere? That's a hard story to swallow," admits Dockins.

Wallace can see the doubt in the policeman's eyes.

But for himself, he is looking for any sign of hope, so he says, "But what if he's telling the truth? Let Clyde show us where the door is. As far as I can tell, it's your only lead."

Dockins looks at the old man and studies him.

Houston adds, "It's worth a shot, right, Officer?"

Chapter 145

Jack's confidence soars. He feels that what Scotty has done is pure genius, and a glimmer of hope now emerges in his eyes. Jack collects the three cups and the ball from the floor as Scotty proceeds to explain the game to the Giant. Then the amateur carny takes a large piece of the drywall and lays it out flat along the floor, producing a makeshift game table.

Once the cups have been set out in a row before the Giant, Amy walks up to Jack and pleads, "Jack, be careful, please! You can't lose."

Jack grins at her and says, "Don't worry, Amy, I've got this."

The narrator meanders over to Jack, as well, and says, "I wish you good fortune, Jack. I see that your friend the apprentice has given you an out."

"Yes, he has," responds Jack, who looks up at the man and then over to Scotty who is still explaining and re-explaining the rules to the Giant.

Never again will Jack think of Scotty as weak. All of those years Scotty had spent with his nose in books had made him smart, in fact, downright crafty. Jack will never take Scotty Carnahan for granted again.

Meanwhile, Mason is sitting on a stump and fiddling with some of the candy remains of the house. Jack sees him and wonders, *What is he thinking? Is he even happy I have a chance? He can't be that angry, can he? Why do I even care? He betrayed me.* Their friendship had been obliterated during the night, and at least once, Jack had sworn to himself that he would never speak to Mason again if they survived. Yet, looking at him now, he feels something odd: sympathy.

Mason's head turns Jack's way, and their eyes meet. They stare at each other for a moment. Then Mason raises his head slightly and calls out absently, "Good luck, Jack." After this, he goes right back to playing with the debris, seemingly uninterested in whatever the results of the game may be.

The gesture may have been halfhearted, but it makes Jack feel that maybe things could be salvaged—if he wanted them to be.

As for the wolf, the beast has made a seat out of a large collapsed section of wall and is cautiously waiting, perhaps intrigued by the strange game. Still, Jack notices that every few seconds the beast stares at Amy, and he thinks, *If I make it through this, we might have to deal with him again.*

Scotty and the Giant finally finish.

Now, turning his attention down at the small board, the Giant addresses Jack, "So, you just happen to have these items with you?" Then after a pause, he adds, "Why do I think I am being set up?" His face is suddenly stern.

"No one is tricking you," Scotty announces. "You have just as good a chance as Jack. It is simply a matter of keeping your eyes on the ball."

He lifts a cup over the ball and then removes it for the Giant to see before continuing. "Like I said, best two out of three. Jack will shuffle the cups first, and you will try and guess which one it is under. Then it will be you turn."

"I guess I am game," The Giant concludes and then chuckles at his pun.

At least the Giant seems like a good sport, thinks Jack. In fact he catches himself thinking that as far as giants go, this one is likable.

Jack kneels on the floor and calls up to the Giant, "Are you ready?"

Scotty, the narrator, and the wolf now crowd around the gaming table.

Amy takes a position right behind Jack, gives him a gentle squeeze on the shoulder, and keeps her hand there.

"Yes," the Giant replies.

Jack pats Amy's hand and she lets go. Then he holds the ball up for the Giant to see. Next, he shuffles the cups—slowly at first but soon picks up speed. With dexterity, Jack wheels the cups. They revolve and dart around each other, and sometimes Jack circles a cup one way and then another.

The Giant's head spins circles as he tries to follow the cups as well as he can. The shuffling goes one for about 20 seconds, and then Jack stops suddenly, confidently, and says, "Okay, under which cup is the ball?"

Jack reasons, *There is no way he could have tracked the ball.*

The Giant reaches a large hand to his chin, almost knocking over Scotty with his elbow, and scratches at his woolly beard.

There is a puzzled look on the Giant's face, and he declares, "You expect me to have followed that? I have no clue."

Jack confidence soars even higher, for this means the Giant would be guessing, a one in three shot.

The Giant ponders for what seems like an eternity.

Finally Scotty announces, "Okay, times up. Which cup?"

"It's a blind guess at best," the Giant explains as he points to the cup in the middle.

Jack's heart soars, for he knows that the Giant has guessed incorrectly.

"Nope," Jack says and beams with pride as he lifts the cup and reveals nothing beneath it. He keeps the cup aloft for a few seconds, relishing the victory.

Amy lets out a sigh of relief.

Scotty slaps Jack on the back, and tells him, "Good job."

Then, like an announcer at an athletic competition, Scotty announces the score for everyone in the room to hear: "One to nothing, Jack leads."

Glowing with pride, Jack looks over at Mason. The boy remains sitting and seems to be paying no attention.

The Giant lets out a good natured laugh, which shakes the entire room, and says, "Well, so much for beginner's luck, I guess. You sure are handy with those cups. I suppose it is my turn to try and deceive you."

The wolf chuckles. He is impressed by the boy's good fortune.

As for the others, they are confident that Jack will win after seeing his ability to quickly confuse the Giant.

Jack, too, is confident in his ability to see the cups. He thinks, *This should be easy. How could the Giant possibly confuse me?*

As if she could read his mind, Amy advises, "Keep your focus, Jack. Don't get cocky."

The massive Giant moves what to him is a pea-sized ball under a cup and with a single finger gently begins to nudge the cups around in a clumsy fashion. On more than one occasion, the narrator and Scotty have to move out of the way of the Giant's arms as he struggles to move the tiny pieces.

"You have an unfair advantage, boy. Maybe I should not have agreed to this," the behemoth declares.

"But you did," Amy quickly adds, smiling with pride.

Silence resumes, and the Giant begins to move the cups a little easier. However, he is still painfully slow, and the spectators are following the movement of the balls just as easily as Jack.

Suddenly, Mason blurts out, "Get this over with, Jack."

The simple words distract the contestant, who thinks, *Where did Mason come from?* For one brief second, Jack looks up at the boy who is now among the spectators. Quickly, though, Jack looks back down, realizing he has made a critical mistake.

"Shut up, Mason!" Amy scolds.

Oh, no! thinks Jack. Mason's distraction has caused him to lose track. He's furious, but since he's unable to take another look up at Mason, he tries to calm his nerves. Jack tells himself, *Focus! Maybe something will tip it off?* He glares at the table and soon thinks one cup is moving more slowly than the rest, which means it must have the ball underneath it.

After another full minute, the Giant stops and says, "Okay, thief, which cup?"

With so much at stake, Jack fights the urge to second guess himself. Before allowing his mind to play tricks on him, Jack points to the cup on the right.

Another moment of intense silence ensues as the Giant clumsily attempts to pick up the cup.

Finally, after several attempts and nearly knocking over the other items, the Giant successfully lifts the cup. The ball is not there.

"What!" Jack gasps. He is momentarily shocked. Then when the realization of what just happened hits him, he looks up and glares at Mason, wondering, *Did he do that on purpose?* Mason looks at Jack and says, "I'm sorry." He actually does look remorseful.

In disbelief, Amy asks the Giant, "Then which cup is it under?"

"I'm not sure myself," he responds and then chuckles.

Jack is disgusted at the sound. He can't help but think about his family. He considers how he is now one mistake away, one lucky guess, one break of concentration, from losing them, losing everything.

Scotty demands that the Giant lift the other cups. The behemoth complies, and there, under the middle cup, is the ball.

"So, I got one by you there, thief."

Jack is stunned. He sees the narrator standing and twirling his mustache, but he can't read the man's face.

Scotty clears his throat and, while looking angrily at Mason, announces the score: "So it's Jack one, Giant one."

"Walter," says the Giant.

"What?" asks Scotty.

"My name is Walter, not Giant."

Scotty nods and corrects himself, saying, "Oh, sorry Mr.—"

"This time, Mason, keep your mouth shut!" Amy scolds.

"I said *I'm sorry*. I really did not mean to," he apologizes again.

Jack closes his eyes. He can't think about Mason now; he has to concentrate. With one hand, he pushes his loose bangs up out of his eyes and then says, "It's now or never."

He looks at Amy. Until now, his thoughts had been centered on losing his family and not being able to go home. But, a new thought reigns heavily upon his brow: *If I lose now, there will be no future for Amy and me.*

Jack proceeds to slowly place the ball underneath the middle cup, and then he begins shuffling.

As before, he spins the cups deftly, moving them in and out, weaving and bobbing. But, this time his hands move so fast that even he eventually has no idea which cup contains the ball. At one point, Jack decides to look at Walter, taking his eyes off the cup. The Giant seams confused. *Good,* thinks Jack.

The boy also takes a look at the others. Amy appears to be almost as nervous as Jack. Scotty, on the other hand, beams with confidence, and Mason is staring at his own hands.

Finally, Jack stops shuffling, confident that no one could possibly guess the location of the ball, but then he goes ahead and moves each of the cups one last time.

Jack looks intently at Walter and says, "Okay then, make your best guess."

"I have been a fool. I should have never agreed to this," the Giant moans.

Jack's confidence soars.

"Well, which one?" Scotty presses.

The Giant rubs his hairy chin. He starts to point at the cup on the far left but then pulls his hand back and says, "Honestly, I have no clue."

The odds seem to be in Jack's favor.

No one speaks for what seems like a full minute. Then Scotty again asks, "Okay, which cup?"

The Giant points to the cup on the right and says, "Okay, show me I'm wrong."

Jack gulps. He realizes his future of freedom or captivity boils down to this moment. Before he lifts the cup, though, he looks at Amy, who has leaned down close to his side. She is not watching. Her head hangs low, and her eyes are closed.

Jack lifts the cup slowly.

There, underneath the cup, is the small red ball.

A fire lights underneath the skin of his face. He thinks, *No! How?*

He looks up, bewildered.

Amy raises her head, and after seeing the ball for herself, she gasps.

Scotty bellows, "No way."

The wolf also lets out a surprised, "Well I'll be."

Mason simply turns away.

Walter laughs lightheartedly.

Never in all of his life has Jack been so stunned.

"Well boy," says the Giant. "Say your farewells, and we shall take leave."

Chapter 146

Jack is in complete shock. The gravity of the moment forces down his shoulders into a slump. He thinks, *No, this can't be. What's going to happen to me? How long will I have to stay here? What are my parents going to do without me?* These thoughts depress Jack even further.

"This cannot be happening," Scotty moans. "Jack, you can't leave us."

However, in spite of his friend's declaration, Jack knows there is no alternative and that the Giant is going to take him.

Nonetheless, Amy makes another last ditch effort to the Giant, "One more game all of nothing. If you win, we'll all go with you."

Mason qualifies this by saying, "No way, Amy, I'm walking out of here."

"Speak for yourself," snarls the wolf in agreement with Mason.

"No," the Giant declares. "I think the time for games is over. You had your one chance. It's time you came with me, boy."

Amy looks Jack in the eyes, and with tears streaming down her face, she kisses him softly and quickly on the lips.

The kiss stuns Jack, but the dread of the moment outweighs the emotion of the kiss.

Amy pleads, "You can't go. It's not fair. Mason distracted you."

"He didn't mean to," Jack counters, although he isn't sure he believes it himself.

"It's time to go," the Giant says and makes a motion toward the gap in the wall.

"Just a second, please," Jack responds. "Scotty, tell my parents what happened here."

Scotty grimly nods and wipes his wet eyes.

Then Jack and Mason eye each other. Finally, Mason offers softly, "No one's going to believe us, Jack.... Jack, I promise I didn't mean to—"

"Forget it, Mason," Jack says.

His previous impulse to deck Mason has been overcome with a feeling that he is sincere.

After another awkward few seconds, Mason muses, "Maybe we can come back and bust you out one day?" Then he extends a hand.

It's clear to Jack that his friend of many years meant no harm. So, Jack obliges and says, "See you someday, Mason," before he gulps back the lump in his throat.

Jack now approaches the narrator. The man who had already saved them once simply looks at Jack and gives a deep nod of concern.

"Look," Jack requests, knowing the answer will be no. "Can you, maybe, help me out with this?"

Chapter 147

The old man twirls his mustache again as Jack anticipates the forth-coming denial.

"Well, Jack, you did steal the goose from the Giant; a price has to be paid. You have to make things right."

The words register with Jack. Suddenly he knows what they mean and says, "You were trying to tell us all night!" This realization rocks his world, and he swallows hard. "You were leading us back so we could return the goose."

The narrator nods.

"So I guess this is the end of my story. This is how I make amends because we ignored your words. I... I don't know what to say.... I'm sorry. Is there no other way?"

The man stares at Jack for a few seconds. Then he raises an eyebrow and almost absently quips, "Well, perhaps I could take your place?"

Jack's head jumps up. His eyes lock on the narrator's. He asks, "What? What did you say?"

"I said maybe I can take your place."

The thought gives Jack temporary hope. He wonders if it's really possible, but as soon as he considers this, he feels a tide of guilt and says, "But you didn't do anything."

"I know that."

"Then why?"

"Well you're so young, and while you've finished this story, you have not finished your story. Jack, it is what I have wanted all along. I want you to finish your story."

Jack's heart rate accelerates. But, in spite of his desire to take the man up on his offer, he says, "I can't. It's not right."

"Yes you can, Jack. You have so much to do. Go back to your family. Go with your friends."

"But what about the vault? What about the books? Do you want me to take your place there?"

"Jack, finish your story—go home."

"But—"

"Then it is decided," the narrator states. He then turns away from Jack, walks up to the behemoth, and says, "Mr. Giant, I have decided to take the boy's place."

The Giant considers this and then replies, "That was not the deal. You are not the thief."

"I understand that. However, you said you simply wanted.... What did you say.... Yes, compensation. I am your compensation. If you are a man, I mean *giant*, of your word, you will accept my offer. I believe it is indeed a fair one."

Amy's countenance is visibly rekindled with hope.

Scotty and Mason look at each other with astonishment.

The wolf looks puzzled by the strange offer.

"Well, I am a giant of my word, I can assure you. If it is your will to take the boy's place, then who am I to argue. It's your choice."

Jack absorbs the conversation in disbelief. The situation has changed so fast and in spite of his objections. He asks himself, *Is this really happening?* Yet, he's led to believe that the agonizing, impending sentence has been lifted from him. The only thing keeping him from screaming with delight is the tidal wave of guilt he feels.

Amy rushes to the narrator and asks, "Are you for real? You're taking Jack's place?"

"Yes."

"I... I...." Amy starts, but she cannot find the words and, instead, hugs the man, like a child squeezing a grandparent. As she releases her embrace, she faintly whispers in his ear, "Thank you."

Scotty joins his sister by the narrator. He also has no clue how to properly react to the action of the man. He ends up shaking the narrator's hand and then solemnly backs away, joining Jack.

By this point, Mason has taken a few steps toward the narrator. Jack is keenly aware that it had been Mason who had doubted the man's sincerity from the moment they had been aware that he existed. Now, Mason simply nods to the narrator.

Meanwhile, the wolf slowly shakes his head in disbelief, taken aback by the strange reversal of fortunes.

"Are you finished with your goodbyes?" the Giant respectfully asks.

To answer Walter's question, Jack approaches the old man. Without saying a word, Jack wraps his arms around the narrator, buries his head into the man's white suit coat, and starts crying.

"Jack, it's my choice," the narrator assures.

"I don't understand. You shouldn't have to do this. I'm the one. I'm the one who stole the goose."

"I know," says the narrator. He pats Jack on the forehead and then gently pries the boy away.

The Giant is already exiting through the wall, and the narrator proceeds to follow him. However, just before the man reaches the wall, he stops and pulls something out from behind his back. It is a box.

The narrator says to the group, "Oh, before I go, I thought I would leave you this."

Chapter 148

The narrator gently sets the brown wooden package on the ground. It's nothing fancy, just a plain box, obviously old, with some tarnished bronze hinges and a latch on the side.

Jack wonders, *What is this about?*

The narrator says, "You have made amends. And now, I must go." Then, with a good-natured wave and smile, the narrator disappears through the gap in the wall to follow the Giant.

Feelings of guilt eat at Jack. He contemplates, *Why was he so willing to take my place? He barely knew us, and yet he gave up his freedom. Who will guard the vault?* However, he decides these questions can wait until later, for at the moment, the group needs to deal with the box. Also, Jack considers that, with the witch and the narrator gone, they might have to protect Amy from the wolf. The boy turns to the beast and is surprised to find that the wolf is not looking at Amy but at him. Jack's body tenses, and he quickly scans the floor for something to be able to hurl. He thinks, *Where is Amy's stick? No time to find it amongst this rubble.*

The intimidating figure of the wolf steps toward Jack.

Jack balls his fist.

However, the wolf's demeanor does not reflect ill will—at least as far as Jack can tell. Still, Jack decides he should remain cautious.

The wolf stops a few inches away from Jack and says, "That was a noble thing the man just did."

Jack is surprised that the eolf is speaking to him in a civil manner. He wonders, *Is this a trick? Something to put me at ease before he strikes?*

After a moment of hesitation, Jack responds, "Uh, yes it was."

The wolf continues, "I also believe it was a noble thing you did, offering to leave to save the rest of us. Thank you."

Jack watches in disbelief as the wolf walks back over to the debris of the fallen house and appears to be searching for something among the ruins. The boy guesses that the creature might be looking for the bodies of the Queen and Victor. The words of the wolf have put Jack at ease a little, but he does not relax just yet, in spite of being grateful that the wolf is no longer greedily staring at Amy. For now, at least, the beast seems occupied with another interest—a large red-striped candy cane that he's found in the rubble. The wolf sniffs at it and takes a bite.

Meanwhile, Mason has approached the box on the floor and says, "Maybe he's left us a prize of some sort?" The boy seems genuinely giddy. His sudden transformation from solemnly watching the narrator walk away to greedily eyeing the box is almost shocking. But this doesn't surprise the others.

Amy, in fact, ignores Mason *and* the box and even seems uninterested in the wolf as she walks over to Jack and quietly takes his hand.

Jack intertwines his fingers with hers.

Then Amy looks into his eyes and says, "I'm so grateful."

"I know," Jack replies. "Believe me, I am, too."

Scotty is standing close by. He coughs and then inquires, "Jack, about you and my little sis?"

"Yeah?"

Jack thinks, *This is it. Time to come clean.*

"We'll talk later," Scotty says and grins.

At this point, Mason lifts the box and declares, "It's not that heavy." He shakes it like a child trying to guess what's in a present on Christmas morning and says, "Yep, something is definitely in there."

"Well, open it already, Mason!" Scotty directs.

"I can't quite get it open. There's a little lock on the latch-thing here."

The wolf stops sifting through the rubble and approaches Mason.

Jack thinks, *Keep your eyes on him. You can't let your guard down.* He uncoils his hand from Amy and makes a slight move toward Mason, who takes a full step back when the wolf gets close to him.

"Allow me," says the wolf, holding his hairy paws out for the box.

Reluctantly, but not wanting to argue, Mason hands the gift over.

The wolf opens his ferocious mouth. The fangs that had earlier sunk into Jack's hand glisten with beads of saliva. Next, the creature lifts the box before his mouth and locks his jaws around the latch. Then, he rips the entire hinge off of the wooden box, and he spits this—along with a good-sized chunk of wood—on the floor.

Afterward, he calmly hands the box back to Mason, saying, "Here you go."

Mason looks startled and a little uneasy. The wolf's saliva is all over the side of the box. Mason grimaces in disgust, but goes ahead and takes it back. After using his shirt to wipe off his hand and the box, Mason pauses. He looks at the others before he opens the top of the wooden box.

"What's this?" he asks and quickly reaches inside.

All eyes in the room are focused on Mason.

"Oh man, it's just a bunch of nothing," he declares with obvious disappointment on his downcast face.

Mason pulls a stack of paper out of the box. He places the sheets under one arm, reaches back into the box and produces an old-looking pen.

Curious, Jack walks over to Mason to get a closer view and says, "Let me see them, Mason."

Even now after all they had been through, Jack half expects another verbal battle, recalling how Mason had been so territorial with the map. However, this time, Mason freely offers the objects to Jack, who thinks, *He's not interested in them.* Jack takes the papers and looks them over. They're blank, and Jack thinks out loud, "He gave us a pen and paper?"

The wolf draws closer, and there's a wild look in his eyes.

Jack sees this and cries, "Stay back!"

"No, can't you see?" responds the wolf, whose countenance has changed.

The creature is no longer glowering at them, and, in fact, he appears to be trying to smile.

Amy looks at the wolf and then at the papers in Jack's hand. Suddenly, she knows what the wolf is thinking and says, "He's right—I get it now! Can't you see, Jack?"

"Wait a minute what's going on?" Mason barks. "Why are you so happy?"

Amy exclaims, "The story! The pages! These are the missing pages!"

Jack examines the papers more closely and sees they have little ridges along one side, as if they had been ripped out of a book. Also, the slight yellow tinge of the pages reminds him of the pages from the books in the ride.

All of a sudden a light bulb turns on for Jack, and he realizes, "Your right, Amy!"

"Let me see," says Scotty, who walks quickly to Jack. He flips through the pages and declares, "But, they're blank."

"Of course they're blank, Scotty, that's the point. May I have a piece?" Amy asks her brother, who happily grants her request. Then she says, "Mason, the pen if you will."

And, after securing this object, too, Amy sits down on the floor and begins to write.

Chapter 149

Amy's expectations rise as she places the pen against the paper. *This* is it, she thinks, and she knows what to do. In fact, she has never been so confident about anything in her entire life. Amy's almost giddy as the ink spills out onto the parchment. As she writes, she reads aloud for the others to hear.

> "The wanderer, Amy, had seen enough of the woods that night.
> She wanted to go home.
> Although it was a long and scary ordeal,
> She knew that night had changed her, changed her for the better.
> She should have never left the ride and gotten herself into this mess.
> She never should have gotten so angry with her friends, especially Jack.
> And, she would not allow herself to feel ashamed of her own appearance any longer.
> She knew she was fine just the way she was.

She was thankful for the narrator and wanted to make sure he would be proud of the choices she would make from that point on.

She would no longer wander; she would stick to the path, and now, this path would lead her out of the woods."

After finishing the text, Amy calmly places the pen on the floor and re-examines the words. She stands, filled with joy.

"What was that all about?" Mason asks.

"Wait," Amy instructs and hushes him by lifting her forefinger. She pauses and looks around the room. She is obviously expecting something, and after a few more empty seconds, a look of disappointment mixed with confusion shows on her face.

"Maybe it has to rhyme? I don't understand," she says.

"Neither do we," Mason adds.

Amy responds, "Mason, just be...."

Her train of thought is broken, though, as another idea comes to her. After looking around for another few seconds, she marches toward a wall. She walks past the gaping hole where the Giant had bulldozed through and approaches the spot where the animatronic narrator had once stood and when she's inches away from it, Amy begins to tug at a piece of drywall on the floor. She rummages through the debris left by the Giants entrance.

"She's gone crazy," Mason says. "Jack, what's she doing?"

Jack doesn't know. He is just as confused as Mason. Then it hits him, and he says, "Of course!"

"What?" Scotty asks.

Amy continues to dig in the rubble, before she suddenly stops. She reaches down and pulls up the long forgotten book that had been held by the old narrator mannequin earlier in the night.

She holds up the book and slightly waves it at the others. Amy brushes the white dust off its cover, and with a look of determination on her face, she flips through the pages. Unlike before, the pages now move. She takes the page she has just written and places it into the book, just before the last page. With a look of self-satisfaction, she firmly closes the book.

All of a sudden, as if a flip had been switched, a dull buzz vibrates on the wall to her left. Then a bright light shines in the dim room. It is a glowing green sign with the word "Exit." A large metal door seems to appear from nowhere under the humming sign. Amy proudly looks at the others. Gone from her countenance are any tears of remorse and signs of guilt, frustration, or worry that had weighed her down during the last few hours. Instead, she triumphantly walks back to her companions.

Scotty says, "Amy, that was—"

"Brilliant, I know," Amy playfully acknowledges.

"How did you know?" her brother asks.

"You know, you're not the only one who inherited some brains," she coyly suggests.

Then she looks at Jack and says, "I'm leaving now." Next, turning to the others, she adds, "You boys don't take too long, okay?"

Jack proudly calls out, "Amy, you're going home now!"

Her gaze returns to Jack with a smile. "Yes," she says and allows herself another moment of satisfaction. "See you later."

"That's it? See you later?" Jack asks. He has a look of confusion on his face.

She knows what she wants to do, but she thinks, *In front of Scotty?* Then she says, "Oh, who cares." Amy walks over to Jack, reaches behind his head with her right hand, and pulls him to her lips. She gives him a kiss—not one of fear or of sympathy, but one of love, genuine love.

Her head spins as she releases the lip lock.

"Better?" she asks.

Looking to the side, she catches a glimpse of Scotty and Mason, both of whom are open-mouthed and speechless.

Amy clears her throat and tells Jack, "Now, see you later, okay?"

"You bet!" Jack replies.

After walking a few paces toward the door, Amy pauses and looks back at her companions one at a time. Jack is smiling, marveling at what she has done, and she shoots him a wink. Mason is grinning, but Amy isn't sure why. She guesses that he's either genuinely proud of her, or he's happy he will get out of here alive. Whichever motive he has for sending her off smiling is fine by her. Scotty nervously stares at the wolf, perhaps expecting some last ditch effort to ensnare. Amy looks at the wolf, too, but she is not afraid; she knows he will let her be. Proving her instinct right, the beast simply tilts his head in a quizzical look and, in fact, gently waves.

Amy turns and walks through the door under the exit sign.

Chapter 150

As soon as Amy disappears through the door, the "Exit" light fades and the door vanishes.

Mason rushes to the spot where it was and exclaims "Wait, let us out!"

After pushing on the wall, he turns to the others, thinking, *This can't happen. Are we all trapped in here now?*

"Mason, finish your story," Scotty calmly tells the tailor.

"Oh yeah, of course," responds Mason, who's embarrassed that he had not figured this out on his own.

He walks over to Jack and snatches a piece of paper from him.

Mason had never been much of a writer. In fact, he only managed to pass his English classes by letting his dad "check" his papers. Titus Chick would not allow his son to fail at anything, so when it came to papers, Titus would only lightly chastise his son for poor effort and then establish himself in front of the computer, totally reworking everything Mason had done. Once Titus had finished "checking" a paper, it in no way would resemble its previous version.

Now, faced with the challenge of finishing his story, Mason thinks, *This is too much like homework.... What do I say? What did Amy write?*

Suddenly, a smile erupts on Mason's face.

He says, "Yes! Finish my story. Oh man, this is gonna be awesome."

He takes the pen from the floor, walks to the nearest wall, and holds the paper up against it for support. As he begins to write in his chicken scratch script, he realizes his future is in his hands. After he's finished, he reads the words aloud for the others to hear, just as Amy had done.

"Mason, the tailor, had been so brave.
Without him the others would have died so many times in
the deep, dark woods. Like lots of times.
But he was, like, so glad to be out of that crazy place.
'Cause that's just what he did as soon as he put the paper
in the book. He left.
He went home to his dad, and grew up living an incredible
life.
He was, like, really, really, popular and good at sports.
He did not even have to go to school, but I guess he did
so he could play sports and stuff.
But he did not have to study any more. That's for sure.

He grew up to be a famous athlete and rock star. He had lots of cars and money. The girls loved him. Like tons of girls.

When he got older he married an incredibly attractive model, and lived a long, long, long, life to the extreme!"

Mason looks confidently at what he has written, the longest piece of literature he had ever finished on his own.

He says, "Now that's a story! This is so cool—like finding a genie in a bottle or something."

He drops the pen to the floor and after re-examining his words with a total sense of self-assurance and pride, he strolls over to the book, mimicking the actions of Amy. As the page is placed into the book, the same humming sign flashes on, and the door appears.

"All right!" Mason says as he pumps his fist in the air. "It worked!"

Next, without even giving a wave to the others, he shoves open the door and walks out of the room.

Chapter 151

Scotty and Jack watch as Mason moves through the door and the sign fades. The two friends give each other an odd look.

"He's one of a kind," Scotty says with a sigh.

"You can say that again," Jack agrees. "I can't believe he wrote that."

"I can," Scotty says and shakes his head. He extends the remaining papers toward Jack after taking one for himself. "I think I'm going to go now."

"Of course," Jack responds.

While holding the paper in his hand, Scotty takes a second to deliberate on what to write. At one point, he looks up from the page and scans the room. *What a crazy night,* he thinks. Suddenly, a feeling of self-satisfaction warms his body. He considers how the four of them had been through a lot, how they had worked together, and how he had done his part to get them to where they are now. Scotty realizes that he, too, just like his sister had written, had changed that night. He knows he is braver and more sure of himself, but not sure of himself like Mason. *No, certainly not like Mason,* he thinks.

After a few more moments of reflection, he slowly places the page on the floor and grabs the pen that Mason had dropped and begins to write, confident about the words he would ink on the page.

"The apprentice had changed that night.

He had always lived his life through the experiences of his friends.

He was scared and unsure about decisions. So he let others decide for him.

He was always a sidekick, but now he was different.

He would make his own choices, make his own decisions.

He would not freeze in the face of crises; he would take control.

The adventure had taught him a valuable lesson.

From that day on, upon leaving the woods, he would no longer be an apprentice.

He would be his own man.

He no longer needed someone else to follow."

Emboldened by his own words, Scotty marches past the wolf and Jack. He slides the paper into the book, and the same mysterious scene plays out for him: the "Exit" sign lights up and the door appears.

There it is, the exit sign waiting for me, thinks Scotty. Before leaving, though, he walks over to where the wolf is standing. In spite of everything, he is still uncomfortable in the presence of this creature, who, Scotty remembers, had slammed him to the floor one too many times.

"Uh, thanks for letting her go," Scotty states.

The wolf nods.

Now Scotty walks over to Jack. He considers there's so much that could be said, but he decides to just ask, "So, um, the pool tomorrow?"

"I'm sure I'll be grounded until I'm 30," Jack replies.

Scotty knows that while there may not be many right opportunities for guys to hug, this is certainly one of them. He and Jack embrace in a brief guy-hug. And with that, Scotty turns to leave. Midway to the exit, though, he stops and looks at the ground. There, barely visible through all of the debris, is Lucky.

"Well," Scotty says, "Mason left you here after all we went through." He shakes his head in disbelief.

"Take him home to the twins, Scotty," Jack calls.

Scotty looks at the bear. It's partially singed with stuffing falling out. The thing looks horrible. "They might get nightmares," Scotty responds. "I should probably keep it.... You know, our last Enchanted Forrest ride."

"Yeah. Good idea."

Scotty smiles back at Jack and then walks on through the door.

Chapter 152

The wolf, who's been a spectator in the bizarre show of the last several minutes, has watched quietly as his former foes escaped. When the narrator left, he wanted so badly to pounce and take the girl. However, the words of the narrator kept ringing in his head: *"You must overcome your instincts."* Thus, he had decided to let her go, the one thing he thought he wanted most in the world. As soon as Amy walked through the exit door, he knew he had made the right choice. Strange as it may seem, he even felt proud for her because she had been so brave. When he thought about it, the wolf considered how the kids had repaid his violent pursuit with kindness, actual kindness, and that the Queen was the real villain.

"Boy," the wolf calls to Jack.

Jack's face, which had been filled with joy as his friend had walked through the door, now looks defensive but not fearful. His tensed hands are clenched.

"Do not fear me," the wolf says, attempting to sound pleasant.

This, however, does not cause Jack to relax.

The beast continues, "I need to tell you something before you leave."

"Wha—What?" the boy stutters.

"Thank you."

Jack's eyes widen, astonished at the words.

The wolf says, "You have shown me kindness in spite of my actions. We were all pawns. You deserve to be free."

Jack looks at the wolf, and with a sincere look in his eyes, Jack holds out a piece of paper and says, "There's more pages here, you know."

Now it is the wolf's turn to be astonished. "More papers?" he asks, grasping the implication.

"Do you think...?" the wolf's voice trails off as Jack continues to hold the paper out before the beast.

The creature ponders, *I can actually write my own story? After all the pain I have caused these kids, the narrator allows me a way out?*

With a deep breath, the wolf takes the sheet and the pen. *But what to write?* he wonders. Many thoughts ramble through his mind, but slowly he begins to sift through the echoing thoughts and focuses on what he could possibly say. He thinks, *It's been so long. Can I even remember how to write?* Taking the pen in his hairy paw, he begins to scribble in a messy script.

> The wolf remembered what had happened so long ago.
> And he is thankful. Not for what he had done.
> But for the second chance.
> He had lived a life of evil, always following his instinct.
> Always chasing what he should not.
> He never realized he could be in control.
> For many years he was trapped in a dream.
> Not remembering the life he had before.
> Now he had a choice, the children had shown him the way.
> Could it be that he could live in something other than darkness?
> What would happen if he walked out those doors?
> He was thankful at least for the chance.
> The chance to choose. He could freely choose light or darkness.
> For the first time in his life, he chooses the light."

Chapter 153

The wolf's paws tremble as he places the page into the book. Once again, the room begins its ritual, and the door appears—but something else is also happening. To Jack's complete shock, the wolf is changing. His entire body contorts. Instead of screams of anguish, though, the wolf is laughing. It reminds Jack of a scene from a werewolf horror movie, but it's not a sinister transformation. The hair on the wolf's face and hands recedes, his face shrinks, his long paws recede back into his sleeves, and his two animal legs straighten out.

Jack watches in disbelief, thinking, *No way! Incredible! This tops everything!*

After a few seconds, standing where there had once been a menacing wolf, is a man, a very noble-looking, handsome man. A smile stretches from one side of his face to the other, revealing not fangs but short white teeth. The man is clean-shaven and square-jawed with short blonde hair visible under his black top hat. And, now, the long black coat gives him the look of a true gentleman. Even Victor in his all of his stately glory is no match for the distinguished look of this man.

"I remember everything now," says the man. "That was never who I was supposed to be."

The graveled voice of the wolf is gone, replaced with an eloquent tone that is almost sad and regretful, in spite of his wide smile. He looks in the air absently.

Then a tear rolls down the side of his face and he looks at Jack and says, "I am free."

With a bow to Jack, the man turns to the door.

As the former wolf opens the door, Jack is astonished. What the door reveals is not a dark tunnel, but a plush green field in the middle of the day with a cottage in the distance.

The man looks back at Jack and says, "It is just as I remember, my home."

He steps out into the field, and Jack sees the man take a deep breath of the clean air and then, as the door closes, hears him let out a whoop of joy and yell, "Home!"

"Amazing," Jack says, although no one is there to hear.

While holding the last piece of paper, Jack looks around the room, noticing the collapsed house and the gap in the wall. He thinks, *If we had just followed the narrator's direction, we might have avoided a lot of trouble tonight.* He reflects on the narrator's sacrifice and wonders, *Maybe if we had just followed him in the first place he would not have had to take my place.*

Guilt washes over him, but there is nothing that can be done now since things have been made right. It may not be the way Jack would have wanted it, but it is finished nonetheless.

It's time, thinks Jack. *No need to spend another second in here.*

Grasping the pen and setting the paper on the floor, Jack begins to write. He has no trouble putting his thoughts to paper.

"Jack was relieved to finally be going home.
But he would never forget the narrator.
The man had saved them from the Queen and the Giant.
And he had given them all the chance to make things right.

Jack left the woods that night a better person.
He knew he should not have deceived his parents.
He knew he should have never gotten out of that cart in
the first place.
He should not have taken the goose.
He should not have let others lead him astray. He is truly
sorry.
From that day forward he would be perfect."

Jack hastily scratches part of the last line about being perfect and continues.

"From that day forward, he tried his best to make wise
choices.
He returned happily to his family, even his sister.
He appreciated the life he had, his home, his friends—and
Amy.
He would not be shy about his feelings for her.
And he would never forget the narrator and what he had
done."

Jack rises and takes his turn at opening the book. An odd feeling encompasses him. In some way, he actually feels a little sad to leave. Still, he goes ahead and slides the paper into its slot, and as he closes the book, the sign begins to glow.

He thinks, *No, it is time to leave this place for good*. While heading to the door, he takes one last look at the room and sees another piece of paper on the ground. This causes him pause, and he wonders, *Who is that for?* The answer is apparent when Jack spies a figure of a man standing just inside the passageway from where they had entered the room. It is Victor. Jack points to the paper and gently rolls the pen to the middle of the floor.

He calls out, "If you ever want to go back home, Douglas."

Jack nods at the man, and then, with one deep sigh, he turns and pushes the door open.

Chapter 154

"Okay, Clyde, you ready? Let's go find your door," Jimmy says. He pulls the long black flashlight from his belt.

It appears to Clyde that Officer Dockins has decided to bring along a couple of the Crime Scene cops in their grey suits to accompany them.

Suddenly, the blustering voice of Howard Snodgrass wails, "Why have I heard nothing about this until now?"

The portly man waddles over to the gathering of officers, followed by Officer Quinn, who looks apologetically at Dockins as Howard plows forward.

He is obviously agitated and asks, "Clyde, why am I being questioned about a secret door?"

Clyde feels he has already been subjugated to enough humiliation for one night and decides not to answer.

Dockins says, "Mr. Snodgrass, what are you doing? For Pete's sake, Quinn, can we keep anyone away from Mr. Spahn?" He gives a sigh.

Snodgrass looks at Clyde and, after waiting several seconds for a response, says, "Okay, Clyde, we're gonna play it that way, huh? Mums the word?"

"Mr. Snodgrass, please come with me," Quinn says and firmly grabs the man by the arm.

Snodgrass holds his ground, though, and says, "Wait just one stinkin' minute, Officer. I have something to say... for the record."

The portly man stands stiff, straightens his tie, clears his throat, and makes a big to do over his next few words.

"Honestly, Officer, I have no idea what this man is talking about. Secret door—ha!" He pauses, looking at his audience to make sure he has their full attention, before continuing, "Officer, if anyone knows this park, it's me. There's no secret door in this building. I know this park almost as well as I do the back of my hand."

The absurdity of the last statement makes Clyde grin a little. As far as he knows, Snodgrass has never even been inside the ride. Still, he understands why Snodgrass is upset. If there turns out to be a secret door inside one of the rides that several children could have disappeared into, the Douglas Finch case might get back on the front page of the paper along with news of this current disappearance of teens. Clyde could see the headlines now, wild stories linking the two incidents, blaming the park for doing nothing about the mysterious door. In fact, there were about three reporters already assembled here ready to write those articles. This could have all sorts of ramifications for Howard Snodgrass and the park's owner, The Newcastle group. *No wonder Howard is on the war path,* Clyde thinks.

Officer Dockins says, "All right, Howard, we get it, enough." After a moment of consideration, he suggests, "Mr. Snodgrass, since you are the authority on this ride, why don't you accompany us inside. Then we can all find out together if there is truth behind what your employee is relating to us?"

Clyde shoots a look at Snodgrass and thinks, *This will be interesting.*

"Uh, no, that's okay. I don't want to get in your way and all," Snodgrass replies.

"It was not a question," Dockins states.

Clyde leads the group into the ride. He is followed by Dockins and the two grey-suited cops from the Crime Scene Unit. Behind them is Howard Snodgrass, and pulling up the rear is Officer Quinn.

The crew, for the most part, remains silent, save for the occasional question.

Inside the Little Red Room, they pass the missing wolf statue.

As they exit this room, Dockins asks, "Clyde, how many times exactly have you seen this mysterious appearing door?"

"Oh, I reckon I've heard the music three or four times. But I've heard the music more than I've seen the door. I have only seen the door this one time."

In the pit of Clyde's stomach there is already despair. *Will it be there?* he worries, but in his heart, he knows it will not be. He considers how he will be dismissed as a fool and forced to spend more time in front of those pesky doctors. *They'll parade me down to the hospital, run those tests. I'll have to talk to a psychologist twice a week for a year,* he imagines. The entire prospect tires him. But, what scares him is thinking, *Worse yet, they may think for sure that I did something to the kids.* Suddenly, a chattering sound emits from a spot Clyde has just passed. *What is that?* he wonders and turns around.

"What is it, Clyde?" Dockins whispers.

"Do you hear that clattering sound?"

Dockins gives a hushed chuckle and says, "It's Snodgrass. His teeth are chattering. He's scared out of his mind."

Clyde experiences a temporary feeling of guilty pleasure but lets it go. He knows they are getting close to the room where the door appeared.

By now, they should be able to hear the calliope music if it were playing, and its absence depresses Clyde. This is ironic for a man who had spent so much of his life praying he would never hear that awful pipe organ again.

The group moves into the room where Clyde had left the kids. It is dead quiet.Clyde breaks the silence by saying, "You know where we are now?"

A dull feeling of heartache builds in the old man. He stops and looks around, thinking, *Here we are again in the room where this whole mess started. One stupid mistake... leaving those kids.*

Jimmy says, "Clyde, we've been through this room several times. It's really not why we are in here now. Where's the room with your mysterious door?"

"Oh, sorry, lost in thought. It's actually the very next room."

There's still no music. Clyde thinks, *This is bad.*

As Clyde pushes to open the door into the next room, he feels something resist, as if something or someone is coming out of the door. He let's go quickly, not knowing what to expect.

"What's going on, Clyde?" Officer Dockins asks.

Suddenly the door bursts open.

The officers fumble with their belts, reaching for side arms.

Howard Snodgrass makes a pterodactyl-like sound and ducks down behind one of the men in suits.

Clyde looks up in total shock as the four teens spill through the opening.

A total and overpowering sense of relief floods through Clyde, who calls out, "Jack!"

"Oh man, Clyde, have we got a story for you," Jack says.

All four of them are standing there, looking like they have just stepped out of a blender.

Good grief, what in the world happened to them? Clyde thinks.

"These are the four kids then, Clyde?" Dockins asks with his radio already nearing his lips.

"Of course they are, Jimmy."

But where had they been? Clyde wonders.

The burden of the night had been lifted and during the procession back to the front of the ride, the kids tell outrageous tales to the policemen, who respond with strange looks and occasional, outright "no ways." Clyde doesn't pay much attention to this conversation, though. He knows he can catch up later. The old man does, however, focus in on one entertaining conversation that Howard Snodgrass is having over his cell phone.

Snodgrass barks, "We found the kids, Pritchard.... No, I'm not sure what the parents will do." Then, in a muffled voice, he asks, "How much is it gonna cost to keep this outta court?"

Chapter 155

Jack's heart races. They have arrived at the last set of doors before the outside. He wants to run. He wants to burst through the doors. Then a thought occurs to him: *My parents are gonna be hacked.* He decides he will just have to face the music and realizes that he doesn't care, thinking, *At this point, they could ground me for a year and I would still be happy.*

Officer Quinn opens the doors, Scotty immediately blows past Jack and leaps into the outstretched arms of his mom. Suddenly, there is a loud round of applause from the onlookers while reporters hold up cameras, trying to capture whatever celebratory shots they can. The entire scene appears chaotic with the crowd forming a blob around the exit party, ignoring cries of the officers shouting, "Stay back!"

Jack navigates his way through the crowd, seemingly oblivious to the pats on his back and the barrage of questions from reporters. He peers through the crowd for any sign of his parents. He also looks for Blair and ponders, *I never would have thought I would long to see her.*

By this point, Amy has joined Scotty with their parents. She, too, gives her mom a giant squeeze around the neck.

"Where have you been?" asks Mrs. Carnahan.

"Are you okay?" Mr. Carnahan asks.

Meanwhile, Mason has found his dad and is already boasting, "You should have seen me in there."

All of a sudden, Jack feels two arms wrap around him from behind. He recognizes the gentle squeeze and exclaims, "Mom!"

Upon turning around, he sees the tear-stained eyes of his mother, which causes him to start crying, too.

He tells her, "I'm so sorry. I know I shouldn't have—"

"Shhhh, later, Jack. I am just so happy you're safe," his mom says.

Wallace Braddock places a hand on Jack's shoulder and says, "You really gave us a scare there, kiddo."

"Dad!" Jack responds. He turns to his father and gives him a giant hug, as well.

Wallace is not used to this kind of attention from his son, and he looks awkward for a second before warmly returning the embrace.

As Jack's cheek rests on his father's chest, he spots Blair and sees that she is tearing up. Jack thinks this might just be the most unbelievable thing he's seen the entire night. He releases his father's embrace and approaches her.

Blair, in spite of her tears, says, "Do you realize how much trouble you've caused me tonight?"

Jack laughs and thinks, *Same old Blair.*

The happy reunions continue as the police get control of the crowd. Now, only the families and some of the officers surround the teens.

At this point, Jack looks at Amy. She catches his gaze and winks before going back to embracing her twin sisters, one of whom is holding a large, and rather tattered, stuffed blue bear. Scotty, at the same time, is attempting to tell his dad about everything that happened but going so fast that Houston Carnahan has to tell him to slow down three times.

Several feet away, Mason continues to confidently tell his father about how many times he had to save the others.

Jack thinks the scene is perfect.

Clyde is in the mix, as well. Policemen are giving him handshakes and good-natured pats on the back. In particular, Jimmy Dockins lauds Clyde's efforts to find the missing kids.

The unbelievable stories relating to a mysterious door do not seem to matter much to the officers or the families, who are just grateful to have their children back.

Still, Scotty pulls his mother towards Jack and says, "Look, mom, we have proof. It's not my imagination. Jack got bit by a snake. It nearly killed him, but I made this medicine."

Hearing this disturbing news, Jack's parents crowd around him.

"You were bit by a snake?" Wallace asks.

Jack moves his shirt to show the bite marks. However, they are nowhere to be seen.

Epilogue

The mayor of Cassidy Falls has been speaking for what seems like an hour.

Standing just behind the mayor on the stage of amphitheater is Clyde, who yanks uncomfortably at his tie. This is the first time he's worn one since his tenth wedding anniversary. A few days ago, Clyde was uncertain about what life had in store for him. As far as he was concerned, the only career he'd known was finished. The park had closed and the rides that could be salvaged were sold, while the others were fodder for the wrecking ball. In their place, the construction of a new mall had begun almost immediately.

For the next couple of mornings after its closure, Clyde continued to wake up, put on his work clothes, and think, *I need to check the bumper cars.* He would even get into his car and start the ignition before remembering that the park had indeed been shut down for good. He considered moving to Virginia to live with his daughter, but then two weeks after the park had closed, he received a phone call telling him to be at the city park at 10 a.m. on Saturday.

Now, standing before what looks to be the entire town of Cassidy Falls, Clyde hears the mayor coming to the conclusion of his long-winded speech, saying, "For all your service to the children of our beloved city, we honor you, Clyde Spahn."

The mayor hands Clyde a plaque, and as the mayor reads the words on it aloud, Clyde cannot help but allow a small tear to well up in the corner of his right eye.

> "For all your years of charity to our children,
> the mayor of Cassidy Falls declares this day,
> August 17, as Clyde Spahn Day."

Thunderous applause fills the nighttime sky.

Shaking his head in disbelief, Clyde is even more stunned as the mayor continues, "Clyde, in addition to this, the city council has decided to offer you a position as the new head of the City Parks and Rec Department."

Once again the crowd applauds in hearty approval.

Clyde is overwhelmed by the offer, but he knows immediately that he will accept it. Then the mayor launches into a self-serving rambling about how the new Parks and Rec Department would be the envy of the state. Clyde takes this moment to scan the crowd and spies Scotty Carnahan.

The boy meets the man's gaze and gives him a smile and a wave. Clyde nods and thinks back to that night.

No one else had believed the four teenagers, for it had all seemed too absurd. The little group's initial story was dismissed as the delusions of four terrified kids. Later, when questioned by the police, they changed their tune and said they had simply got lost in the dark, so their initial musings to the cops were officially recorded as "mutual hallucinations," which were understood as the effects of being lost in a ride with so many troublesome images. In accounting for why it took so long to find the group, the official explanation was that the kids had gotten lost in a dark part of the ride and apparently continued moving around just out of sight of the various search parties.

Clyde continues looking around, and his eyes make out a person who appears to be Howard Snodgrass. *No,* thinks Clyde, *he wouldn't be here. It's not him.* He allows himself a chuckle when thinking of the man's fate. Howard had been re-assigned to work in the new mall as head of security, a crystal clear demotion. The Newcastle Group obviously frowned on the fact that Titus Chick had left the closing park with a parting gift—one giant lawsuit. Clyde relished the thought of Snodgrass spending the rest of his working life watching closed circuit TVs and running off loitering teens at the new Storybook Hollow Mall where "shopping dreams come to life."

Just behind the crowd, he spots his other present. The city park had bought the Dutch Swings and Blackbeard's Pirate Ship, and as part of his new job, Clyde would still get his fix of tinkering with these old amusements.

While hoping the mayor would finish any moment now, the old man spots a young couple holding hands and standing halfway back amongst the crowd. Clyde catches Jack's eye and gives him a wink. He whispers something to Amy, and she grins.

The mayor at last concludes his speech, and applause breaks out yet again.

"Congratulations, Clyde, you deserve this," says the mayor, shaking Clyde's hand.

Someone in the crowd calls out, "Speech!"

However, Clyde just waves uncomfortably and waltzes off to the side of the stage.

He is swarmed by a throng of well-wishers, but as people congratulate him, his only thought is that he wishes Edna could see this, although she would have been just as embarrassed as he is by all the attention.

It takes Clyde a full 30 minutes to navigate through the crowd toward the front of the park. As he makes his way toward his car, a local construction crew catches his eye. They are struggling to place a large black metal archway at the entrance to the park. Clyde feels a small twinge of uncomfortable recognition when he sees what is etched into the cast iron frame:

The Enchanted Forrest.

About the Author

Todd Loyd currently serves as the President of the National Conference on Youth Ministries. He grew up in Nashville, TN, and loved every minute of a childhood filled with trips to Fair Park and Opryland. In 1986 Todd was cast in the Film "Ernest Goes to Camp" as Chip Ozgood. Rarely does a week go by that someone does not remind him of the movie. In 1994 he graduated from Lipscomb University with a Bachelors degree in Communications. For nearly 20 years Todd has worked as a student pastor working with teens and speaking all over the United States. He and his wife, Amanda, have three boys and are very active in Special Needs charities like "Best Buddies of Middle Tennessee" and Athletes for Special Kids.